the image maker

A LOVE STORY

HOLLYWOOD HEARTS
BOOK ONE

KATHERINE OWEN

THE WRITING WORKS GROUP

For Lauren Nicole Owen, always.

other books by the author

Other Books By Katherine Owen

<u>The Hollywood Hearts Series</u>

The Image Maker – Book 1

The Image Breaker – Book 2 (Fall 2025)

The Image Keepers – Book 3 (Fall 2025)

The Image Masters — Book 4 (Winter 2025)

<u>The Truth In Lies Series</u>

This Much Is True (Truth In Lies, Book 1)

The Truth About Air & Water (Truth In Lies, Book 2)

Tell Me Something True (Truth In Lies Book 3)

<u>Standalone Novels</u>

When I See You

Seeing Julia

Not To Us

<u>Works-In-Progress</u>

Saving Valentines (Fall 2025)

The Image Breaker – Book 2 (Summer 2025)

The Image Keeper – Book 3 (Fall 2025)

Another WIP (still untitled)

More information about the books including play lists, excerpts, and extras at:
http://www.katherineowen.net.

contents

the image maker - synopsis

THE IMAGE MAKER

HOLLYWOOD HEARTS ~ *1*

KATHERINE OWEN

When elite public relations strategist Isla Ryder accepts a career-defining opportunity to rebrand Hollywood's most notorious *'bad boy,'* Roman Lysander, she expects a challenge—but not the earth-shattering chemistry that ignites between them from the very start.

Isla has built her reputation on control, strategy, and keeping her distance. Roman has perfected the art of living up to his scandalous reputation while hiding his true self behind the glittering facade. But when their professional arrangement becomes intensely personal, both discover that some connections cannot be managed or manufactured.

With a multi-million-dollar film project hanging in the balance, powerful Hollywood dynasties at war, and secrets that could destroy everything they've worked for, Isla and Roman must decide if what's burning between them is worth risking their carefully constructed worlds. Because in a city built on illusions, the most dangerous gamble isn't with their careers—it's with their hearts.

Sometimes the best strategy is simply telling the truth. But in Hollywood, the truth can be the most dangerous weapon of all.

author's note: pronunciations & caveats

Author Note: Pronunciations & Caveats

Dear Reader:

Okay, I have chosen some unusual names for this novel. And in my mind, certain ways that names are to be pronounced. Names are pronounced phonetically, for the most part, but, of course, with the *Katherine Owen* twist in the style of things for some names, surnames, and nicknames.

Isla - ees-lah. The 's' sounds more like a 'z' in my mind. 'eez-lah.'

The Spanish pronounce it this way: 'ees-lah' with more emphasis on the 's'. I'm kind of *blending it.* /ēz/-lah. So, when Samantha calls Isla by her designated nickname, **'Iz'**, it's pronounced as 'ease' /ēz/.

Roman's nickname **'Ro'** pronounced 'row' for Roman, which is Brandon's nickname for him.

Lysander surname. 'li-SAN-der'. So, it's like 'lit' without a the 't'. li-SAN-der, Yes, I'm aware it should be phonetically, 'ly-SAN-der' as in, 'Lye-SAN-der'. I don't like that, and I am unwilling to change.

The Caveats

Yes! Oh yes! There is a lot of swearing in this book because it is part of the two protagonist's characteristics, used as a coping mechanism one could say. I think we covered my proclivity for swearing, at one point, in my earlier works and definitely at my website right on the home page. Here's the author note that further explains my style.

> *Author's Note: I write pretty dark stuff. I love to write about impossible situations. My storylines will twist you up and tear you apart, and I will surely make you cry. You may begin to wonder if there will ever be a happy ending. My heroes tend to be great, and my heroines tend to be f^cked up. And, I like that word, and you'll have to get used to that or you may just want to pass on my work. I don't mind. Truly. Not really. Okay, a little.*

It's not your mother's romance; it's mine. My novels are filled with angst, complex situations, passion, and love, as well as the reader's constant worry… will they *ever* get together? However, in this novel, *The Image Maker, Book 1*, the storyline is a little different. There's a reason for that. Hang on! There's more. That's all I'm sayin'.

THE IMAGE MAKER
A Love Story
Hollywood Hearts ~ 1

PART ONE

ordinary world

"The apartment below mine had the only balcony of the house. I saw a girl standing on it, completely submerged in the pool of autumn twilight. She wasn't doing a thing that I could see, except standing there leaning on the balcony railing, holding the universe together."

J. D. Salinger, A Girl I Knew

CHAPTER 1

the catch & opportunity

Isla Ryder

"Same Mistakes" - Laurel
"Same Old Love"- Selena Gomez

Tuesday Morning 9:00 a.m.

MY PHONE BUZZES AGAINST MY EAR, a frantic vibration mirroring the chaos humming through the Powers & Winston Public Relations agency's office. "No, no, no," I say in frustration into the phone. My voice is tight but controlled. "Absolutely not. We are not issuing a statement about 'the musical artist being out of control' and the music producer being unhappy with his behavior. We are *pivoting*. Robbie *adores* karaoke. It was *a mutual connection*. It's just been a misunderstanding. *Not a love fest. Not a hook-up.* Got it? Send it to me. *I'll fix it.*" I end the call.

Around me, the sleek, modern space pulses with stressful energy. Phones ring, hushed urgent whispers snake through the air, and the click-clack of keyboards provides a relentless, staccato beat. The panoramic windows overlooking Manhattan stream sunlight and promise. It's a cruel irony against the storm raging within these walls.

Another celebrity meltdown.

Another day at the office.

It's like a drug, this crisis management gig. The familiar adrenaline floods my veins. It's an addictive rush that requires laser focus in a quest for absolute control in the face of utter pandemonium.

It's not for everybody, but I'm one of the best public relations strategists around, and I love it—or *need it*—one of those.

I quickly craft a draft of a tweet designed to soothe the internet hordes and then send it off into the ether to my team to proof and seek the client's approval within the next fifteen minutes. My narrative is something along the lines of the singer being 'overwhelmed by the enormity of the role' and needing 'a fun night out to recalibrate that just got out of hand'.

Spin.

Always spin.

Idiot, I think again, picturing my client.

His drunken night with some blonde where they were singing karaoke on stage and practically fornicating—*practically* being an optional term—was captured on video by some devoted fan, igniting this whole fucking mess.

But aloud, on yet another phone call about the very same thing, my voice remains a smooth, soothing assurance with the guy's manager. "Yes, Adam, it's completely contained. Damage control is our specialty. Consider it *handled*. Because *it is*."

My team is a well-oiled machine, even when the engine is sputtering and about to burst into flames. I am the primary strategist, but we all play a constant game of three-dimensional chess with the media, with public opinion, and with reality itself.

I juggle two calls simultaneously on two different phones, barking instructions with precision, delegating tasks like a general deploying troops. Through my interior office window, I spy Samantha Harper on her way to her office. She gives me her familiar wave as she rushes past and then stops for a moment in my open doorway. I give her a questioning look, roll my eyes, indicating I'm still on a phone call.

"Drinks most definitely later." She gives me this strange, conspiratorial look, as if she has a secret and wants to tell me all about it but can't.

I know she met with Kimberley earlier this morning, so I assume that is what we'll talk about over drinks later. I nod and watch her leave.

Ten minutes later, she comes back around with a fresh Starbucks cup, enters my office, puts it on my desk, and winks at me. I give her a grateful smile. "Coffee. You're going to need it," she says mysteriously.

Again, like she has a secret. "What's up, exactly?" I end my latest phone call.

"Drinks later. *Lots* of drinks. Later." Then she just backs out of my office with a sly grin.

I hear her familiar stiletto heels fiercely tap down the marble hallway and smile to myself. Samantha, always in motion, is probably in search of the next crisis to deal with before I even have to know about it. She constantly has my back with all the continual chaos that is public relations and the subsequent controlled narrative.

She knows me too well because beneath the carefully constructed surface; I am a tightly wound spring, vibrating with barely suppressed tension. Public relations isn't just my career—it's my identity, my sanctuary, the one realm where I maintain perfect control when everything else in my life has been utter chaos. Peace was stolen from me at seventeen and almost a decade later, I am still haunted by its absence.

Each crisis is a high-wire act for me because one wrong word, one misspoken quote, or one secretly taken photograph can quickly shatter whatever carefully crafted narrative my team and I have put together. The stakes always feel personal. When a client's image collapses, something in me fractures, too. It's why I'm relentless, why I push myself and my team beyond reasonable limits. We're here to pick up the pieces, reset the tactics, and execute the overall strategy again when we have to. That's the job. *My job.* The only thing I've truly excelled at since my world collapsed nine years earlier.

I sip the coffee Samantha brought me, grateful for her intuitive thoughtfulness. She's been my best friend since we were freshman at Penn and my right hand since we started at Powers & Winston together as interns five years ago. While other people come and go in this industry, burning out from the pressure, Samantha stays. She understands what drives me without me having to explain it. She is one of the only two people in my life I can count on, the other being Kimberley.

My phone buzzes again, and I check the screen. Another crisis brewing with another client. The cycle never ends, and truthfully, I prefer it that way. The constant demands keep me from dwelling on my past.

That rainy Tuesday in December when I was seventeen remains a blur in my memory—the police at my dormitory door at the boarding school in Switzerland, the words "accident," "plane crash," "no survivors," and "I'm sorry for your loss" floating around me like debris. In an instant, my playwright father, whose words had moved millions, my mother, whose costume designs garnered prestigious awards, and my eight-year-old brother Thomas, who followed me everywhere—*all gone.*

Kimberley swept in right afterward, and then after college she brought me and Samantha into her world of public relations and image management. She taught us both that while we couldn't control the randomness of life and death, we could control narratives. We could shape how the world perceived things. We could create order from chaos.

I became obsessed with mastering this art. By twenty-five, I'd become the youngest lead strategist in the firm's history, channeling my grief into becoming the perfect PR protégé. My personal life remains practically nonexistent, except for the one we don't talk about like ever. I'm not a monk. There are occasional dates that I pretty much ensure never develop into relationships, but friendships are limited to Samantha and a few industry contacts. I've built my reputation on being unflappable, on turning disasters into opportunities.

My father's words—from his last play about loss—sometimes haunt me: "We create stories to make sense of the senseless." That's exactly what I do every day. I create stories, craft narratives, and control perceptions. It's the only way I know how to survive.

I glance at my watch and down the rest of my coffee. Three more fires to put out before I can meet Samantha for those drinks, she promises. Whatever secret she's keeping can wait. Right now, there's work to be done, and that's all that matters.

It's not life and death.

It just feels like it.

My personal mantra.

I say it every morning in front of the mirror while I try to project unwavering confidence to the world. Control. It's the only thing anchoring me in this swirling vortex of manufactured drama and high stakes.

Finally, the immediate fire simmers down to mere embers. The pop star's apology tweet goes live within a half hour of my writing it. Perfectly worded. Perfectly timed.

The Internet, fickle beast that it is, begins to sniff out a fresh scandal.

Not ours.

I lean back in my ergonomic chair. The tension within me eases ever so slightly. It's a temporary lull. *This* I know. Yet today, the feeling of victory feels hollow for some unknowable reason. It's a win, but it feels flat instead of triumphant.

Forty-five minutes later, the insistent sound of my office intercom slices through the relative quiet I've been enjoying.

"Isla," Samantha says with veiled enthusiasm. "Kimberley wants to see you. *Now.*"

Kimberley summoning anyone *now* is never a casual request. My stomach tightens with anticipation. "Do you know what it's about?" I'm still wondering about her strange behavior less than an hour ago. "Thanks for the coffee, by the way. I owe you big. How did the meeting with Kimberley go? Are you getting a raise?"

"Something like that," she laughs a little. "Just go talk to Kimberley, so then I can talk to *you* about everything. Drinks later, remember? I made reservations at Ophelia."

"Ophelia, huh? What are we celebrating? And surely my best friend would give me a heads-up if it was anything bad with Kimberley, yeah?"

"You'll see. Drinks at 5:00 p.m. at the Ophelia Lounge," Samantha says knowingly.

Whatever it is, must be big news, because Samantha normally tells me everything straight away. The anticipation coils tighter inside me.

I smooth down the front of my black power suit and the deep burgundy lace camisole I'm wearing. My armor for today. I check my reflection quickly on my phone screen. I still look like I have it together, even though I've been up since 2 AM.

But I am in control.

This is Kimberley Powers' world.

Her domain.

And in her domain, composure is currency.

Kimberley's office occupies the top floor—larger and more opulent than anyone else's except for her agency partner, Julia Winston. It's a study of controlled elegance with expensive abstract art adorning the walls, some daring—depicting nudes, all deliberately unsettling. *On purpose.* It makes me smile a little.

The panoramic window encompasses the sprawling cityscape, a glittering kingdom laid out at her feet. The scent of jasmine and lavender, her signature perfume, permeates the air.

The atmosphere is cool, controlled, and subtly intimidating. She maintains a waiting list of celebrities, CEOs, and politicians eager to work with her. She's selective about all of her clients—those she takes on, those she turns down, and those she turns out.

Kimberley sits behind her massive mahogany desk, an imposing fortress in itself. Today she wears a tailored ivory cream power suit that manages to be both severe and outrageously chic. Her sharp topaz blue eyes assess me as I approach. A glimpse of something I can't quite decipher graces her features. *Pride? Calculation? It's always a guessing game with Kimberley.*

I've learned from the best. She trained me, after all. She has mentored and guarded me since that rainy day in Switzerland, when my entire world collapsed.

"Isla," she says smoothly, indicating with the slightest wave of her hand I should close her office door. "It's time. I knew this day was coming, and I thought I was prepared. I know you're ready," she says with a wistfulness I have not witnessed in a long, long while.

"What is going on with everyone today? Samantha is acting all weird and now you look far *too sentimental.* What is it, exactly?" I ask, revealing minor frustration.

I don't like surprises pretty much on any level.

She slides a sleek manila file across the polished surface of the desk towards me, cutting straight to the chase. "Lysander Entertainment.

Trent Lysander's empire." She gets this elated smile, as if she's won an Oscar without even really trying. *A winner's triumph.*

She waits while I quickly scan the file she's given me. I feel the weight of the assignment just by the thickness of the folder and all its contents, already discerning the unspoken significance of it all.

"Lysander Entertainment. This isn't just *any* client. This is something else entirely," I say, more to myself than to her. She nods emphatically.

More impatient now, she launches into her obviously prepared speech. "We've landed the Lysander Entertainment account, Isla." She clasps her slender, manicured hands together. Her excitement grows with every word. Her gaze unwavering as she looks upon me, intently gauging me for my reaction. "And I'm putting *you in charge.*"

And there's the bombshell.

"Me? In charge of an account like that? Lysander Entertainment is the film production company Trent Lysander runs, right? It is a massive West Coast empire based in the heart of Hollywood. *Literally.*"

"Yes, exactly. It's huge, Isla. And it's all yours." Her hand sweeps across her desk as if she is Vanna White, turning the lit-up letters.

And then I land on the name she's glossed over in her fine little speech.

My stomach drops.

Roman Lysander.

The name itself is a red flag. A blaring siren in the otherwise carefully orchestrated symphony of one's professional PR life.

Mine.

Roman Lysander. Hollywood's notorious playboy. The tabloid regular whose exploits range from trashing hotel rooms to public altercations with paparazzi. The man who reportedly showed up drunk to his last film premiere.

"Roman Lysander?" I ask faintly. Just saying his name tastes like there's suddenly chalk in my mouth. I try to keep my voice neutral, professional, and respectful, but my composure starts to shatter.

My carefully controlled world precariously sways at this news. Images of my ex, the famous Chad Jameson, flash through my mind—the empty promises and humiliating betrayal that almost went public. If not for Kimberley's masterful intervention, the tabloids would *still* be talking about it.

Roman Lysander.

No.

Absolutely not.

"Kimberley, with all due respect…" My mind already racing to say in a polite, professional way, *no.* As in, no fucking way *no.*

"It's too much for me to handle. And you know *why.* After the Chad situation…" I trail off, not wanting to elaborate. "Roman Lysander is not just a difficult and obviously challenging client. He's a five-alarm fire." I whisper. "Just like the baseball player."

I hang my head in shame, remembering the strident intervention Kimberley and Julia had to take on my behalf with the whole mess that threatened to unravel my life like a lightning strike during a particularly dangerous electrical storm.

"No. *Completely* different. *Different* person. *Way* different circumstances. *Isla.*"

I look up upon hearing the heartfelt way she says my name. "I wouldn't ask you to manage the Lysander Entertainment account if I didn't think you could handle it. *Including* Roman Lysander. *Especially* Roman Lysander. This is *different.* So much bigger. Life changing, in fact."

"Kimberley, I appreciate the opportunity. Truly, I do." My voice is firm and reasonable. "But Roman Lysander… he's a disaster. He's exactly the kind of client we usually try to avoid. As you know, my focus is on building positive narratives, on crafting lasting brands, and not damage control for another Hollywood train wreck. For the most part." I have to add the qualifier because of my morning spent on the pop star fiasco. I keep my tone even and professional, but my resistance is clear.

Still, Kimberley just gazes at me like a mother bird, assessing the strengths of her baby bird for its first flight.

"You can do this." The 'no argument' salvo.

"This is *not* what I want. This is not what I signed up for," I say helplessly, shrugging my shoulders. "I don't know how to manage an account this size on my own. It's at least a million-dollar account in annual billings, probably *more.*"

I'm trying to understand why Kimberley is doing this as I quickly scan the file again, she's handed me under her studied silence.

Studied silence.

It's a tactic I've seen a thousand times that she uses on misbehaving clients or ones she is about to resign. Kimberley's lips curve into a slow, knowing smile. It sends a shiver of unease down my spine. She leans across the mahogany expanse of her desk. Her gaze sharpens.

"Isla, sweetie, you've been playing it *too safe* for a long while now."

I'm surprised by the endearment of *sweetie*. We're careful at the office in not acknowledging that we are related. I'm her niece. We don't talk about that. *Like ever.*

Then I zero in on her implication.

"*Too safe? Too safe? Me?* I don't understand. Has my work been suffering? Have I been sub-par in any way?" *It's unimaginable.*

Kimberley laughs softly. "No. No, Isla. The exact opposite, in fact, but this is your chance to shine. It's your opportunity for the freedom you so desperately crave. I'm *giving* you the Lysander Account. It's yours to run under your own agency. On your own terms."

"I'm not following." I suddenly feel completely outplayed. "What do you *mean* by my own agency?"

Kimberley's perfectly manicured nails tap against her desk, a rhythmic sound that always signals her impatience. "The Lysander Entertainment account will be your anchor account with the launch of your own boutique PR firm in Los Angeles. *Your firm.* Your *dream*, Isla. The one you've talked to Samantha about since college."

My mouth goes dry. "Our own firm? In LA?"

"With Lysander Entertainment as your anchor client. Billing one million annually, guaranteed. It's a retainer of $100,000 per month and is the perfect launch vehicle for you." She slides another document toward me. "The lease is already secured for your office space in West Hollywood. It's all arranged."

I scan the paperwork, my hands trembling slightly. "This is... everything Samantha and I have talked about for a long while now." I swallow hard.

It seems too good to be true.

"Almost everything," Kimberley corrects. "There's more."

What more could there possibly be?

There's a catch.

Of course, there is.

"I've told Trent Lysander that you will personally handle Roman Lysander's rebranding. You'll be responsible for completely transforming his image from Hollywood's 'bad boy' to being considered for more serious roles as an actor." She pauses, letting her words sink in. "Isla, you have the power to make or break Roman Lysander's career."

The catch.

CHAPTER 2

no roots

Isla Ryder

"No Roots" – Alice Merton

Tuesday Afternoon

"THE POWER TO MAKE OR BREAK Roman Lysander's career?" The words taste foreign in my mouth, like speaking a language I've never learned. "I'm not understanding how I have the power to do that or why I would want to." A laugh escapes me, hollow and uncertain. "I mean, I can be a bit of a hard-ass, but only sometimes. And I have good intentions behind everything I do."

The leather chair creaks beneath me as I shift, suddenly hyperaware of every sound in Kimberley's pristine office. The distant hum of Manhattan traffic through the windows feels like white noise against the storm brewing inside of me.

"Of course you do. You're the best. You have more patience and tolerance than I ever will." She sighs. It's a sound that carries weight I can't quite decipher, then transforms her. She gets this radiant smile, the one that usually precedes her most dangerous propositions. Kimberley shakes her head from side to side as if she can't believe it herself. "Okay, here's the amazing part. Remember your screenplay contract? When we negotiated the rights of your screenplay…"

"Yes." The word comes slowly as understanding dawns, cold and electric in my veins. "I have the final say on casting for the roles for *Vendetta* if the film ever gets made." I roll my eyes, but something in Kimberley's expression makes my breath catch. The way she's practically vibrating with barely contained excitement. "Wait."

No. She couldn't have…

I can barely breathe. "Are they finally ready to *greenlight* the film?"

"Yes." She raises her hands in triumph like she's conducting a symphony of pure possibility. "I've spoken to Trent Lysander several times, more lately, on your behalf, about the *Vendetta* film project, but I didn't want to get your hopes up. You know how these films go. It can take years to get a project of this scale going. Well, Trent Lysander has secured the funds along with a few select investors, including Powers Media, our little side project, and they have *greenlit Vendetta*, with Everest Bishop directing. Baby girl, it's happening."

I swear she practically sparkles.

It's happening. The words hit me like a physical force. My novel and then the screenplay—that I wrote in those sleepless nights after my family perished in a plane crash where I channeled grief and my father's legacy onto the proverbial page—is going to become a film.

"Everest Bishop as director? That's fantastic." Excitement soars through me. It's the exhilarating feeling of being at the top of the best roller coaster ride, that moment when you're suspended between earth and sky, when anything feels possible. This feeling of utter triumph races through me—a rush I rarely allow myself to experience. "Wow. This is incredible news, Kimberley."

She nods, but something shifts in her expression. A shadow crosses her features that makes my stomach tighten. "Isla, darling, I *need* you there. You're going to want to be there to ensure the film comes to life, creatively, like you want it to."

"*There?* As in, Los Angeles?" The question comes out more wary than I intend, but something about her tone sets off every alarm bell I've learned to trust.

"Yes. You're going to want to be there for all of it." I sense her hesitation, the way she pauses, like she's choosing her words with surgical precision. "Well, like I said, there's a bit of a catch. There are rumblings that Roman Lysander should be strongly considered for the lead role for Steven

Stryker. Apparently, Everest Bishop is on board with that. He worked with Roman on one of his earlier films and believes in Roman's acting ability and talent. And Trent Lysander is pressing pretty hard for it, too."

It's more than a rumor then.

And definitely more than just rumblings.

My elation doesn't just fade—it plummets, crashing down like a plane losing altitude. For a moment, I cannot breathe. The room suddenly feels too warm and too closed in, the walls pressing in ever closer. My chest tightens as if someone is squeezing my ribs from the inside, and I taste something metallic and sharp—rage, pure and molten.

And I'm rightfully pissed.

"Wait. What?" I surge up from my chair, the movement sharp and violent. "But *I* have final say about the casting of the main characters, *especially* Steven Stryker." The anger inside me builds and spreads through my bloodstream like poison.

I pace the floor, each step across Kimberley's plush carpet sending reverberations up my legs, matching the tremors of rage I'm fighting to contain. The Persian rug beneath my feet feels too soft, too luxurious for the fury building inside me. *This is exactly why I negotiated that clause. This is exactly why I don't trust anyone.*

I whirl around to face Kimberley, and the words explode out of me. "*Roman Lysander* as Steven Stryker in *my film?* What the actual fuck? He's a fuckboy. He might be Hollywood's heartthrob, but how is he capable of taking on a serious role like Steven Stryker? *Vendetta* is a *serious film,* requiring a *serious actor,* not some rom-com playboy who goes through women like flavors of ice cream at Ben & Jerry's. This is exactly *why* I wanted full casting authority! So, the lead roles don't fall into mediocrity, where the uniqueness of the storyline gets lost and becomes yet another forgettable film, like so many others. Fucking politics. Fucking Hollywood. Oh my God, this is *exactly* why. There is no fucking way that is happening to *my film.*"

The outburst drains me and leaves me visibly shaken. I collapse back into the chair with a resigned 'humph'. I feel as if I've just run a marathon through my own worst nightmare. "Sorry." The usual remorse seeps in. I've lost my temper with the only other person, besides Samantha, who always has my back.

The elation of getting *Vendetta* greenlit completely disappears. It's replaced by a cold, heavy dread that sits like a stone in my stomach. I shake my head emphatically at Kimberley, who simply watches me with that calculating expression I've seen her use with difficult clients.

She's not at a loss for words. No.

She is studying me, trying to figure out how best to handle me.

I've seen it hundreds of times.

With difficult clients.

I am one of those now.

Difficult clients who are on the losing end and fail to realize it.

Until it's far too late.

Fait accompli.

"Well, I see I have your attention *now*," Kimberley says. Her voice carries that particular edge she reserves for moments when she's about to deliver a killing blow. "Isla, this is the big leagues. This is how the game is played. It's why I negotiated on your behalf about the final say on the lead roles, especially Steven Stryker. Your identity as the writer—and the screenwriter for the film, *Vendetta*—remains *undisclosed*, but *these people*, well, they do this for a living. They will not let a non-disclosure agreement and a casting clause within the film rights contract hold all the power over a lucrative project like *Vendetta* without a fight. Legal or otherwise."

She leans forward, her gaze intensifying until I feel pinned beneath it like a butterfly on a collector's board. "So, we need to be present, on the ground in LA, play the politics, and get a lay of the land. Trent Lysander and his team have invested a hundred million dollars, and he intends to make three times as much with its release. Right now, he is willing to put up some serious cash, a monthly retainer of $100,000—pittance compared to the money raised for the film's production, but still worth *our time...*" Her smile turns predatory. "In order to fully remediate his son's image and make him more palatable for middle America. You're the best at that kind of branding. And that's why we must take a stand. You want to retain your power and creative control over *Vendetta*, right?"

"Abso-fucking-lutely. Yes, I do. And I *will* retain my rights over casting power no matter what Trent Lysander and his company try to do." The vehemence in my voice surprises even me, but it feels good to say it, to claim that power.

"Well, you have to be *out there* for that. *In LA*. Where these big dogs play. So yes, I pitched Trent Lysander the idea of sending my very best out there to handle the image problem of his son. He knows it's an opportunity he cannot afford to *not* take. Double negative there. Sorry about that." She laughs, but there is no humor in it.

"Trent Lysander has acknowledged and agreed to your dual role as PR strategist to his son." Kimberley's voice takes on the confident cadence of a master negotiator sealing a deal. The sound makes me hyperaware—I know that tone. It means I'm already part of her plan, whether I like it or not. "Roman will be your project, so to speak, but you'll be under contract to Lysander Entertainment."

She leans forward slightly; her manicured fingers steepled as she delivers the crucial details. "He obviously knows you are the screenwriter for *Vendetta*, under your pen name, Ashley Thomas. He's fully aware of that connection. Most importantly, he's under a non-disclosure agreement. He can't divulge your true identity without running into serious legal trouble with us and our lawyers under the contract he signed with Powers Media regarding the film rights."

The weight of what she's saying settles over me like a heavy blanket, suffocating in its implications. Trent Lysander knows exactly who I am, yet he's agreed to these terms. The irony isn't lost on me—the man whose son I'm supposed to rebrand also holds the keys to my screenplay's success as a film.

It's too neat.

Too convenient.

Too complicated.

"The contract includes both the casting clause parameters and the protection of your identity under the NDA," Kimberley explains, her tone becoming more businesslike, as if we're discussing quarterly reports instead of my entire future. "He has agreed to you being in the dual role of PR strategist *and* as the screenwriter with final casting decision for the film *Vendetta*."

She pauses, letting that sink in before continuing. "He agreed to all of those terms in the public relations contract—retaining you at a hundred grand a month for a year, fully aware of who you are but also recognizing what you can do for Roman."

The complexity of the arrangement makes my head spin. I'm not just taking on Roman Lysander as a client—I'm walking into a situation where his father knows I hold all the cards for his son's career-defining role, yet he is paying me handsomely to potentially save that very career. The circular nature of it feels extremely dangerous, like standing in the eye of a hurricane, temporarily calm but surrounded by devastating winds. *Like being seventeen again and having the ground disappear beneath my feet.*

Kimberley gets that familiar gleam in her eyes. *Winning*. She smiles. "I think we can assume that he is desperate to rehabilitate his only son's image, and I convinced him you are the only PR strategist who can do this successfully."

"Well, yes, with clients who actually *follow* my strategy and *cooperate*." The words come out sharper than intended. "I'm not exactly sure what I can do for Roman Lysander. He actually has to *want* to change. And, as you very well know, my track record in working with 'bad boy' behavior is less than stellar."

Without thinking, I touch my neck, feeling the phantom weight of the diamond necklace that the famous baseball player once clasped there—a gift before the betrayal. The flash of this unwanted memory stings like a yellow jacket wasp, sharp and immediate. The pain fades quickly, but the poison remains, spreading through my system as a reminder for every reason I don't trust anyone. *Especially not Hollywood playboys who think they can charm their way out of consequences.*

She shakes her finger at me with the authority of someone who has cleaned up more messes than she can count. "Chad Jameson was an *anomaly*. A narcissist of the worst kind. He fooled us all. Just poor judgment calls on *all our parts*. I never should have taken him on as a client. Let alone assigned him to you. But he's in the past. It's over and done with. Lessons learned all around." She waves a dismissive hand.

She sighs. And for a singular moment, looks uncertain. Very un-Kimberley-Powers-like. But then, she doubles down, exhibiting defiance. "Let's *focus* on the finer points here. It *is* in your best interest to ensure that *Vendetta* gets made the way you intend it to. And you *cannot do that* from the East Coast, wasting your incredible, magical PR talent, taking care of some obnoxious pop star who is fucking a fan on a karaoke stage at two in the morning."

She's already heard about my morning.

Of course she has.

Nothing happens in this building without Kimberley knowing about it within the hour.

I lean back in my chair, the leather cool against my palms where they grip the armrests. The smooth texture grounds me, giving me something solid to hold on to while my familiar world seemingly shifts. I attempt to compose myself, to really take in what she's saying, but it feels like trying to catch smoke with my bare hands.

"You're the best narrative building strategist around and you have very good instincts for all of it," she says proudly, rewarding me with her best smile—the one that used to make me feel safe when I was seventeen and drowning in grief. "You'll win Roman Lysander over. And Trent Lysander, too." She frowns, and uncertainty crosses her face. *Very un-Kimberley like.* "Although Trent Lysander is an enigma all his own. He and Roman seem to have a very complicated relationship."

"Not exactly selling me on this idea, Aunt Kimmy." I lift my chin in defiance and stare at her, my arms crossed like armor across my chest.

Aunt Kimmy was my nickname for her when I was a little girl. Oh yes. I'm playing the nepotism card now. *'Don't make me do this'* is being telepathically sent across the desk in her direction. *Clearly.*

I watch her closely, studying the micro-expressions that cross her face. She hesitates for a few seconds. I can practically see the gears turning behind her eyes as she intently studies me from across that massive mahogany desk.

Another power move.

The desk.

She shared this with me once—how the physical barrier gives her a psychological advantage over a client, or an employee, or her niece, even.

I know exactly when she changes tactics. I watch it happen in real time, like watching a master chess player sacrifice a pawn to win the game.

"Isla, darling." Her blue eyes sparkle with untold determination and supreme confidence.

Here we go.

"Let's stay focused on the bigger picture. The *opportunity* here. The facts are these: Roman Lysander is *not a train wreck,*" she says softly, her voice taking on that hypnotic quality she uses when she wants to reprogram someone's entire worldview. "He's a *goldmine.* He is the epitome of untapped potential. He is raw charisma. A walking sex god. He has millions of fans—men and women alike—who would fuck him in a heartbeat if he asked them to. The guy is on the cusp of a massive career breakthrough, has massive appeal, and loads of untapped talent for his craft. *Vendetta* could *redefine him*, and you're the only one who can help him, so that it does."

"So, you want me to fuck him if he asks?" The words slip out before I can stop them. Sharp. Insolent. One could say disrespectful.

If she wasn't my aunt, I wouldn't be saying it.

The words hang in the air between us, nearly visible in their audacity. The silence stretches, taut as a wire, and I can hear my own heartbeat.

Kimberley laughs—her most wicked laugh, the one that means she's about to say something that will either scandalize or enlighten. She shakes her head from side to side in wonder. "You can fuck whoever you want." She grins at me, arching an eyebrow with the practiced ease of someone who has never been shocked by anything. "However, I believe that is a strategy to be used very carefully and most wisely. But you do what you want, Isla Jane, whatever you think is needed here."

It's practically a dare, coming from Kimberley at this point.

"Funny, ha-ha. Whatever. I'll keep that in mind," I say with noteworthy sarcasm and the fakest smile I can muster.

The scent of her jasmine perfume suddenly seems too strong. It makes my head swim. Or maybe it's the two hours of sleep I got before all hell broke loose with said pop star and probable fornication on a karaoke stage at two in the morning. *My life has become a series of other people's bad decisions.*

"Isla. It's not just Roman Lysander's film career that is on the cusp of a meteoric rise; it's *your film, Vendetta,* which could be the breakout film of the summer. A blockbuster. That's what Trent Lysander is predicting, at least, on the conference call about *Vendetta* being greenlit that we had earlier today," she says. Her tone intensifies with every word she utters.

"Isla, this is the dream. *Your dream.* And I just want you to be happy, carefree, live a full life, and earn gobs of money from your amazing talent and see all your dreams come true. This isn't the time to hold back. Or play it safe. This is the time to go big and not be afraid. Surely, you'll make mistakes. Make lots of them. Just learn from them. Life is too short, as we both know all too well."

Life is too short.

The words hit like a physical blow, bringing with them the smell of rain and the sound of police officers' voices, explaining that planes sometimes fall out of the sky and take everything good with them.

She frowns, and suddenly she looks less like the powerful PR maven and more like the woman who tried to figure out how to raise a traumatized teenager while building an empire. "I'm sorry I wasn't much of a mother to you when you were seventeen. I should have taken you out of that boarding school in Switzerland and brought you back to New York… sooner. I just didn't know what to do—"

"I liked it there." I interrupt her before she can venture further into emotional territory that neither of us knows how to navigate. The words come out too quick, too defensive.

I don't talk about my family. Like ever.

Because talking about them makes them real and making them real makes losing them hurt all over again.

My throat constricts, and for a moment, I'm seventeen again, smelling the old wood in the headmistress's office, tears streaming down my face as those impossible words echo in my memory: *'There was a plane crash. There are no survivors.'*

"You were barely older than I am now. How could anyone handle a seventeen-year-old who'd just lost everything and everyone? But you made it work. You've always made me feel like I'm part of your family with Brad and the kids. And I appreciate everything you've done for me. I always have. Thank you."

We are way out of our normal emotional depth here.

We do not share often.

We don't do feelings.

We do strategy and damage control and carefully constructed narratives that keep the messy truth buried where it can't hurt anyone.

She pauses for a long moment, and I watch her subtly wipe a tear from her eye with the back of her hand. *Regrouping.*

We both are.

She recovers first. She always does. Her smile returns, teary but determined. "Think of it, Isla. Los Angeles." She gestures expansively, somehow invoking imagined sunshine and the glittering promise of the West Coast with the wave of her manicured hand. The diamond there sparkles just like her eyes when she's about to close a deal. "Your own boutique PR agency. I know it's what you want. What you crave. You've been under my guidance for years, darling girl. Do you think I don't know and understand the need to fulfill your own dream? Believe me, I do. Well, this is your chance. With Lysander Entertainment as your anchor account. You can build your own firm any way you want.

Lysander Entertainment just gives you that initial start, a base to build from. It will be your gig with my backing, but you can run it any way you want. No interference from me."

She has played her ultimate trump card, the one she knows effectively pierces through all my carefully constructed defenses and any remaining resistance I may have. Kimberley is offering me the very thing I crave the most: freedom and independence.

The chance to prove I don't need anyone. That I can survive on my own terms.

Like I always have.

"I know, but... *Roman Lysander*." Just speaking his name invokes negative feelings and immense trepidation, like reciting a curse aloud that might summon evil. "It will be a *lot of work*. These kinds of clients always are. It's an almost impossible task turning his 'bad boy' image around."

"But *not* impossible. You have exceptional talent and natural instincts for what needs to be done for someone of his stature. I *know* you'll be able to help him."

"Thank you. But that's the least of it, yeah? What about the casting power and politics around all of that? I guess I can't worry about that part of it. I'll have to compartmentalize and just concentrate on the immediate issues with his image and branding. Go for some quick wins out of the gate and then focus on more long-term strategies from there. Then, I can determine if he is the right fit for the role of Steven Stryker for such a serious film, like *Vendetta*."

I'm already strategizing. Already planning. Already caught up in her strategic plan.

Kimberley looks pleased. She knows I've already 'crossed over' into working on the strategy of how to fix Roman Lysander's image problem.

My mind races ahead. "So, as far as casting decisions in relation to *Vendetta*, it's essential that I find out what he's like in person and spend some time studying his body of film work and review his screen tests. Then, I can meet with Everest Bishop and get his input as well. Executing on all of these tactics will help me in making the right casting decisions for *Vendetta*, even as it relates to Roman Lysander. I imagine I will have *some time* before Lysander Entertainment and company are looking for those decisions about casting. And Roman Lysander either has the acting chops to play the role of Steven Stryker or he doesn't. We'll see."

"Exactly. Just know, that little condition in your screenwriter's contract about final say on casting is your superpower. And yours alone," she reminds me softly, and there's something almost maternal in her voice. "You understand the character of Steven Stryker better than anyone else. *You* get to decide if Roman is right for the part after you've spent some time with him. You'll know either way. You have good instincts for film as well as public relations in identifying talent," Kimberley says. "And Trent Lysander and his team have assured me they will trust your judgment either way. They cannot afford to make a mistake here, Isla. There is too much money involved. I think that's why he's become so willing to retain you in order to rebrand Roman. He and Lysander Entertainment need to get this right. So, your vested interest on both ends of the spectrum in terms of redefining Roman Lysander's image and determining if he has what it takes to take on a serious role like Steven Stryker for *Vendetta* is paramount. It is in everyone's best interest, at this point, to get it right."

"But it's my decision. Solely mine." The words intimate power, responsibility, and danger all at once.

"Yes," she says emphatically, and the single word carries the weight of a promise and a threat.

"Does Roman Lysander *know* that I have this power?"

"Doubtful. Remember, Trent Lysander is under an NDA with us." Kimberley tilts her head to one side, slipping into her thinking mode. "He is being a little cagey. I don't think he even wants Roman to know that he has put such a vested interest in all of this by hiring you to address his image and reputation. But we'll see."

Of course he's being cagey. Rich, powerful men are always cagey when their reputations and their sons' careers are on the line.

She leans forward, directly meeting my gaze. "The other thing to be mindful of is that you get two percent of the gross when the film releases next summer. *Gone Girl* grossed $365 million. *Vendetta* could be just as big, especially with Everest Bishop directing."

"I don't care about the money."

"Yes, *but everyone else does.* Just be aware of that. Power and money and fame—the three things that rule the world of the rich and famous, especially in Hollywood."

I brush aside what she's saying to a certain extent. Power, money, and fame are not my focus. But she's right; they're everyone else's.

Final say is my power.

Control is a table stake.

Power over Roman Lysander's fate? Not my focus right now.

And *Vendetta*. My secret passion project, born from grief and love and the desperate need to honor my father's legacy. Who knew my novel would become a bestseller? That Kimberley would convince me to write the screenplay and be so earnest in protecting my rights when Lysander Entertainment picked it up two years ago?

I owe her. So much.

My mind races, a whirlwind of conflicting emotions that threatens to tear me apart from the inside.

Elation.

Trepidation.

Triumph.

Terror.

The freedom and the independence that come with all of that feel both thrilling and terrifying. It's the dream Samantha and I have been talking about for so long, and it's finally within reach.

It would be our own firm—our agency.

The dream.

Built on the foundation of managing Hollywood's most notorious 'bad boy'.

And the film, *Vendetta*, is finally *greenlit. My film.* The story I wrote to make sense of senseless loss, to give meaning to meaningless tragedy.

But the opportunity is in LA, not Manhattan. *Not ideal.*

Roman Lysander. *Again, not ideal.*

Understatement of the fucking century.

The thought of working with him, effectively managing his chaotic lifestyle and his image, feels monumental. I shiver with a strange mix of dread and anticipation, like standing at the edge of a cliff and knowing you're about to jump. I can do it though. If anybody can take on a challenge like Roman Lysander, it's me. *This, I know.* Ego aside, I'm *good* at what I do.

And the opportunity is there.

Glittering like a diamond amongst a pile of sand and rocks.

It's a gamble, a terrifying leap into the unknown. The lure of independence, of finally being able to prove myself and control my own destiny, is irresistible. I can't turn down the opportunity. And *Vendetta*. The novel I wrote to honor my parents' love and my father's writing legacy. I can't let anyone, especially a self-destructive Hollywood 'bad boy', ruin it. At the very least, he'll need my guidance, so he doesn't.

I can finally step out of Kimberley's shadow and into my own light. I need to go to LA and find out who I am dealing with. There's no other way. And, of course, Kimberley knew this all along.

I take a deep breath and slowly exhale. The air seems different somehow, charged with possibility and danger in equal measure.

"It's a lot to take on. But the opportunity is unbelievable." I sigh and then smile in gratitude at Kimberley. "Okay. Yes, I'll take on the Lysander Entertainment account in the rebranding of Roman Lysander. And I will do everything I can to help him with rebranding his image either way. If he doesn't make the cut for Steven Stryker, there will be other roles for him," I say with a nonchalant shrug.

If he doesn't make the cut, I'll make sure he knows exactly why.

"Fabulous," she says, clasping her hands together like she's just closed the deal of the century. Kimberley comes around her massive desk and hugs me tight, and I'm taken aback by the unexpected display of affection. She never displays this much emotion in the office. Most of the employees at Powers and Winston don't even know we're related.

We are way out of bounds here.

The familiar scent of her perfume envelops me, and instead of feeling overwhelming, it's comforting now—like being wrapped in expensive armor.

She steps back from me, her hands lingering on my shoulders. "Start packing, Isla Jane. Los Angeles awaits and Powers & Winston PR is picking up the one-year lease on Julia's place in Malibu for you, as well as an apartment at The Harland in West Hollywood. You'll probably want to stay in West Hollywood during the week and save the place in Malibu for weekends. It's a bit of a drive, and LA traffic is part of the lifestyle."

She stops talking when she sees my face, which must look like I've just been told I need to learn to breathe underwater.

"A bit of a drive? *Traffic? What?*" The words come out faint, like they're being squeezed through my constricting throat. My stomach drops as if I'm already navigating those infamous LA freeways, trapped in metal and glass and exhaust fumes. *Another challenge I will have to figure out. Another way this city will want to kill me.*

"It's LA, darling girl. There's a nice little Porsche in the garage in Malibu. Julia's already dealt with car insurance. You're going to be *fine.* Your executive suite office space will be in West Hollywood, and they'll be able to help with the logistics you'll be needing."

"Thanks?" I'm still reeling about the mention of traffic and driving and office logistics. Still trying to process the fact that my entire life is about to change in the span of forty-eight hours.

Holy shit. This is really happening and at warp speed.

So, like Kimberley.

"Oh! I almost forgot the best news. I've talked to Samantha already, and I'm sending her with you to LA. You'll need help setting things up with your own agency, and that is Samantha's superpower. She's thrilled about LA. She'll follow you out there, in the next day or two, once you've settled in a bit. I asked her to allow me to talk to you first before she said anything."

Relief floods through me like cool water on burning skin. *Samantha. At least I won't be completely alone in this.*

"Well, that explains her strange behavior earlier and the coffee delivery right after dealing with the pop star disaster this morning." The memory of Samantha's mysterious behavior makes me smile despite everything.

"Yes. Yes, it does."

"Samantha and I have always talked about starting up our own PR agency someday. We should definitely go in as full partners." The words rush out before I can stop them, carried by a sudden surge of hope and determination.

"She mentioned that in her always effervescent enthusiasm," Kimberley says with a little laugh that sounds almost fond. "But that's between you two. I'm just here to support you both in any way I can. Julia is, too. We're both on board. Whatever you decide about a partnership for your boutique firm is up to you and Samantha. It's your gig, Isla."

Your gig.

Your responsibility.

Your chance to succeed or fail spectacularly.

Kimberley picks up her phone and dials an extension, her movements crisp and efficient. "Willow? Could you come in, please?"

Willow Adams, Kimberley's assistant, sails into the room with the grace of someone who's spent years navigating the treacherous waters of high-stakes PR. She hands me another thick file; her smile warm and encouraging. "Congratulations, Isla." The words carry genuine warmth, and for a moment, I feel like maybe this isn't completely insane.

"That file has your itinerary, plane ticket for the red-eye tomorrow night, a decent amount of cash, bank account information for money transfers," Kimberley says, ticking off items like she's reading a shopping list. "And, more importantly, the dossier on Roman Lysander, and all the background information on Trent Lysander and Lysander Entertainment, too."

The file feels heavier than it should, as if weighed down with all the possibilities and dangers it contains. My fingers tingle where they touch the smooth manila surface, like I'm holding a live wire.

"You've thought of everything. Thank you. It's all... so generous. I won't let you down."

I hope.

I pray.

As I leave Kimberley's office, the thick files clutched against my chest like armor, I realize the New York skyline suddenly feels different through the panoramic windows. More... confining. This city that has been my sanctuary, my carefully constructed safe space, but now it seems like a cage I need to escape.

Los Angeles. Sun. Opportunity. Freedom. It's a fresh start and a chance to build our boutique PR agency, to do things our way, on our own terms, like Samantha and I have always talked about during those late-night strategy sessions fueled by too much coffee and too many dreams.

And I have the right to wield my power by having the final say on who gets the lead role for *Vendetta.*

No small thing. Too big to fully comprehend.

The power to make or break someone's career.

The power to protect my father's legacy or watch it burn.

Then I think about the connections. All the connections.

Lysander Entertainment.

Roman Lysander.

Vendetta.

Money and power and fame—the holy trinity of Hollywood corruption.

There is something about this amazing opportunity that feels... dangerous.

Treacherous *even.*

Exciting, *yes.*

Thrilling, *yes.*

Life-changing, absolutely.

Even so, *it is undeniably dangerous.*

Why?

Because I have the power to make or break Roman Lysander's career.

Because his father is paying me to save the son while I hold the keys to his destruction.

Because I've never trusted anyone, and now I'm walking into a world where trust is a currency I cannot afford.

The power feels too wieldy, too sharp, like holding a blade by the edge instead of the handle.

That's the undeniably dangerous part.

To him.

And to me.

I press my hand against my chest, feeling my heartbeat beneath my palm—rapid and irregular, like a bird trying to escape a cage. Its frantic rhythm tells me I'm about to step into something that could change everything.

Hopefully, it's something good.

CHAPTER 3

resurrection

Isla Ryder

"Young And Beautiful" - Lana Del Rey
"The Chain" - Fleetwood Mac
"Beautiful People Beautiful Problems" - Lana Del Rey, Stevie Nicks

Tuesday Evening

THE CLINK OF ICE IN MY WATER GLASS seems amplified in the relative quiet of our corner booth at the Ophelia Lounge. The sound reverberates through me, like the persistent echo of Kimberley's words from earlier today. Samantha slides a vibrant pink cocktail aptly named *'Resurrection'* across the polished marble table towards me. Her own *'Resurrection'* is already halfway gone. Her energy practically vibrates off the plush velvet seating.

Samantha Harper embodies the ethereal beauty of a younger Lily James from *Cinderella*—that same luminous quality that makes strangers stop her on Manhattan sidewalks, convinced she must be related to the actress. At 5'9", she possesses that willowy elegance and natural sex appeal, but there's something more potent radiating from her: an effervescent energy, an 'I can conquer the world' confidence that feels almost supernatural.

Others view her as the blonde version of Wonder Woman disguised as a Texas debutante—raised on her family's sprawling ranch with five protective older brothers who taught her to ride horses, drive trucks, and rope cattle with equal finesse. The only girl, the baby of the family, she fled Texas after delivering a resounding 'no' to her high school sweetheart's marriage proposal. At Penn, she latched onto me like we were destined soulmates, and after graduation, she followed me to New York City as if the metropolis had been calling her name all along.

Samantha lives in designer everything, knows every fashion house worth knowing, and maintains this relentlessly romantic worldview painted in shades of rose gold and endless sunshine. She sees possibility where I see pitfalls, magic where I see manipulation.

My world, by contrast, exists in black. It matches my dark mahogany hair, my carefully curated wardrobe, my pragmatic outlook. At 5'7", I occupy that perfect middle ground—neither too short nor too tall—and I've learned to maximize what I have through strategic styling. I'm the mirror image of my mother and Kimberley, except for my father's emerald eyes, a genetic gift that occasionally earns me comparisons to Keira Knightley. Though my hair runs darker, my bone structure more angular, my eyes are emerald green while Keira Knightley's are brown. I never quite understand the comparison. Still, being likened to the star of my beloved *Pride and Prejudice, 2005,* feels like an unexpected compliment.

'Average but gifted'—that's how I described myself in my college personal essay.

I manage chaos for a living; I don't create it. *Usually.*

My natural inclination is to prepare for catastrophe, though I do it with style. I'm the friend you want when the apocalypse arrives—I'll be distributing water rations and organizing survivor hierarchies while maintaining perfect lipstick. Samantha will be planning the evening's entertainment. We'd both be essential for survival, but we'd serve completely opposite functions. The yin and yang of crisis management.

"Okay, spill *everything.*" Samantha leans forward. Her blue eyes are wide with vicarious excitement. "Kimberley swore me to secrecy until you knew, and I thought I was going to spontaneously combust. *Los Angeles.* Our *own* agency. Can you believe it?"

I take a measured sip of the potent mix—vodka, Campari, passion fruit, hibiscus. *Resurrection.* The fancy drink burns a path down my throat, warming me, even as a chill of uncertainty spreads across my skin, despite it being the third week in August in Manhattan.

Fitting name, *Resurrection*, although perhaps the word feels too optimistic for the chaotic rebirth Kimberley has clearly orchestrated.

"I can believe Kimberley *arranged* it." I keep my tone even. "Down to the very last detail, I'm sure. Including talking to you *first*."

Samantha waves a dismissive hand. "Details, details. Focus on the big picture here, Iz. Sunshine. Movie stars. Ryder & Harper Communications LA. And..." She pauses for dramatic effect, lowering her voice to a conspiratorial whisper, "Roman *freaking* Lysander."

A now familiar tightness coils in my stomach at just hearing his name. My fingers involuntarily clench around the smooth glass, knuckles whitening. It's not just the tabloid headlines flashing through my mind—the trashed hotel rooms, the paparazzi altercations, or even the drunken premiere. It's the echo of Chad Jameson, the professional and personal fallout I barely survived, and only thanks to Kimberley and Julia's intervention. But the inherent risk of tethering our nascent agency, *our* independence, to such a volatile variable still exists.

It's real. It's a potential disaster, or a challenge. Dress it up however you like.

It's a risk. And I don't like those.

"He's the catch, Samantha." I swirl the liquid in my glass. The pink vortex mirrors the churning in my gut. "The multi-million-dollar, blue-eyed, walking PR disaster of a catch."

"Are you *kidding* me?" Samantha leans even closer, her blonde bob framing an incredulous expression. "He's literal Hollywood royalty. That face? Those eyes? That man's *body*. Forget PR disaster. He's a PR *opportunity* if there ever was one. Think of the headlines *we* can generate. The *good kind*." She fans herself dramatically. "Half of America wants to climb him like a tree."

"And the other half wants to watch him fall," I say emphatically. The words taste bitter on my tongue, like the Campari in my drink. "He's not just young, gorgeous, and rich, Sammy girl. He's reckless. He jeopardizes productions. He's the antithesis of the serious, lasting brands we try to build. He's a liability. Especially *now*."

"Especially *now*? What do you mean?"

I take a deep breath, fill my lungs with needed air, and slowly exhale.

Control. I need control.

I look at my best friend in earnest and then slowly smile, nodding. "Because *Vendetta* is officially greenlit." My words carry both the amazing thrill and the heavy burden. My heart pounds against my ribs like it's trying to escape. "Everest Bishop is directing."

Samantha gasps, her hand flying to her mouth. *"No way. Isla!"* She's breathless with excitement. *"Your book? Your screenplay?* It's actually *happening. Oh, my God.* Why didn't you *lead* with that?" Her initial excitement about LA seems momentarily eclipsed.

"Because…" I lean in, lowering my voice, "Trent Lysander is pushing for Roman to play Steven Stryker. Everest Bishop is apparently considering it, too. And while I technically have final say…"

Understanding dawns on Samantha's face. "Whoa. Okay. That *is* complicated." She stirs her drink thoughtfully. "So, you're his publicist, charged with fixing his image, *and* the secret screenwriter deciding if he's worthy of the lead role in your passion project? *Wow!* Yeah, that's *a lot.*"

"Exactly. Exactly." The repetition escapes me, a nervous tic betraying my anxiety. "Trent knows I wrote *Vendetta* as Ashley Thomas, but he signed an NDA. And Roman?" I shake my head, exhaling heavily. "Roman may just know some New York PR strategists are showing up to reform his image, but I seriously doubt he sees that in a positive light. Instead, he'll view us as a hostile takeover of his life." I laugh a little.

"We're not that hard-ass, though." Samantha looks thoughtful.

"Well, he's not going to be happy. He's probably going to resist every strategy and tactic we come up with. It's not going to be easy convincing him that we have the solutions to his image and reputation problems because he probably doesn't view them as problems, or *himself* as the problem, for that matter. I'm sure, in his mind, we're just the hired guns—*the babysitters*—wreaking havoc on his social life and lifestyle. For no good reason at all."

"Well, you can relieve him of that notion in short order. I know you can," Samantha says with extreme confidence. "Truly, you're the best at that kind of thing. Look who just sent you a gorgeous bouquet of red roses this afternoon, promising better behavior from here on out."

She's referencing the fornicating pop star without naming him since we're in a public place. We're careful with our clients that way. Discretion above all else, while we solve the fucking problem. Literally, in this case.

"Right? And if he only knew how much I hate flowers." I grin at her.

"Well, I brought them to the apartment. Since I *knew,* you were going to promptly throw them out."

"Rescuing flowers now, are we?"

"Someone has to." Samantha's gaze sharpens. "So. Back to Roman Lysander," she whispers, so we won't be overheard. "He has no idea you're the one making the call on casting?"

"None. There's an NDA in place protecting my identity as the screenwriter. And frankly, right now, that cannot be our focus. We need to be laser-focused on his rebranding. The casting is a separate thing. He needs to embrace our strategy, surrounding his public relations, before the other part, the casting part for *Vendetta,* comes into play."

I take another sip, feeling the burn of the cocktail match the simmering anxiety throughout my body. The pressure behind my eyes builds, threatening a headache. "But if Roman Lysander screws this up, he doesn't just tank our new agency. He tanks everything I've created with *Vendetta.* The film could become a joke before the cameras even roll."

A scenario I will not tolerate.

Samantha considers that, then leans back, looking all thoughtful. Her eyes grow dreamy, and her voice softens. "Isla, I know you think he's a risk as far as *Vendetta* goes, but... I can totally see Roman Lysander as Steven Stryker. Think about it. Evelyn Stryker falls in love with *exactly* that kind of reckless charm and that heartbreaking intensity. That's why the vendetta feels real. It's not just about revenge. It's about love. It's that amazing love he has for Evelyn that drives the entire storyline for Steven Stryker."

"Thank you. You're my best friend and biggest fan rolled into one. Love you, girl." I smile but then it falters. "But it's fiction, Samantha. In real life, that kind of intensity blows up in spectacular, headline-grabbing fashion." My shoulders tense up. A familiar knot forms between my shoulder blades just thinking about the challenges being presented with Roman Lysander like the rolling credits after a movie ends. There are so many. It's overwhelming.

She shrugs, undeterred. "Maybe. But Roman's got real acting ability *despite* the lifestyle drama. And you've got the exact skills—personally and professionally—to channel all his chaos into something incredible. I *know* you do."

I look down at my drink, the vibrant color swirling dangerously close to the glass rim. Samantha always sees the potential—the passion in life. I tend to look for the traps and the downfalls. I wish it could be that simple. But where she feels excitement, all I feel is the heavy weight of responsibility and the constant quest for absolute control of the chaos. The challenge of it all settles in on me, making each breath a conscious effort.

"Or it could all just explode spectacularly," I murmur. "It could all just… fall apart."

Samantha reaches across the table, squeezing my hand. Her touch is warm, sympathetic. "Yes. But that's life, no? We take chances and experience the spectacular rise as much as the fall. It's the ultimate rollercoaster ride. Isn't that half the fun?"

Cup half-full girl meet cup half-empty girl.

"Easy for you to *say*." A reluctant smile tugs at my lips. "*Easy* for you to say."

"Kimberley wouldn't set you up to fail." Samantha's insistence and her unwavering loyalty ground me. "She knows you can handle this. It's like she said, right? Big leagues, big plays."

"Yes. Big leagues, big plays," I echo. "She also said Trent Lysander has millions invested and won't hesitate to steamroll me if my 'final say' clause becomes inconvenient. This isn't just about managing a difficult client. It's about navigating Hollywood politics, protecting my creative control, launching our agency, and managing the guy who could embody—*or destroy*—the most important project of my life. All the while pretending those last two parts aren't connected."

"Okay, deep breaths," Samantha says, reaching across to squeeze my hand briefly. "It's a lot. But it's also *everything*. Our own firm. Your movie. This is the *dream*, Isla. The messy, complicated, terrifying, potentially amazing dream."

I pull my hand back, needing the space. The air around me suddenly feels too close, too warm. "The logistics alone… Kimberley's already leased office space, an apartment for me at The Harland, another for you at Nine Thousand One, *and* Julia Winston's place in Malibu for my weekends? Plus, a Porsche?" I shake my head. "It feels less like freedom and more like being repositioned on her chessboard."

"Maybe," Samantha concedes with a shrug, "but it's a *really nice* chessboard, and she's giving you the *queen* piece, the most powerful piece. The one with all the power and all the moves. And frankly, I'm relieved we don't have to find apartments and a car ourselves. At least, right away. We can hit the ground running. You focus on the strategy—for Roman, for *Vendetta*, for Ryder & Harper Communications LA. I'll handle the operational end of things—the day-to-day stuff while you work your PR magic on Hollywood's most notorious 'bad boy'. Partners, remember?"

I manage a small smile. The tension in my shoulders eases slightly. "The perfect team." I clink my glass against hers. "You're the best, Sammy girl."

"Now tell me more about the *rest* of this conversation with Kimberley. You said there were 'some fireworks' in your text."

I laugh. "It was warpath material. I completely lost it when she told me about the part where I'm tasked with rebranding Roman Lysander, and then she lays out the catch about casting rumors where they are considering him for Steven Stryker. I was like, 'what the actual fuck? Are you *serious*?'" My hands gesture wildly, nearly spilling my drink.

"I was livid. Not normally my style, but I'm pacing her office, cursing up a storm." I laugh again, shaking my head. The memory plays vividly in my mind—Kimberley's unflappable expression as I unraveled in front of her.

"Then, it's epic Kimberley. *Seriously.* She looks me dead in the eye and says Roman Lysander isn't a train wreck—he's *'raw charisma'* and a *'walking sex god'* 'with millions of fans who'd fuck him if he asked.' He's apparently the golden ticket if we rebrand him right for *Vendetta*, according to Kimberley's logic, said in that commanding way of hers. You know which tone I'm talking about."

"Yeah, I know that one." Samantha nods knowingly.

"So, I'm a little pissed, feeling completely outgunned, so I throw her logic back at her, and deadpan: 'So, you want me to fuck him if he asks?'"

Samantha nearly spits out her drink with her sudden laughter. "You didn't!"

"Oh, I so *did*." I smile wryly. A flush of heat rises to my face at the memory. "I wouldn't dare, but she's my aunt, so *oh yeah*, I pulled the nepotism card, knowing she wouldn't fire me outright. But Kimberley just laughs—this wicked, scandalized laugh—and says, *'You can fuck whoever you want. However, I believe that is a strategy to be used very carefully and most wisely. But you do what you want, Isla Jane, whatever you think is needed here.' she says.'"* I mimic Kimberley's arched eyebrow and teasing tone perfectly.

"Samantha claps a hand over her mouth, eyes wide. "She practically dared you!"

"Right?" I roll my eyes dramatically. "So, I flashed her a totally fake smile and told her I'd 'keep that in mind.'"

"Green light on Roman Lysander." Samantha laughs. "Classic Kimberley."

"Right? So *not happening*." I laugh.

"But then, she just calmly tells me to go to LA, reform Roman Lysander, build our empire, and maybe have some fun while I'm at it. She actually told me not to be afraid to make mistakes."

"She's right, you know," Samantha says, her expression suddenly serious. "You're always *so careful*, Isla. Always planning ten steps ahead. When was the last time you did something just because you *wanted* to or had fun doing it?"

I open my mouth to respond, then close it again. The question reverberates through me, exposing a void I never openly acknowledge. "I can't remember," I say with a groan. "I can't remember the last time. That's bad, yeah?"

"That's terrible," she says with a gentle laugh. "Maybe LA is your chance to let loose a little. Take some risks. Live a little. Have some *fun*."

"My risk-taking tends to end badly." The memory of Chad surfaces again—all his promises, and yet the ultimate betrayal ending it all. Badly. The shame that followed. I swallow hard, pushing it away.

"Chad Jameson was a narcissist. We all fell for his charm. You're no longer naïve. You're seasoned, as it were." She gets a little smile.

"Indeed." I grin. "More cynical. More controlled. And I appreciate you believing in me and having my back at all times." I take a sip of my 'Resurrection' cocktail. The sweetness lingers, a counterpoint to the bitterness of my thoughts. "What would I do without you, Sammy girl?"

"I think you'd be fine, like you always are," she replies cheerfully, but then she turns serious. "But look, Isla, maybe this *is* your chance to loosen the reins a little. You're always so controlled and mapping every contingency. Kimberley told you not to be afraid to make mistakes, right? When was the last time you took a real risk that wasn't meticulously calculated out in the first place?"

I stare into my drink, the pink liquid mocking my tightly wound insides. Chad was a risk, born of loneliness and bad judgment, and it nearly cost me my career. Since then? Risks have been purely professional, strategic, and always weighed and measured.

Samantha lives life. I *manage* it.

"It's been a while," I admit quietly.

"Exactly," Samantha says gently. "I'm not saying let Roman Lysander wreak open havoc on your life, personally or professionally. But maybe... be more open to possibilities? To LA. To launching our own agency. To the possibility that things might not go exactly according to plan, and that might not be the worst thing in the world. Embrace the joy."

Her words resonate, echoing Kimberley's push towards independence. Freedom isn't just about being out from under Kimberley's direct supervision; it's about shedding some of the emotional armor I've assumed since I was seventeen. The armor that's kept me safe but also kept me isolated. But the thought of lowering my defenses, especially with someone like Roman Lysander in the vicinity, feels reckless. Even dangerous.

My heart races. My breath catches as I feel the undue pressure for perfect execution, like always.

"Okay," I say finally, meeting her gaze. The word feels heavier than it should, laden with promise and possibility. "I'll try to be *open*. Maybe even embrace the joy." The word *joy* still feels like a foreign word. It's unfamiliar and strange to me. But I smile anyway.

"That's my girl!" Samantha raises her glass. "To Ryder & Harper Communications LA. To *Vendetta*. And to whatever beautiful chaos awaits us on the West Coast."

I clink my glass against hers. The sound is sharp, decisive.

Chaos. *Yes.*

Beautiful? *That remains to be seen.*

The opportunity? *Immense.*

The dream? *Tangible.*

But so are the stakes. I have the power to make or break Roman Lysander's career, and in doing so, perhaps my own.

It's a dangerous game, and I need to play it perfectly. Failure is not an option, not when my independence and my father's legacy are on the line.

Los Angeles awaits. And I need to be ready for anything.

I need to be ready. I need to be ready. I need to be ready.

But am I?

CHAPTER 4

your eyes open

Roman Lysander

"Your Eyes Open" - Keane

Thursday Morning 11:00 a.m.

MY HEAD IS A GODDAMN WAR ZONE. Each pulse of pain behind my eyes feels like a fresh artillery blast. I groan, shoving my face deeper into the silk pillowcase, trying to block out the sliver of sunlight that's somehow penetrated the fortress of blackout curtains. It's a losing battle. The light stabs anyway, a tiny, insistent dagger. I open my eyes briefly, then immediately squeeze them shut again. *No. Too much.*

My tongue feels like it's been dragged across the Mojave Desert. *Sandpaper.* That's the only word for it. And my stomach is currently engaged in a Cirque du Soleil routine, flipping and twisting in protest. Last night's tequila shots are staging a full-scale revolt. I swallow hard, willing myself not to revisit them prematurely.

I don't want this. I don't want any of this.

Disoriented, I open my eyes again, just a sliver this time, and take in my surroundings. Familiar surroundings, unfortunately. My bedroom. Or what's left of it. It looks like a bomb went off in here, and the bomb was filled with empty bottles and possibly some bad decisions. Empty bottles of tequila, mostly. And beer cans, crushed and scattered across the Persian rug like fallen, metallic leaves. Crushed red Solo cups litter the bedside table, overflowing with cigarette butts—even though I supposedly quit, again. Is that goddamn lipstick? Bright red lipstick smeared across the rim of a cup like a drunken kiss goodbye. Or hello? Who the hell knows?

———

I go downstairs for bottled Evian water and an espresso, noting in disgust the discarded clothes draped along my staircase and tossed over my dining room chairs. Not my clothes.

One guy—I think it's Mark, what's-his-name. The agent from CAA may have even thrown up in my hall coat closet. There's a distinct stench coming from behind a rack of my designer jackets. Nice. Classy. Late last night, I placed a call to the cleaning crew telling them about that mess and requested they come two hours early with double the staff, promising to triple their normal rates to get things in order twice as fast. They'll be here around noon. The remnants of last night's party are a chaotic tableau of regret, and another hangover, adding to a work-in-progress masterpiece of poor life choices.

The air itself is thick, viscous almost, with the stale, cloying smell of booze, cheap cigarettes, and something vaguely floral. What *did* I even drink last night? Besides tequila, obviously. There's a sickly-sweet undertone to the floral scent, like someone spilled a gallon of cheap perfume to mask the stench of sex and sin.

Or maybe that's just my imagination, fueled by dehydration and the faraway feeling of self-loathing buried so deep within the recesses of my mind, I barely feel anything anymore.

My body aches, a dull, throbbing pain that radiates from my temples down to my fingertips. I feel like shit. Physically, obviously, but also, just generally. This hollow ache in my chest, the one that booze, and meaningless hookups are supposed to silence, is becoming a constant companion, like a shadow I can't shake. The kind that reminds me of white birthday cake I'll never taste again the way it was meant to be— made by my mom's hands.

The cold marble countertop beneath my palms grounds me for a moment, the sensation cool and real against my skin. I close my eyes and breathe in. Then out. The cool surface offers momentary relief, like a brief respite amid the chaos.

I don't want this. I don't want any of this.

I climb the stairs and return to my master bedroom and survey my reflection in the mirrored wall opposite the bed. It's brutal, unforgiving. Bloodshot eyes stare back at me, red-rimmed and puffy. Stubble, more like a five-day-old beard, bordering on homeless chic. My hair is a disaster, sticking up at all angles.

Yeah, definitely looking my goddamn best. Hollywood's golden boy, right here.

'Image is everything in this town,' My best friend and manager Brandon Chase's voice echoes in my head, even before he's physically here to deliver his usual morning sermon about my fuckups. The irony isn't lost on me. Not even in this tequila-induced haze.

My messy bedroom, the overflowing ashtrays, the lingering scent of expensive perfume, whatever Hollywood's scent of the month is, and the random castoff clothing across my expensive furniture all screams "Hollywood's 'bad boy'."

It's the brand I've cultivated, the image I've so carefully—or so carelessly constructed. I run a hand through my already wrecked hair, wincing again as my fingers snag on a knot.

This is getting old. This whole charade. Partying to oblivion night after night, hooking up with nameless faces I'll never remember, pretending to the paparazzi and the gossip blogs that I'm having the best goddamn time of my life. It's all bullshit. A carefully crafted, expensive, self-destructive lie. But it's the role I've been cast in, and apparently, I play it well. Too well. The lines between Roman Lysander, Hollywood heartthrob, and Roman Lysander, actual human being, are blurring into nothingness at a fast clip rate.

For a fleeting moment, as I stand under the shower and review the wreckage that is my life, I'm assailed by the physical manifestation of internal chaos. A wave of something close to despair washes over me. This isn't me. Not really. This isn't who I want to be. This is just… noise. Distraction. From what? The silence that screams inside my head when I'm finally alone.

It's the silence that no amount of noise can ever truly drown out. From the ghost of my mother's laughter that I can almost, but not quite, remember. A phantom echo in the chambers of my heart. I shove the feeling down, crush it like a cigarette butt in one of those overflowing ashtrays.

Don't go there, Roman. Not now.

Never, if I can help it.

That darkness is a bottomless pit, and I'm already too close to the edge of it.

The hot water scalds my skin, turning it a shade of red. I welcome the pain. It's real, at least. Something to feel besides this endless, aching emptiness. The steam rises around me, a temporary cocoon obscuring the world outside. For a moment, I exist only here, in this haze, this liminal space between numbness and feeling.

I don't want this. I don't want any of this.

I haul myself out of the shower and quickly dress in a white t-shirt and jeans. The cotton fabric feels impossibly soft against my still-damp skin, a small comfort in the wreckage of the morning after.

It's then I hear the loud, insistent banging on the front door. It jolts me. Not a polite knock. A full-on, police-raid style assault. The sound reverberates through my skull like a jackhammer, each impact sending fresh waves of pain through my temples.

"Roman! Open up! I know you're in there!" Brandon's voice booms through the two-story glass mansion, laced with his usual brand of exasperated impatience and just a hint of genuine concern, buried deep, like a diamond in a pile of rocks. It's the one and only Brandon Chase, my talent manager, and my best friend since our days at UCLA.

He doesn't even wait for an invitation, or even a verbal confirmation of life. The door, thankfully unlocked because I'm a goddamn idiot, swings inward with a crash, banging against the wall. Brandon strides in, black suit immaculate as always, even at—I glance at the clock on the bedside table—almost noon. Noon? Shit. The cleaning crew will be here soon enough.

His face is a thundercloud, dark and ominous. He surveys the scene, his nostrils flaring, his eyes scanning the room, taking in every detail of my spectacular morning-after fuckup. "Geez, Roman," he says finally, his voice dripping with disgust and weary resignation. "This is… seriously impressive. In the worst possible way. Well, let's look at the bright side. You've showered and even shaved. Thanks for not looking homeless."

"Good morning to you, too," I mumble, trying for nonchalance, but my voice comes out raspy, betraying the tequila-soaked truth.

Brandon is, unsurprisingly, not amused. Not even a little. "*Morning?* Roman, it's almost noon."

"Look at the bright side. It's not quite noon yet. It's 11:41 a.m., still morning." He ignores my smart-ass comment about the time and continues to glare at me.

"There *is* no bright side, buddy. We're on a clock here. It's more like how best to avoid the nuclear fallout that will soon be on its way here. *We* had a meeting scheduled for *nine* this morning. With Everest Bishop, the director. About *Vendetta*. Your dad was there, too."

My stomach, which had just about settled into a fragile truce, plummets. *Vendetta*. Shit, I forgot. *Again…*

How the hell do I keep forgetting about the single most important thing in my entire goddamn career right now? Am I actively trying to sabotage myself? Probably. Sounds about right.

"Look, Brandon. I'm sorry, but I—"

"Save it." He cuts me off before I can even get the words out. "You don't *understand*. That's the problem. I did my best to cover for you, but this must stop. This self-destruction you've got going. And these leaches you hang with. They're just using you—drinking your alcohol, freeloading on your food, and trying to get an introduction to your dad. You think they care about you and your star power? And this goddamn death wish you seem to have for your own career; I just don't understand it. Why? Why are you about to throw away the biggest opportunity of your life?"

"It's not intentional," I say in the breach of his sermon. I already know he is just getting started.

"God, I hope not, though I do wonder. Your career, the one you supposedly care so much about, the one you whine about being taken *seriously* for—it's all hanging by a thread at this point. *Vendetta* is everything for you. It's your shot at breaking out of this pretty boy trap you've built for yourself."

He gestures wildly around the room with a sweep of his hand, encompassing the wreckage that is my living room that still exudes the overall aura of some mindless partying with nameless faces of people I do not even know very well, if at all. Disgust is etched on every line of his usually composed features. It's a dangerous game I play. We've talked about this so many times.

"Because right now, all you are proving is that *you are* a goddamn unsalvageable mess."

My jaw clenches. Anger flares and looks for a way out. "It's so *damn easy* for you to stand there in your tailored suit and *judge* me. You don't live this life. You don't have the paparazzi camped outside your gates 24/7, reporting every goddamn move you make. Easy for you to say, bro. You're not the one living under a microscope, where every move I make, every breath I take, is analyzed and twisted around and distorted by the goddamn media. This is *my* life. Maybe it's my way of blowing off steam."

"Steam?" Brandon asks, the sound sharp and dismissive. "*Steam?* Roman, you're not blowing off steam, you're detonating a goddamn bomb on your own career, on your own Hollywood golden boy life. And you're taking everyone around you down with you, including me. Everest Bishop is now having doubts. About *you*. And Lysander Entertainment…" He practically spits out the name of my father's company. "The studio is getting nervous. Your dad just told me he is *not thrilled* with your 'image rehabilitation' progress. And he's willing to do whatever it takes to turn things—*you*—around. Whatever it takes," Brandon hisses.

The air in the room thickens. The tension between us ratchets up another notch. The brightness of the California sun streaming through the windows feels like a mockery, illuminating the darkness I'm trying to hide from. This is not just about Brandon being my manager or my best friend anymore. This is about my family. My father. Lysander Entertainment isn't just some faceless corporation to me; it's my legacy, my father's legacy, even though he's buried himself in work in his Hollywood Hills estate ever since… Mom died. He has millions invested in this upcoming film, *Vendetta*, he's backing. And now that he's so involved in *Vendetta*, it means… pressure. More pressure than ever to make this right. For my dad. For Brandon. For me.

"*Vendetta* is not just another *film*, Roman. It's different this time." Brandon's tone shifts slightly, becoming more serious, more urgent, the anger receding, replaced by an intensity I rarely see from him. "It could mean everything for you. Lysander Entertainment—*your dad*—wants to see its release next summer. They think it will be next *summer's blockbuster*." He actually sounds like he believes it, which is saying something for Brandon. He is the ultimate pragmatist—the king of calculated moves.

"And this role of Steven Stryker is tailormade for you. It could be your McConaughey moment. But everyone is beginning to think that you're going to piss it all away, that you are going to flush your entire career down the toilet if you don't get your act together. *Now*." He stares at me, his gaze boring into mine, unwavering. "You've got to want it, Roman? Do you even want *Vendetta*? Because this is your chance. Do you want it?"

Do I want it? The question hangs in the air, heavy and suffocating.

Do I want *Vendetta*?

God, yes. More than anything.

More than another night of oblivion. More than another fleeting, meaningless connection with some girl.

It's not just about the fame, or the money, or even the acting. Although those things are definitely part of the appeal, I'm not going to lie. It's about something else entirely. Something deeper. A chance to prove myself. To everyone who thinks I'm nothing but a spoiled rich kid coasting on my father's name and my dead mother's fame. To everyone who's ever written me off as just another Hollywood heartthrob with an expiration date.

To myself. Yeah, maybe mostly to myself. And maybe, just maybe, to find something real in this fake, glittering, goddamn world. Something that actually means something.

But saying it out loud, admitting to that vulnerability, that raw, desperate need feels impossible. I'd be too exposed. It's too risky to even admit to Brandon, my best friend and manager, how much I want the lead role in this movie.

So, instead, I shrug, trying to play it cool, to project that effortless, careless charm that everyone expects from Roman Lysander. "Of course, I *want* it, Brandon. Don't be ridiculous. It's *Vendetta*. Every young male actor in Hollywood wants the lead role in *Vendetta*."

Brandon sighs, heavy with resignation. He runs a hand through his own perfectly styled, slicked-back dark hair. He's beginning to give up on me. I can see it in his eyes. He's fought for me, defended me, cleaned up my messes for years, and he's finally reached his breaking point. *And who can blame him?*

"Okay, fine. Play it cool. Continue to play the goddamn Hollywood rebel. But I'm telling you, Roman, you're walking on a razor's edge here. One more screw-up, one more headline about your drunken escapades, one more missed meeting, and *Vendetta* could slip right through your fingers. And then what? Back to smiling vacantly at the cameras while your actual talent rots away in another forgettable romantic comedy film. Is that what you want?"

His gaze still locked on mine, he waits for my answer. But I just stare back at him, the hollowness inside me echoing his words, amplifying the emptiness. I don't want to feel like this anymore. If I could just silence the screaming inside my head. If I could just find something or someone real. If I could just be seen as something more than just a walking tabloid headline surrounded by empty bottles and empty people.

I don't want this. I don't want any of this.

But I know I want *Vendetta*. I want it so badly it physically hurts, a different kind of pain than the hangover—deeper, more persistent, more real.

Brandon throws a manila folder onto my marble kitchen counter I'm standing next to. It lands with a soft thud. "The crack PR team your dad has hired will soon be on their way here to LA from New York. Kimberley Powers of Powers & Winston PR out of NYC is sending her very best. Apparently, your dad is pulling out all the stops, like I said. The suits at Lysander Entertainment are terrified you're going to sink the whole goddamn ship before it even leaves port, and this miracle worker of a PR wonder has been hired by your dad to allay all those fears." He pauses, his eyes narrowing, watching my reaction, gauging my response. "Her name is Isla Ryder."

"You're sure she pronounces her name as eez-la and not eye-lah?" Brandon gives me this thunderous look. "Unusual name, Isla Ryder, is all I'm saying."

Brandon sighs in frustration. "It's eez-la. And Isla Ryder is the most accomplished PR strategist in Kimberley Powers' arsenal. Like I said, Kimberley Powers is sending her very best. For *you.* She's 26. A bit mysterious. There are literally no photographs of her online. She doesn't do social media at all, although there was a bit of gossip about her dating Chad Jameson a few years ago."

"The Yankees' first baseman? Isn't he a bit of a player? No pun intended." I smirk at my best friend.

"Funny. Yeah, I guess you're competing against his 'bad boy' reputation on the *opposite* coast. But he has an $80 million dollar baseball contract that you don't have. Let's not lose focus here, Roman.

We're focused on *you* and your acting career. Your dad has hired this Isla Ryder, PR princess, for Lysander Entertainment, and her first assignment or quasi project out of the gate is *you*."

"So, this Isla Ryder is being sent to *fix* me? Rather, my reputation? Why would I be okay with any of that?" I ask in defiant frustration, running my hand through my damp hair. "What the actual fuck?"

"*Vendetta*. That's why. Your dad doesn't want to leave things to chance any longer. Isla Ryder is tasked with ensuring that doesn't happen." He pauses again, letting the name hang in the air, heavy with unspoken implications.

"She's here to *help you*, Roman. To perform some kind of goddamn miracle PR makeover and turn you into something palatable for middle America. Don't screw this up." Brandon looks royally pissed, but then he shrugs with notable indifference. "I'll call you later to check in. I have to get to the office and prepare some stuff for Isla Ryder's arrival. Apparently, she flies in tomorrow."

Brandon turns to leave and then turns back. "Oh, Happy 28th Birthday, by the way. That's the excuse I've finessed for them to buy you some cover. I told them you wanted to sleep in on your birthday and you had a ton to do for your party tonight. Your dad said he was going to try and make it."

"No, he's *not*. You know damn well he'll have some dinner meeting and never show. Like always."

"He said he'd *try*. I'm just relaying to you what he told me this morning." I shrug and Brandon continues his litany of do's and don'ts. "Don't drink tonight, Roman. Let's make it a dry night for you. There is too much on the line. The caterers should get here around five with hors d'oeuvres and a giant cake just the way you like it—white cake, Italian buttercream frosting with a cream center filling. And I ask, is this a birthday party or a wedding?" Brandon laughs at his own joke.

"You know how I feel about white cake." I try to smile, masking the instant pain that still aches at losing my mom years ago. She always made me a white cake with Italian buttercream frosting. Every year.

"Yeah, I know, buddy." Brandon gets this sympathetic look. "Anyway, I'll be back around four this afternoon. Happy 28th Birthday, Ro."

My best friend turns and leaves for a second time, striding back through the wreckage of the party and out the front door of my Malibu beach house. He shuts the door behind him with a quiet click. It's his way of saying sorry. 'Sorry for yelling at you.' 'Sorry for making fun of your request for white birthday cake.' 'Sorry about your mom.' 'Calling out your loser friends and generally being a dick to you for the past half hour.'

It's what he does in response to what I do.

I'm left alone in the wreckage. Physically, metaphorically. The silence surrounding me rings louder than Brandon's lecture.

Isla Ryder. Her name seems to hang there, as if suspended in the morning sunlight that streams through the upper windows on the east side of the house.

My dad's hired gun from New York sent to 'fix' me. Great. Some PR strategist who thinks she can walk in and remake my image? Tell me how to live? How to breathe? What exactly is her plan—follow me around with a clipboard, documenting every screw-up? Monitor my drinking? Screen my friends? Dictate who I can and can't be seen with?

Isla Ryder. No pictures online, Brandon said. A ghost. Probably some uptight suit who thinks she knows everything about a world she's only seen from the outside and has been so far away on the East Coast that she will never fucking get it. Fucking great.

Let her come.

Let her watch.

Let her judge.

My world's already under the microscope. What's one more pair of eyes scrutinizing the mess?

The shadows stretch across the floor, darkness and light playing their eternal game. Metaphorically, I stand in the middle of it all, caught between who I am and who I'm supposed to be, between the spotlight and the shadows.

I don't want this. I don't want any of this.

Maybe she *can* perform miracles. Or maybe she's just the next person who gets to see how fucked up this all really is before inevitably giving up on me like everyone else has.

Isla Ryder.

Right.

We'll see about that.

malibu landing

Isla Ryder

"Born Without A Heart" - Faouzia
"West Coast" - Lana Del Rey

Thursday Morning 7:00 a.m.

THE AIR HITTING MY FACE AS I STEP OUT of the hermetically sealed environment of LAX isn't as hot as New York's humid August heat. It feels different. Lighter somehow, but scented with exhaust fumes, jet fuel, and something vaguely tropical, like blooming night jasmine struggling against the urban sprawl. The sunlight isn't the sharp, angled light of Manhattan slicing between skyscrapers. It's a wide, hazy, almost relentless blanket thrown over everything, bleaching the colors, and promising heat.

I am not home.

But where is that, exactly?

I feel strangely detached, like I'm watching myself in a movie as I navigate the chaos of baggage claim and then on to the limousine services area. The sheer scale of LAX, the symphony of languages, the frantic energy of travelers—it's overwhelming in a way that JFK or

Newark never quite manages. New York's chaos is compressed, vertical. Los Angeles feels sprawling, horizontal.

It feels like a kinetic ocean wave threatening to pull you under if you don't keep moving.

Sunlight, blindingly bright, streams through the terminal windows, bouncing off the polished floors and chrome, creating a dizzying glare. Palm trees, *real palm trees,* sway languidly outside, visible through the glass walls. *Palm trees.* It's almost surreal.

This isn't New York. This isn't real. Or maybe this is a different kind of real. A manufactured, sun-drenched illusion of reality.

I fish my Gucci sunglasses out of my laptop bag and slide them on. The tinted lenses instantly mute the harsh glare, making the world seem slightly less… intense. *Irony, intact.*

It's a small act of control in a landscape that feels utterly foreign. Around me, the terminal buzzes with unique energy, different from JFK. It's less frantic, more… relaxed. Languid. Even the announcements over the PA system seem to drawl, stretching out the vowels in a way that feels distinctly Californian.

Finding my commissioned driver proves easy. 'Isla Ryder' is displayed on his handheld placard. Soon enough, I'm sinking into the plush white leather seats of a black Escalade, the cool air conditioning a welcome relief from the heat. "Malibu, please," I tell the driver, a man with sun-weathered skin and mirrored sunglasses, who nods silently and pulls smoothly into the chaotic flow of LA traffic.

The traffic flows differently here than in New York's concrete arteries. Less urgent somehow, more resigned to its fate. Cars drift past with windows down, spilling fragments of beach pop and mellow hip-hop into the warm air like musical breadcrumbs marking their passage.

Everyone seems to exist in slow motion, unhurried by the relentless clock that governs Manhattan's pulse. It's either genuine California calm or the most elaborate performance of relaxation I've ever witnessed.

I find tucked between the pages of my travel itinerary, Kimberley's handwriting on a small note card:

"Blend in. Or at least, enjoy the sunshine. K."

Blend in.

Funny.

The irony isn't lost on me. Here I am, a New York strategist armed with vintage Gucci sunglasses and enough emotional baggage to sink a yacht, and yet I'm supposed to seamlessly integrate into this sun-bleached landscape of manufactured dreams. Practicality clearly takes a backseat to image in this city where even the traffic jams look like music video backdrops.

I study the faces in the cars beside us—tanned, relaxed, seemingly unburdened by the weight of expectation that presses down on my chest like a stone. They make it look effortless, this California ease. But then again, I've learned that the most convincing performances often require the most practice.

I recite the address to the driver Kimberley has provided to the house in Malibu, arranged through Julia Winston, Kimberley's agency partner and best friend. Malibu—a respite for weekends—will also serve as a temporary base while the finishing touches are put on my apartment at The Harland in West Hollywood.

"Get your bearings, soak in the Pacific, then hit the ground running Monday," Kimberley had instructed via text.

The subtext clear: *Relax. Rest up. Enjoy yourself.* It's like an inside joke —at least two of those things I never do.

The driver pulls out of LAX and merges onto the freeway. It immediately becomes an exercise in defensive driving, and I wonder if I'll ever be able to navigate it myself—another variable to factor into my LA strategic planning.

Next Monday's problem.

I'm still on Thursday's.

***

The transition from Los Angeles to Malibu unfolds like a smooth silk ribbon. The concrete jungle of LA gradually disappears in the rearview mirror as the Escalade navigates onto the Pacific Coast Highway. What was once a chaotic symphony of horns and endless cars softens into the rhythmic percussion of waves meeting the shoreline.

The road snakes along the coastline, hugging cliffs on one side while the vast, glittering expanse of the Pacific Ocean stretches endlessly on the other. The sheer, natural beauty catches me off guard.

After years of Manhattan's vertical ambitions of gleaming glass and metallic angles of steel, this horizontal infinity of ocean blue and white sand feels completely disorienting and yet I'm completely drawn in already. The Pacific Ocean extends beyond comprehension, impossibly blue, with constant waves crashing against the shore in a hypnotic pulse that seems to whisper, *'slow down, breathe, stay awhile, Isla.'*

It's a postcard-perfect panorama that no Instagram filter could possibly enhance. Palm trees, impossibly tall and slender, line the road. They sway in the gentle breeze like elegant dancers, as if just performing for passing travelers. The air transforms with each mile—cleaner, saltier, fresher—carrying hints of sea spray and sun-warmed sand.

I lower my window slightly, letting the Pacific breeze tangle my long, dark hair, not caring for once about the imperfection of it all.

Pelicans glide effortlessly overhead, riding invisible currents with a mastery that makes me envious. They belong here. I wonder if I ever will.

Opulent houses, architectural marvels of glass and steel and stucco, cling to the cliff sides with breathtaking audacity. Glimpses of infinity pools that seem to merge with the ocean flash by. Manicured gardens defy the coastal winds. These aren't just homes; they are statements. Dreams materialized in concrete and glass, each one competing with the natural splendor surrounding them.

Malibu. This is the playground of sun-drenched privileges, dramatic coastlines that stretches twenty-one miles with all its hidden enclaves. *This is where Roman Lysander lives.* It's not likely I'll run into him. Twenty-one miles of coastline should be enough separation for us both.

Malibu. It feels both idyllic and vaguely threatening, like a beautiful mask hiding something complex and potentially dangerous underneath.

The long thirty-six-mile drive from LAX to Malibu allows the initial shock of arrival to settle, although it's soon replaced by the swirling vortex of thoughts I've been trying to keep at bay about Ryder & Harper Communications LA. Our names, printed on the hypothetical letterhead I've already mocked up a dozen times in my head. It's real. Terrifyingly, exhilaratingly real. The weight of the opportunity Kimberley handed me and Samantha—or perhaps strategically placed in our path—is huge. A million-dollar annual retainer. Independence. The chance to build something from the ground up, exactly as Samantha and I envisioned during all those late-night strategy sessions fueled by ambition and takeout Thai food.

But the price… *Roman Lysander.*

The name still sends a discordant jolt through my system. It's not just the professional challenge, which is formidable enough. It's the echoes of Chad Jameson—the easy charm, the public adoration masking inherent recklessness, the potential for personal and professional catastrophe if boundaries blur. My stomach tightens at the memory, the sting of betrayal still sharp after more than two years.

Control. Maintain control.

That's the mantra.

Roman Lysander is the client. The *anchor* client. The success of Ryder & Harper Communications LA hinges on my ability to navigate this, to sculpt his narrative without getting sucked into the chaos of his orbit. To tame the chaos that surrounds him. No small feat.

And then there's *Vendetta.* The story I poured onto the page in the dark aftermath of losing my family, a tribute to my father's memory hidden behind the pseudonym Ashley Thomas. Some nights, I still wake up with Dad's voice in my head, hearing fragments of conversations we never got to finish.

The ache of that loss never really fades.

It's become something I carry.

———

Kimberley's announcement that Lysander Entertainment has greenlit *Vendetta* and then that Roman Lysander's name is being floated for Steven Stryker adds a layer of complexity that feels almost unbearable. The idea of him embodying Steven Stryker, a character born from grief and a yearning for justice, feels all sorts of wrong. I'm not sure there's a path to reconcile that feeling.

But Kimberley's right—succeeding with Roman, proving my strategic value to Trent Lysander will afford me leverage down the line. Leverage to vehemently protect my work. Leverage tied to the casting clause Kimberley so brilliantly negotiated—the secret power I wield, the ace up my sleeve. But actually, using it, even thinking about it now, feels premature and dangerous.

The focus must be on the strategic public relations side of things.

Establish Ryder & Harper Communications LA.

Deliver phenomenal results for Trent Lysander with success in better positioning Roman's image and reputation—a table stake. Success with that objective is essential.

Protect the flank before planning any kind of attack, or needing one, for that matter.

The driver's voice, smooth and unnervingly calm, tells me, "We're almost there."

We leave the Pacific Coast Highway and head up a winding canyon road. The houses here aren't just houses; they're compounds, hidden behind imposing gates and lush, meticulously manicured landscaping.

Here in Malibu. Privacy is clearly the ultimate luxury. The privilege. The cachet.

Finally, the driver says, "Here you are, Ms. Ryder. We've arrived."

Julia Winston's house isn't merely stunning. It's an architectural statement. All glass, sharp angles, and clean lines, perched precariously on the cliff side, seemingly floating above the ocean below. Floor-to-ceiling windows dominate the facade, promising panoramic views that probably cost more than my entire Penn education. Designed in keeping with Julia Winston's impeccable taste, no doubt. Understated, expensive, and intimidatingly perfect.

A sleek, minimalist gate silently slides open as the Escalade approaches, presumably recognizing the car's transponder. The driveway curves up to a massive pivoting front door that looks more like an art installation than an entrance. My sensible two rolling suitcases and garment bags feel ridiculously out of place against the backdrop of such opulence and luxury. I tip the driver generously, take his business card, because come Monday I will have to deal with all of that, and I might need another ride. I watch him and the Escalade retrace the contours of the drive and disappear up the road.

And I feel alone more than ever. For a myriad of reasons, I do not share aloud.

Inside, the house reveals its true character—cool travertine floors gleam underfoot as the main living area opens into an expansive floor plan furnished with low-slung Italian white leather sofas and curated art pieces. But the real centerpiece is the view—an entire wall of glass slides open onto a sprawling deck, with the Pacific Ocean dominating the vista, an endless expanse of blue meeting the horizon. The sound of the waves creates a constant, soothing percussion.

A small, discreet electronic tablet sits on a console table near the entrance, displaying a welcome message:

"Welcome, Isla. Make yourself at home. Essentials are stocked. Wi-Fi code: Sunset78. Let me know if you need anything. Have fun. Relax. :)–JW."

Have fun. Relax. I smile. She must be talking to Kimberley, coordinating the *'we-need-to-coach-up-Isla'* messages. *Funny.*

I leave my suitcases by the door, suddenly reluctant to unpack, to claim this space. It feels too temporary, too borrowed, too tied to the reason I'm here.

After a brief self-guided tour of the premises—a pristine kitchen that looks untouched, with serene bedrooms, and spa-like bathrooms—I return to the living area, drawn by the magnetic pull of the ocean view.

I slide open the glass wall, stepping out onto the expansive deck. The sea breeze whips long strands of my dark hair across my face, carrying the scent of salt and sea. Below, the waves crash onto a secluded stretch of beach. It's undeniably beautiful, a picture-perfect postcard of California dreaming.

But the beauty feels distant, somehow impersonal. It doesn't soothe the knot of anxiety in the pit of my stomach. It just highlights the strangeness of it all—me, Isla Ryder, transplanted from the frenetic energy of New York City to this serene, sun-drenched cliff side. And now tasked with rehabilitating the image of Hollywood's most notorious 'bad boy'.

The scale of the challenge feels suddenly overwhelmingly real. This isn't just another crisis management gig at Powers & Winston. This is my agency. It's my reputation on the line from day one. And my anchor client is a volatile, unpredictable actor with the potential to either make or break Ryder & Harper Communications LA before we even officially launch.

Deep breaths.
Seek control.
Strategize.

I retreat inside. The silence of the house presses in on me. For a moment, the emptiness of the space echoes something deep inside me—that hollow place that opened up when I lost Dad, Mom, and Thomas. It's that space that's never quite filled, no matter how much success or ambition I pour into it.

No. Not now.

I press my palm against my sternum, feeling my heartbeat, willing the wave of grief to recede. Some days it still catches me unaware, rising from nowhere, threatening to pull me under. I can't afford to drown today.

Pouring myself a glass of sparkling water from the ridiculously well-stocked refrigerator, I retrieve from my laptop bag the thick manila files Kimberley gave me, simply labeled: LYSANDER, R.

Settling onto one of the obscenely comfortable but aesthetically severe sofas, I spread the contents across the low, polished travertine coffee table. It feels like preparing for battle, laying out the intelligence reports, assessing the enemy's strengths and weaknesses.

Except Roman Lysander isn't the enemy. He's the client. The asset. The project. Framing it that way is crucial. Detachment is my best strategy. For all the reasons.

The file is exhaustive, a testament to Powers & Winston's thoroughness. Tabloid clippings scream from glossy pages, a curated collection of Roman's greatest hits—or rather, misses. Paparazzi shots of him stumbling out of nightclubs, looking bleary-eyed and defiant.

Headlines chronicling fleeting, tumultuous relationships with co-stars and models. Quotes attributed to him that range from charmingly arrogant to petulantly dismissive. Soundbites from disastrous interviews where his boredom or disdain practically radiates off the page.

I force myself to look beyond the sensationalism, analyzing the patterns. The incidents often cluster around periods of high professional pressure or, conversely, long stretches of inactivity between projects.

Trigger points? Possibly boredom, or a reaction against expectation. The relationships seem intense but short-lived, often ending publicly and messily. A pattern of self-sabotage? Or a deliberate cultivation of the 'rebel' image?

His defiance in photos seems practiced, almost a performance in and of itself. Who is the real Roman Lysander behind the carefully constructed, or is that deconstructed, facade?

Then there are the other sections of the file. Clippings from earlier in his career, reviewing independent films he starred in before hitting the mainstream jackpot. Critics praised his 'raw talent,' his 'magnetic screen presence,' his 'surprising depth.' Quotes from respected directors lauded his potential, his charisma, and his natural instincts.

What happened between then and now? The meteoric rise to fame after that blockbuster Greek god role seems to coincide with the escalation of his off-screen antics. Was it the pressure? The intense scrutiny? Or something deeper?

A subsection details his family background. Trent Lysander, the formidable CEO of Lysander Entertainment. A brief, almost clinical mention of his mother, Kelly Lysander, the beloved actress who died tragically when Roman was sixteen. The file notes the timing—his rebellious phase seemed to begin in earnest shortly after her death. Grief manifesting as self-destruction? A classic, almost cliché narrative, but entirely plausible.

I know what grief can do.

How it can tear you apart from the inside.

And the relationship with Trent? Described as 'strained,' 'complex,' marked by high expectations and, according to anonymous sources quoted in older industry profiles, 'a lack of paternal warmth'.

Does Roman act out, seeking his father's attention, or in defiance of it? Understanding that dynamic will be key. Trent hired me, but Roman is the one I need to reach, to manage, and reshape.

There are notes on his known associates. Brandon Chase, his manager and former UCLA classmate, described as fiercely loyal but increasingly frustrated. A potential ally? Or an enabler? Various agents, co-stars, industry figures—a complex web of relationships to navigate.

Melody Parker, the current *It-Girl* actress whose name keeps popping up alongside Roman's name in recent gossip columns—a genuine connection, or a PR-driven pairing orchestrated by the studios or even Trent?

The file suggests the latter, a strategic move to soften Roman's image that seems to be backfiring due to their combined volatility. This was briefly covered during Wednesday's conference call with Trent Lysander and Brandon Chase, Roman's talent manager, with Kimberley and me. It's just another complication added to an ever-growing list of potential issues that will need to be addressed.

I study the photographs again, moving beyond the paparazzi shots to official headshots, stills from his films, red carpet appearances. The man is undeniably, almost unfairly, good-looking. That 'golden boy' moniker isn't just hype. Blond hair, blue eyes, a jawline that could cut glass, and a physique that clearly benefits from either genetics or rigorous training, likely both. But it's the eyes that hold my attention.

In some photos, they're blazing with confidence, charm, almost daring the camera to look away. In others, particularly the older, pre-scandal shots, there is a glimpse of something else—vulnerability? Intensity? A momentary glimpse of the 'serious actor' Brandon Chase, and even Kimberley Powers, believes still exists beneath the surface.

Or am I just projecting, searching for something redeemable in the face of a guy whose reputation precedes him so loudly?

The file contains a preliminary strategy proposal drafted by Kimberley's team; the one Trent Lysander apparently approved. It focuses on controlled media appearances, carefully selected interviews emphasizing his dedication to his craft, philanthropic involvement, which is currently non-existent, and needs immediate implementation.

Not a giver, this guy.

And a strategic distancing from the party scene and problematic associates is definitely needed, which he is going to hate me for even suggesting. Standard procedure for image rehabilitation.

Solid, but predictable strategy. But the preliminary strategic plan lacks finesse. It treats the symptoms, but not the cause.

To truly rebrand Roman Lysander, to make it stick, we need to understand the *'why'* behind the behavior, not just manage the fallout. We need a narrative that feels authentic, even if it's meticulously crafted.

My mind works, connecting dots, mapping out potential angles.

The *'Redemption Arc'* is obvious, but risky—it acknowledges past sins, requiring genuine buy-in from Roman, which seems unlikely based on his defiant persona.

The *'Misunderstood Artist'* angle—focusing on his craft, his passion, painting the scandals as distractions from his true calling—has potential, especially leveraging those early positive reviews.

The *'Focused Professional'* narrative requires tangible proof—landing serious roles, demonstrating discipline, which loops back to the *Vendetta* situation. If he *could* land and excel in a role like Steven Stryker, the narrative writes itself. But *getting him to that point* is the Herculean task.

How to approach him? The file paints a picture of someone resistant to authority, cynical about the industry, and likely dismissive of a *PR fixer* sent by his father.

Coming in strong, laying down the law might trigger his defiance. Building rapport seems essential, but treacherous. He's undoubtedly charming—the file is littered with examples of him winning over skeptical journalists or hostile crowds, only to implode later.

Charm is his weapon, and likely his defense mechanism, too.

Duly noted.

The memory of Chad Jameson, never distant enough, whispers a warning in my ear. *Charming. Magnetic. High-profile. Toxic.* The parallels are unnerving. But this time, I'm not the naive girlfriend who got swept off her feet by the charming narcissist. I'm the strategist. I hold the power—not just the contractual power of the Ryder & Harper Communications LA retainer, but the knowledge and the objectivity. And the secret casting clause for *Vendetta* is a silent weight in my back pocket with immense power.

Still, my hands tremble slightly as I shuffle through the papers. I clench them into fists, willing the physical reaction away. Chad's betrayal left emotional scars deeper than I like to admit. The humiliation. The public spectacle. The way my professional judgment by some of my peers was questioned because I'd let my personal boundaries dissolve.

Never again.

The professional risk has massive implications. For me. Roman Lysander, with his higher profile and deeper ties to industry power through his father, could easily derail my entire agency if I misstep, if I let those boundaries blur even for a second. He represents both the biggest opportunity and the biggest threat.

I open my laptop and begin a brief essay-style version of a client strategy plan. It can serve as a working draft for this weekend for Samantha and me to work from in preparation for the formal presentation already scheduled with Trent Lysander next Wednesday.

We'll be ready.

It's going to be fine.

Sure, sure.

Roman Lysander: *Strat Rehab Plan*

Navigating the complex landscape of Roman Lysander's public image demands a nuanced approach, one that balances authenticity with strategic rebranding. As the anchor client of Ryder & Harper Communications LA, the stakes for Roman's transformation are monumental, not just for his career, but for the agency's burgeoning reputation. The goal is to shift public perception from Roman as a 'Hollywood 'Bad Boy'' to a 'Serious Actor,' worthy of roles like Steven Stryker in films, like *Vendetta*.

The challenges are substantial. Roman's image is deeply entwined with negative tabloid narratives that paint him as volatile and resistant to authority. His relationship with his father, Trent Lysander, is fraught with potential conflict, adding layers of complexity to the task. Moreover, Roman's current associations with the party scene and figures like Melody Parker could undermine efforts to establish credibility. Therefore, authenticity is paramount; any rebranding must resonate as genuine, requiring Roman's active buy-in.

Fortunately, Roman's undeniable talent and charismatic presence are significant assets. His earlier work received critical acclaim, suggesting untapped potential that can be leveraged. High public recognition is a double-edged sword, but with the right narrative, it can be transformed into an advantage. Additionally, Trent's considerable resources and industry clout provide a powerful backing for this endeavor. Brandon Chase, Roman's loyal manager, could also serve as a valuable ally, provided his goals align with the overall strategy.

The initial phase of the rebranding will focus on building rapport and establishing Ryder & Harper's authority. Listening to Roman, understanding his motivations, and identifying leverage points are crucial steps in fostering professional trust. Setting clear boundaries will define the roles and expectations, framing the rebranding as a partnership aimed at achieving Roman's goals of securing more respected roles.

Quick wins will be essential to signal change. This could involve managing Roman's social media presence and orchestrating controlled media appearances that highlight his dedication to his craft. Tightening information control and aligning with Brandon Chase will limit unofficial statements and prepare for potential issues.

Narrative exploration will form the backbone of the strategy, seeking to tell a compelling story that weaves in themes of overcoming adversity and personal growth. Identifying philanthropic interests could further bolster Roman's image, adding depth and authenticity to his public persona.

While the *"Vendetta"* factor is a potential future opportunity. It should be completely separate. The primary focus is on the contracted public relations work for Trent—the PR strategy with Roman. Success with Roman's rebranding and image rehabilitation is key and will lead to high level success with everything else in relation to his film career.

I lean back, feeling more satisfied and at ease just in reading back through my notes. This is good. We can pull from these notes and put together a PowerPoint deck to present and discuss early next week with Trent Lysander, Roman Lysander, and Brandon Chase.

The sun begins its slow descent toward the horizon, painting the clouds in fiery shades of darker yellows. It's half-past two. The sheer beauty of the sun over the Pacific is momentarily distracting. 'A fresh start', Samantha had called it. A chance to build something that is ours, away from the ghosts of New York, away from Kimberley's shadow.

But the biggest ghost isn't the New York skyline or my family's tragedy, which fuels my ambition but stays locked away. It's the potential for history to repeat itself, the fear of vulnerability that Chad Jameson exploited. Roman Lysander represents that fear made manifest, packaged in Hollywood glamour and tied directly to my professional future.

I close the files and gather all the paperwork and place all of it on the desk in the office down the hall. The image of Roman Lysander's challenging gaze lingers in my mind. He's not just a client. He's a test. A test of my skills, my control, my ability to navigate the treacherous intersection of fame, power, and personal demons—his, and perhaps, my own.

My throat tightens unexpectedly. For a moment, I allow myself to feel the weight of it all—the pressure, the expectations, the fear of failing. I wrap my arms around myself, feeling suddenly small in this vast, empty house perched on the edge of the continent.

I miss my family.

I miss who I was before grief rewrote me.

These thoughts come unbidden, intense and painful. I push them away. There's no room for that kind of vulnerability now. *Not here.*

But it comes anyway. So, I open one of the garment bags—the one that contains my mother's wedding dress. And it's like she's here. I smell the faint scent of her signature perfume.

I sit with her wedding dress for a little while. I let the tears fall and communicate my fears about LA out loud to the answering silence. *All of it.* And it's like she's right here. *Listening.*

The calm comes, eventually. It always does.

I drape her dress over one of the living room chairs. I'll deal with putting it away later when I finally unpack.

When I finally accept that I'm here.

"And it's going to be okay," I say aloud in the empty room.

Funny.

Who says that?

Who believes that?

It's never really okay.

But I say it again like a mantra. *"It's going to be okay."*

My thoughts drift back to the present reality in which I find myself.

Ryder & Harper Communications LA. The name feels heavy, weighed down with the reality of this first, monumental task of rebranding Hollywood's golden boy, Roman Lysander.

Failure is not an option Kimberley entertains.

And neither do I.

Okay, Roman Lysander, let's see what you're really made of.

The game is on.
And I play to win.
I look out at the dark blue ocean and feel solace.
A knowable connection. Peace even.
For a few minutes.

CHAPTER 6

soul meets body

Isla Ryder

Thursday mid-afternoon

THE SILENCE IN JULIA WINSTON'S borrowed palace of glass and travertine is feeling less like peace and more like a low-grade fever of anxiety beneath my skin. The sheer weight of the Lysander dossier, and the daunting reality of launching Ryder & Harper Communications LA with *him*—Roman Lysander, Hollywood's prodigal son—as the anchor client, while the unfamiliar, sprawling vastness of Los Angeles and even Malibu presses in from all sides. It's simply too much to process sitting still.

My thoughts are a tangled-up mess, a Gordian knot of ambition, apprehension, and the lingering ghost of Chad Jameson whispering unwelcome warnings in my ear like insidious backseat driving, which is its own type of irony, since I don't drive at all. A secret I carry alone.

Control feels tenuous, slipping through my fingers like the fine California sand just beyond the deck.

I need to move. Urgently. To sweat out the accumulating tension, shake off the residual stiffness from the cross-country flight, and maybe, just maybe, find a fleeting moment of clarity amidst the crashing waves and the endless horizon. A run. On the beach. It's the perfect antidote, the necessary physical exertion. It's a desperate counterpoint to the relentless mental gymnastics I've been performing since Kimberley dropped the Los Angeles bombshell two days ago.

I change quickly, pulling on sleek black short leggings with a light grey and black animal leopard print. It is Lululemon's latest spring line one-of-a-kind offering—the matching black cropped sports bra and outer tank top—my usual running attire, chosen as much for performance wicking as for the illusion of effortless competence and the style it projects, even during exercise. The brand must be maintained always.

Control.

It's the cornerstone of my existence, professionally and personally.

Stepping out onto the expansive deck and descending the twenty private wooden stairs leading down to the beach below feels like crossing a threshold into another dimension. The sand, pale gold and surprisingly soft, beneath my high-performance running shoes, shifts slightly with each initial step, demanding a different kind of balance than when navigating crowded Manhattan concrete sidewalks.

The Pacific stretches out before me, an immense, breathing entity of deep, mesmerizing blue. Its surface glitters under the relentless California sun like scattered diamonds. It's like a talisman. The waves crash onto the shore in a powerful, rhythmic roar, a constant, primal sound that drowns out the frantic static buzzing in my head.

I run parallel to the shoreline, seeking the firmer, damp sand near the edge where the waves surge and retreat in an endless cycle. The sun beats down, warm and insistent, on my shoulders. The ocean breeze is a cool caress against my skin and carries the clean, briny scent of salt and sea.

It's invigorating. Wilder. More elemental than anything I'm accustomed to. This scene is in direct contrast to the steel and glass canyons I left behind in Manhattan. The air itself feels different here. It's lighter. Somehow charged with possibility. Yet so vast and slightly intimidating.

For a few precious moments, the accumulated weight of everything lifts. Trent Lysander the client, Roman Lysander the project, even the daunting task of launching Ryder & Harper Communications LA, as well as maintaining the carefully guarded secret of being the screenwriter with casting privileges for *Vendetta*—*these things I carry*—recede into the background. The endless noise of the waves and the distant cry of seagulls effectively offset everything that plagues me.

Instead, it's just the rhythmic pounding of my feet on the packed sand. The steady cadence of my breathing that seemingly matches the ocean's pulse. The endless blue expanse of ocean stretches to my left along with the vast, open sky that arches above the horizon and on my right, the golden sand stretches along the long line of palatial houses built along the cliffs.

This startling sense of absolute peace washes over me, so utterly foreign it feels like a revelation. It's a momentary cease-fire in the internal war I constantly wage with myself.

This isn't the contained, frantic energy of a Central Park loop, where I am hemmed in by skyscrapers and the city's relentless vibration.

This is a natural, untamed space. It is freedom in its element. A lightness I haven't felt in… maybe ever, since my world tilted on its axis nine years ago.

Lost in the rhythm and in the unexpected reprieve from all the stress I'm under. I'm focused solely on the hypnotic dance of the waves chasing my feet and retreating again. I'm mesmerized by the sheer scale of the ocean to my left as I run north, effectively captivated by nature.

I attempt to stay out of the path of unpredictable waves by looking down and then to my left more than usual. So, I don't see the figure running towards me until it's catastrophically too late.

<hr>

One minute, I'm immersed in the run, finding a fragile equilibrium between exertion and the environment. In the next, I slam *hard* into something incredibly solid and unyielding—a wall of warm granite disguised as a muscled human chest. The impact is jarring, brutal, and knocks the wind out of my lungs with shocking force.

Momentum gone. Air gone.

Control utterly, humiliatingly gone.

I stumble backward, swept off my feet by the unexpected wall of no-forward momentum. My balance completely obliterated. I go down hard, and land awkwardly. A sharp, searing pain instantly flares with my right knee as it violently connects with something jagged hidden beneath the sand.

"Fuck!" The word bursts out uncensored, torn from my throat before the usual filters can even engage. A pure, primal reaction. I clutch at my knee instinctively. Hot, streaming red wetness immediately coats my fingers and makes a beeline towards my high-rise short leggings.

Blood.

My blood.

My stomach lurches violently at the sight of the warm red slickness between my fingers as I take turns staring at my hands and then reapplying pressure to the at least three-inch jagged cut at my knee. "Fucking fantastic. God dammit."

"Whoa, hey! Are you okay? I'm so sorry, I guess I wasn't looking where I was going... I didn't see you." A deep voice, masculine and laced with genuine concern, cuts through my pain-fogged haze.

It sounds close. Very close.

"Sorry for the swearing," I say, gasping between jagged breaths, suddenly mortified by my involuntary profanity, almost as much as the sudden, unexpected injury.

Tears blur my vision with the too-bright, picturesque scenery. It's a humiliating combination of intense pain and profound shock. My throat constricts, chest tightening as the full impact of the collision registers in waves of agony. I groan as the injury intensifies with terrifying speed and becomes a sharp, persistent pain.

I blink away the tears but struggle to focus through the watery film. A guy kneels in the sand beside me now, his presence large and immediate, somehow towering even on his knees. My gaze travels instinctively upwards, from strong, tanned legs clad only in bright red board shorts, up a ridiculously sculpted torso glistening with sweat from his own run to a face that seems unfairly blessed by the genetic lottery.

Sun-streaked blond hair, windswept and artfully messy in a way that probably costs a fortune to achieve. Eyes the exact color of the summer sky overhead, unexpectedly framed by faint laugh lines at the corners. A square jaw dusted with just the right amount of rugged stubble. He looks like he just stepped off a movie poster advertising the California dream itself.

His attention, however, is focused entirely on the jagged cut at my knee. He gently, carefully pushes my bloodied hands aside. "Damn.

Looks like you caught a shard of glass, or something sharp when you fell. It's bleeding quite a bit."

"Quite a bit. Like *a lot*?" I cannot quite keep the growing alarm out of my voice. He seems to sense my sudden panic.

"Just quite a bit, not a lot."

"Quite a bit. Not a lot. You're sure there's a difference in those two descriptions, though?" My voice is getting thready because the blood is becoming a problem. *For me.* It feels like my leg is soaked in blood at this point.

He ignores my semantics discussion. Instead, he assesses the wound with a surprising, almost clinical calmness, his touch unexpectedly gentle despite his obvious strength. "Doesn't look deep enough for stitches, though. Lucky break."

"*Lucky?*" I echo faintly, momentarily distracted from the throbbing pain by the sight of the blood still oozing steadily from the cut, staining my leggings a darker shade of black. My mouth goes dry, a metallic taste coats my tongue. "How *could* you possibly *know*? It feels... distinctly *not* lucky right now. Not lucky *at all*. Not even a *little bit lucky*."

"Trust me, I've seen worse," he says simply. His reassuring calmness is slightly jarring, given his Adonis-like appearance. It's strangely comforting, though. "Just needs cleaning, pressure, and a decent bandage dressing."

"Yeah?" I press my hand back against the wound instinctively, trying to staunch the flow, feeling slightly dizzy and lightheaded from the shock, the sudden loss of control, and *all the blood*. My fingers tremble against my knee, betraying me.

"Can you maybe not do the play-by-play quite so much?" My voice is more thready and more faint sounding, despite my best efforts. "I'm *not great* with blood... especially *my own blood*, if I'm being honest."

"Take off your tank top. We should tie it off with that to stem the bleeding."

"*What?* No. It's *Lululemon*."

"We'll buy you another. Bleed out here. Or tie it off?"

"But... it's *Lululemon*," I say again with a decided groan, as if this should explain everything.

"With me?" He holds his hand high. "Without me." He lowers his hand.

"*With* you? *Without* you? Oh... the *movie*. Tom Cruise. *Funny*." I sigh big. "Tie off the gaping wound with my *Lululemon* tank top, which is one of a kind. You can't order another one. It was the spring line. Once it's out of stock." I shake my head in frustration. "It's gone forever. *With me? Without me? Fuck,* what a day," I say under my breath.

With sudden earnest and loads of wishful thinking, I press harder at the blood flow with the palm of my hand to see if I can get it to stop, while he just watches me do it with this faint smirk on his face. And yet, the blood continues to run down my leg in a steady stream and now threatens the inside of my running shoes because I'm half sitting up. I kind of sweep the blood back up towards my knee.

But then, my vision dims again because of the *blood… all the blood.*

"Tie it off with your Lululemon tank top or bleed all over the sand here. The blood is already soaking your *matching* leggings as it is." He tries again with the schtick, raising his hand up and then lowering it. "With me, without me."

"And logic, too! Good for you. So, the whole outfit is basically ruined. Good point. Good point. With me. Without me. *Cute.*"

My vision gets dark around the edges. My breath gets really thready now. I close my eyes tight as if this is somehow going to somehow help me from completely blacking out.

I open my eyes in defeat because *that is not working* either, and he is just staring at me. "Oh, my God. Oh… 'kay. *Fine.* Great. Fucking great. Let's move." I'm pulling my tank top off, kind of thanking God I have a sports bra underneath as my sight darkens even more. He even helps me take the tank off, but just the contact with him on my increasingly weak arms has my skin tingling for some unknowable reason.

He quickly makes good use of my precious $80 Lululemon tank top and ties it off around my knee like a paramedic would.

"*See?* It worked. Problem solved. Part of it, anyway."

"Thanks?" The momentary distraction keeps me from thinking about the blood, but that kind of returns to me again. "I feel… not so good."

Because proper use of the English language has left me, too!

I grab his forearm and lean into him, trying to chase away the blackout feeling once more, as my hearing diminishes, too. I feel like I'm going to faint as if on cue for the next scene where I literally pass out on the sandy beach with a stranger in unfamiliar surroundings.

"Don't pass out. Don't pass out." I've said this aloud.

"My place is *right there.*" He glances up the beach and gestures vaguely over his shoulder with a tanned arm towards one of the stunning architectural marvels perched precariously on the cliffs overlooking the beach. It looks even larger and more dramatic than Julia's temporary loaner house.

"Let me help you. I can clean up your wound and get you bandaged up. It's going to be okay."

"It's going to be *okay*," I mock him. "Like it's ever okay. Like it really is ever okay. Like fucking never is it okay though, right? Like fucking never." He studies my face for a few seconds, probably assessing my sanity at this point. "Oh God. Sorry. Sorry. Rough, fucking day."

"My place. Right there," he says calmly.

My internal alarm system, honed by years navigating the treacherous waters of public relations and permanently scarred by one disastrously public relationship with a charming, manipulative professional athlete, immediately comes to life. Letting an impossibly handsome stranger lead me off the relatively public beach to his secluded, multi-million-dollar Malibu mansion? It sounds suspiciously like the opening scene of a horror film, far different from the thrillers my father used to write, and my mother helped costume.

"You're not... like, a serial killer or something, are you?" The question slips out before I can censor it, fueled equally by pain, disorientation, and a lifetime of ingrained caution operating on overdrive. "Because saying 'it's going to be okay' seems like something a serial killer would say right before the big killing scene, yeah?"

He actually laughs, a warm, throaty sound that echoes slightly in the open air and surprisingly, genuinely, puts me slightly more at ease. "Nah, wrong zip code for that," he says, with a nice smile that even crinkles the corners of his too blue eyes. "We specialize in other kinds of predators here in Malibu."

He stands up smoothly. Effortlessly. Then offers me his hand. It's large, tanned, surprisingly calloused—a working hand, incongruous with the polished movie-star looks.

"Come on. Let's get you cleaned up before you attract sharks. Can you stand?"

I hesitate but also feel a distinct lack of better options. So, I run my hands through the loose wet sand to wipe off some of the blood and then take his offered hand. His grip is strong and steady as he pulls me to my feet. I wobble precariously, landing momentarily against his solid chest, *again*. And once again, it's like leaning against warm granite, solid and unyielding. My entire being pulses with a heat that has nothing to do with the California sun.

I quickly push myself back, trying desperately to regain some semblance of composure. I'm acutely aware of my sweaty appearance, still slightly blood-stained hands, bloody workout gear, my precious Lululemon tank top tied tight around my right knee, my disheveled hair now coming out of my hair tie in all directions, and the embarrassing tears I'm still trying to surreptitiously wipe away with the back of my free hand which is now sandy and still bloody.

"I'm sorry," I mumble again, studiously avoiding his gaze, focusing instead on a distant sailboat on the horizon. The world tilts slightly. My vision swims at the edges. "I never... I'm usually much more aware... of my surroundings. East Coast time, I guess. Still adjusting." I take a shaky, unsteady breath. "And I'm not usually this clumsy. Or emotional."

God, I sound utterly pathetic.

Pathetic and small. Completely unlike me.

He just laughs again, seemingly completely unfazed by my rambling apology or my general state of disarray. He slips a supportive arm around my waist, easily taking most of my weight as I put tentative pressure on my injured leg.

"Happens to the best of us. Wipeouts are practically part of the Malibu initiation process." He guides me slowly, patiently, towards the imposing cement stairs leading up from the beach to his property, his hold firm and reassuringly steady. "Don't need you to take another tumble. Just lean on me. You're okay."

I'm never okay.

Not really.

But we'll go with that for now.

His unexpected kindness is profoundly disarming. There's no calculation I can detect from him, no hidden agenda I can sense, just straightforward and uncomplicated helpfulness.

He's just a Good Samaritan in red board shorts, possessing a cover model physique.

I hobble along beside him, letting him take most of my weight, feeling ridiculously vulnerable, and, against all my better judgment, strangely grateful for his intervention.

CHAPTER 7

blood in the cut

Isla Ryder

"Blood In The Cut" - K. Flay
"Blue Jeans"- Lana Del Rey
"Same Old Love"- Selena Gomez
"Dreams" - Fleetwood Mac

Thursday mid-afternoon

THE STAIRS LEADING UP TO HIS HOUSE seem impossibly long and steep. There are like a hundred steps and taking each one sends a fresh jolt of pain through my knee. The house itself as we ascend and get ever closer is even more imposing than Julia's place—a modern fortress of glass, steel, and wood cantilevered dramatically over the cliff face, commanding an obscene panorama of the coastline.

We stop at his outdoor shower, and he unwraps my leg and rinses the cut and my bloody short leggings under the warm water using a little soap. Dignity disappears like everything else.

"Need to clean it. You don't want staph bacteria to get in there," he says.

"Staph? What? In Malibu?"

"It's an ocean," he says patiently, like he is dealing with a child. "The bacteria don't make a distinction by the location that I know of." He laughs again.

"Right. Sure, okay. Got it." I'm kind of getting dizzy all over again, watching the blood, *my blood*, go down the outdoor shower drain. I hold on to his shoulder while he leans down and does whatever he's doing to my cut and my bloody clothing. "Sorry for all of this. God, I'm usually not this much trouble."

"No problem." He grabs a dark navy blue beach towel from the hook and towels me down with it and then wraps it around my waist.

I'm looking up at the sky, concentrating on a seagull flying overhead. Then he's wrapping another smaller navy-blue towel around my leg. I step back and helplessly watch him rinse out my Lululemon tank top in the outdoor shower spray.

Blood again. From my cherished tank top. I stare back at the bird overhead and try to take steady breaths and concentrate on anything else but the blood. I can feel him watching me do it.

Then, he practically carries me inside as these massive sliding glass doors whisper open automatically as we approach, revealing an interior that screams expensive, sophisticated, and again with the minimalist taste, with lots of white and glass and chrome everywhere.

A vast, open floor plan with a living area that flows seamlessly into a dining space and then into a state-of-the-art kitchen dominated by a massive freestanding island made of what looks like gleaming white marble veined with dramatic dark grey and blues. Beautiful. Expensive. Unique.

It's clearly a house built for entertaining on a grand scale, though unlike Julia's pristine, almost sterile perfection, there are subtle signs of recent life here—a couple of stray cocktail glasses on a low side table, a luxurious cashmere throw draped artfully, or perhaps hastily thrown over the arm of a sleek Italian white leather sofa.

There is a faint, lingering scent in the air that's a complex mix of expensive cologne, salt air, and... the hint of lemon. And maybe the ghostly remnants of some recent party.

He settles me carefully onto one of the tall, espresso brown leather-upholstered bar stools at the island, his movements efficient and surprisingly gentle.

I watch, slightly mesmerized and feel increasingly out of my depth, as he wets a thick wad of paper towels at the oversized stainless-steel sink and returns with them.

"Okay, let's take a proper look at that battle wound."

He removes the smaller dark towel from my leg and then gently begins dabbing away the blood with the wet paper towels. The blood flow has started up again as soon as he undid the towel. He cleans away any remaining sand from around the cut on my knee and dabs gently at the cut itself. His touch is surprisingly deft, and he's focused on it. After a moment, he carefully places my hand over the makeshift compress he's fashioned out even more wet paper towels.

"Keep pressure right there, okay?" he instructs softly. "Don't peek." He studies my face for a second, his blue eyes searching mine. They're so blue. Impossibly blue. The kind of blue that makes you forget yourself for a dangerous moment. "You're not going to pass out on me, are you?"

"That's not really my style," I say, trying for a firmness I don't entirely feel. My knee is throbbing insistently now, a painful drumbeat beneath the pressure of my hand.

Don't pass out. Don't lose control. Don't fall apart.

"Good to know." He grins, a quick, devastating flash of white teeth against tanned skin that does funny things to my equilibrium. "Okay. Stay put. I'll find the first aid kit."

He retrieves a sleek, minimalist bottle of water from a Sub-Zero refrigerator that looks bigger than my entire first New York apartment kitchen and hands it to me. "Hydrate. Doctor's orders." He disappears for a few minutes, rummaging efficiently through lower cabinets nearby.

He returns quickly, holding a well-stocked, professional-looking first aid box. He kneels on the cool floor in front of me again, opening it and selecting a bottle of antiseptic and a package containing large sterile bandages.

He uncaps the antiseptic. The sharp smell stings my nostrils. "This might sting." His blue eyes meet mine again. "Got to clean out any sand or nasty ocean gunk, for sure." Before I can fully brace myself, he efficiently, decisively pours the clear liquid over the wound.

"Holy shhhiiittt, that stings," I hiss involuntarily, sucking in a sharp breath as the stinging intensifies, sharp and immediate. It feels like liquid fire. My entire leg seems to ignite, and the pain shoots up from my knee to my hip in a blinding flash.

"Sorry," he says again, though he doesn't look particularly

apologetic. He seems more focused on the task at hand. He blows gently on the wound—an oddly intimate, unexpectedly soothing gesture that sends a strange, confusing flutter through my chest—before carefully applying three vertical butterfly bandages to close the gaping three-inch wound at my kneecap and then covers it with a large sterile pad. Finally, he secures it firmly with strips of surgical tape. His movements are precise, economical, and confident. He seems to know exactly what he's doing.

Where did a guy who looks like him learn first aid like this?

"There," he says finally, sitting back on his heels for a moment and surveying his handiwork with a nod of satisfaction. "All bandaged up. Should hold you for now. How does it feel?"

"Better," I lie. I try to flex my knee tentatively beneath the bulky bandage. It still hurts like hell, a deep, throbbing ache, and the bandage feels tight and restrictive, but at least the bleeding seems to have stopped. "Thank you. Seriously. You're… surprisingly good at that."

He shrugs, standing up smoothly. "Picked up a few basics. Occupational hazard, sometimes."

I nod, slide off the bar stool, undo the towel around my waist and drape it over the bar stool. Then, I busy myself with throwing away the bloodied paper towels into the kitchen wastebasket under his kitchen sink cabinet, that I find after a small search.

Overstepping. Uninvited to make myself at home, and yet I have.

<hr>

I wash my hands at his kitchen sink and stupidly watch my own blood from my bloodied hands swirl down in the stream of water into the drain. I kind of put my head down on the edge of the sink and try to regain my equilibrium because I'm almost ready to pass out *again*.

"You okay over there?" he asks, sounding worried.

"Fine. Just fine." Finally, I turn to him, and pause for a moment, and swiftly become lost in his amazing blue-eyed gaze as he scrutinizes me closely.

"You don't look so fine."

"Sorry, blood on my hands. Here's a tip: don't watch your own blood as it swirls in the streaming water and goes down the drain. *Blood in the cut.*" I flash to K. Flay's song and hum a few bars under my breath.

Nervous as all get out now. I walk back around his gigantic island, drying my hands on each side of my leggings, and retake my designated place on the bar stool sitting on the damp towel.

The hand washing effort did a number on me, though. Now I feel light-headed all over again after seeing the blood on my hands and inadvertently watching it swirl down the drain.

"Sorry. Sorry. Problem with seeing the blood. Just need a sec." I sound weak and pathetic. I'm fighting passing out all together from moving too fast and the kitchen sink episode just now.

He reaches out and steadies me with his hand. "Sure, you're, okay?"

"Just a sec." I lean slightly forward from the waist, bending my head horizontally, hoping it's enough to stop the threat of the blackness that is visible around the edges of my vision all over again. I close my eyes.

"Just breathe. Take a deep breath. Exhale. Do it again." His commanding voice helps. "I think you should lie down."

I keep my eyes closed, trying to outrun the blackness. "I'm *not* lying down on your *white* Italian leather sofa. I'll be okay. Just need a minute."

"It's been like *five*."

I slowly raise my head and finally open my eyes. He's studying me intently.

"You, okay? You're sure?"

"It appears the sight of blood is worse than the cut itself. I'm good. I got it under control now."

"Sure, you do. You could just lie down on the sofa for a few minutes."

"I'm good. I'm fine. *Really*. I just need another minute." I close my eyes again under his blue-eyed studious stare. Still holding onto his arm as he is holding onto mine. I breathe deeply in and out. "Come on. Get it together," I've said this aloud again. I open my eyes, and he is staring at me in this intense kind of wonder.

Probably thinking, what is with this girl?

"You, okay? *Sofa*. Right there. You could just *lie down*, like I said *ten minutes ago*."

"I'm okay. Really. I'm good. I *got* it." I straighten at the waist and kind of fling my arms out to each side, demonstrating my steadiness. A sitting sobriety test, so to speak. "I *got* it. *See?* I'm good." I smile in absolute triumph.

He shakes his head, laughs a little, and smiles back. Then he lets go of me and leans casually against the island beside me, crossing his well-muscled arms over his impressive bare chest. He studies me for a long moment.

Open curiosity finally appears in his eyes now that the immediate crisis is over. "So, the accent definitely gives you away. East Coast, right? New York?"

Here it is.

The opening.

This is the moment to establish the carefully controlled narrative *about me* with a stranger.

Keep it vague.

Professional distance is paramount, even from a kind, ridiculously handsome stranger who just played paramedic.

"Something like that." I aim for a breezy nonchalance that feels utterly fake. Meanwhile, my heart hammers against my ribs, like a trapped bird seeking escape.

"Just got into town, actually. Staying nearby for a bit while I get settled. Work brought me out here to LA." I gesture vaguely towards the door, hoping to convey temporary status. "Still finding my bearings, obviously, given the dramatic beach entry. *Scene*, as it were."

He nods slowly. His gaze lingers on my face for a beat too long, making me slightly uncomfortable. "Yeah, Malibu can be tricky to navigate at first. It's beautiful, but it definitely keeps its secrets close." He pushes off the counter, moving towards the door. "Well, I should probably let you get back and rest that knee. Need help getting home? Which way are you headed on the beach?"

"No, no. I'm fine getting back. I'm fine now. *Really*." I slide more carefully, more gingerly now, off the high bar stool. I carefully fold up the damp towel and leave it on the bar stool. The cool, solid floor feels good beneath my bare feet. We left our running shoes outside on the deck, so we wouldn't track sand into his house.

Stability seems to have returned to me, slowly but surely.

Whew. Good news all around.

We walk out onto the deck together. I grab my wet Lululemon tank top and drape it over my free arm and then retrieve my running shoes from the corner of his deck by the outdoor shower. I carry my running shoes in each hand like twin ice cream cones, then carefully balance myself as I start across the deck, heading toward the massive set of stairs.

I'm already anxious in contemplating the massive set of stairs. Navigating them comes with intense trepidation. And I already *know* he's going to be watching me descend them the entire time.

I stop in the middle of the deck and turn around and face him. "Thank you again, though, for everything. The first aid, the water... the rescue." I pause, realizing I don't even know his name, this Good Samaritan of Malibu. "I'm sorry. I don't even know your name. I'm Isla. Isla Ryder." I offer my name, thinking it sounds casual, unremarkable, just another name in the sea of people he must encounter.

His expression changes subtly as soon as I say my name. Not recognition, exactly, or at least not immediately. More like... *interest?* A spark of something unreadable, maybe a glimpse of faint familiarity, but it's quickly masked.

But how can that be?

I'm just hallucinating now.

What with the cut and the blood and the pain.

Ugh. Don't think about... the things.

Especially from this kind stranger, whose face is suddenly starting to look incredibly, unnervingly familiar, triggering a faint but insistent alarm bell in the back of my mind. Have I seen him somewhere before? Has he been to Manhattan? There's something about the intensity of his gaze, the specific configuration of his features. What *is* it?

He extends his hand formally. His earlier easygoing charm replaced by a slightly more focused intensity. His gaze is sharper now, clearly assessing me. I quickly put both shoes in my left hand and shake his hand. My usual firm grip is weak, still dwelling on... *all the... things.* I feel unsteady again within seconds, thinking about *all the things* again.

"Roman," he says, his voice a low, resonant rumble that seems to vibrate through the air between us. His hand engulfs mine, warm, strong, the calluses rough against my skin. "Just Roman."

Roman.

The name hits me hard. My stomach drops and steals the air from my lungs at the same time. It's feels almost identical to the force of the initial collision with him on the beach. *Roman.*

Not just any Roman. Because how many guys named *Roman* could a girl actually *know?*

Zero.

The name is unusual, just like mine.

The sun-streaked blond hair, the impossible sky-blue eyes, the physique that looks as if it has been sculpted by the gods, the ridiculously opulent Malibu beach house… it all clicks into place with horrifying, stomach-plummeting clarity.

Fuck. Fuck. Fuck.

Roman Lysander.

My client. My project. The notorious Hollywood 'bad boy' I'm supposed to strategically rebrand. The man whose extensive files I was just dissecting a little more than two hours ago, meticulously cataloging his scandals and cynically strategizing his public redemption. The actor whose name is being whispered in connection with *Vendetta*—my *Vendetta*—makes my blood run cold and my protective instincts flare.

He's standing right here. Inches away from me. He just rescued me, tended to my wound with unexpected kindness and surprising competence, utterly oblivious to who I truly am or the immense, secret power I wield over his professional future. His kindness wasn't a performance designed to charm the PR handler his father hired. It felt unsettlingly genuine, almost spontaneous.

Which makes everything infinitely more complicated.

Now.

My carefully constructed professional composure, what is left of it, threatens to shatter into a million pieces. My mind races, frantically trying to reconcile the charming, helpful stranger kneeling at my feet moments ago with the volatile tabloid caricature described in his dossier file. My mouth goes desert dry. My pulse thrums loudly in my ears. My breath hitches. I think I'm about to hyperventilate for the all the reasons… *all… the things.*

He can't know.

He absolutely cannot know I'm the 'fixer' sent by his father to manage him.

Not yet.

Not like this.

My entire strategy hinges on establishing control, on setting the terms of engagement from a position of strength, not hobbling into his kitchen, crying, bleeding, and flustered, and washing my hands at his kitchen sink like I own the place. *And almost passing out. Twice.*

I pull my hand back from his, perhaps a little too quickly, forcing a smile that feels brittle and tight around the edges. "Well, thank you again, *just Roman. Lysander.* For playing the Good Samaritan so effectively." My voice sounds slightly strained, breathless, even to me. "I should… I should get going now. Need to find some ice for this knee."

He nods, though his gaze remains searching, even more curious now, perhaps sensing my sudden shift in demeanor, my abrupt eagerness to flee. "Yeah, ice is definitely a good idea. And maybe try to stay off it for a bit, let it rest." He starts walking with me towards the massive set of stairs. His presence beside me suddenly feels charged and dangerous. My gait is unsteady. I'm busy gasping at the air but trying to hide it.

"Which house did you say was yours again? I can walk you back and make sure you don't face plant in the sand again before you make it home."

"I'm not going to *face plant* in the sand anytime soon," I say tartly.

"You sure about that?" he asks. "You almost passed out at my kitchen sink and again almost at the kitchen island."

Those episodes did not go unnoticed. Great.

"Yes... I'm fine. Really. Fine. Absolutely fine." I say, maybe a little too forcefully, as desperation creeps into my tone. The words tumble out in nervous repetition.

Need for distance. Need to escape this unexpected, deeply compromising proximity before I say something monumentally stupid, or worse, revealing, and before he puts two and two together about the unusual name, he just heard.

"It's just down the beach that way." I gesture vaguely southward again, trying to project confidence I don't actually feel.

"Which house exactly?"

"The one with the... uh..." My mind goes completely blank.

Jet lag, shock, extreme pain, blood, *oh the blood*, and the overwhelming presence of Roman Lysander have scrambled my short-term memory. I flew in early this morning, went straight to the house, dumped my bags, reviewed all the files, and then went for this disastrous run. I barely registered the exterior details beyond *'expensive beach house'*.

"It has... a deck?" I offer weakly. I swing my arm like Vanna White pointing out his.

Roman raises a skeptical eyebrow. A hint of amusement plays around his lips. He seems to recognize my flustered state.

"Okay, narrow it down for me, East Coast. Big deck, small deck? Wooden chairs, metal chairs? Any distinguishing features? Hot tub? Weird sculpture? Crying gnome?"

"Um..." I close my eyes, trying desperately to conjure up an image. Panic mixes with embarrassment. How could I *not* remember? My chest tightens, and my breath comes in short, shallow gasps all over again. The control I pride myself on seems to have abandoned me entirely.

I open my eyes. He's studying me hard now.

"Sliding glass doors... like these?" I gesture helplessly at his own wall of glass. "A pool... I think? On the right side of the deck, if you're facing the ocean. And... maybe a table? Yes. That's right. There was a table, outside, on the left side. Round glass table. With an umbrella. A big umbrella is in the middle. Of the table. Blue and white stripes. Definitely blue and white stripes! Whew. Got it." The detail surfaces like a lifeline.

Roman nods slowly, his expression thoughtful as he scans the coastline in the direction I just indicated. "Blue and white striped umbrella... round glass table... pool on the right..." He points. "Okay, I think I know that one. Julia Winston's place?"

My relief is quickly followed by a fresh roaring wave of unease. Of course, he knows Julia Winston. Kimberley's agency partner and best friend, who, indeed, arranged this house for me. My skin shivers with cold sweat despite the warmth of the day.

The connections are closing in fast. Too fast.

"Yes, that's it." I try to keep my voice even. "Just borrowing it for a few days while my apartment gets sorted."

Keep it temporary. Keep it vague.

"Right." He grabs my arm and carefully leads me towards the massive stairs that lead down to the beach. "Come on then, *neighbor.* Let's get you home before you bleed out or forget where you live all together." He lets go of me and steps out onto the top landing of the stairs, waiting for me, his earlier offer now sounding more like a gentle, insistent command.

Defeated, and frankly, not entirely sure I trust my knee or my sense of direction right now, I give in. "Okay. Thank you."

He has this bemused look on his utterly too handsome face. "Are you sure you're, okay?" he teases. "You look a little pale." Then, he just waits for me at the top of the stairs. "I'll go first, in case you faint or something. I can catch you if you faint."

"I'm *not* going to faint."

"You almost *did. Twice.*"

He steps in front of me and makes his way a quarter of the way down the stairs while I gingerly follow. My right knee throbs with massive amounts of pain. The bandage is so damn tight with the insane amount of gauze and tape he used. I'm beginning to suspect he used too much *on purpose*. It's making it difficult to walk, let alone take the stairs.

I wince. He sees it.

"Oh… I should have given you Advil," he says with a groan. He stops a little more than halfway down the cement steps that lead to the beach. "Sit down. Wait here. While I get some. You might not have any, and that is going to hurt *a lot more* later."

"Hey," he says, turning back to me at the top of his steps, where I now sit like an obedient child waiting for him. "Did you eat on the plane?"

I shake my head from side to side. Fresh tears fill my eyes for no reason at all that I can think of.

"I'll bring you a sandwich. There's some catered food leftover from last night's festivities. And I'll get you some more gauze and tape." He grins wickedly at me.

I watch him disappear back into his house. My world suddenly, terrifyingly, feels upside down.

I hate this—hate the vulnerability, the dependence on someone else, the complete loss of control. I hate how exposed I feel. I hate that I've met Roman Lysander this way instead of on my carefully prepared terms.

Control. *Gone.*

Plans. *Demolished.*

Professional distance. *Obliterated.*

And somehow, sitting here on the concrete steps of Roman Lysander's Malibu mansion, I feel more lost and out of control than I've been in years.

CHAPTER 8

too good to be true

Isla Ryder

"Too Good To Be True" - Kacey Musgraves
"Snow On The Beach" - Taylor Swift, Lana Del Rey
"West Coast" - Lana Del Rey
"Just What I Needed" - The Cars

Thursday Mid-afternoon

I AM HAVING TROUBLE RECONCILING this charming rescuer of a man with the Roman Lysander 'bad boy' image I am supposed to be fixing.

I am confused.

Exhausted.

And vulnerable.

I wipe at my face again and again, as these tears of mine will not fucking stop. My hands shake as I tie the shoestrings of my running shoes together and hang them over the wet Lululemon tank top draped over my arm.

What a scene. Pathetic and helpless.

I'm carrying *half* my running gear.

What the fuck is wrong with me? This is so unsettling. I am out of control.

I stare out at the endless ocean that stretches out before me. The vast blue emptiness mirrors the hollow feeling inside of me. I stare, transfixed and stupefied.

What is happening here?

This is *not* a Kimberley Powers move.

I can hear her 'beyond amused', wicked laugh in my head already.

Isla, baby girl, *what are you doing*?

Her voice sounds so clear I turn to see if she's standing behind me.

And then he's back, now wearing a fresh white t-shirt, looking me over even more closely. His cerulean blue eyes study me with an intensity that puts me on edge right away. Without comment, he drops three Advil into my outstretched hand. The pills are small and burnt orange against the palm of my hand. I put them in my mouth, and the sweet flavor dissolves slightly against my tongue.

He hands me the water bottle I absentmindedly left on his kitchen counter, while he juggles the plate with the wrapped sandwich from his kitchen in his other hand, along with a fresh roll of gauze, tape and two kinds of bandages. I wash down the Advil with the proffered water while he watches. The liquid is cool against my throat.

He nods, satisfied. Apparently, he is *all in* on playing my medical advisor now.

"I'm sorry. I'm an absolute mess. This is so unlike me."

He holds out his free hand and pulls me up from where I've been sitting on his stairs. The contact sends a jolt through me all over again.

I angrily wipe at my face. *Again.* I hate this feeling of being undone. Of losing control.

"Probably the time change. East Coast to West Coast is a bitch. It's probably why I like to work in films, mostly based in LA, which are becoming so rare these days." His laugh is this deep husky sound I find completely disarming, like soft velvet against my jagged nerves.

"Well, I haven't slept since Monday, really. Tuesday 2:00 a.m. work crisis. Duty calls ever since… That's what I'm going with…" my voice trails off.

He is looking at me with far too much interest.

I am in way over my head at this juncture.

I think he knows it, too.

He has this bemused smile going and I'm sure if he's put things together enough, he's thinking, *'she's the ace PR strategist Kimberley Powers sent? No fucking way.'*

We walk slowly along the shoreline's edge. The companionable silence from before now charged with my internal panic and his thoughtful quiet. He adjusts his pace to my hobble, occasionally glancing down at my bandaged knee as if assessing its structural integrity. The pain pulses with each step, a steady throb that keeps me grounded in this surreal moment with him.

He stops for me every few minutes, and we rest. Me, carrying the bottled water, my tied together running shoes slung over one arm along with my soaked, ruined Lululemon tank top. He, carrying my sandwich for later and all of my medical supplies.

My mind replays the entire encounter on a continual loop, analyzing his behavior. Was there recognition in his eyes when I said my name? Did he connect Isla Ryder with the PR strategist his father may have already mentioned? Or was it just surprise at the unusual name, the East Coast accent, or the sudden appearance of a bleeding woman on his stretch of beach?

He seems relaxed, unconcerned, and still genuinely helpful. But he's an actor. A very famous one. How much of this is real, and how much is performance? I've seen him transform completely in films, become someone else entirely. Is this just another role he's playing?

I glance up at him. He's studying me as if to commit this encounter to memory for examination and scrutiny later. Our eyes meet. I feel that same jolt again, that same unsettling recognition we seem to share but do not openly acknowledge.

"You're not what I expected, Isla Ryder." He gets this uncertain look, vulnerability flashes across his features, before disappearing behind the practiced charm.

"Oh? What did you expect, Roman Lysander?" My voice comes out steadier than I feel.

"Someone completely different, not so goddamn beautiful. You're fucking ethereal. I wasn't planning on that."

His words hit me like a physical force. I feel heat rise to my face and spread down my neck. "I've never been told I was *'fucking ethereal'* nor *so goddamn beautiful* before. Thank you? I think? Mr. Lysander, you're so very kind."

The sarcasm serves as a shield. It's a thin barrier against the unexpected compliment.

"You know what I mean. Sorry about the fucking ethereal comment. It's a compliment. You remind me of her. Keira Knightley, *Pride and Prejudice, 2005*," he says with this discernible reverence.

"My favorite film." I look over at him in surprise.

I find myself unable to stop the flow of words that follow. They tumble out in a rush of unexpected emotion. "Thank you, that's very kind of you to say, considering the sight that I must look at this particular moment. I'll *take* the compliment, although I doubt Kiera Knightley swears as much as I do." I laugh a little and so does he.

I sigh. "I watched *Pride and Prejudice, the 2005* version with my mom when it first came out. I think I was seven. I'll never forget it. Loved it then. Love it now. Love Kiera Knightley. She is one of a kind. An amazing actress, *actor*, whatever inclusive term they deem using these days." I roll my eyes and laugh again, a nervous sound.

"Agree with everything you've said. I watched it with my mom, too. I think I was nine. She loved it. I loved it, too, although I'm a guy, so what do I know?" His voice is raspy with emotion, and there's a fresh turbulence in his ocean blue eyes.

I stare at him and slowly nod. And then I'm talking *again*. I can't seem to stop. It's like the words are being pulled from some deep, hidden recess inside of me. "That scene where Mr. Darcy professes his love to Elizabeth Bennet, and she turns him down? That, to me, is one of the most emotional love scenes ever captured on film, in all of time."

"Wow. Matthew Macfadyen did it for you, huh?" He sounds surprised.

"Well, yes. The vulnerability of him in that film was absolutely stunning. It's a rare thing for a man to be that honest and open with his feelings. And to be turned down. To be rejected outright. It was so unsettling to watch the heartbreak travel across his handsome face. He was utterly destroyed, but silent about it, you know? He was gasping for words and decorum. It was so genuine. The emotion captured on film in that moment was beautiful and heartbreaking at the same time, *in the rain*. It felt *real*." I shake my head from side to side.

"I'll have to watch it again."

"It's a great scene." I look up at him and slightly smile. "Of course, to say nothing of how the character of Darcy completely blew it with Elizabeth. He was oblivious—obviously as part of the time period—but surely when he insults her family, her status, and fails to see her for who she was *at all*. Although you can see them fighting the attraction they had for each other. So well done. But he pissed her off, well and good. And that made it easy for her to turn him down when she lost her temper with him. It's clear he didn't understand her." I sigh a little.

"It wasn't just Matthew Macfadyen's performance, though. Keira Knightley in that scene at the end, as he leaves her and strides away, how her whole body reacts as she falls against the stone wall and kind of caves inward in the realization of what she's done. No words needed. The audience can feel her misery as much as his. It's brilliant. I mean, that five-minute scene pretty much sums up the entire complexity of relationships between a man and a woman for all of time. Of course, it's just a film, but it's artful in the way it portrays real-life experience with complex relationships where love is involved. I suppose it's an acquired taste for guys, the film, *Pride and Prejudice*, I mean." I laugh a little and tuck a flyaway strand of my long, dark hair back behind one ear.

He watches me do it in this studied fascination and seemingly takes in every word I've just said at the same time. I feel exposed, as if I've revealed too much of myself in this simple exchange about a film.

"It's coming back to the theaters for the twenty-year commemoration," he says. "We should go see it."

"Absolutely. Love to."

The words hang between us. It's a promise of something that cannot yet be defined.

We keep walking a little further in this—*weird for me*—now companionable silence. The fine sand shifts beneath my bare feet, soft and warm. The ocean breeze caresses my face, carrying the scent of salt and sunlight. My knee throbs with each step, but I welcome the pain because it keeps me present and alert and stops me from drifting too far into this strange connection that seems to be forming between me and Roman Lysander.

Then, he stops and points out the house. "There you go. Casa Winston. Blue and white stripes standing proud. And the *only* beach house *for miles* where the sliding glass doors are *closed* on a perfectly warm day in Malibu."

"Ha-ha. But I *did not lock* them, like I would have in Manhattan." I grin up at him. "Progress is being made. In real time here. Thank you."

Delayed relief washes over me as I recognize the distinctive umbrella on the deck of the house nestled against the cliff. "Thank you," I say again. I feel genuinely grateful, but I am also desperate for him to leave so I can collapse and hyperventilate in private at all the unforced errors I've made with him in the past hour.

"I'm okay now. *Really.* You've been great about all of this, Roman, and you've gone way beyond the call of duty." My voice catches slightly on his name. *Roman.* Not Mr. Lysander. Not the client. Just Roman, the nice guy who bandaged my knee and walked me home.

"Oh no, you get the full Roman Lysander treatment." He takes my arm and helps me climb the deck stairs. There's a fresh wave of pain through my knee with each step.

Then, he pushes open the enormous glass sliding doors and steps inside as if he owns the place. "This is great. Perfect, actually. Not so ostentatious as mine. I was going through a phase when I bought my place, trying to prove something to my dad, I guess, and myself. I bought it after my first big hit movie and first gigantic paycheck. Paid cash. Probably foolish, but it's all mine. Brandon, my manager and best friend, thinks I should have dumped all that cash in the stock market, but I wanted a place of my own in Malibu far enough from LA, but still doable."

"I did that, too. Paid cash for a brownstone two-bedroom apartment in Manhattan. After I turned 25... We just sublet it to some Wall Street guy Samantha knows, who refuses to take the friend zone hint and still holds out hope for Samantha Harper." I laugh a little. "Samantha is my best friend from college. We've lived at the brownstone for the past year or so. Anyway, we've been working together... And now, we'll be here. And I should definitely stop talking so much." I shake my head slightly, feeling the familiar tightness in my chest that comes when I reveal too much of myself.

I've said too much.

Details about myself, I normally would never say.

I never do this. I never do this. I never do this.

"You're not talking too much. I enjoy hearing about your life in New York City—*Manhattan,* I mean. I thought about living there once, a long time ago, but my dad's here, so there's that. He still lives in Hollywood Hills on this palatial estate. He stayed there even after my mom died."

He hesitates. A shadow crosses his face. "We should go there sometime. It's an experience. They collected art together. They did everything together. Cooked. Entertained. It was a different Hollywood life back then, more glorious, and I loved growing up there." He stops and gets this haunted look. "Now, *I'm* talking too much. And you look like you could use a nap. Not that you look bad. You look incredibly gorgeous, but I'm pretty sure you said you took the red-eye, and it might be catching up to you now." He reaches over and tucks another stray strand of my hair back behind my ear.

The gesture is intimate, too intimate. I feel the warmth of his fingers against my face, and something inside me threatens to break wide open. I swallow hard.

"Big fan of artwork here. I would love to see it sometime. I'm sorry about your mom. How are you doing with that?" He looks confused by my question. "I read somewhere once that grief isn't something you get through; it's something you *carry*. It's always there. So, how are you doing with it *today*?"

"I'm doing all right. I miss her, you know? Especially today. Earlier when we were talking about *Pride and Prejudice*, the memory of her and me watching that film… well, it feels like it happened just yesterday. I'm nine years old again and hanging out with my mom. She was the only one who truly *got* me. I miss her, you know?" He sounds wistful and a little sad.

"It's an incredible loss. It never goes away. She was an amazing actress. I've seen *all of her films*, probably at least a dozen times. I bet she was an even more fantastic mother to you."

"My mom was everything. To me. To my dad. Yes, we miss her terribly. Still."

"Of course you do." I nod. Something in his voice, in the raw honesty of his admission, breaks through my carefully constructed defenses. I feel a familiar ache in my chest, involving that hollow space that never quite fills back up.

"People think because I lost my family nine years ago that I'm over it. That holidays without them are now normal for me. That I'm *used* to it. But you never are. You've lost something you'll never get back. Your future is forever changed. Earlier. I was overwhelmed by how alone I am here. I brought my mom's wedding dress with me." I point to the garment bag and the dress still draped over the chair.

He walks right over to it and trails his fingers along the long line of pearl buttons. "They're real pearl buttons, yeah?" he asks, looking over at me.

"Yes. Real pearls. Vintage dress. I keep the dress in that garment bag and just keep it close to me. It's like she's still here in some form." The words pour out of me, unstoppable. "Still. The loss. All those future plans. Gone." I frown. "My mom won't be here to help me do up all those pearl buttons on the dress. My dad won't be walking me down the aisle, giving me away… to… Matthew Macfadyen."

I'm suddenly desperate to lighten the moment because of the intense way he is looking at me right now.

It's as if I reached him on a soul level somehow with my little revelation.

Completely out of character for me to even talk about my family. The vulnerability is too much. Too exposed.

I've shared too much of myself. Again.

"So, it's going to be Matthew, huh? He's like in his late 40s, and I believe already married, Isla." Roman grins.

"Don't ruin the fantasy, Roman. Samantha has five older brothers. They love me. One of them will come through for me. Someday." I smile at him.

He returns my smile but then, he gets this troubled look. "I'm so sorry about the loss of your entire family. And here I am going on about the loss of my mom when I still have my dad. So, how are *you* doing with all of that today?"

The genuine concern in his voice catches me off guard. I feel the familiar sting of tears and blink rapidly, willing them away.

I will not cry. Not here. Not now. Not in front of him.

As if me crying less than a half hour ago was just an illusion.

"It's not a tit for tat thing, you know. It's not a trade in whose grief is worse. Mine or yours. I read once that the grief you carry is as big as the love you have for those you've lost. That really stayed with me. I'm doing my best." I say, going for nonchalance. "Today? I met this famous guy who was generous with bandages, antiseptic, and gauze, as well as a sandwich, but most generous with his time and attention when I needed it the most. So today is good. Thank you for asking. My mom *loved* LA. With the dress… it's like she's still here. With me, you know? And she would be thrilled that I am here." I smile ever so slightly but awkwardly step back from him.

We both fall silent.

I think we have over shared in unexpected ways that feels like it will come back as a boomerang of regret within the next hour. The silence stretches between us. It's filled with unspoken words but with this uncanny, shared understanding.

Finally, I say, "thank you again for the paramedical rescue, the sandwich, the water, the Advil, and for walking me back." My voice is barely audible over the distant crash of waves.

"Happy to help a neighbor in distress," he says slowly, heading toward the sliding doors.

I follow him out. Together, we walk back across the deck toward the stairs, his presence large and unavoidable.

He glances around the deck, then back at me. "So, Isla Ryder, new to LA, staying at Julia Winston's place… what kind of work brings you out to our sunny shores, if you don't mind me asking?" His tone is casual, conversational, but the question feels pointed and direct.

My heart rate picks up. I feel a bead of sweat form at the base of my spine.

Keep it simple. Keep it vague.

"I'm in communications," I say, choosing the broader term. "Consulting, mostly. Exploring some opportunities out here. But LA is clearly a different beast than New York."

"Communications," he repeats slowly, thoughtfully. "Interesting field. Especially out here." He studies my face again, that intense blue gaze making me feel pinned and exposed, like a butterfly preserved on a board for future study.

Then, as if making a decision of imminent importance, his expression clears, replaced by that easy, charming smile. The killer one that Kimberley would identify as raw charisma.

"Actually, Isla. Ryder. Speaking of LA opportunities and welcoming new arrivals… I'm having a little get-together tonight. Nothing too crazy, just some friends over. A celebration of sorts. My place." He gestures back down the beach towards his house. "You should come. Get your first real taste of Malibu life in action. Consider it *reconnaissance.*"

Reconnaissance.

The word hangs in the air between us, loaded with meaning.

Is it a test? *Yes.*

A casual invitation? *No.*

An opportunity for him to figure out who this mysterious Isla Ryder really is? *Yes.*

My publicist senses engage and override my instinct to politely decline. This could be invaluable. A chance to observe him in his natural habitat, see who his 'friends' are, gather intel, and better understand the dynamics I'll need to navigate.

I can call it a professional obligation disguised as attending a social event.

And frankly, after the flight, the stress, the injury, the sheer weirdness of this entire encounter, the thought of immersing myself in the superficial chaos of a Hollywood party feels strangely appealing.

Before my strategic brain can fully analyze the myriad of risks versus the potential benefits, before I can construct the perfectly calibrated noncommittal response, the words are already out of my mouth.

"Maybe," I hear myself say.

My attempt to sound casual, like I'm just considering it, let-me-check-my-calendar-and-see-if-I-can-fit-you-in, somehow fails miserably on all fronts. I sound too eager, too interested, like that of a dazed fangirl. I cringe inwardly at my own transparency.

"What time were you thinking?"

"Right before sunset. Half-past seven. Everyone likes to catch that." Roman shrugs, the picture of the casual, perfect host. Then he smiles again, that charming, slightly all too-knowing smile that reaches his eyes this time. "So, sunset is around 7:45 p.m. tonight. It gets dark fast out here on the beach, so it is probably best to take the road, not the beach. Especially with that cut." He glances down at my bandage pointedly. "Don't want you getting lost or tripping in the dark. The ocean's beautiful at night, but deserves respect, especially if you're unfamiliar with the territory. Which, let's face it, you still are."

"I'm going to let that insult of my knowledge of the Pacific Ocean pass," I say tartly. He laughs, the sound warm and genuine. "But I'll keep that in mind, take the road, not the beach. Got it."

"Anyway, just follow the music if you get lost. I've put together a special playlist for tonight. Kind of an homage. You really can't miss it." He offers a casual wink, a practiced, fleeting gesture that probably sends hearts fluttering across entire continents and puts the gossip columnists into overdrive.

Then, before I can even properly respond or process the full implications of accepting his invitation, before I can fully grapple with the bizarre, dangerous turn my first day in Malibu has taken, he gives a final, brief nod and mysteriously smiles at me. "See ya later, *Isla. Ryder.*"

He turns and jogs lightly back down the stairs, heading back towards his own glass fortress down the beach, leaving me standing alone on Julia Winston's deck, slightly breathless, and definitely off-balance. My knee throbs with a dull, insistent pain while my mind is still reeling from the collision, both literally and metaphorically.

Roman Lysander. My client. My incredibly handsome, unexpectedly kind, potentially volatile, multi-million-dollar problem. And I'm going to his party tonight. *Maybe.*

I watch him disappear into the shimmering heat haze rising from the sand, a solitary, golden figure against the vast blue canvas of the Pacific.

Who is he, *really*? And how am I going to be able to handle this?

This isn't just complicated.

This isn't just difficult.

This isn't just challenging.

This is treacherous territory, and I've already stumbled blindly into the minefield of it all on day one.

The game is on, and the stakes feel terrifyingly, impossibly high.

I close my eyes and let the sound of the waves wash over me. For a moment, just a moment, I allow myself to feel the full weight of everything—the grief I carry, the pressure of this job, the unexpected connection with Roman, and the fear of failing. It crashes over me like a wave, threatening to pull me under.

I can do this. I can do this. I can do this.

But can I?

The doubt seeps in, cold and insidious.

I open my eyes and stare out at the endless blue horizon, feeling more alone than I have in a long time.

PART TWO

catalyst

"She was BEAUTIFUL, but *not* like those girls in the magazines. She
was beautiful, for the way she *thought*. She was beautiful, for the
SPARKLE in her eyes when she talked about something she *loved*. She
was beautiful, for her ability to make other people smile, even if she was
sad. No, she wasn't *beautiful* for something as *temporary* as her looks.
She was beautiful, deep down to her soul."

F. Scott Fitzgerald

CHAPTER 9
'
i'm not over

Roman Lysander

"I'm Not Over" - Carolina Liar
"Wouldn't It Be Good" - Nik Kershaw
"Cake By The Ocean"– DNCE

Thursday Late Afternoon

ISLA RYDER. POST ISLA RYDER'S unexpected visit to my domain. Now, I'm thanking God that the cleaning crew arrived at noon, two hours earlier than usual, just as I requested. I'm relieved that I watched them file in with their vacuum cleaners, sprays, and various cleaning supplies, attacking the battlefield of empty bottles and crushed red Solo cups with practiced efficiency. The mess in the hall closet was dealt with first—Mark's unfortunate contribution to last night's festivities. I really need to stop inviting these people over. New plan after tonight's event. Thank God, Isla Ryder does not know of the chaos that was my home just a few hours before her unexpected arrival in it.

Now, after another quick shower, I retreat to the sanctuary of my home theater because everything has been cleaned and put back into perfect order for the next event. *Tonight.*

And she might be coming. Isla Ryder might come to my party.

My birthday party.

I collapse into one of the plush recliners. My head still pounds from last night's tequila indulgence, despite the copious amounts of Advil I've consumed. My run earlier was a last-ditch effort to burn off the remnants of my hangover, but then that was cosmically interrupted by playing paramedic to the beautiful stranger on the beach. *Isla Ryder.*

The theater is my refuge—a state-of-the-art setup with soundproofing that muffles the vacuum cleaners and chatter from the cleaning crew as they return from their late lunch break to finish upstairs. The massive screen dominates one wall, currently blank and waiting.

My fingers hover over the remote control. I should be reviewing lines for an upcoming audition scheduled next week for another romantic comedy. I should be watching something intellectually stimulating to prepare for the next *Vendetta* meeting since I missed the one this morning. I should be doing anything but what I'm about to do.

Instead, I navigate to the digital store, searching for *"Pride and Prejudice, 2005."*

Pride and Prejudice. The film I watched with my mom when I was nine. The film Isla Ryder mentioned with such passion on the beach earlier this afternoon.

I hit purchase without hesitation, and within moments, the opening credits begin to roll. I've seen it before, of course, but it's been years. My mom loved this movie. She made me watch it with her multiple times, insisting it would teach me about 'real emotion' and 'authentic acting'. At nine, I was more interested in superheroes and explosions, but I sat through it for her sake many times.

Now, I find myself leaning forward, watching with fresh eyes. Not just remembering my mother but searching for something else—the scene Isla Ryder described with such intensity. The rain. The rejection. The raw emotion.

I fast-forward impatiently until I find it—Elizabeth Bennet and Mr. Darcy standing in what appears to be some kind of stone gazebo, rain pouring down all around them. The tension is electric, the air between them charged with equal doses of spoken accusations and unspoken feelings.

Isla Ryder is right. Darcy doesn't see Elizabeth in that scene at all.

What did she say? 'Of course, to say nothing of how Darcy completely blew it with Elizabeth… He fails to see her for who she is at all; he made it easy for her to turn him down… I mean, in that five-minute scene, it pretty much sums up the entire complexity of relationships between a man and a woman for all of time.'

"'I had to see you," Darcy says, his voice strained.'

And then it unfolds—his declaration of love, awkward and heartfelt, followed by her rejection. *Brutal. Uncompromising.* I watch Macfadyen's face transform. His hope drains away. It's replaced by shock, then pain, and then a desperate attempt to maintain his dignity.

"'Forgive me, madam, for taking up so much of your time.'"

I rewind. Watch it again. And again. The sixth time through, I'm no longer just watching—I'm studying. The micro-expressions. The way Macfadyen holds his body, the subtle shifts in his posture as rejection washes over him. The restraint. The controlled breathing. The way he conveys so much without saying a word.

It's masterful. It's exactly the kind of acting I've always wanted to do —*needed to do*—but have never quite managed to access. Something real. Something that requires more than my looks or my charm.

Isla Ryder is so right. The vulnerability is stunning. It's the antithesis of everything Hollywood has wanted from me, everything my career has been built on. Zeus, in *"God of Thunder"* required abs and a smoldering gaze. Not this. Not the potent, unguarded emotion that Macfadyen delivers in his performance.

I can't help but wonder what Isla saw in my face when we talked about this scene. Did she see the same longing I feel now—to be taken seriously, to do work that matters? Or did she just see Roman Lysander, Hollywood's golden boy, another pretty face with an expiration date whose reputation needs fixing?

***

My phone buzzes, interrupting my racing thoughts. My dad's name flashes on the screen. My thumb hovers over the answer button. I don't want to talk to him. Not today. Not on my birthday. But I answer anyway. I always do.

"Hey, Dad."

"Roman." His voice is crisp, businesslike. No 'happy birthday, son.' No warmth. Just my name, a statement of fact. "I'm calling about tonight."

"Let me guess—you're not coming." I try to keep the bitterness from my voice, but it seeps through anyway. It always does with him.

A pause. "I have a dinner with the Paramount executives. It couldn't be rescheduled."

"Of course." I run a hand through my hair, unsurprised, but still disappointed. *Always disappointed.* "The business comes first."

"This dinner could directly impact your career, Roman. Including potential opportunities beyond *Vendetta.*"

"Right. Always thinking of me." The sarcasm is thick, but he either doesn't notice or chooses to ignore it. He's good at ignoring things. *My feelings. My birthday. Me.*

"I've arranged for a gift to be delivered. Something special."

"Thanks." I know better than to ask what it is. Probably another watch for my already extensive collection—something expensive and impersonal. Something to add to the pile of things I don't need.

"And Roman—" he pauses, and for a brief, foolish moment, I think he might say something fatherly. Something real. "Try to behave tonight. Brandon informs me that he told you about the PR strategist from Powers & Winston PR. She arrives tomorrow in LA. Isla Ryder. She's the best in the business, and I'm paying a fortune for her services. Don't give her more work than necessary on her first day."

My grip tightens on the phone. "Isla Ryder," I repeat, the name rolling off my tongue with a familiarity I shouldn't possess yet. "She's your hired gun."

"She's a professional. One of the best. She'll help you clean up your image for *Vendetta.*"

"And that's what matters, right? The image. Not the reality."

Another pause. "The reality is that you're sabotaging yourself, Roman. You have talent—*real talent*—but you're burying it under tabloid headlines and bad behavior. Ms. Ryder can help, but only if you let her."

I swallow hard, unexpectedly affected by the rare acknowledgment of my talent. "I'll be on my best behavior." A promise. Probably broken already. The lie comes easily now. Practiced. Perfected. Another performance for the man who values those above all else.

"Good. Happy Birthday, Roman." The words sound rehearsed, an afterthought. "I'll call you tomorrow."

The call ends, and I'm left staring at the frozen image of Macfadyen's devastated face on the screen. I hit play again, watching as he walks away from Elizabeth Bennet, dignity intact despite the rain and rejection. Then, I focus on Kiera Knightley, just as Isla Ryder described, noting the way she stumbles back against the stone wall, holding herself together, realizing what she's done without a single word of dialogue. Isla Ryder is so right about everything going on in this emotionally charged scene. It's great acting. *Inspiring.*

Would my father even recognize real emotion if he saw it? *No.*

Would anyone in this town?

Would Isla Ryder?

I close my eyes, envisioning Macfadyen's devastated face. Seeing my own.

I almost hope she doesn't come. *Almost.*

———

With the house immaculate once more, the cleaning crew having erased all evidence of last night's debauchery, I stand in my bedroom, staring at the options laid out on my king-sized bed: a casual black t-shirt and jeans, a more dressed-up navy button-down with tan trousers, or the white linen shirt that photographs well against my tan.

I'm overthinking this. It's just another birthday party, another excuse for Hollywood's elite and hangers-on to drink my alcohol and network under the guise of celebrating me. I shouldn't care what I wear. But I do. *Because she might come.*

I grab my phone and call Brandon.

"What's up, birthday boy?" Brandon answers, the sound of LA traffic humming in the background.

"Tell me more about Isla Ryder," I say without preamble. Without pretense. I need to know.

A pause. "Why the sudden interest?"

"My father just called to remind me she's flying in tomorrow. If she's going to be following me around, *fixing me,* I'd like to know what I'm dealing with here."

Brandon sighs. "I gave you the file, not that there's all that much to go on in there. But like I said before, she's 26 years old, graduated from Penn with honors in communications and English literature. She's worked directly under Kimberley Powers at Powers & Winston for the past five years. Handled some major crisis management situations for celebrities, politicians, the occasional disgraced CEO. She's very private. She has no personal social media presence. There's no public dating history except for that thing with Chad Jameson a couple of years back."

"The Yankees player, right?"

"Yeah, Yankees' notorious first baseman. Big scandal when they broke up, though the details were mostly kept under wraps. Powers & Winston made sure of that. That shit was shut down real fast."

I frown, trying to reconcile this information with the woman I met on the beach. The one who spoke so passionately about *Pride and Prejudice*, who seemed genuinely moved when talking about grief. The woman who looked at me and saw… something. Something real.

"What does she look like?" I ask, keeping my tone casual. Too casual.

"No idea. Like I said, no photos of her online. Why?"

"Just wondering if I'll recognize her when she inevitably shows up to babysit me."

Brandon laughs. "I doubt she'll be that obvious. Powers & Winston are known for their subtlety. She'll probably observe you from a distance first and get the lay of the land, so to speak, before approaching you directly."

Little does he know.

"The subtle approach, yeah? Okay." I take a beat not giving anything away. "When are you getting here? You said *4:00 p.m.* and I thought we were going to hang out a bit?"

He sighs big. "Yeah. Well, some things blew up. Sorry. I'll probably be there around six-thirty. I've still got some calls to finish up. The caterers are set for five, right?"

"Yeah, Julie's handling it. Everything's under control."

Nothing is under control.

Not really.

Not me.

Not my feelings.

Not this strange pull I feel toward a woman I've just met.

"Good. And Roman—" His voice takes on that cautionary tone I've come to hate. "Keep it low-key tonight, okay? No tequila shots, no tabloid-worthy stunts. Let's try to keep it together so Isla Ryder doesn't have a PR problem with you on her first day next week, yeah?"

"I'll be the perfect angel." A promise. *What are those? The lie comes so easily.* I smile to myself. "See you at six-thirty."

I end the call and toss my phone onto the bed. My gaze returns to the clothing options. After a moment's consideration, I choose the white linen shirt and tan trousers. Classic. Understated. The kind of outfit that says I'm not trying too hard, even though I clearly am.

As I dress, my mind drifts back to the beach, to Isla's shocked expression, when she realized who I was. There was recognition there, but something else too—wariness, perhaps. *Caution.* As if she understood immediately the complicated dynamic between us.

She knows who I am now. Not just Roman Lysander, the actor, but Roman Lysander, her project. Her assignment. The problem she's been hired to fix.

Will she come tonight?

Part of me hopes she won't—that she'll keep her distance, maintain the professional boundary that should exist between us. But another part, a larger part than I care to admit, hopes she will. That she'll step into this circus of my own creation, this carefully constructed façade of my life and see through all of it.

The doorbell rings, pulling me from my thoughts.

"Julie." I greet the head caterer with a warm smile as she and her team file in, carrying trays and equipment. "Right on time, like always. Thank you."

Julie Matson returns the smile. Her efficiency is evident in the way she immediately begins directing her staff. At forty-something, she's a no-nonsense professional who's been handling my events for the past three years. She knows exactly how I like things—the food, the presentation, and the timing.

"Happy birthday, Roman," she says, setting down her clipboard on the kitchen island. "Twenty-eight, right? Any special requests this year?"

"The usual setup is fine," I say, gesturing around the open-plan living area. "But you remembered the white birthday cake with Italian buttercream frosting and cream filling, right?"

She raises an eyebrow. "Like last year?"

"Exactly like last year." I don't elaborate. Julie doesn't need to know that white cake with Italian buttercream was what my mother made for me for every birthday until she died. That I've insisted on it every year since. It's a tradition I maintain, even though it's never quite the same. Never right. Never enough.

"Yes, Roman, we have your birthday cake, just like you ordered last year. No worries. We got you." She laughs. "We'll set up the bar here, buffet along the island, dessert station by the windows. DJ's area is clear?"

I nod. "Joey's coming at six to set up. He's got the playlist I put together already."

"Perfect." She studies me for a moment, her expression softening slightly. "You okay, Roman? You seem a bit… tense."

"I'm fine," I say automatically, then reconsider. Julie's one of the few people in my world who treats me like a normal human being, not a meal ticket or a celebrity. "Just the usual birthday existential crisis. Another year older, another year of wondering what the hell I'm doing with my life."

She laughs. "That's just being in your twenties. Trust me, it gets worse."

"Great. Something to look forward to." I glance around the kitchen. "I need everything to be perfect tonight."

"It always is," she assures me. "But for any particular reason? Someone special coming?"

I hesitate. "Maybe. I'm not sure yet."

Julie's eyes light up with interest. "Not Melody Parker again?"

"God, no." I grimace. "Someone… different."

"Well, now I'm intrigued." She picks up her clipboard again. "Don't worry, we'll make sure everything is flawless. Your mystery guest will be impressed."

"Thanks, Julie." I step back, allowing her and her team to work their magic. "Oh, and can you save me two pieces of cake for later? At least one corner piece with extra frosting, yeah?"

She gives me a knowing look. "One for you, one for the mystery guest? You got it."

"Thanks, Julie."

She smiles and returns to directing her staff, leaving me to wander through my own home, feeling strangely like a visitor.

My house is impressive—I know that objectively. Six bedrooms. Eight bathrooms. A home theater. A gym. Floor-to-ceiling windows overlooking the Pacific. It cost a fortune, paid for with my *"God of Thunder"* money, as I proudly told Isla Ryder earlier. Empty rooms full of expensive things. But despite the breathtaking views and designer furniture, it's never quite felt like home. Just another set. Another place to perform.

I step out onto the deck, breathing in the salty air. The ocean stretches out before me, vast and indifferent. I've always loved that about it—how it makes everything else seem small and inconsequential. My problems, my career, the constant pressure to be something I'm not —all of it diminishes against the backdrop of that endless blue of the Pacific.

My phone buzzes again. Another birthday wish, this time from my agent. Then another from a co-star from my last film. Then three more from people I barely know. The messages are all similar—generic well-wishes, often accompanied by reminiscences of wild nights out or inside jokes that aren't actually funny.

None of them know me. Not really. They know Roman Lysander, Hollywood's golden boy, the supposed party animal, the tabloid regular, most of which is without any of my own doing. I'm just the data point, easy to follow and speculate about, half the stuff they just make up about me. They don't know the guy who watches *Pride and Prejudice* in his home theater, analyzing the nuances of Matthew Macfadyen's performance. They don't know the guy who still misses his mom, who still craves his father's approval despite himself.

They certainly don't know the guy who spent his afternoon bandaging up a beautiful girl on the beach, feeling more alive in that unexpected, surprising hour than he has in months.

I wonder if Isla Ryder sees through the façade. If she recognized something real in me, the way I think, I recognized something real in her. Or if I'm just another project to her, another damaged celebrity, to rehabilitate for the sake of her career.

The doorbell rings again. Joey Landini, my DJ, has arrived.

"Roman!" Joey greets me with our usual handshake-into-half-hug. "Happy birthday, man! Twenty-eight, huh? Getting old."

"Tell me about it." I laugh a little. I lead him over to his designated area near the sliding glass doors. "Got everything you need?"

"Always." Joey begins setting up his equipment with practiced ease. He's been my go-to DJ for years, understanding exactly the vibe I want for my parties. "The playlist you sent over is killer. Taking it back to the '90s, I see."

"It's an homage," I explain, watching him work. "Top songs from 1995 until now, plus top songs of the misunderstood, including Nirvana and some others."

Joey nods appreciatively. "Nice concept. Very personal."

"That's the idea." I hesitate, then add, "I might want to make a special request later, though. Something not on the list. I'll let you know."

"Sounds good." He continues setting up, connecting cables and adjusting levels. "So, big crowd tonight?"

"The usual suspects. Industry people, some friends. Nothing crazy."

"Right." Joey's tone suggests he doesn't believe me. "Just like last year's 'nothing crazy' that ended with you taking a swim in the ocean at 3:00 a.m."

I wince at the memory. "Different vibe this year. I'm turning over a new leaf."

"Sure, you are." He grins, not unkindly. "Whatever you say, birthday boy."

I leave Joey to his set-up and return to the kitchen, where Julie's team has transformed the space into a catering masterpiece. The bar is stocked, the buffet artfully arranged, and a magnificent white cake sits prominently on the dessert table.

Everything is perfect. Controlled. Just the way I like it.

So why do I feel so goddamn anxious?

Brandon arrives at half-past six on the dot, looking every inch the successful Hollywood manager in his Tom Ford tailored black suit with a freshly pressed white dress shirt and a cerulean blue silk tie. He surveys the setup with approval before turning to me.

"Looking good," he says, eyeing my attire. "Clean, classic. A very reformed 'bad boy'."

"That's exactly what I was going for," I say in a deadpan tone. "The *'I've seen the error of my ways'* aesthetic."

Brandon sighs. "I'm just trying to help you, Roman. This *Vendetta* opportunity—"

"I know, I know. It's the chance of a lifetime. Career-defining. My shot at legitimacy." I've heard the speech so many times I could recite it in my sleep. The words have lost all meaning. "I get it."

"Do you? Because your behavior lately suggests otherwise."

I feel a flash of irritation. "I'm here, aren't I? Sober, dressed appropriately, hosting a perfectly respectable birthday party. What more do you want from me?"

"Consistency," Brandon says flatly. "One night of good behavior doesn't erase months of tabloid headlines."

"Which is why my father hired Isla Ryder, right? To wave her PR magic wand and make all those headlines disappear?"

Brandon studies me. "You're really fixated on this PR woman. Why?"

I shrug, avoiding his gaze. "Just trying to understand the plan. Know my enemy."

"She's not your enemy, Roman. She's here to help you."

"By completely reinventing me? Turning me into someone I'm not?"

"By helping you become the person you are." Brandon's voice softens slightly. "The person I know you are, underneath all the... performance."

The sincerity catches me off guard. Disarms me. I don't know how to respond when people see through the act. I don't know who I am without it.

I shift gears. Redirect. "It's weird turning 28. I feel like I should have more to show for it. Where's my life going, you know?"

"Well, that's some heavy existential stuff to be pondering before a hundred guests arrive. But I know what you mean. I have a plan. I want to get married by the time I'm thirty."

"You have to *actually continue* seeing a girl to make that happen, Brandon. What happened to Ava? She seemed pretty cool."

"Ava doesn't want to have kids. That pretty much sums up while I am not seeing her anymore. I mean, kids are a part of my plan. Two, at least. Maybe three."

We don't ever talk about this kind of stuff. Too far away from where we are actually at in life. Too personal. Way beyond the *'what-kind-of-scotch-is-your-favorite?'* conversation. But, at 28 years of age, you need to be thinking about those things. Not the scotch. The kids.

So, I know this is going to shock my best friend. "I want five kids."

"Five kids?" Brandon asks. *"Do not lead* with that one, whoever you decide to deem worthy of marrying, Lysander. And why, *five?"*

"Well, I have always wanted a big family. I *wish* I had siblings. So, I'm glad I have you, bro. As for the number of kids? Well, one is not enough and two isn't really either; three is two against one, yeah? And four is two against two. Five is an odd number, and it just seems like a good number—a passel of kids to play with, raise, and watch grow up. One big happy clan, as it were."

"The Lysander clan." Brandon laughs. "I'm thinking that leaves out Melody Parker."

"That *definitely* leaves out Melody Parker." I grin. "My heart isn't breaking over that one."

My mind flashes to the green-eyed goddess from this afternoon. A crazy thought. *Isla Ryder is...* I catch my breath and hold it.

I cannot define Isla Ryder. At all.

Brandon is watching me closely now. "You okay, Roman. You look kind of shook up. Are you feeling all right?"

"I'm good. I'm fine. Absolutely fine."

Now, I'm mimicking her responses.

What is going on with me?

This girl, Isla Ryder, is occupying far too many of my waking thoughts at present, literally all afternoon, since I left her back at Julia Winston's place.

The doorbell rings again, rescuing me from the serious conversation Brandon and I were having. The first guests have arrived.

"Showtime," Brandon says, straightening his tie. "Remember—"

"Best behavior," I finish for him. "I know the drill."

And just like that, Roman Lysander, Hollywood's golden boy, slips back into place like a well-worn mask. I plaster on my signature smile, ready to greet the parade of beautiful, empty people who will fill my house for the next few hours.

But as I move toward the open door, I can't help but glance farther down the street, wondering if, somewhere inside Julia Winston's borrowed house, Isla Ryder is deciding whether to accept my invitation. *Or not.*

The party fills up quickly. The usual mix of industry insiders, actors, models, and people whose connection to me is tenuous at best. I play the role of gracious host, moving from group to group, accepting birthday wishes with practiced charm, laughing at jokes that aren't funny, and feigning interest in projects I couldn't care less about.

It's exhausting. It's always exhausting.

Brandon watches me from across the room, his expression a mix of approval and caution. I'm playing my part well, but he knows me well enough to see the cracks in the facade, the moments when my smile doesn't quite reach my eyes.

I pour myself a drink. Just one. A promise to myself. To Brandon. To the father, who isn't here.

Melody Parker arrives fashionably late, making an entrance in a red dress that leaves little to the imagination. She makes a beeline for me, air-kissing both cheeks.

"Happy birthday, Roman." Her hand lingers on my arm. "You look amazing."

"Thanks, Melody. So do you." The compliment is automatic, empty. Like everything between us.

Meanwhile, I'm thinking of Isla Ryder and the way she held onto me pretty much through her entire bloody cut ordeal and how endearing and surprisingly sexy I found that to be. Needing me, hanging on to me in her unexpected crisis. She was just so *real. Amazingly real.*

Melody leans in closer, her perfume overwhelming. "I have a special birthday present for you later." Her meaning is unmistakable.

I force a smile, already planning my escape. "Looking forward to it."

That is so not happening.

I'm not looking forward to anything except the possibility of seeing Isla Ryder walk through my front door. A woman I barely know. A woman hired to fix me. A woman who might see through all of this.

Brandon catches my eye from across the room, giving me an approving nod. The Melody Parker connection is part of the strategy—a "stabilizing influence" in the public eye, according to the studios. Never mind that there's zero genuine chemistry between us, that our 'relationship' is as manufactured as everything else in this town.

As the night wears on, I find myself increasingly distracted. My gaze drifts toward the sliding glass doors, searching for a face that hasn't appeared. I take sentry turns watching the front entrance and the back entrance. The clock ticks past eight, then eight-ten. Maybe she's not coming. Maybe she saw through the invitation, recognized it for the test it was.

Or maybe she just doesn't care. Maybe I'm just another job to her, another celebrity ego to manage, not worth the effort to attend a party on her first night in town. The thought stings more than it should.

I drift through my own party like a ghost, present but not really here. The music is perfect—Joey's executing the playlist flawlessly, charting the course of my life in song.

But all I can think about is who's not here.

My father. My mother. Isla Ryder.

I play my part, but my heart isn't in it.

It's somewhere else.

With someone else.

What is going on with me?

Maybe she's not coming. Maybe I read her wrong. Maybe the connection with her I felt on the beach was just another performance.

Mine? No, I wasn't performing.

Maybe she was.

I slip away from the crowd, seeking a moment's solitude on the deck. The night air is cool against my face. The sound of the waves is a welcome respite from the noise inside.

I lean against the railing, looking out at the dark ocean, wondering what I'm doing, and why I care so much about whether this girl shows up at my party.

CHAPTER 10

lucky

Isla Ryder

"Lucky" – Britney Spears
"Ocean Eyes" - Billie Eilish

Thursday Afternoon into Evening

BACK WITHIN THE COOL, SILENT SANCTUARY of Julia Winston's borrowed glass palace, the adrenaline from the beach encounter finally recedes, leaving behind a confusing residue of throbbing pain, lingering disorientation, and sharp, insistent calculation and deep analysis.

My knee pulses with a steady, unwelcome rhythm beneath the surprisingly professional bandage Roman applied. A physical testament to the collision that threw my meticulously planned first forty-eight hours in Los Angeles completely off-kilter.

I've been here before. I've done this before. Calculating odds, assessing risks, and planning for the contingencies.

But not like this. Not with someone like him.

I limp towards the massive wall of windows overlooking the Pacific, the sun's slow descent towards the horizon painting it in dramatic streaks of yellow, orange, pink, and the hint of deepening purple. The sheer beauty of it is majestic and calming, a stark contrast to the churning chaos inside me.

Roman Lysander.

He's not just a name in a file anymore, not just a collection of tabloid headlines and analytical notes. *He is a real person.* A ridiculously attractive, unexpectedly kind, surprisingly competent *real* person who knelt at my feet, cleaned my wound with gentle efficiency, and offered to help me without a trace of the arrogance or dismissiveness his reputation would suggest.

And that? That is infinitely more dangerous to me personally than the predictable 'bad boy' outlined in Kimberley's dossier.

The guy in the file? Professionally, I could strategize against him. I could anticipate his defiance, plan contingencies for his volatility, and build professional firewalls against his expected charm offensive.

The guy on the beach? He bypassed all of my defenses entirely. His kindness felt genuine. It was disarming. His competence was unexpected. His physical presence was overwhelming. *To me.*

I close my eyes and allow myself to feel the lingering sensation of his hands on my skin. Clinical, yes, but still… there.

That easy confidence, the lack of pretense in his actions, and the straightforward way he took charge of the situation. None of those perfectly align with the image of a self-destructive party boy coasting on fame.

My mind races in an attempt to reconcile the two Romans.

Was the beach encounter the performance? A calculated charm deployment, instinctively recognizing a potential challenge or simply responding to playing the Good Samaritan to a stranger?

Or is the tabloid persona the act? A shield he's constructed to keep the world at bay, and hide something more complex about himself underneath?

I press my forehead against the cool glass and breathe deep. The sharp contrast between the cool surface and my flushed skin grounds me momentarily.

Understanding which is which—or acknowledging the possibility that both are true facets of a complicated whole—is now paramount to my successful strategy in rebranding him and to the success of Ryder & Harper Communications LA.

Intertwined.

Complicated.

He knows my name. He knows I'm staying at Julia Winston's house. He knows I'm new in town, working in 'communications.' How long until he, or more likely, his manager Brandon Chase, or his father Trent, connects the dots for him? If he hasn't already? Isla Ryder, the PR strategist from Powers & Winston, Kimberley Powers' top gun, hired specifically to rebrand him.

The clock is ticking.

Or time has already run out.

His invitation to the party tonight wasn't just casual neighborly politeness, despite the effortless charm with which it was delivered. *'Reconnaissance,'* he called it, with that knowing glint in his eyes.

Was it a test?

An attempt to size me up outside of a formal meeting?

A chance to see if the new arrival would sink or swim in his natural habitat?

Yes, to all of those.

Truly? It doesn't matter what his motives are or might be. Professionally, attending isn't optional; it's mandatory. It's an unexpected, invaluable opportunity to observe him unfiltered, surrounded by his chosen circle. Who are his friends? What are the power dynamics? Who holds influence? What are the potential pitfalls and pressure points I'll need to navigate?

This is field research, pure and simple. Strategic intelligence gathering disguised as social mingling.

I push away from the window as the decision solidifies within me.

I have to go.

Forget I'm running on fumes and haven't slept for more than two hours in the past three days. Forget the throbbing knee, forget the lingering disorientation, forget the unsettling excitement his proximity causes me for some unknowable reason I cannot name. This is business. Ryder & Harper's first, most critical mission.

But beneath the professional justification, the intrigue of something else ignites—personal curiosity. Annoying, unprofessional, but undeniably present.

Who *is* Roman Lysander, really? The kind stranger or the tabloid train wreck? A questionable fit for *Vendetta*'s demanding lead as Steven Stryker or a misunderstood talent trapped in a gilded cage.

My phone buzzes on the sleek console table where I left it. I glance over and quickly hobble over to pick it up. *Samantha.* Right on time. Relief washes over me, a welcome anchor in the swirling uncertainty of the past two hours.

"Okay, *spill.* I've got twenty-five minutes before they call for final boarding." Her voice comes through the line, crackling with energy despite the cross-country distance and the background hum of JFK airport. "You sound breathless. Did you trip again? Did you meet Aquaman this time? Tell me everything about literally colliding with Roman *freaking* Lysander!"

I sink onto one of the low-slung, ludicrously expensive sofas, the cool leather a stark contrast to the residual heat already rushing up my neck to my face. "You're not going to believe it, Sammy."

And I tell her everything—the run, the collision, the unexpected solidity of his chest, the fall, the blood, the surprisingly gentle first aid administered by the man himself, the realization of *who* he was, the walk back, and finally, the invitation.

"He cleaned your cut? Your gaping wound? With his own famous hands?" Samantha squeals. Pure delight radiates through the phone. "And he invited you to his party *tonight*? Iz, this is fate. *It's cosmic.* The universe is practically screaming at you."

"The universe is presenting a strategic, intelligence-gathering opportunity, Sammy girl." I try to inject professional objectivity into the conversation, mostly for my benefit. "He's the client. Or the son of the client. The project. Going to his party is pure *'reconnaissance'.*" I blush at using his word. "It's a chance to observe him, his environment, and his network. *It's work.* Really."

"Work involving potentially the hottest man currently alive and breathing on the planet, who also happens to be stratospherically charming *and* princely kind enough to rescue my little running gazelle best friend, profusely bleeding and in distress on the beach." Samantha's voice practically vibrates with excitement through the phone. "Sign me up for that kind of work."

I can practically see her bouncing in her seat at the airport terminal, eyes sparkling with all kinds of romantic scenarios. Her ability to find fairytale magic in the most mundane professional situations never fails to both amuse and exasperate me.

"Sammy—"

"No, seriously, Iz. A gorgeous Hollywood prince literally swept you off your feet—okay, technically *onto* your feet after you face-planted—and then played sexy paramedic? This is like every romance novel we've ever secretly devoured rolled into one perfect meet-cute."

Her infectious enthusiasm makes me smile despite myself. "You're being ridiculous."

"I'm being *realistic*. About the cosmic significance of a hot guy with first aid skills appearing exactly when my workaholic best friend needs rescuing." She pauses dramatically. "Plus, *hello*? Intelligence gathering at a Hollywood party? This is like Christmas morning for ambitious PR girls."

The boarding announcement booms in the background, but Samantha's excitement remains undimmed. "Promise me you'll actually *enjoy* this reconnaissance mission. Seriously, though, you *have* to go. Think of the intel. You can scope out his inner circle, see who the real players are, and get a feel for the vibe that surrounds him. It's perfect. It saves us weeks of trying to figure out the landscape of Hollywood and all its players as it relates to him. And it's definitely cosmic."

"That's what I was thinking, maybe not the cosmic part, but it saves us time in learning who the players are in his world."

I'm secretly relieved she sees the professional necessity.

"It feels... weird, though, right? Just showing up at his house hours after he bandaged me up, knowing I'm the PR person hired to manage him, but maybe him *not knowing*... yet."

"All the more reason to go *now*. Get the lay of the land before the official meeting. You'll have an advantage. And hey," her voice drops conspiratorially, "you get to see him in his natural habitat. Report back on *everything*. Especially the abs. Were they as good in person as they look on screen? Details. Stat."

"*Samantha*, I was a little focused on not passing out with all the blood. I wasn't looking at his abs, per se." Even though a reluctant smile tugs at my lips. "Boundaries. Strictly Professional. Remember?"

"Right, right. Professional observation of abdominals, *only*. *Got it*." She laughs through the phone. "But seriously, Iz, go. Be brilliant. Be observant. Be the strategic goddess you are. Just... be careful, okay? He might be nice about bandaging up a girl's bleeding cut knee, but his reputation exists for a reason. Don't let the charm fool you, my gazelle girl."

"Trust me." My voice hardens slightly. "The charm is noted, analyzed, and filed under 'Potential Manipulation Tactics.' My guard is up so high it's practically orbiting the planet. *This* is strictly business."

"Good. Good. So, what are you wearing? This requires the perfect blend of *'effortlessly chic LA cool'* and *'don't mess with me, I run shit'*."

<hr>

We spend the next ten minutes dissecting my limited wardrobe options. My usual arsenal of sharp power suits and understated black cocktail dresses feels all wrong for a Malibu beach party, especially with a conspicuous bandage marring the line of my leg.

"Okay, the Free People top—the pearly sequin one—it catches the light, very LA," Samantha says decisively. "And the black leather jeans. *Yes*, the ones I made you pack. They scream cool confidence, are a little edgy, and they're unexpected. Shows them all you're not some stiff East Coast suit."

"Leather jeans? To a beach party?" I picture myself sweating profusely.

"It's Malibu, Iz, not the Sahara. And it gets cool at night by the ocean. Plus, they hide the bandage better than anything else, right? Pair them with the Iggy Crystal strappy silver stilettos. Subtle bling, killer heels. It says, 'I'm here, I'm fabulous, and I could crush your strategy deck and your heart simultaneously.'"

"Subtle." I laugh despite myself.

"Exactly what we're going for here. Hair? Sleek ponytail. Maybe that twisted braid thing you do. Keep it polished but not too severe. Makeup? Emphasize the eyes. Smoky, maybe? Keep the lips neutral or just a hint of gloss. You want to look observant and intelligent, but slightly mysterious all at the same time."

"Are you sure you're not moonlighting as a Hollywood stylist?"

"Just looking out for my partner here. Got to make sure Ryder & Harper Communications LA makes the right first impression, even unofficially. Speaking of, did FedEx get there with the package?"

"Just arrived. I haven't opened it yet."

"Well, do it *now*. Our business cards are in there. Take them with you tonight—you're going to be blown away by what I came up with for the design." She laughs. "Dammit all to hell. I've got to run. They're calling for final boarding. And *my name*, specifically. Text me updates. Be safe.

Have fun... professionally speaking, of course. *Or not,"* she adds wickedly.

The line clicks dead, leaving me alone again in the echoing silence of the house. Samantha's whirlwind of advice settles in all around me.

Leather jeans, it is.

I retrieve the FedEx package from the entryway table and open it, smiling as I examine Samantha's handiwork. The business card is a 2" X 2" minimalist, white heavy card stock that is embossed in gold with a Gordian knot graphic. No names, no titles, no address. Just a QR code in the same embossed gold on the back. It will take genuine effort and a serious genius to contact us for public relations services.

Samantha Harper has thought of everything.

It's a statement. It's fucking fabulous. It's so perfectly Samantha—a little borrowed from that scene in *Hitch* with Will Smith but entirely transformed by her unique sensibility and creativity. I load about ten business cards in my black sequined clutch, though I'm not convinced I'll give any out. We are not beggars, and we will be selective about our clientele.

An hour later, after a quick shower, which was quite a trick not getting the bandage wet, I stand before the full-length mirror in the cavernous master bedroom suite examining my fashion choice. The outfit Samantha prescribed works surprisingly well. The sequined top catches the ambient light, shimmering subtly. The black leather jeans fit like a second skin, surprisingly comfortable, and effectively camouflage the bandage wrapped around my knee. The silver stiletto sandals add height and a touch of glamour, elongating my legs. My hair is pulled back into the intricate braided ponytail Samantha recommended, not too severe but stylish. The makeup is exactly as she suggested, too— smoky eyes, neutral lips.

I look... different. Less like Isla Ryder, Powers & Winston's formidable PR strategist, and more like... someone who belongs in Los Angeles. Someone who might actually attend a Malibu beach party thrown by a movie star without looking completely out of place.

The transformation is slightly unnerving. It feels like putting on a costume, another layer of a carefully constructed image.

My stomach tightens with the familiar knot of anxiety.

I know this feeling. I've been here before.

I stare at my reflection as the tendrils of doubt snake their way back in. The confidence instilled by Samantha's pep talk starts to fray around the edges. This isn't just about choosing the right outfit. It's about stepping onto a new stage, playing a high-stakes game where I don't know all the rules or all the players.

Was leaving New York the right move? Powers & Winston was familiar territory, a place where I'd earned my stellar reputation, where I understood the landscape, where Kimberley's formidable presence was both a shadow and a shield.

Here, I'm exposed. Ryder & Harper Communications LA—our dream, yes, but now resting entirely on my shoulders, on my ability to navigate this treacherous first assignment. The weight of expectation—Trent Lysander's, Kimberley's, Samantha's, my own— feels crushing.

I am alone. Again. The thought cuts across me in a peculiar, ominous way.

What if I fail? What if Roman Lysander proves unmanageable? What if his charm isn't just a tactic, but something genuinely insidious? Taking on a client with his profile—is it strategic brilliance or reckless hubris?

Control.

Maintain control.

The mantra feels less like a statement of fact and more like a desperate prayer.

And then there's *Vendetta*. My secret, my tribute, my soul poured onto the page. The thought of Roman Lysander inhabiting Steven Stryker, a character born from my deepest grief and fiercest ideals, still feels all sorts of wrong. But my power to influence that casting, the clause Kimberley secured, is tied directly to my success here, with him. I need to fix Roman's image to gain the leverage needed to protect my own creation from... well, from him. The irony is bitter, almost suffocating.

I take a deep, deliberate breath, forcing the panic back down. The air fills my lungs, cool and sharp. I hold it there, letting the pressure build before releasing it slowly.

This isn't about fear. It's about ambition. It's about building something of my own, stepping out of Kimberley's shadow, proving I'm more than just Joshua Ryder's orphaned daughter, and more than just a victim of tragedy who inherited a fortune. I want Ryder & Harper Communications LA to succeed. I want *Vendetta* to be realized—authentically and powerfully. Additionally, I want control over my own narrative and my own destiny.

The fear is still there, a low hum beneath the surface, but as I continue to stare at my reflection, determination begins to overlay it. The smoky eyes looking back at me hold a new resolve. Tonight isn't just reconnaissance; it's the first move on the chessboard. It's claiming my space in this town on my terms.

The queen chess piece with all the moves. Often underestimated, while players focus on protecting the king. It makes me smile. My dad always said, "The queen has all the power, Isla. Never forget that."

Isla Ryder, Image Maker.

That's the role I need to play tonight.

Cool, observant, strategic, and unfazed.

I grab the small, black sequined clutch Samantha insisted I buy for 'LA emergencies', slip my cell phone, passport ID, and credit card inside, along with the square business cards. The long silver chain strap goes over my shoulder, crossbody style, leaving my hands free. Practicality disguised as fashion.

A final check in the mirror. The woman looking back is ready. Or as ready as she'll ever be.

It's just before 8:00 p.m. and I missed the sunset. I'm pushing past fashionably late. Time to face the music—literally, if Roman's promise of a loud playlist holds true. Time to step into the glittering, treacherous world of Roman Lysander.

As I walk out the massive front door, clicking it shut behind me, the night air is cool. It's filled with the rhythmic roar of the ocean. Down the coastline, lights blaze from Roman's house, spilling onto the street, accompanied by the faint, thumping bass line of music carrying on the breeze. It looks less like a house and more like a cruise ship that's run aground, ablaze with light and sound.

Glittering promise, or a glittering trap?

A little thrill courses through me that is equal parts apprehension and anticipation. I can feel it in my chest, my throat, even the tips of my fingers. My heart beats faster. My skin shivers with notable excitement. This could be fun.

The game is officially underway. And tonight, I need to learn the rules fast. Because losing isn't an option. Not for Ryder & Harper Communications LA. Not for *Vendetta*. And certainly not for me.

There is less of myself with every loss. I won't lose this time.

CHAPTER 11

come as you are

Roman Lysander

"Come As You Are" – Nirvana
"Blood In The Cut" - K. Flay
"It's All I Can Do" - The Cars
"Perfect Day" – Hoku
"Fade Into You" – Mazzy Star
"Meant To Be" – Bebe Rexha

Thursday Evening

THE BASS OF NIRVANA'S "Smells Like Teen Spirit" thumps through the floorboards, vibrating up my legs and into my chest, but it's just noise tonight. All of it. Usually, these lyrics hit something deep, something undefined.

Tonight, they're just part of the droning symphony of Hollywood bullshit I'm supposed to be conducting. Eighty, maybe ninety people cram my living room, spilling onto the upper and lower decks. The usual Malibu crowd: agents with slicked-back hair and slicker smiles, actresses with faces frozen in that almost-famous pout, producers running on fumes, and a scattering of generically beautiful people who just... exist. They laugh too loud, drink too much, talk deals, projects, who's hot, and who's not.

Fake cheer on surround sound. And I don't want any part of it. Not tonight.

I lean against the wall near the sliding glass doors to the upper deck, nursing a lukewarm club soda with lime—Brandon's orders. Pathetic. My best Roman Lysander smile is plastered on the practiced and perfected golden boy grin that makes gossip blogs drool and casting directors nod. Tonight, it feels like a lead mask.

"Looking good, man." Gary sidles up, his cologne is an assault. He's a producer, or claims to be, always sniffing for a break or a free drink. "Big night, Roman. Place is jumping. Happy Birthday, by the way." He gestures with his amber liquid. Definitely not club soda for Gary.

"Thanks. Yeah, *jumping*." The word tastes bitter. Jumping with superficiality. Jumping with empty calories and emptier conversations. I nod, smile–puppet motions. Gary rambles on about some streaming deal, dropping names like paid endorsements.

I tune him out. I'm relieved when he finally drifts away.

My gaze sweeps through the crowd. *Searching. Restless.*

She's not here. It's a quarter-past eight.

Brandon materializes. Suit still impeccable, expression tight. "Looking good, Roman," he echoes Gary, but his tone is pure warning. "Just... keep it clean tonight, okay? The studio is watching. Lysander Entertainment is watching. *Everyone* is watching."

He means *my father* is watching through his cohorts, anyway. I've already seen a couple of Lysander Entertainment VPs boosting my bar tab. The unspoken pressure—*Vendetta*, the lead role, everything hinges on it—hangs between us, an albatross we both carry. I've never seen Brandon this stressed about a movie, about *my* landing a part. It's like he needs it as much as I do. His anxiety infects mine, feeding a resentment that grows between us like a tumor. It's going to blow up someday. I feel it coming.

He starts to move off, then turns back. "Happy Birthday, by the way." A smile flashes. "I'll do a toast in about ten minutes."

"Well, thanks, *by the way*," I say, charm dripping like honey, masking a fuse lit deep inside. The rage towards him feels almost physical. "No worries. Practically a saint tonight. Club soda, mostly. I'll toast with champagne. No Patron, even though it *is* my birthday. Playing Saint Roman, patron saint of image rehabilitation. *For you. And you, alone."* I take a pointed sip of my pathetic drink.

Brandon's eyes narrow, unconvinced. "Saint Roman is usually three sheets to the wind by now. Just… behave yourself. I'll do the toast. We'll sing 'Happy Birthday' Elvis style and do the cake presentation. I already looped in Melody Parker for that. Then, I'm taking off. Early meeting. Another client."

"You have *those?"* Sarcasm floods my voice. I am, literally, his meal ticket, financing his entire fancy lifestyle with my twenty percent cut off millions. He usually does a good job, mostly good by me. But lately? His attitude for treating me like some fucking show dog he needs to train—fetch, sit, and beg—is beyond irritating.

"A few others require attention, bro. Not my *undivided* attention, like *you,* of course." He sighs, dramatically big. "Anyway, you've got this. Think of *Vendetta,* Roman. Remember, it's all about *Vendetta."* Annoyingly, he's not wrong.

"Well, thanks, *bro,* for setting me straight."

"Roman… I didn't mean anything by it." Fear appears in his eyes— the fear of his cash cow bolting. "You've got this."

Yeah, you did.

"I've got it under control, okay? Relax. My dad isn't out to screw me over." The implication hangs: *but will you?* We'll see. The ties that bind us feel like they're fraying. Cliche, maybe, but true.

Vendetta. Yeah, I remember. The role, the movie, the potential lifeline. The thing that is supposed to pull me from this self-destructive spiral. The magic talisman everyone keeps dangling in front of my face. Tonight, even *Vendetta* feels distant. Abstract. It's just another role in the Hollywood charade that is out of reach.

I reward him with a curt nod. Brandon finally backs off, melting into the crowd. But he keeps glancing my way like he's on a fucking timer, or a nervous bodyguard. *Control freak.* But he has a point. Behave. Play the game. For *Vendetta.* For my career. For… something. I'm not even sure what anymore.

A wave of boredom washes over me, suffocating. I scan the room again. Faces blur—with Botox borrowed smiles. Same people, same talk, same goddamn party on a different Thursday night. Even if it is my birthday.

And she didn't show.

The disappointment is a physical ache. I refuse to examine why this is.

Ten minutes crawl by. Brandon gives his toast, sings my praises, throws in digs about me turning 28 years old—he's four months younger. He thinks he's hilarious. The crowd laps it up. Candles flare. I blow them out dutifully. Cake gets cut. Melody Parker, the current 'It-Girl', my dad and even Brandon sometimes keep pushing my way for image repair, latches onto someone else near the bar. *Fine by me.*

I hate this pressure. I hate being discussed like I'm not even in the room. Right now, I hate everyone. I'm 28 years old, my dad didn't show, and my best friend, after giving me a quick thumbs-up post-toast, bolts. His duty is done. Another item for the secret list of unforgivable shit I keep a running tally on in my head. His hired car is probably idling at the curb.

I'm about to ditch this whole charade, retreat to my bedroom to stare at the ceiling, and further contemplate my life, when I see her.

Isla Ryder is here.

Late. Past fashionably so.

It's half past eight.

I said seven-thirty. And I've been counting.

The boredom haunting me all night vanishes, instantly replaced by… something else. Intrigue. Curiosity. A spark ignites these almost dead embers I carry at a soul level and becomes a roaring fire.

Funny. I didn't mention running into her this afternoon to Brandon. I didn't see the need to stir up trouble unnecessarily. He definitely wouldn't have left if he knew she might show. I'll deal with the fallout tomorrow. Because there *will* be fallout. Brandon needs to control everything and everyone. And right now, he's not controlling me, which is exactly why we're both silently seething. He left. His choice. On my birthday.

But Isla Ryder is here.

My night just got a whole lot better. Exponentially better. I don't stop to examine too closely why that is.

I detour to the DJ setup near the deck doors. Joey Landini, my go-to guy, is working the crowd. "Hey, man. Happy Birthday, Roman." He shouts over the music. "Love the set. They're already dancing."

We do the guy handshake. I lean in. "Hey, playlist changes. Can you work in Nirvana's "Come As You Are" in about fifteen minutes? And, then this one, "Blood In The Cut" with K. Flay and then The Cars "It's All I Can Do" and then, "Fade Into You" with Mazzy Star, and then "Perfect Day" with Hoku? Oh, and this one, Bebe Rexha's Meant To Be."

He nods, grinning. Now, he's writing them all down because it's turned into an actual playlist deviation of sorts and a huge request. "Nice. Sure. Got it. Somebody special?"

"Something like that." I grin back. "Thanks." I pay him well, and he's reliable. And he doesn't ask too many questions. I appreciate that about Joey.

Next, the caterers at the kitchen island buffet. Nobody really eats this amazing food, but Julie Matson and her team are great. They always pack up the untouched leftovers into meal-sized boxes for my fridge. *Bonus.* Julie smiles, handing me the two plates of cake she saved for me —a huge corner piece for me, a decent slice for my guest, matching decorative plates, silver forks, and linen napkins. Details matter. "Happy Birthday, Roman."

"Thanks, Julie."

My gaze finds Isla across the room, near the fireplace. She stands out like an exotic black orchid in a field of daisies. Her long dark hair is pulled up in a chic, twisted ponytail. Her sleek, pearly white top stops at her midriff, paired with black pants—understated, screaming sophistication amidst the barely there cocktail dresses. She languishes against the wall, radiating utter coolness, and an aura of intelligent detachment.

Even I feel a hint of intimidation. I check my reflection—white linen shirt, tan trousers, favorite leather loafers. My clothing choices suddenly feel… all wrong.

You're trying too hard, dude.

Get it together.

Just bring her some cake.

Isla Ryder. The woman I practically *ran* down this afternoon on the beach. Isla Ryder. The name Brandon keeps me apprised on. The PR woman from New York. Kimberley Powers' best. Sent here to 'fix' me. The image maker.

It doesn't quite square with the woman whose cut knee I bandaged up just hours ago, while she wiped away tears and swore like a sailor, the one I gave Advil and water and a sandwich to. The one who *talked* about *Pride and Prejudice* with such unexpected passion and reverence. She seems... different from the professional shark Brandon painted her to be.

Now, she stands there, observing this Hollywood circus like she's from another planet and seemingly sees right through the bullshit.

She's not my type. Not blonde, bubbly, eager to please, like Melody Parker, who's now giggling at some other actor by the bar.

Still, for some unknowable reason, I'm attracted to Isla Ryder.

My gaze snaps back to her. It's not just that she's beautiful—though she is unsettlingly so. Elegant. Ethereal. *Fucking ethereal*, like I stupidly told her this afternoon.

Why does it matter so much to me that *she* know that *I* see she's above all of this? I don't know.

But it's something deeper. There's something about her. Layers and layers of intrigue that surround her. The set of her jawline, the way she holds herself, the intelligence flashing in those amazing emerald green eyes of hers. She looks... completely untouched by the Hollywood machine.

She's real.

Then an unexpected truth hits me. I *want* to know her. *Really* know her. Not in the casual, meaningless way in which I usually approach women. Not in another fleeting conquest for the self-destruction highlights reel. No, to all of that.

Instead, I want to peel back the layers of cool composure and better understand the mystery that radiates from her like moonlight through fog, which feels so unattainable, and yet she illuminates everything around her.

It's a ridiculous impulse. I'm supposed to be charming Melody Parker, the chosen set piece, and play the reformed 'bad boy' in order to land the lead role for *Vendetta.*

Instead, I'm fixated on the woman my father hired to *fix me*—the ultimate insult. Trent Lysander *can't* even bother to show up, but he has possibly *made* damn sure to send his PR mercenary.

Part of me wants to resent her on principle. She's the enemy, right? Paid to reconstruct me into something palatable for the middle America film audience.

But the woman on the beach—the one who talked about the film *Pride and Prejudice,* and carrying grief, who looked at me like I was a real person and not some project—she felt *human. Real.*

It's throwing me off balance. It's confusing as hell.

Instead of resentment, instead of keeping my distance, I'm carrying two plates of birthday cake across my crowded living room to her. And I'm drawn to her as if she's the only authentic one in this room full of beautiful, empty people.

please please please

Isla Ryder

"Please Please Please" – Sabrina Carpenter
"A Drug From God" – Grimes, Chris Lake

Thursday Night

ROMAN'S HOME–A MANSION, REALLY–is perched higher above the ocean than Julia Winston's. It is all glass and sharp angles, designed for views, entertaining, and posing, probably not so much for actual living.

The music of Nirvana is almost a physical thing. The throb of the bass guitar and Kurt Cobain's melancholic lyrics for *"Smells Like Teen Spirit"* instantly presses against my ribs as I step through the front door entryway, engendering a sentimental nostalgia that infuses the crowd. Many sing along in real time.

There's a theme here. I am intent on figuring it out before the night ends.

Roman Lysander appears to be a man of many layers. He doesn't just chase the latest popular music. His not favoring the mindless rap music is also a plus. The lyrics, the bodies, and the heat engulf me as I slowly make my way through the crowd. It is a suffocating wave of Hollywood excess, but also an apparent penchant for the past I wasn't expecting.

The party is a swirling vortex of precisely curated chaos. The music is so loud that conversations must be yelled to be heard. Every surface gleams with reflected light, bouncing off champagne flutes, and strategically placed spotlights, and too-white teeth.

I feel out of place. My pearly top and black leather jeans ensemble, while sleek and chic, feels understated, almost… somber amidst the flashy sequins and endless show of bare skin.

My hair is pulled back into a loose ponytail with a silver clasp, a deliberate choice as I strive for some semblance of control. But now, it feels too severe in this sea of artfully tousled waves.

The coolness factor is undeniable. It's a *'see and be seen'* crowd composed of Hollywood's finest.

And it seems they're *all* here.

Even my club soda with lime, clutched in my hand like a child's favorite Kool-Aid, feels like a declaration of war against the free-flowing champagne and plentiful tequila shots being handed out like party favors by black tuxedoed waiters that carry the libations on silver trays throughout the crowd. I drink it down quickly. Then, put the empty glass on a tray near the bar as I pass.

A server in a black tuxedo, complete with a black silk bow tie and sash, stops in front of me. "Ms. Isla Ryder?" I nod in stunned surprise. "I'm Danny. Danny Vazzano. Mr. Lysander wanted to ensure you have whatever you want upon arrival and throughout the evening." His face turns red, realizing what he's just said.

"He did. Did he?" I laugh, despite my plan for affecting a nonchalant coolness factor in my demeanor tonight. "Hello, Danny Vazzano." I shake his hand while he balances his tray with the other. He grins.

Danny Vazzano has a little doppelgänger look going on with said host. Blond hair, blue eyes, ready smile, just not as tall or as imposing. He would be the sidekick in a film. Not the standout. Not the lead.

Danny offers me three choices in libations, unless I want something from the bar. "There is Veuve Clicquot champagne, the French 75 cocktail made with gin, champagne, lemon juice, and simple syrup. And, of course, Mr. Lysander's favorite tequila, Patron El Cielo Silver."

Of course, Patron El Cielo Silver is the host's favorite tequila. I try not to roll my eyes at Danny when he proudly tells me this. However, the French 75 cocktail and Veuve Clicquot champagne and even the Patron El Cielo Silver tequila are impressive choices for an event like this one. Whatever this event is. On a Thursday.

Nicely done, Roman Lysander. Very classy.

My favorite cocktail to order in a bar is the French 75. Just one of those packs a serious punch. I can socialize for a good hour or two with just one.

I take one of the French 75 cocktails and a flute of the Veuve Clicquot champagne from Danny's tray. He smiles at me. "Very good, Ms. Ryder. Please let me know if there is anything else you need. I'll check in with you periodically."

"Thank you, Danny. You're very kind, and I appreciate it more than you know." I smile at him somewhat gratefully as his enthusiasm puts me at ease.

"Welcome to Malibu. Mr. Lysander mentioned you were new here."

"Something like that." Instantly realizing my quest for anonymity at this party has already evaporated.

———

Danny disappears through the crowd while I try not to read too much into the fact that Roman Lysander has assigned a server to my every request for the night. And yet, I must admit it's thoughtful.

Unnecessary.

Unexpected.

Unexplainable.

A lot of *un*'s.

There are, indeed, surprising layers to the one and only Roman Lysander.

Layers. Lots of layers.

Granted, Samantha would be over the moon with such attention to detail spent on a rarefied guest. It makes an impression on me, too, but I try not to dwell on that aspect.

Because. Well. I'm already struggling with all these emotional walls I've put up for defense for situations like this one. I can already sense it may not be enough. They might not be strong enough. They might not be high enough.

I miss my wingman. Need her here.

I set the flute of champagne up on the mantel. Then I take a position nearby and casually sip the French 75 while I covertly look around.

———

Roman is nowhere to be found. However, the attentiveness of Danny the server proves to be somewhat restorative. The warmth of the gin and champagne combination course through me soon enough. The feeling of being on edge begins to dissipate.

As if on a time schedule, another tuxedoed server with a silver tray, who seems especially tasked with gathering the empty glassware, comes by and retrieves my empty cocktail glass just as I finish it. He smiles at me, too.

Is the entire team of tuxedoed servers tasked with taking care of me?

Or am I being paranoid?

More than usual?

This is quite the party. It seems to run more like a choreographed and finely tuned operation. There must be more than a hundred people here, now. Quite a few arrived when I did, which explains why so many cars were already starting to park down as far as my driveway. Twelve houses away. *But who's counting?*

As Samantha predicted, the party is a research goldmine. Everyone, who is anyone in this town or trying to be, is here. And it will most definitely serve as a way to observe Roman Lysander up close and personal once again, so I can better analyze his carefully constructed persona in his natural environment.

Fifteen minutes later, I recognize Roman's talent manager, Brandon Chase, as he takes a position in the center of the crowd. Some tech guy places a microphone in his outstretched hand. Brandon taps it, asking for everyone's attention. The music dies down to a normal pitch and Brandon asks the crowd if they can hear him. A raucous "Yes!" is heard all around. And we're off and running on to this next surprising, choreographed part of the show.

Brandon Chase has this slicked back dark hair; it's styled just so. He is handsome with a wide smile and sexy likening to a younger Bradley Cooper without too much of a stretch. Longish hair, darker, but has that handsome, engaging look. He exudes both sophistication and power. I imagine the twenty percent cut he gets from Roman's gross earnings helps a lot for his obviously very expensive lifestyle.

I am catty tonight.

No. It's a fact. I know this from my research earlier.

It's one fact I actually looked up while trying to learn who the players are in Roman Lysander's universe.

Brandon is tall, around 6'2" with an athletic frame, though slighter than Roman's by a good ten pounds of muscle, which gives away his propensity for work over play. He's a serious guy. I definitely felt his intensity from our brief conference call with Kimberley, Trent Lysander, and him just yesterday.

I'm undecided if he is a friend or foe to Roman.

Or to me.

Time will reveal that in short order once I've presented my plans for Roman's rebranding strategy.

Now, I watch as Brandon raises his glass and calls out to Roman, who appears out of nowhere from the far side of the room, pulling the somewhat famous young actress, Melody Parker, along with him.

Brandon begins his speech by reading from an index card.

Prepared.

But is it spoken from the heart? *Unsure.*

"Roman, I've known you since our days at UCLA. You've always had my back, and I will always have yours. To my best friend, my best client, who requires *so much of my time*," he pauses, giving the crowd time to react to his little dig, "but I don't *mind. Really. Most* of the time."

Like happy party goers, there is laughter and applause at the guy's timing and his attempt at a joke at Roman's expense.

Foe? Unsure.

There are more shrill whistles and claps all around. "Anyway," Brandon says, "we're gathered here on this very special occasion to celebrate the one and only Roman Alexander Lysander. Happy Birthday, Roman! Here's to you on your *28th birthday*. Of course, no one will believe you now when you say, 'I'm only 28', two years from thirty, but who's counting now?" Brandon says with a hearty laugh. "Happy Birthday, Roman! Cheers, my friend!"

Birthday? Oh…

This sinking feeling settles in on me for a nice long stay.

I am so off my game today.

Meanwhile, the crowd goes wild, and everyone raises their glasses in salutation to the birthday boy, Roman Alexander Lysander. I guess even the false types of Hollywood like birthdays and parties.

Roman takes the microphone from Brandon, thanking him, and raises up a fresh glass of champagne a server has just handed him, while everyone says, "Cheers, Roman."

He laughs and then drinks it right down and says in good natured fashion, "To being 28! Like Brandon said, two years from thirty. But who's counting, besides everyone in this room? Here's to honesty and good times and good friends. How many do I see in this room? Not sure I can count that… high or any at all." The crowd laughs with him. "And thanks to my best friend and manager, Brandon, for always having my back since our raucous days at UCLA. You are the best. I love you, brother. Thanks everyone for coming to my little birthday celebration. Cheers!"

Melody then takes Roman's hand and leads him over to his humongous birthday cake, where there must be at least twenty-eight candles all lit up for him. He blows them out in short order while the crowd sings 'Happy Birthday' in perfect time to the disc jockey's planned rendition of *"Happy Birthday"* sung by the late Elvis Presley.

It's sweet.

He's good about it.

All of it.

I watch closely as the head caterer, Julie, cuts a giant corner piece of birthday cake just for him. He smiles widely and thanks her. He says something to her, and she nods and puts his designated piece of cake and another plate of cake aside on the opposite counter, away from the guests.

I met Julie Matson earlier, when I first arrived. I make it a point to connect with catering staff—partly professional courtesy, partly genuine interest. In Manhattan, you're only as good as your network, and the best caterers are worth their weight in gold for client events. We'd exchanged business cards and, surprisingly, recipes.

Samantha will be thrilled. She'll be pleased I've already made a new contact here in LA. We're always looking to expand our culinary repertoire for entertaining potential clients, especially since we're new to LA, and Julie had been refreshingly generous with her knowledge.

What touched me most was when she offered Kelly Lysander's recipe for Italian buttercream frosting and the white cake that accompanied it. She'd confided that it was Roman's special request every year—the same cake his mother used to make—and that she felt the weight of getting it exactly right for him.

"I bake as a stress reliever," I'd told her, surprised by my own honesty. "I'm always looking for something new to try. Can't sleep, so I bake in the middle of the night. Often."

Julie had laughed; a sound filled with understanding rather than judgment. "Come and bake with me anytime then. I can't sleep either."

Fast friends with Julie Matson.

There's something comforting about that instant connection—two insomniacs finding solace in flour and sugar, creating something beautiful from simple ingredients in the quiet hours while the rest of the world still sleeps.

"He's a good guy," she said softly, and I followed her gaze to where Roman had commanded an audience outside on the deck, bathed in moonlight and magnetic charisma.

I managed a slight smile. "Indeed." A noncommittal, but safe, response. Yet it struck me as intriguing how the people working behind the scenes—the ones actually close to him—seemed fiercely loyal. Julie spoke of him with genuine affection, not the calculated admiration of someone seeking favor.

It was sweet. Fascinating, actually. Another layer of Roman Lysander I needed to better understand if I hoped to navigate the complexities ahead.

Now, Roman walks past the buffet, completely ignoring Melody Parker, who is casting about, wondering what she should do now.

Huh.

There are cheers and good wishes all around for the only prince holding court in the place, Roman Lysander. He makes his way through the crowd, stopping every few minutes to accept best wishes for his 28th birthday from his party guests.

So, it's his birthday.

He didn't mention that to me earlier.

And I didn't do all my homework.

This is Kimberley Powers' 101 PR teachings.

We're supposed to know everything about the client.

Everything.

Dossiers on clients can run two hundred pages. They are done on everyone. It's Kimberley Powers' superpower and mine. But I was busy packing up my life in Manhattan, both the personal and the business side of things.

Out of sorts.

Me.

Most definitely.

Samantha gave me all the files on both father and son, but I just glanced through both documents. Each file ran over three hundred pages each. I spent time on all the other intel gathered, including the gossip bloggers' articles. And yet, I forgot to devote as much time and attention to the dossiers—the most important documents in my arsenal in understanding and working with clients. Our job is to know more about them than they know about themselves. That's the job.

Okay. Technically, Trent Lysander is my client in this scenario. He's the one I'm on retainer to. But it doesn't excuse being sidetracked and not knowing absolutely everything about Roman Lysander as part of my assigned objective in rebranding him at this point. That is my job. That's why I am here. In LA.

Geez, Isla, do your fucking homework!

Get it together, Isla Ryder.

I debate another drink.

Like a signal on a timer, Danny swings by and dutifully hands me another French 75 cocktail.

I am most definitely out of my element at this point. And I should just go home. I check my watch. It's almost nine. I've been here for almost an hour.

I can hear Samantha's voice in my head telling me I have to stay. 'You *can't* go yet, Isla. The party is just getting started.' Her famous words at every party we've ever been to echo through me now.

I am somewhat shaken. My perfect execution in *'reconnaissance,'* as Roman called it earlier this afternoon, is not going well at all.

I didn't know it was his birthday, signaling how unprepared I actually am.

And, somewhere along the way, I've concluded my outfit will not set off a high fashion trend in LA any time soon with this flashy crowd. Melody Parker helped with that conclusion when we passed each other in the far hallway near the guest bathroom at the far end of the house. "You'll learn," she said to me, looking me up and down as if I was some kind of rival. Costly mistake. To be reflected upon later.

Hollywood, tonight, has made me uncertain.

Hollywood, tonight, has made me feel less than.

The thoughts come unbidden, a remnant from another time and another failure. I push the thoughts away from me and swallow hard in an attempt to get it together.

Get it together. Get it together. Get it together.

With resigned solace, I finish the second French 75 in short order.

Soon, Danny appears yet again and retrieves my empty glass from my outstretched hand. "No more gin for me tonight." I shake my head from side to side and try to smile at him.

"Did you want to try the Veuve Clicquot champagne instead?" he asks, helpfully.

"Yes, please. I'm a little off my game tonight, Danny. Thank you." I take the flute of champagne and reward him with a grateful smile.

"It's an intimidating crowd," he says with a sympathetic smile. "But you're doing great. Just let me know if you need anything else. Like I said, Mr. Lysander wants to ensure you have a good time tonight."

"Thank you, Danny. I'm having fun. You're the best." He grins, apparently pleased I've remembered his name.

We're fast friends. The only one I have here, for sure, besides Julie, the caterer.

I'm now convinced that libations are going to turn things right around for me. I think Danny agrees with me. He winks at me before he turns and disappears into the crowd again.

In need of a reset, I take a position near the massive stone fireplace, vying for a strategic vantage point that overlooks the swirling masses so I can recover some of my poise. From here, I can observe people without being immediately drawn in. I can just play the silent observer in the heart of this spectacle at the famous actor's *birthday party.*

The air is thick with the cloying scents of expensive men's cologne and overly sweet perfume; they compete for dominance along with the aromatic richness of brioche and the tangy citrus combination of Veuve Clicquot's finest champagne, which overflows at this point throughout the party atmosphere.

Visually, it's a sensory assault: flashing lights, designer labels screaming for attention, faces frozen in practiced smiles, eyes darting this way and that, always searching for someone more important, someone more valuable to talk to or impress.

And then there's Roman. He hasn't seen me yet, or he's pretending not to. Now, he's holding court by the giant sliding glass doors that lead out to his patio, talking to his DJ about something while the ghostly streaks of the moonlight from the massive living room windows paint him in a silvery light. A god in his element.

Even from this far distance, his charisma is a tangible thing—a magnetic pull that provokes envy and holds attention with just about everyone in this room. The practiced charm is on full display: the amiable smile, the casual hand gestures, the way he leans in to listen, making each person feel like the center of his universe, even if just for a fleeting moment.

I watch him closely, assessing his every move with what is supposed to be a detached, professional eye. The 'bad boy' archetype is being laid on thick, almost too perfect with the slightly too-long hair that makes every woman want to run their hands through it, and the artful way his body moves in his casual designer clothes that gives off his sensuality without even really trying.

There's the hint of a smirk that suggests he's always on the verge of breaking the rules or already has. It all seems so carefully crafted. It's a performance honed over the years that encourages paparazzi flashes and tabloid headlines effortlessly.

It's the ultimate display of the chase of the predator and the prey.

Who's the predator?

Who's the prey?

It's interchangeable.

And that's the point.

My professional assessment kicks in, cold, and clinical, though maybe slightly dulled by the second cocktail. I conclude that damage control is needed. Extensive damage control. The scandals, the rumors, the public perception of reckless self-destruction—it's a PR nightmare.

But beneath the layers of manufactured rebellion, I sense something else, a hint of... boredom. Even detachment. His smile doesn't quite reach his eyes. The effortless charm feels... automatic, as if he's going through the motions, playing a role. A role, perhaps, he's grown tired of inhabiting.

He moves through the room with practiced ease. Women flock to him like moths to a flame. Melody Parker plays the ever-rising starlet. She is positioned near the birthday boy, so eager to play her part. My lips press together. As I recall, Trent Lysander somewhat enthusiastically mentioning her on our conference call as a possibility as Roman's *potential strategic distraction*. They do those things here. Fake relationships in order to closely manage the narrative and have fresh fodder to feed the fans.

It's entertainment.

To them.

It's the worst kind of deception to me. Absolute nonsense. But Kimberley warned me about all of it and told me I would have to adjust and possibly make an accommodation to my overall strategic plan. After that conference call, finding it so appalling, I almost turned down the whole goddamn opportunity, but Samantha talked me down from that proverbial ledge.

"We'll figure it out," she'd said. My best friend's wisdom about everything in life and love is her superpower. "Let's just go to LA. We'll get a feel for things out there and we can go from there. Isla, you *cannot back down*. You play the game that you want to play. That's what makes you so damn good at this PR thing. Don't forget that. And now, you're playing for *our gig*. You've got this."

Need a personal cheerleader?

Samantha Harper will always be mine.

Now, I focus on the play-by-play with dear Melody Parker. She has her arm intertwined with Roman's. Her blonde hair gleams under the track lighting. She giggles at something he's said. Perfect arm candy, manufactured for maximum media impact. Predictable. Superficial. And everything I despise. *Pretty much.*

You're trying too hard, sweetie.

And yet... with Roman Lysander, there's that magnetism, the unmistakable allure. Despite myself, despite my ingrained aversion to his type, I feel a faint tug of curiosity. It's not attraction, not exactly. More like professional fascination. Like studying a complex specimen under a microscope with an almost maniacal need to know just who he is and what he thinks.

The champagne burns pleasantly down my throat, but the sensation triggers something unexpected—a memory of another party. Two years ago. Chad Jameson and his public betrayal. The night everything fell apart. *I've been here before. I've done this before.*

But this is different.

Is it?

The room suddenly feels too warm, the collar of my Free People pearly top is too tight against my throat. I've been the outsider before, the one who misjudged, who failed to read the situation correctly. And I paid for it. We all did.

I'm not that person anymore.

I'm not starting over.

I'm building on what I've learned.

———

I set my glass down with fingers that tremble slightly, press my palm flat against the cool stone of the fireplace. The roughness grounds me and effectively pulls me back to the present.

I need to understand what makes Roman Lysander tick, to understand all the layers of his carefully constructed image, to find his character strengths, and discern his vulnerabilities so I can properly focus on rebuilding his brand.

I would prefer to do it without a potential strategic distraction like Melody Parker.

I'm not winning that one.

Yet.

Obviously.

meant to be

Roman Lysander

"Meant To Be – Bebe Rexha
"Blood In The Cut" - K. Flay
"Come As You Are" – Nirvana
"It's All I Can Do" - The Cars
"Fade Into You" – Mazzy Star
"Perfect Day" – Hoku

Thursday Night

I MOVE TOWARDS HER. I'M DRAWN TO HER as if trapped in an imaginary tractor beam in space, clearly in her orbit, despite the insistent warnings going off in my head. There is less of myself with every step because there is something surrendered in this gravitational pull that I can't—*don't want to*—resist. I weave through the crowd. My best Roman Lysander smile back in place, weaponized and ready, proffering my simple offering of my birthday cake.

As I get closer, I notice details about her I missed from across the room. The way her pearly top and black pants skim her body, hinting at curves beneath the severe lines of her long legs. The delicate silver chain around her neck, a tiny, almost fragile elegance. The sparkle of diamonds at her earlobes and her expensive silver sandals on the most delicate feet I've seen in a long while.

I already know she's even more striking up close. Those emerald green eyes, framed by dark lashes, are even more mesmerizing. They're assessing me now, too, coolly, clinically, as I approach. No sign of recognition, no hint of the beach encounter from earlier. Just professional detachment. She's in image maker mode, and she's fully engaged.

"Blood In The Cut" plays. I try not to smile too much. Hopefully, Joey's been able to weave in the rest of my playlist changes.

As I get closer, I realize she's wearing *black leather jeans*. She truly *is* a goddess.

Fucking ethereal. Indeed.

Get it together, bro.

It's just a girl.

Yeah, but she's fucking ethereal.

"Excuse me," I say, my voice thankfully smooth and practiced. The Roman Lysander charm turns up a notch.

The guy she's talking to—Agent Slick Smile—finally notices me. His eyes widen just a fraction in the instance of Hollywood recognition and proper acquiescence. He nods, a quick, deferential nod, and melts away, leaving Isla and me alone in the swirling vortex of the party.

Good riddance.

"The girl from the beach I so unceremoniously ran down," I say softly. "Thank you for coming, Isla Ryder. Welcome to my home. I didn't think you were coming."

Her gaze comes to rest on me, cool and appraising. "Nice song choice. Playing one of my favorites, I see." She gets a half-smile. "But *you* didn't *tell me* it was *your birthday*."

A major oversight on my part. Apparently.

I shake my head from side to side and get a wide smile. "*You* aren't on Instagram. I think 58 million fans know it's my birthday, but not *you*, Isla Ryder. I don't know whether to be hurt or relieved," I say with a laugh. "Anyway. Thank you for the birthday wishes. What are you drinking?"

"Champagne." She dutifully points to the flute that rests on my mantle. "I had two of those French 75 cocktails when I first got here. My absolute favorite. To stymie my nerves."

"Your absolute favorite is a French 75." She nods. "You're nervous?" I ask in surprise.

"It's an intimidating guest list. Let's face it; I've been off my game all goddamn day. Still am. Didn't know it was your birthday, for example."

I grin at her swearing and relish the pink flush rising on her upturned face. "Didn't get that far, huh?" I tease, shaking my head slowly from side to side. She looks up at me and smiles. This secret smile that gives nothing away.

"How's the cut? Did you take some more Advil?" I am still ready to perform my medical duties if need be.

"I took a shower, while carefully avoiding getting the bandage wet. A feat in itself." She inclines her head. "I took some more Advil, even attempted to take a nap, which I *never* do. All done on the advice of my Good Samaritan, Roman Lysander, from earlier this day."

"Right as rain then." I hand her a plate of birthday cake. She looks uncertain, bemused, and a little surprised. I watch this cascade of emotions cross her striking features one by one.

"Right as rain," she echoes. "Cake for me? Thank you. You like the corner piece, I see," she says with deference.

"I'm a sucker for white cake and frosting, especially Italian buttercream. And covet the corner pieces. Have since I was five. The more frosting, the better, yeah?" I take a large bite of my birthday cake. It's so good, and I haven't really eaten all day—too busy playing paramedic to Isla Ryder's cut knee, feeling out of sorts after meeting her, and my mind's been caught up in the significance of the *Pride and Prejudice* scene we discussed, replaying it over and over. Then working out logistics with the catering staff took up the rest of my afternoon, since Brandon didn't get here until half-past six and was no help at all.

I grab a glass of champagne from a passing server's tray. The glass feels cool against my palm, a counterpoint to the heat spreading through my chest as she watches me with those emerald eyes of hers so full of depth and mystery. The bubbles rise and pop like the tension building between us—effervescent, impossible to contain.

Somewhat nervous for some unknowable reason, I've already scarfed down my cake. I set the empty plate aside and quickly notice that she's barely eaten hers.

"Do you want to finish my cake?" she asks, looking at my already empty cake plate.

"Only if you're not going to," I say. "It *is* my birthday."

"Indeed." She laughs and dutifully hands me her plate of mostly uneaten cake. I finish her cake in record time.

"You have a little frosting right there." She points to the left side of my face. I grab one of the linen napkins and wipe at my face. "Still there." She laughs a little. Then she just leans in and wipes the frosting off my face herself with her thumb and index finger, like she's drawing on me with a piece of chalk. Her hand is cool upon my face. It sends a strange sensation through me, as if she is wired with an electrical current.

"Thanks."

"No problem. Just a hidden flaw of mine. One of several." She inclines her head again. "Must make things right, yeah? Spinach on your teeth after you have just finished eating a salad and the guy, you're on the date with, doesn't tell you?" She makes a slicing gesture across her throat. "Bad move."

"Catastrophic for the guy for not telling you." I laugh and then smile at her in absolute awe and unveiled fascination.

"Abso-fucking-lutely. Sorry, Samantha's favorite word. Becoming mine." The honesty I see in her face just draws me in further. "No tolerance for cowards. Gladiators only need apply."

The key to her heart just given away with those words alone.

My God, this girl is pulling me into her orbit, and I'm not sure I'm going to be able to escape or if I even want to.

We stand in front of each other in this companionable silence, studying each other.

But then, she tilts her head to one side, which I now recognize as her thinking mode, and she smiles like she holds a secret or has discovered one. "The theme of your playlist. I got it. Top songs for every year you were born, yeah? Except "Come As You Are" that came out in 1993." She frowns, trying to figure that one out.

I laugh and shake my head. Amazed at her depth and at her absolute fucking brilliance.

"But I love that song, "Come As You Are" and Kurt Cobain. Nirvana," she says with notable sadness. "So, I will add to my answer, the misunderstood. All the Nirvana stuff was before your time, but so were The Cars, Foreigner, and Fleetwood Mac." She shrugs with nonchalance.

I give her a questioning look.

"Final answer. The misunderstood and top songs from the time you were born 1995 until now." I nod slowly. She smiles at me. "My dad played music whenever he was writing, so my entire childhood is filled with memories of the music he always played. Anyway, I was wracking my brain for the theme. The homage you mentioned this afternoon. Glad we got that solved." She takes a swig of her champagne while I chase down the right words to acknowledge and embrace all she's just said to me.

I'm beyond impressed that she's figured it all out.

And me. A little bit.

Which, if I'm being honest, is a little terrifying.

"You got it, Isla Ryder. Nobody else here will." I laugh. "Yes, it's an homage. Some of the top songs from every year of my life starting with 1995, the year I was born, but also songs my mom would play for me, of, yes, *the misunderstood*. Especially Kurt Cobain." I hesitate at first, but then I say it anyway, "Although "Blood In The Cut" and "Come As You Are" and the next four songs are for you. "Blood In The Cut" because you were humming that song earlier this afternoon. Thought we should pay it homage, too."

"Songs for me? I don't know what to say to that." She listens to The Cars sing "It's All I Can Do" and intently stares at me as if by studying my face, I will provide her with the answers she seeks.

I'm not going to tell her. I'm not sure I know myself why I chose these songs for her.

I offer my take on music, though. Something I never do. "I think music is a glimpse into someone's soul."

She simply nods *once*. "Exactly that." She holds her breath and then her green eyes suddenly shimmer with unshed tears. Her lips part, and she attempts to smile, maybe as part of a distraction or a defense mechanism.

Enchanted all at once by all of her, I watch as a single tear escapes her lower lash and rolls down her beautiful face. I reach out and catch it with my hand before she can wipe it away.

She is mesmerizing in the most unusual ways.

She is the type of girl I am unused to having to impress.

She is real.

Real in a way that makes everything else in this room feel like a cheap imitation of life and art equally.

She laughs when she hears Hoku singing "Perfect Day." "You're funny, Roman. Really, the *perfect day*? I interrupt your run, occupy your entire afternoon, bleed all over your stairs, deck, and house, and almost pass out at your kitchen sink and again almost at your kitchen island. *Perfect day?*"

"It was to me… a… *perfect day.* And it's nice that you can finally admit to almost passing out. *Twice.* Three times if we count the beach."

"Ha-ha. Not admitting to any such thing." She grins. "I *do* love this song. Loved *Legally Blonde,* too. Reese Witherspoon is next level."

"She is. She's a friend of mine."

"Really? That's nice. You're very funny. I like that. I have trouble remembering the punch line to a joke, but I appreciate good humor and that little hint of sarcasm you seem to drop in. You surprise me, Roman Lysander. I'm not usually one for surprises, but these have been good surprises. Thank you for the songs. I love them."

"You're welcome." I hesitate, and then say, "I'm so glad you came." I lean in. "Thanks for coming to my birthday party, Isla Ryder."

"Thanks for inviting me."

And now, I am entirely too focused on coming up with witty things to say and coming up empty more times than I care to count.

"Meant To Be" with Bebe Rexha and Florida Georgia Line starts playing. An intense desire to dance with her comes over me and the song's title feels almost prophetic. She tilts her head again, listening to the lyrics, and I find myself hoping the words resonate with her as much as they suddenly do with me.

"Let's dance, Isla Ryder." I hold out my hand to her, an undeniable impulse, and then, drawn in by an invisible thread, I gently pull her along to the darkened deck outside where people are dancing. She seems to truly revel in the open air, and she moves around the deck with me with a surprising grace, and a lightness that feels almost ethereal. There's that word to describe her once again.

Holding her hand in mine feels less like a simple touch and more like a quiet revelation, a whisper of something destined, as we move in sync across the quasi-dance floor. The moonlight plays with her dark hair, casting a bewitching glow, and my fascination in learning all about her takes on an even more determined, almost dreamlike, quest.

I know the cut on her knee is acting up, so we stop dancing after all her songs have gone through the rotation Joey set up for me. We spend a little time on the deck talking in the moonlight, looking out over the dark Pacific. It's this kind of shared experience of peace I've never known before.

———

Eventually, we return inside and retrieve our drinks from near the fireplace. The crowd shifts in rhythm and intensity, and I note several players at this party are far too interested in our conversation. I incline my head toward them, hoping she gets the drift our conversation needs to take.

"Roman Lysander," I say to her. I extend my hand, the practiced gesture of a thousand red carpets, a million photo ops. "We… bumped into each other earlier. On the beach?" I add the beach detail, just to throw off the gathering onlookers who might wonder why I brought cake over to a stranger no one yet knows. "Thanks for coming to my party," I add.

Around us, the Hollywood hum continues, a low buzz of conversations and laughter. Isla seems to notice a couple of women, dressed in impossibly chic outfits, subtly watching us from across the room, their eyes sharp and assessing. I follow her gaze.

"That's Morgan Grant. The platinum blonde one and her sidekick, Brenna. Be careful of those two in particular. For Morgan Grant, I am her 'go-to' headline for entertainment and a salacious scandal. She should *pay me* for the amount of clicks she gets based off of me. Only some of them are true," I say in a low voice. "And to think we went to high school together, but that doesn't seem to matter to her. I am her number one target for gossipy headlines."

"There's a story behind it, I'm sure," Isla says. And then she subtly points her slender finger to a man with salt and pepper hair. "And that guy?"

"He's a producer, competition to my dad," I say. "He wanted to go in on the *Vendetta* film action pretty badly, and my dad turned him down." I incline my head in the guy's general direction, confirming her questioning glance that he's listening intently to our conversation. "The reconnaissance has begun, whether you want it to or not," I whisper to her.

"And where is your dad?" Isla scans the crowd.

"He didn't make it," I say, the words hollow in my chest. "He's a busy guy, probably had a dinner meeting run late, and figures this will all die down by the time he could get here." The familiar ache of his absence settles in on me like an old friend. Expected, but no less painful.

"I see." One of the servers drops off a glass of club soda for her, although I see her eyeing the flute of champagne she's left on the mantel. "Thanks for letting me know about the curiosity surrounding us," she says with a cool smile. "I appreciate it more than you know."

I sense an even bigger shift in the atmosphere as the interest in our conversation garners more attention. The familiar game begins, the one where I'm both player and prize. New and more dangerous players take notice, including Morgan Grant, who moves even closer to us now. I lower my voice slightly, my gaze still fixed on Isla, but with a new undercurrent of caution.

"So, Isla Ryder," I say, my tone now deliberately casual, as if we are truly just meeting for the very first time, "East Coast girl in the wilds of Malibu. What brings you to our sunny shores?" It's a repeat of our earlier conversation on Julia Winston's deck, but I gesture vaguely around, encompassing the party, the beach, the whole LA scene, hoping she understands the signal—everyone is watching.

Isla catches on immediately.

She mirrors my casual demeanor, her professional mask falling into place, but now with a subtle layer of practiced charm overlaid. "Business, mostly. Though the sunshine is definitely a perk." She offers me a small, polite smile. "Ryder & Harper Communications LA. We're just opening up a West Coast office."

"Ryder & Harper Communications LA," I say, as if considering the name for the first time. "New firm in town? Ambitious. What kind of PR?"

"Image management, brand building, crisis control. The usual." She keeps her tone light, noncommittal, a practiced deflection. "Though we specialize in... well, let's just say, *challenging clients.*" She lets the word hang in the air and gets a subtle smile.

It's a playful jab. We both know it.

I laugh. "Challenging, huh? Hollywood is full of those. You'll fit right in." Her green eyes twinkle with amusement, but there is something else there too, a spark of genuine appreciation that I tipped her off. "And you're from...?" I prompt, drawing out the question, playing the role of the genuinely interested party host.

"New York City. Well, Darien, Connecticut, actually. Born, raised and grew up there." She grimaces ever so slightly. It's so subtle. It's a good thing I'm looking so intently at her, or I would have missed it. Too personal? A secret she isn't supposed to disclose. Or just regret, as if she's disclosed something personal, she doesn't want people to know about her. *Noted.*

"I suspect Malibu is going to be a very different environment. A different jungle of sorts." She glances around the room, a slight and almost imperceptible smirk crossing her lips.

"Hollywood *is* a different jungle, entirely. Don't underestimate the players. Or the animals that roam here," I say with double meaning.

Her green eyes flash with just a fraction, a hint of something... amusement? Maybe. "I'll keep that in mind. Again, my name is Isla Ryder," she says, her voice cool, low, even more efficient than her single word greeting earlier. She takes my hand, her grip firm, surprisingly strong. A jolt of something unexpected shoots up my arm. Static. Again, I feel a faint electric charge in the superficial air of my Malibu living room. *Not just static. Something more. Something dangerous. Something I need.*

"Isla Ryder," I repeat. Her name rolls off my tongue, as if I'm testing the sound of it. Once more. She is so intelligent, so elegant, and still a bit mysterious. All these things I've already tabulated about her since this afternoon.

We smile at one another. We share the secret, as if she isn't the same woman who was in my kitchen six hours before, getting her knee bandaged up by me, wiping tears with the back of her hand from her most gorgeous face, looking fragile, and in desperate need of my careful ministrations.

"Ryder & Harper Communications LA, right? Brandon mentioned you were coming to town."

Smooth, Roman.

Play it cool.

Play the game.

She wants you to.

"That's right," she says. Her voice is still cool, still efficient, betraying nothing. "Here for... business." She lets the word hang in the air, heavy with unspoken implications. Business. As in the business of fixing me. The business of cleaning up my messes. The business of image rehabilitation.

"Well, like I said before, welcome to Malibu, Isla Ryder. Just business though, or some pleasure?" I ask her, while a slow smile spreads across my face, the real Roman smile, the one that's not manufactured, not weaponized, and is just curious.

I want her to say business. I need her to say business. But God help me, I'm hoping for pleasure. The contradiction tears at me even as I maintain perfect outward composure.

"Like you said, strictly business, Mr. Lysander." Her voice is low, steady, and unwavering. She hesitates for a beat. "Unless… you have something else in mind?" The question hangs between us, charged with unspoken attraction.

Her lips curve, that faint, almost imperceptible curve again, but this time, there's a hint of something else in her green eyes. Challenge. Maybe even… amusement.

She's teasing me.

Playing a game.

Danny, the tuxedoed waiter, the quasi-B-list actor, who has acted with me in a few of my films, that I assigned to take care of Isla should she ever show up, swings by. Danny seems smitten with his assignment, while I keep my gaze clearly fixed on Isla.

"More champagne?" I ask. How can she say no? She can't, and we both know it as the surrounding onlookers teem with growing interest, trying to figure out our connection.

I recall from earlier: the Veuve Clicquot being served is her second favorite, Taittinger her first. I ask Danny to retrieve a chilled bottle of Taittinger Champagne, an ice bucket, and two champagne flutes in short order.

***

When Danny returns, he makes a big deal about opening the bottle of Taittinger as if to impress Isla. I avoid rolling my eyes, but it's close.

She's mine, Danny. Back off.

I hand her a flute of the Taittinger with a bit of a flourish. She smiles. A reward, in and of itself.

"Happy Birthday, Roman Lysander." She clinks her glass to mine.

"Thank you, Isla Ryder. Like I said, thank you for coming."

Maybe Isla Ryder is just what I need.

Something seems to shift between us. I wonder if she is the spark that's going to set this whole goddamn charade on fire.

Either way, game on. Definitely game on.

And for the first time in a long time, I actually feel… *alive.*

As if something real is finally about to happen in this fake, glittering town. And it's all thanks to Isla Ryder's arrival. Who would have thought that image rehabilitation could be so… captivating?

The game has begun.

CHAPTER 14

the malibu experience

Isla Ryder

"Blood In The Cut" - K. Flay
"Come As You Are" - Nirvana
"California Nights" - Best Coast
"It's All I Can Do" - The Cars
"Fade Into You" – Mazzy Star
"Perfect Day" – Hoku

Thursday Night

ALMOST NINE. I'm holding my breath, just watching him. Intrigued. Mesmerized. Enchanted. Admittedly. And then, he turns, his gaze sweeps across the room, and for a split second, our eyes meet. There's recognition on some level between us, and then the faintest spark of something… amusement? Intrigue? It's gone as quickly as it appears, replaced by the practiced Roman Lysander charm as he returns to the buffet table and retrieves the two plates of cake from the head caterer, Julie, who set them aside for him earlier. And then, he seemingly moves in my direction, carrying the two plates of untouched cake.

Indeed.

He approaches me in this indirect way. He weaves through the crowd, but his smile widens as he gets ever closer to me. The song, *"Blood In The Cut"* with K. Flay singing plays.

A special request?

Or something else?

A message of some kind?

Oh yeah. Me humming the lyrics to this song earlier must have stayed with him.

The guy I've been talking to, well, *he's* been talking, and I've been trying to look like I'm interested in what all he's been saying, but if there were a test on the topic of conversation; I would fail. *Utterly fail.*

Truly, I'm trying to keep an eye on my surroundings and on all these party goers and Roman Lysander. He approaches me, like a prince intent on talking to the cinder girl by the fireplace. *Me.*

Like a hidden protocol or implied hierarchy, the guy who's been talking to me moves off, as if on cue, as soon as Roman reaches us.

"The girl from the beach I so unceremoniously ran down." Roman's voice is smooth, a low rumble that cuts through the party noise. "Thank you for coming. Welcome to my home. I didn't think you were coming." The surprise in his tone is expertly feigned, almost believable, if I wasn't trained to see through every layer of manufactured sincerity.

"Nice song choice. Playing one of my favorites, I see." I half-smile. "But *you* didn't *tell me* it was *your birthday.*"

He grins and then laughs. "*You* aren't on Instagram. Fifty-eight million fans know it's my birthday, but not *you*, Isla Ryder. I don't know whether to be hurt or relieved," he teases, and then he smiles in the most disarming way I've ever seen.

I laugh openly because I drank two French 75 cocktails in the last half hour, way beyond my usual rate of one in three hours. "Happy Birthday, Roman Lysander."

"Thank you, Isla Ryder. What are you drinking?" he asks, looking pointedly at my empty hands.

"Well," I say airily, "I'm a gin girl, so I tried the French 75 cocktail when I first arrived and just finished another." He gives me a quizzical look. He seems surprised by that admission. "And now it's on to champagne. Veuve Clicquot is a very nice touch. Very classy. I'm a Taittinger girl by nature, but Veuve Clicquot is my second favorite." I point to the half-full flute that rests on his fireplace mantle.

"I'll keep that in mind," he says, looking amused.

"I'm sorry. You're the host. I'm being rude. I *love* Veuve Clicquot champagne. It's an excellent choice. And the French 75 cocktail is my absolute favorite. I normally just teetotal that one along, but like I said, I drank two right down to stymie my nerves."

"Not rude. Very honest." I incline my head. "You're nervous," he says, and raises an eyebrow as if doubting me.

"Well, it's an intimidating guest list. Let's face it; I've been off my game all goddamn day. Still am. Didn't know it was your birthday, for example."

"Didn't get that far, huh?" he teases.

I smile at him, despite myself, and shake my head slowly from side to side.

Then, he gets this concerned look. "How's the knee? Did you take more Advil?"

"It's kind of throbbing. I should have worn flats instead of stilettos. But who *does* that?"

"Who does that?" he asks with a quiet laugh.

"Anyway, I took a shower, which was quite a trick not getting the bandage wet. I took some more Advil, attempted to take a nap, which I *never* do. All done on the advice of my Good Samaritan, the one and only Roman Lysander."

I grin up at him. He's tall, at least 6′4″ another fact I realize I should have already tabulated.

"Right as rain then," he says.

"Right as rain. I am right as rain."

Then, like a little boy offering a prized toy, he hands me one of the plates of cake he's been carrying. "Here, I brought you some cake. You look like a white cake and Italian buttercream frosting kind of girl, in addition to loving French 75 cocktails and Taittinger champagne."

"Something like that. And, wedding cake, as long as it's white cake and without layers of chocolate or, God forbid, carrot cake." I laugh softly. He does, too.

"No chocolate cake. Never carrot cake. *Noted.* I love white wedding cake. It's the only reason for a wedding in my book."

"Right? So, there's that." I nod in emphatic agreement. "And the corner piece? You like the corner piece of your birthday cake, I see." I point to his plate with my free hand.

"I do," he says, surprised. "Did *you* want the corner piece?" He starts to offer me his plate, though I see a sliver of reluctance cross his features.

"No, no. It's your birthday," I say, shrugging. "I'm good. Maybe I can snag a corner piece of cake 'to go' later."

"I'm a sucker for white cake and frosting, especially Italian buttercream. And covet the corner pieces. Have since I was five. The more frosting, the better, yeah? I'll tell Julie to save us all the corners." He sets down his cake plate on the nearby travertine table and pulls out his phone, sending a text. I watch in fascination because he *solves* this conundrum of cake and corners in fifteen seconds flat.

"Do you actually have your caterer on speed dial?" I ask him, truly impressed.

"The caterer, the house cleaning crew, my driver, and my dry cleaners. It takes a village—essentially, all of Malibu—to run this place, and this scene. These are the finite details and services I do not delegate."

"Wouldn't a live-in assistant help? Oh. I got it. Like Alice from the Brady Bunch," I say without thinking it through. "I'm sorry that didn't come out right. You don't need a *nanny*, per se, just someone like Alice."

Who is this girl talking like this?

We don't flirt.

We don't bring up the Brady Bunch.

Stop it, Isla. Just stop… talking.

The French 75s strip away my carefully constructed walls and have set loose all these thoughts I keep locked away. Professional distance dissolves like sugar in the gin. I'm unraveling, and part of me really doesn't care.

"Yes, I could use someone like *Alice*, but then I wouldn't be living alone and wouldn't be able to walk around naked whenever I want."

Now, I'm picturing Roman walking around naked, probably as he intended me to.

The game is definitely on.

So, I up it a little intentionally, fueled by those fast-acting French 75s.

"That's the feeling I *had* when I first entered the front door of Julia Winston's gorgeous beach house today. Of course, I'm sad I won't be living with my best friend Samantha like we were in Manhattan, but Kimberley has her all set up at a Nine Thousand One apartment in West Hollywood. And Samantha is thrilled about pretty much *everything* to do with LA. I guess that's the trade-off for me as well. I'll be able to walk around naked whenever I want in my own place, at least in Malibu. The hidden bonus, as it were. But not when I'm at The Harland during the week."

"I have no words." Roman closes his baby blues for a few seconds. "I'm just picturing that. You. Naked. Julia Winston's beach house." He opens his eyes and looks at me. "Wow. I can still see that image. Very nice. You *are* most intriguing, Isla Ryder."

"Don't mean to be," I whisper. "That's the French 75 talking." I grin up at him but realize by the look of intensity in his eyes that I need to change course like right now. "Eat your cake, birthday boy, before it dries out or I change my mind about *that corner piece.*"

He grins and takes a large bite of his birthday cake as if to prove it's his and his alone. Soon there's white and blue frosting on his lips. I resist the urge to wipe it off and watch in fascination as he enthusiastically digs into his birthday cake. *Literally.*

I've only taken two bites of the white cake he brought me while he's already finished his. I look up from my plate and catch him watching me.

"Do you want to finish my cake?" I ask.

"Only if you're not going to."

I shake my head from side to side and hand it to him. A smile spreads across his face. Mine too. I can't help it. It's endearing to see someone enjoy their birthday cake this much.

After he finishes my cake, I cannot take it anymore. "You have a little frosting right there." I point to the left side of his mouth. He grabs a linen napkin and wipes at his face. "Still there." Nervous laugh. Finally, I lean in and wipe it off myself with my thumb and index finger. His face is warm against my hand. And the contact between us takes us to a whole new level of awareness.

"Thanks."

"No problem. Just a hidden flaw of mine. One of several. Must make things right, yeah? Spinach on your teeth after you have just finished eating a salad and the guy, you're with on the date, doesn't tell you?" I make a slicing gesture across my throat. "Bad move."

"Catastrophic for the guy for not telling you."

"Abso-fucking-lutely. Sorry, Samantha's favorite word. Becoming mine." I laugh. "No tolerance for cowards. Gladiators only need apply."

He's staring at me as if he's memorizing every word, I've been saying for the late-night test scheduled for later.

Must change course.

I listen to the music for a few minutes and then I nod all at once. "The theme of your playlist. I got it. Top songs for every year you were born, yeah? Except for "Come As You Are" that came out in 1993." I frown, trying to figure that one out, but then I just nervously laugh and shake my head. "But I love that song, too. And Kurt Cobain. Nirvana. So, I will add to my answer, the misunderstood. All the Nirvana stuff was before your time, but so were The Cars, Foreigner, and Fleetwood Mac." I shrug with nonchalance. Roman gives me a questioning look and stares at me intently now.

"Final answer. The top songs from the time you were born in 1995 until now as well as the misunderstood. Especially Kurt Cobain. Anyway, I was wracking my brain for the theme. The homage you mentioned this afternoon. Glad we got that solved."

"Exactly that. You got it, Isla Ryder. Nobody else here will." Roman smiles, but he looks a little disconcerted. "Yes, it's an homage. Songs starting with 1995, the year I was born, some of the top ones, and some of the most nostalgic ones and all the songs my mom would always play for me, of yes, the misunderstood. Especially Kurt Cobain." Then, he runs his hand through his hair and says," Although, "Blood In The Cut" and "Come As You Are" and the next four songs are for you. "Blood In The Cut" because you were humming that song earlier this afternoon. Thought we should pay it some homage, too."

"Songs for me? I don't know what to say to that."

He openly hesitates, and then he says, "I think music is a glimpse into someone's soul."

"Exactly that." His revelation and obvious reverence for music overwhelms me all at once. He understands music the way my dad did. Music. Its significance. The lyrics. The messages in song. Tears gather at my lashes. One slips down my face and Roman gently wipes it away with the back of his hand before I can. I attempt to smile at him, but I can't. Not right now.

"My dad loved music," I finally say. "He played it all the time when he was writing." *Too much information.* Things I never say to anyone have come rushing out.

Get it together, Isla.

Like right the fuck now.

"Your dad sounds like he was just an amazing guy. Your mom, too. Your little brother?"

"Thomas. He was eight. Followed me everywhere." I try to smile, but it isn't really working. Instead, I listen to the music playing, trying to better decipher the signals that he's giving me with each song choice. "It's All I Can Do" by The Cars is playing. I try not to look at him as I'm trying to understand why he would pick this song for me. *Don't read into it.* I half-smile at him.

Then, "Perfect Day" with Hoku starts playing and I sort of laugh out loud upon hearing it. "You're funny, Roman. Really, the *perfect day*? I interrupt your run, occupy your entire afternoon, bleed all over your stairs, deck, and house, and almost pass out at your kitchen sink and your kitchen island. *Perfect day?*"

"It was to me. A… perfect day. It's nice that you can finally admit to almost passing out. *Twice.* Three times if we count the beach."

I grin. "Haha. Not admitting to any such thing. I *do* love this song, though. Loved *"Legally Blonde"* and Reese Witherspoon is next level."

"She is. She's a friend of mine."

"Really? That's nice. You're very funny. I like that. I have trouble remembering the punch line to a joke, but I appreciate good humor and that little hint of sarcasm you seem to drop in. You surprise me, Roman Lysander. I'm not usually one for surprises, but these have been good surprises. Thank you for the songs. I love them all."

"You're welcome." He hesitates, and then he says, "I'm so glad you came, Isla Ryder."

I don't even know what to say to that and by the way he is looking at me; I decide it's best to not say anything. I smile instead, which seems to work like a 'go' signal.

He leans in. "Thanks for coming to my birthday party, Isla Ryder."

Careful, Isla.

"It's quite an event you have orchestrated here. It seems you ensure everyone is having a good time." I try to maintain a cool and even tone. I attempt to ensure my professional detachment is firmly back in place. *Again.* After whatever that was with the walk around naked reference and the frosting. *A transgression. A definitive crossing of boundaries. Twice.*

Boundaries? Where exactly are those?

I work on keeping my expression neutral, mirroring his practiced charm with my own carefully constructed composure. At least, I give it the old one, two try.

"Thank you. That's the idea—that everyone has a good time. I was just thinking… this party could use a little more… *sophistication* though. And then, poof, you *finally* appear."

He gestures to my pearly top and black jeans attire. His gaze lingers for a fraction too long on my ensemble. His smile deepens, a flash of white teeth in the fading light.

"Sophistication is always in short supply in… Hollywood," I counter, my tone dry, a subtle jab. His smile falters for a split second, a flicker of genuine surprise in his eyes before the charm clicks back into place.

Good. He's not used to women who don't fawn over his practiced lines.

"Touché," he says and then laughs, a low, appreciative sound. "You know, I owe you an apology. About this afternoon. Beach runs are apparently hazardous to sophisticated women in pearly white tops and black leather jeans and silver sandals that must have set you back a cool grand. You look incredible, by the way. Ethereal."

"Ethereal?" I raise an eyebrow, teasing lightly. "Just ethereal? Or is there an unspoken modifier?" My voice is no more than a distinct murmur, and he has to lean in to hear me say it.

He grins as we share the memory of what he said at the beach. Then, he gestures to my mostly empty champagne glass. "Speaking of which, a sophisticated woman like you deserves another glass of champagne. And I have Taittinger." He raises an eyebrow, a playful challenge in his eyes.

"This is it for me," I say, taking a deliberate sip, my gaze unwavering. "Especially when I need to keep my wits about me, since I'm new in town and all, in an unfamiliar place among strangers." Another subtle jab, hinting at the chaotic nature of his party, the undercurrent of recklessness that permeates the air.

He laughs again, a genuine sound this time, a hint of amusement in his eyes. "Wits about you, huh? Intriguing. Tell me, what exactly are you keeping your wits about you for?" He leans in closer, the practiced charm replaced by something more intense and entirely too focused. On me.

The game is escalating.

"Just… general Hollywood mayhem," I say, my voice light, dismissive, but my gaze holding his. "One can never be too careful in this town, so I've been told."

"True enough," he agrees, his gaze still locked on mine. "But sometimes… a little mayhem is exactly what you need. To loosen things up. To break the ice."

He signals Danny, who is passing nearby, and requests Taittinger champagne, two fresh glasses, and an ice bucket.

Because when you're the star, requests like that are fulfilled instantaneously.

In short order, my newfound friend Danny is back with two fresh glasses; he opens the Taittinger like a professional sommelier, and after procuring Roman's approval, he slowly pours the coveted champagne into the fluted glasses.

Danny sets the silver ice bucket and bottle of Taittinger on the travertine table nearby and swiftly leaves after ensuring that Roman and, especially me, require nothing else.

"I see you've made a friend in Danny," Roman says, looking amused.

"Danny has been taking care of me since I got here. Thank you for ensuring I had a good time."

"Danny is great. He takes care of all my special requests," Roman says with a mischievous grin.

"I'm a special request now?" I ask.

"Something like that." He holds up the flute of champagne. The golden liquid shimmers in the low light. "Taittinger champagne. Your favorite. To break the ice and calm your nerves, I think. You've had a long day, Isla Ryder."

He's not wrong, of course. It's been a long day. For me.

Roman's charm is off the charts. A rare trait? Or pretense? *We'll see.*

He's thoughtful. Real or not? *Undecided.*

And now more champagne. *My instincts scream: No more champagne, Isla.*

But a reckless impulse beats inside me, a rebellious spark in the face of his charm. And Samantha's words from earlier echo in my mind: *the party is just getting started…* Besides, one more glass won't hurt. It's just a way to better understand my client. Reconnaissance, like Roman said this afternoon.

"Alright," I concede, a slight curve to my lips. I take the proffered flute, the crystal cool against my fingers. "To… breaking the ice further. And, Happy Birthday, Roman Lysander."

He clinks his own glass against mine, the sound still sharp and clear in the noisy room.

"To breaking the ice further, and thank you, Isla Ryder, for the birthday wishes," he says. His blue eyes hold mine for a long moment, and a glimpse of something deeper, something dangerous, sparks beneath his surface charm.

Careful, Isla.

The champagne is undeniably good, crisp and dry, effervescent, a welcome contrast to the cloying sweetness of the party air. The bubbles tickle my nose as I sip it. The fine champagne spreads through me slowly, not as fast as the two cocktails earlier.

Good call. I'm fine.

It's been a long day. A long flight. And the enormity of this encounter, with the pretense of being just another party guest, is strangely… liberating.

"So, girl from the beach," he says, his voice softening, becoming more intimate, the practiced charm shifting into a more seductive gear. "Tell me, what brings a sophisticated woman like you to a chaotic Hollywood party like mine on a Thursday night?" He leans closer. The scent of his cologne, musky and expensive, assails my senses.

"Curiosity. Intrigue. It's Malibu. It's a party. And you invited me. But like I said, you didn't tell me it was your birthday." I meet his gaze, matching his intimate tone with my own carefully controlled persona. "I didn't get you a *present.*"

Another calculated move, mirroring his flirtation, keeping him intrigued, keeping him off balance.

"Birthday presents are always a good thing. I don't think anyone brought me one, so you're good there. Brandon paid for the cake. His present is enough," he says. A slow smile spreads across his face. "I'm glad you came, although you were fashionably *late.* I wasn't sure you were coming at all. But your being here is a present, in and of itself. Thank you. I'm glad you came to my birthday party, and you let me finish your cake. *See?* You gave me a present, after all."

"Well, it has been a long day for me. And now I'm glad I didn't miss your party, since it's your birthday and all."

"Meant To Be" with Bebe Rexha and Florida Georgia Line plays. It's one of the songs he said he chose for me, and my analytical mind immediately flags it. *Meant to be?* The phrase itself, so deceptively simple, yet laden with a significance I can't easily dismiss. It's quietly seductive, two people deciding to take a chance on each other in that country twang of a song. So simple. So direct.

I tell myself not to read into it, not to dissect the lyrics as if they're a coded message, but the thought lingers like a persistent melody in my head. Is this another one of his calculated moves? Or is there something else, a whisper of genuine intent that my strategic brain is ill-equipped to decipher?

He seems to sense my momentary stillness, my internal debate, especially after all the boundaries we've already crossed. His gaze with those startling blue eyes softens, and he holds out his hand, a silent invitation. "Let's dance, Isla Ryder."

His words, a gentle command, pull me from my spiraling and wayward thoughts. He leads me, almost instinctively, to the darkened deck outside, a sanctuary of open air and moonlight. The chaos of the living room recedes, replaced by the soft balm of the night.

Here, under the vast sky, the music feels different, less like background noise and more like a current pulling us along.

Roman is an amazing dancer, his movements fluid, confident, completely at ease. We glide across the deck, losing ourselves in the rhythm of this song and the next. His large hands, warm and secure, engulf mine, just like at the beach earlier today.

I shouldn't be relaxing quite this much in his arms. He's the movie star, the famous actor, the client, the walking PR crisis I'm here to manage. But a rebellious part of me whispers, *you don't say 'no' to this.* And the truth is, I'm enjoying myself. Truly, deeply. I can't remember the last time I simply *danced*, lost in the moment, without a strategic thought or the necessity of a purpose at play.

His presence feels… safe. A strange, unexpected comfort in the whirlwind of this Hollywood night. Letting go. Just being. It's a feeling I haven't allowed myself in so long. I already know it's dangerous. It's this beautiful sense of surrender I'm not yet ready to name. A fleeting pang from my cut knee reminds me, regretfully, that even perfect moments have their limits.

"Your knees acting up. I can tell you're in pain. We can go back inside if you want."

"The cut is acting up. Yes. Sorry. But I really enjoyed this. It's been way too long since I've been dancing. So, thank you for the dance." I smile at him in the cast of the moonlight shimmering across his handsome face. Then, somewhat impulsively, I wistfully ask, "Can we maybe stay out here for a little while longer? Unless you need to go see to some of your other guests. I don't want to monopolize all of your time."

"You're not monopolizing my... time. I'm good. We can stay out here as long as you want. I am exactly where I want to be."

"Me, too."

Boundaries. Boundaries. Boundaries.

Where did you go?

Our conversation *begins* to flow more easily, almost effortlessly now, fueled by champagne and a growing, undeniable chemistry.

We dance around the edges of our true selves, veiled in playful banter and subtle probing, a familiarity lingering from this afternoon's rescue and his chivalry. I don't make things up. Instead, I dole out facts to him, feeding his suddenly insatiable curiosity, letting my guard down slightly, letting him in. How I'm from New York City. Went to Penn, graduated with honors in communications, then went to work for Kimberley Powers.

He asks about New York, about my 'life back East,' painting me as this sophisticated city girl, out of her element in the chaotic sunshiny glitz of Malibu. I let him believe it, playing the role of the intrigued outsider observing this bizarre Hollywood world with detached amusement. It's mostly true. But he's getting a little too close to that vein of insecurity I hide from everyone.

I, in turn, ask about his work, about 'the film industry,' carefully avoiding any mention of *Vendetta*, of Steven Stryker, or the many reasons I'm actually here.

It seems he knows most of them already. And we avoid all of that because we're both very aware of the onlookers at this party.

He talks about acting, about the creative process, about the pressures of fame, revealing glimpses of vulnerability beneath the layers of his so practiced charm. He's intelligent, and there is so much more depth to him than I expected. His self-awareness is surprising, a stark contrast to the 'Hollywood golden boy' image plastered across the tabloids, along with an endless parade of rebellious behavior.

Early in our extended conversation, he *tips* me off as to who's who at the party. The ever-ruthless Morgan Grant, the gossip blogger who follows Roman around constantly looking for a salacious scandal. He told me they went to high school together. There's a story there that I must investigate. It's the same with some guy who was turned away from being a part of the *Vendetta* film project by his dad, Trent Lysander, that I must better understand.

Roman is the perfect host, squiring me around, promoting my business to the right people and deftly propelling me away from the ones with their own agendas. We dance a little more on the back deck to the mesmerizing lyrics of Best Coast's song, "California Nights". But then, the cut at my knee continues to throb just as he predicted it might earlier this afternoon. I wince and he sees it again, as if it is now a film scene we've practiced together. Now, truly responsible for all my medical needs, Roman brings me three more Advil and a bottle of water, repeating the scene from early this afternoon all over again.

The party winds down around half-past eleven, and the catering staff subtly starts to put food and drink away. The music dies down enough that conversations can be had without yelling.

We still talk in low tones, very aware of the onlookers still hanging on. But even Melody Parker has exited the stage. Roman touches the small of my back and leads me over to the kitchen, where he asks the staff to box up two of the cake corners, he requested earlier. I'm not sure what his intentions are, but he grabs another chilled bottle of Taittinger champagne and puts it all in a black bag "for later," he tells me mysteriously.

"Well, Isla Ryder, you've looked around and met my friends. What do you think?"

"Hate to break it to you, Roman, but none of these people are your friends."

"I know." He gives me a conspiratorial look. "Brandon's my friend, my best friend, but our friendship becomes strained when it's defined by my success and the financial gain for both of us instead of everything else. You know what I mean?"

"I do. Trust should be the only currency. Samantha? Like I may have said, she's on a flight from NYC to LAX as we speak. Pulled up stakes at Powers & Winston PR so we can launch our own gig here. Samantha is my best friend. She always has my back, no matter what. But I wonder sometimes if that will end. It seems like it always does. Even now. Starting Ryder & Harper Communications LA, out here; I worry because she's giving everything up in Manhattan. What if we can't make it work? Now, I've ruined my career and hers, too."

The fear of loss clings to me like a shadow. I keep collecting people, then losing them, one by one. Each departure takes a piece of me with it. I'm not sure how much of myself is left to give.

"That's a lot to process," he drawls.

"Sorry." I shake my head and laugh. "It's your *birthday* and I'm monopolizing all of your time with my problems. Where's your best friend, Brandon?"

"He had to go. Early client meeting," Roman says, shrugging with indifference. "He's like that sometimes. Coordinates the show and then bows out with other plans." His blue eyes study mine more carefully now. "You're... so intriguing," he says suddenly. "But it's like you're holding something back."

He's closer than I anticipate to the truth.

"Everyone has their secrets." My voice is low and betrays nothing. "I have mine. You have yours; don't you?" I turn the question back on him, deflecting, probing in return.

He hesitates for a moment. Something dark crosses his features, a shadow beneath the charm. "Secrets are the currency of this town," he says, his voice softening, losing some of its playful edge. "Everyone's got them. The trick is... knowing who you can share them with."

"That would be quite a trick," I say. "I don't know... I find you can't trust anyone, you know?"

The champagne has loosened me up. *Too much...* The physical proximity, the glances that linger a touch too long, the charged undercurrent of flirtation—it's all creating a heady, intoxicating experience between us.

I respond to his charm, to his intensity, indulging in this simple attraction. It's just research, I try to remind myself, a necessary step in understanding my... client.

But a small, rebellious voice whispers in the back of my mind: *maybe it's more than that.*

He touches my arm, a casual brush of his fingers, but the contact sends a jolt of electricity through me. My pulse quickens. I tell myself it's just a visceral reaction I should ignore. Dismiss it as the effects of the champagne and his proximity.

But it's more than that. It's the danger. The forbidden thrill of indulging in something I know I should avoid. It's the allure of the 'bad boy', the magnetic pull of the archetype I've sworn off.

He is most definitely the type of man who has the power to dismantle my carefully constructed personal life and break my heart into a thousand pieces in no time at all.

The warnings are real.

Alarm bells clang in my head, loud and insistent.

I finish the last of my champagne, feeling a dizzying swirl inside my head. The party becomes a blur of noise and faces, fading into a hazy background as my focus narrows and lands on Roman. I shouldn't be attracted to him. He represents everything I'm trying to avoid. And yet, the pull is undeniable.

***

The party has definitely wound down. The crowd thins out even further. The music softens to simple background noise. He leans in, his voice low, intimate. "So, girl from the beach, Isla Ryder," he murmurs, his breath warm against my ear. "Are you ready for your… Malibu experience to continue?" He raises an eyebrow, a seductive challenge.

"I'm not sure if the Malibu experience would be any different from what I left behind in New York. That one broke my heart." My words are stark, completely revealing.

I am laid bare and broken by his expensive champagne and his goddamn charisma.

And I *realize* I've just revealed my innermost soul to *a client*.

I'm still finding pieces of myself scattered across Manhattan, and here I am, risking the fragments I've managed to gather. The shards pierce me anew with each memory that surfaces and the ones I'm actively creating now.

My rational mind screams no. *Walk away. Maintain control. Focus on the mission.*

But the champagne has loosened my grip on reality, and the dangerous thrill of the forbidden is too tempting to resist.

"What did you have in mind, Mr. Lysander?" My voice is husky, a hint of breathlessness creeping in.

He smiles, a slow, knowing smile that sends a shiver down my spine. "How about I walk you home?" His suggestion is a godsend. His gaze locks on mine, holding me captive. "You're on East Coast time. It's way past your bedtime."

"True. Do you mind walking me home? My cut is getting the best of me. I shouldn't have worn stilettos. *Clearly.* And I need some more Advil," I say with a rueful smile.

Roman takes my hand, his fingers intertwining with mine, the contact sending another jolt of electricity through me, stronger this time, more undeniable. "Then let's not waste any time. I'll walk you back. We'll take the beach. It's quieter and no one will notice us." His voice is low and steady.

He grabs the black bag off the counter. He stops and gives instructions to the cleaning crew—who seem to materialize precisely at half past midnight—telling them to clear out the remaining guests and lock up.

And just like that, we leave through the sliding glass doors and head into the cool night air toward the moonlit beach and the uneven beckoning shoreline.

CHAPTER 15

snow on the beach

Isla Ryder

"Snow On The Beach" – Taylor Swift, Lana Del Rey

"Birds of a Feather" - Billie Eilish

"Fade Into You" - Mazzy Star

"Perfect" - Ed Sherman

"Deep In Your Love" - Bebe Rexha, Alok

"Soul Meets Body" - Death Cab by Cutie

"Landslide" – Fleetwood Mac

Early Friday Morning 1:00 a.m.

ROMAN CARRIES THE BLACK BAG with the cake and champagne in one hand. His expensive brown leather loafers dangle from the other. I clutch my silver Iggy Crystals sandals—one in each hand like precious treasure. The cool night air whispers against my bare feet as I step along the cool sand. *Sobering.*

"Sand and salt water will destroy those," he warns, as if I have never been around an ocean before.

This makes me want to laugh—a real laugh that starts deep in my chest but stays trapped there.

Hollywood people live in such a tight, self-centered bubble, utterly unaware that life exists elsewhere. And that, perhaps, there's another ocean besides the Pacific. The Atlantic, for instance, where my family's estate still sprawls along one of Darien, Connecticut's finest shorelines. The property I still own but haven't been back to in almost a decade. Another piece of myself I keep locked away.

The walk along the beach feels otherworldly. The pulsing music from his birthday party fades behind us, replaced by the rhythmic crash of waves. The Malibu night air is fresh and salty—a stark, welcome contrast to the suffocating heat of bodies packed into his home for the past four hours. The almost-full moon hangs low in the sky, casting silver streaks across the dark water, illuminating our solitary path.

The sand is cool and yielding beneath my feet. We walk side by side, close enough that our arms brush occasionally. Each accidental contact sends something electric through me. Something I don't want to name.

It's as if there is a transference of some kind between us with each contact. The commingling of selves we'll never get back.

The champagne and our strangely direct conversation have created a charged atmosphere. I think we both recognize this for what it is—a temporary escape from reality. It's just a pocket of time where anything feels possible.

This feeling won't last.

It's too fragile.

Too improbable.

Too tenuous.

Too impossible.

The conversation shifts. Playful banter recedes like the tide, and something deeper rises to the surface. The champagne has definitely done its work.

Edges blur. Defenses lower.

Mine, especially.

It's no longer about witty comebacks and veiled challenges. Now, the air vibrates with something more honest and infinitely more dangerous.

"You know," Roman says, his voice softer now, more introspective as the waves crash rhythmically beside us, "this whole town, Hollywood… it's just a performance." He kicks at a shell, sending it spinning into the darkness. "Everyone playing a part. Smiling for the cameras. Saying the right things. Being marketable."

I turn to study his profile, caught off guard by the sudden shift in his tone. My skin shivers with awareness as much as the cool breeze.

"And you're tired of performing?" The question comes out barely above a whisper, though genuine curiosity stirs within me.

He stops walking, turning to face me fully. The moonlight catches the blue of his eyes, making them almost luminous against the night.

"Tired? Yes. Truly exhausted. Suffocated by it at times. Sometimes all three at the same time." He runs a hand through his hair, the gesture surprisingly unguarded. I notice how he does this—a quick, almost defensive motion that betrays his uncertainty. It's the third time tonight I've seen this tell.

"Everyone wants a piece of Roman Lysander, the image. No one really sees... me. Who I actually am."

The confession hangs between us, revealing and unfiltered. I study him in the moonlight, seeing past the carefully constructed facade of Hollywood's golden boy. The vulnerability in his eyes catches me off guard. There's something deeply human about watching someone this famous, this perfect, reveal the cracks in the emotional armor beneath the surface.

He shifts his weight, looks down at the sand, then back at me—another tell. The Roman Lysander from magazine covers wouldn't fidget. Wouldn't look down with uncertainty. Wouldn't let the mask slip.

The two French 75s and the glasses of champagne, two, I think, soften my edges, make me receptive in ways I normally don't allow. My professional boundaries blur with each wave that crashes against the shore. I should redirect and maintain some distance between us and, most assuredly, remember why I'm here. But I don't do any of those things.

Instead, I find myself drawn in by his authenticity. The champagne has created this strange bubble where I'm not Isla Ryder, PR strategist, and he's not Roman Lysander, movie star. We're just two people on a beach, sharing truths we normally keep hidden.

"Being seen is terrifying." I surprise myself with the confession. "Sometimes hiding behind the image is safer."

His eyes find mine, holding them with unexpected intensity. "Is that what you do? Hide behind your image, too?"

The question penetrates deeper than it should, stirring something

I've kept dormant for years. There is less of myself with each revelation. His honesty about hiding behind his image is unexpected. It cuts deep. Something in my chest constricts painfully.

Is this part of his charm offensive?

Or is there something genuine beneath the practiced façade?

"Everyone does," I whisper, aware that I'm stepping into dangerous territory. "Some of us are just better at hiding behind the image than others." We start walking again. Side by side, staying out of the waves creeping ever closer as the tide comes in.

"And who *are* you, Roman?" My voice sounds strange to my own ears—too soft, too interested.

He hesitates, looking out at the dark ocean for a long moment, the waves hissing and sighing around our ankles. "I don't know anymore." His words float between us, barely audible above the surf. "I lost him somewhere along the way. Under all the headlines and the expectations and… the bullshit. And now I'm 28 years old."

"It's just a number."

"Says you at *26*." He looks at me in the moonlight. "I'm two years from thirty. My God! It's surreal how fast time goes."

"I'll be 27 in three months. November. Scorpio here." I attempt to smile. "And then, I'll be saying, and now I'm 27 years old." I groan and get a wry smile. "So, don't listen to me. Tell me why you have a problem with being 28 years old."

He sighs, but the sound is immediately swallowed by the ocean's rhythmic waves crashing onto the shore. "I thought I'd be farther along in my career by now. *Truly*. I mean, my dad *runs* Lysander Entertainment. He does some of the biggest movie deals in town. He can make things happen, but I feel like he's holding out on me. Like I'm not good enough for him to bother helping."

He laughs, a short, harsh sound that scrapes against the night, then shakes his head. "I sound like I'm whining. I *am* whining. It's just… Geez, Isla, even you can see the parasitic side of life in Hollywood, can't you? And you just *got* here. Don't you *feel* it already? It's real. It will suck out your soul and leave you hollowed out inside. And for me, the only thing I have is acting. It's the only thing I'm really great at, and yet I just keep fucking it up. *Sometimes. On purpose.* Like I fight the soul sucking, but in the end, I give in, and yet, the only one losing out is me."

We've stopped walking, keeping a wary eye on the encroaching waves.

"Maybe you're overthinking it. Your father loves you. And he's enlisted my expertise to help you. It's a substantial contract and I'm really good at what I do. That's a *whole lot* of public relations help. The thing is, I'm here to help you figure it out. Navigate through it all and create a better narrative for you. It's all about strategy and tactical navigation and—"

He looks down at me, surprise quickly hardening into something that radiates towards me like anger. We're in a dangerous place, and it has nothing to do with the dark ocean swirling near our feet.

"You're not *serious*, are you? *Change my narrative? Rebrand me*? Like I'm *a fucking product*?" His voice cuts through the night air. "I'm a *real* person. How *exactly* are you going to help me figure things out for the real Roman Lysander, the one buried alive beneath all the trappings of Hollywood?"

He takes a deep breath and sighs heavily, then looks at me in true frustration. "Isla. You tragically lost your entire family, and yet, you are so closed off, so busy playing the badass PR princess, you don't even really deal with that on any kind of emotional level. *At all.* Lady, you need more help than I do."

I'm stunned into silence by what he's said. My chest constricts. My lungs burn. I cannot even breathe.

He is too close to the truth.

The truth about me.

My only defense is to lash out.

"*No*. You don't get to judge me. You don't *know* me. You don't know what I go through on a daily basis. I thought you might be different, but you're all just the same. Another fucking guy. Well, fuck you, Roman Lysander." The words are torn from me.

"You don't know the first thing about me. But you're ready to fuck me, anyway. And if your dad tells you to fuck Melody Parker, so you can land the role of Steven Stryker, you'd do that, too. *Twice*, if asked. As if that would help you at all," I say with disdain.

"You don't have any friends because parasites surround you— people who would soon cut your throat to get ahead of you! Really! And you think you know me? Oh, my God! Just go home, Roman. And leave me the fuck alone."

I turn away from him as deep-seated anger and all-consuming despair and never-ending grief take a firm hold of me from the inside, desperately seeking a better way out. I visibly shake with uncontrollable rage. My nails dig half-moons into my palms because my hands are clenched so tight.

He's hit a nerve.

He's triggered something deep inside me I must outrun.

The vast desolation of disappointment and disillusionment in him and what all he's just said to me—*the truth of me he's discovered*—rages outward, like an all too violent, out-of-control storm.

Devastation imminent.

Everyone take cover.

My heart hammers so hard in my chest it feels painful. Like an actual heart break.

Reasons not forthcoming.

All reasoning irrevocably lost.

I race up the beach toward Julia's place despite the searing pain of my cut. But suddenly, clouds drift across the moon, plunging the sand into deeper darkness. I slow down while my knee throbs with fresh pain. A dry sob escapes. Then the tears come. Hot, silent, unstoppable. Because I'm fucking tired. Still on East Coast time. I drank too much and ate too little. I ate the sandwich he gave me more than ten hours ago.

Blue and white umbrella.

I grip the handrail and pull myself up the twenty deck stairs as best I can. My cut knee throbs in protest with every step.

Out of breath, I make it to the glass sliding doors and push them aside. Thank God, I *didn't lock* them. The New Yorker in me almost did. Now, I'm glad I *trusted* Malibu just enough to leave them unlocked.

I head straight to the Subzero refrigerator and take a long drink of water directly from the glass pitcher. *Because I can.*

In the next, I slam the pitcher onto the counter a little too hard, satisfied by the sound, marveling slightly that it doesn't shatter.

I wipe my mouth with the back of my hand, turn, and look out toward the living room windows, seeking the dark ocean's solace. Needing peace.

And there's Roman.

———

He stands in the middle of the living room, hands on his hips like he owns the place.

"Now. Is. Not. A. Good. Time." I hold my hand up to ward him off from coming any closer to me.

Then I turn away from him, embarking in a frantic search through the kitchen cabinets, trying to remember where the Advil might be. I glance at the stairs, contemplating the climb, knowing there's a bottle on the bathroom counter upstairs. I can feel Roman watching me.

I drink directly from the pitcher again.

Because I can. That's been established.

"I just want to say—"

"I. *Don't.* Want. *You.* To. Say. *Anything.*" My voice is tight and controlled. The opposite of what I feel.

"I'm just trying to understand— "

"There. Is. Nothing. To. Understand. About. Me."

He gets this little smirk. It plays with his gorgeous lips. It pisses me off even more. "Oh! You! I've got you pretty much figured out. It's going to be *a lot of work,* and I'm not sure your dad is *paying me enough.*"

"What are you so afraid of, Isla Ryder? That's what I want to know." His voice is quiet now. *And dangerous.*

"I'm not afraid of anything!" I scream the words at him. My voice breaks on the last syllable.

We both know this isn't true.

We stare at each other.

He, looking like he's trying to figure out how to rewind time and effectively disarm the bomb within me that he's already detonated.

Me, mindlessly casting about for the professional emotional armor I normally always wear, the shield that prevents *anyone* from learning the truth about me, which is, I fear loving anyone, even myself sometimes, because of the overriding fear of loss that inevitably follows.

The old fear claws up—love means loss.

Always loss. There it is…

It's an emotional fog I can't shake.

I haven't in more than nine years.

The rage I've been feeling leaves as fast as it *comes* on, like an ocean wave recedes from the shoreline. That is how it works with me. One moment my anger burns hot, in the next it is icy cold.

Remorse takes over.

Remorse for taking my rage out on a stranger.

Oh, and my client's son. My project.

My mind races, searching for all the reasons for my outburst without a knowable answer and lands on the immediate solution instead. *The token apology.* Restoring equilibrium becomes my quest.

"There is no explanation for any of this. I'm sorry." I visibly shake now as the energy drains from my body. My hands tremble. My knees feel weak. I grip the countertop for support in holding me up.

Roman retreats, apparently deciding pursuing what I'm afraid of is a dead end.

That's right, buddy. Fucking figure that much out about me.

Instead, he sets down the black bag on the countertop across from me and gingerly retrieves the boxes of cake. Two of them. He opens both. "The corner pieces, just like I asked," he says, smiling like a little kid who's been given exactly what he wants.

I watch in wonder as he uncorks the champagne bottle with a practiced, quiet hiss, like a sommelier on the side, just like Danny. Then he's searches through my kitchen cupboards, crossing all my personal boundaries, just like I did at his place earlier this afternoon.

Hours ago. A lifetime ago.

He gets this triumphant look when his search produces crystal flutes, glass dessert plates, and forks. He carries everything over to the white leather sofa and sets it up on the travertine coffee table.

He gestures for me to sit down and just relax.

He gives me that charming Roman Lysander smile and then this imploring look. "Isla, look. I created a picnic in your gorgeous living room at one in the morning. We'll have some more cake and champagne, and everything will be as right as rain."

I give him the how-is-that-going-to-help-me? stare.

"I can't find the Advil." This has become a problem as big as solving world peace. *For me.* "There's some upstairs in the master bathroom, but not down here."

My feeling of helplessness is overwhelming.

Get it together, Isla.

What is wrong with you now?

"I'll get you some Advil. I know your cut is acting up. You're wincing again."

Roman takes the grand stairs two at a time and disappears. My ability to even care as he invades my personal space, even my bedroom, completely evaporates.

Instead, I cross over to the living room and sit down like he suggested. I lean my head against the back of the sofa and rest my hand over my closed eyes. The world slightly spins.

I am alone in this world.

The realization makes me sad. Again.

It's terrifying.

A few minutes later, I hear him as he sits down next to me. I withdraw my hand from my face, slightly turn my head, and stare straight at him. We repeat the scene as he drops three Advil into my outstretched hand, just like twice before. I swig champagne to wash them down. "Thank you," I say quietly.

I feel him watching me like a doctor monitors his worst patient, ensuring I follow his instructions to the letter, looking for compliance. *He has a vested interest now.*

Me, injured.

Add *psychologically damaged* to my list of ailments.

My wayward thoughts causes me to smile—a tired, wry, out of sorts smile.

"Better?" he asks, his voice gentler now, still watching me.

A grudgingly one-word answer is given with tremendous effort. "Better."

A long silence stretches between us. It's heavy with unspoken words and unacknowledged feelings that threaten to spill over in all directions for us both.

Then I finally say, "I'm sorry I yelled at you. Well, went completely ballistic if one were grading the extent of my anger. That was inappropriate. With a client."

I watch him closely, trying to gauge his understanding.

Of me.

Why?

We don't know.

"My dad is your client. I'm the project, remember?" he says with a slight grin, shaking his head.

Roman tops off our glasses with champagne and carefully sets them on the travertine coffee table. Then, he busies himself with serving the cake. He hands me a plate and dives into his own.

"I only have cake on my birthday. White cake, Italian buttercream frosting, and cream filling. My mom's favorite. Mine, too. My mom made this cake every year for my birthday. Now, it's never the same. Julie tries, my friend, the caterer. But it's not my mom's, you know?"

"I love white cake, too. Always have. Julie gave me your mom's recipe for the cake, the cream filling, and the Italian Buttercream frosting. We could give it a try. I bake at night when I can't sleep, which is… pretty often." My voice is lighter now, warming to his attentiveness, somewhat appreciative that he's basically ignoring all the whys for my earlier meltdown.

"You're going to try to follow my mom's recipe and make her cake? *Tonight?* With the frosting and the cream filling?"

"To the letter."

"Why? Why would you do that for me?"

"Because I'm a fantastic baker, just another skill set I can fall back on when my public relations business falls through because of all these challenging, uncooperative clients I have." I look at him pointedly now.

He laughs and then shakes his head in wonder. "I don't know what to say. Bake a cake tonight? It's going above and beyond the call of duty to try to replicate my mom's cake."

"It's not a *duty*, Roman. It's something I already do. I accept the challenge of trying to get the cake right because I probably can do it," I say with a nonchalant shrug. "I bake all the time. Because I'm stressed all the time, and it's a stress reliever for me. *To bake.* I'm always looking for people to eat my baked goods. Friends. Clients. I made cinnamon rolls for Robbie Anton the other night after a particularly rough PR crisis. It's just what I do. So, it's fine. Okay? We'll give it a try."

"Robbie Anton. The singer? You made him cinnamon rolls. When?" He sounds curious, but there's something else too. His blue eyes get this certain glint to them. *Jealousy?*

"On Tuesday at four in the morning. Yes. It's just something I do. For myself. For the client. Sometimes…" My voice trails off because of the way he's looking at me. He's not keen on hearing I made cinnamon rolls for Robbie Anton in the middle of the night, apparently.

I avoid analyzing his gaze further and pick up the plate of cake he's prepared for me. The first bite melts in my mouth—sweet, comforting. "Hmmm… this is good. Okay, so tell me what's missing in Julie's cake for you. I'm curious now."

"It's not the same," he says grudgingly. He's seemingly still stuck on the thought that I made cinnamon rolls for the pop star singer. "My mom's cake was heavier, not as light as Julie's. And the frosting was sweeter and had a creamier texture. Not like whipped cream, like Julie makes hers."

"Just a sec." I get up and go to the office. Grab my MacBook and return to the living room. Roman's finished his cake.

"She emailed me the recipe." I open the MacBook and look up the recipe in Julie's email. "There are ten steps to making this cake."

"Is that a lot?" Roman asks. He's sitting right next to me, looking over my shoulder at the screen. I can smell his cologne, and it's distracting in this sensuous way.

I look over at him, half-smiling. "That's a lot. But it's just a matter of breaking it all down. Seems to be a timing thing. Your mom's particular about the temperature of the egg whites. That's in her notes. She didn't use the yolks. That's what keeps the cake white. She used real cream; that's what would make the cake heavier." I get up, taking the laptop with me. "Not sure what I have in the way of supplies. Let's go check it out."

In a matter of minutes, I find all I need in the way of ingredients and all the baking supplies from the pantry. Roman carries the Kitchen-aid mixer from the pantry and places it on the counter, while I measure out all the ingredients, including separating the egg whites, so they get to the room temperature like his mom specified.

I task him with getting the cake pans ready. Roman is stoked that we're going to do three layers.

Within a half hour, the three round cake pans are in the oven. I've put in the baking sheets below the cake pans with water, just like his mom's recipe called for.

Now, Roman's looking at me in this studied wonder all over again. I take a sip of champagne and quietly watch him.

"What's up?" I ask warily.

He comes up to me and wipes my face with his thumb. "You had some flour right there. That's all."

"Thanks?" I say. "Why are you acting so weird right now?"

"I'm not," he says, looking down at the floor with this uncertain look. It's the tell again that he's nervous, like at the beach.

"You are. Why?" I ask, catching his blue-eyed gaze when he looks over at me.

"No one... no one has ever *baked a cake* for me at half-past one in the morning because I asked them to. No one... has ever done *anything* for me at half-past one in the morning before. And I'm just wondering why you are doing this... for me? When I said all those terrible things to you at the beach? Why would you do this for me, Isla?"

"Because I'm up at half-past one in the morning. *Usually.* Because I can do this for you. It's not a burden. It's something I do. There're no strings attached. No hidden agenda. It's just something nice to do for someone. Who will actually appreciate it, I guess. I didn't know it was your birthday. And birthdays are important. So, consider it my gift to you."

We're about a foot apart. He's looking at me so strangely still. I wipe my face with the back of my hand. "Is there still flour on my face?" I ask with a little laugh. He shakes his head from side to side. "What then?"

He starts towards me just as the oven timer for the cakes goes off.

"Whew," I say, taking a needed breath. "Cakes may be done. Let's check." I grab the towel and pull out the oven rack. I show him how we test to see if the cake is done by lightly touching it with an index finger. "If it bounces back, it's done. The steam may make it take a minute or two longer. We'll see." I test the cakes individually with my finger while he watches me. "See? They're done. They bounce back, just like they're supposed to when they're done."

My heart is racing because I know he was going to kiss me before the timer went off. We're still in this strange place, this strange bubble, and all my emotional armor feels alarmingly unstable right now.

I place each cake pan on the cooling rack, running a knife around the edge of each cake pan, turn them out so they can cool, while Roman again just watches me. We've already whipped up the cream filling and the frosting. It's just a matter of cooling the cakes and putting it all together.

"How long do you think?" Roman is truly excited about this cake.

"Probably a half hour at a minimum. The worst thing we can do is rush it. The cakes must be cool before we put the cream filling between layers and frost them, or it will be a complete disaster."

We return to the living room to wait for the cakes to cool. He tops our champagne flutes with more champagne and hands me mine.

I lift up my plate of unfinished cake. "We can do a little taste test comparison between Julie's cake and our cake. Then we can figure out what else we need to do to get it to taste exactly like your mom's cake."

"You don't think it will taste exactly like my mom's cake?" he asks.

"I don't know. Baking is tricky that way. You have to follow a recipe exactly to get it just right."

He's playing with his phone. All at once, music comes on. He's figured out the Bluetooth connection for Julia's surround sound music system. Billie Eilish's "Birds of a Feather" starts playing. He pulls me up from the sofa and starts dancing with me.

"Killing time until the cakes are cooled," he says, as he gently moves me around to the music. "We'll take it slow, so we don't stress your cut, okay?"

"Okay." I don't know what to say.

Roman's moves are beyond me. It seems like he's apologized to me in a thousand different ways without actually apologizing.

He clasps my hands in his and intertwines his fingers with mine. We move around the living room with ease. The songs just blend one into the next and we just float along.

I'm enchanted by the way he's looking at me as we just move to the music. Moonlight streams through the open sliding glass doors in these filmy streams and the ocean waves perform this complimentary symphony as if it's all planned out.

My knee starts throbbing again. But it's like we're connected in some way. He already knows.

Roman stops dancing and looks down at my knee. "It's hurting again already?" He looks concerned.

"Well, we kind of pushed it with six songs," I say with a laugh, stepping back from him.

I go to check on the cakes. They're cool to the touch. I search around and quickly find a fancy cake plate turntable in the pantry and start putting the cakes together. He comes up beside me, almost touching me, and just watches me in fascination as I put together the cake layers with the cream filling, as if he's nine years old again. It's cute. Distracting. But I keep going. Determined to get this right for him.

I've got half the cake frosted and I'm spinning the cake plate to get the other side done. While he goes over to his phone to change the music, I light a candle I found. I've put everything away and turn off the overhead kitchen lights.

His cake just sits there on the fancy cake plate with the single lit candle. "Happy Birthday, Roman Alexander Lysander," I say when he returns to the kitchen. "Make a wish."

He closes his eyes, blows out the candle in one go and opens his eyes. I smile at him. Then, grab plates and forks and a sharp knife. "No corners with a round cake. Forgot about that," I tease.

"I'll live," he says with a low laugh.

I hand him his plate of a giant piece of cake, knowing how much he loves the frosting. We move over to the sofa. He takes a bite of our cake. "Hmmm…it's so good. Heavier cake, sweeter too, just like Mom's. The frosting is sweeter, too." He tries Julie's for comparison. "*Huge* difference."

I taste our cake. I nod with supreme satisfaction. "It's pretty close, yeah?"

"I think we got it," he says with a wide smile. "Wow. Thank you. This is… the best birthday gift I've had in… a long time. Isla… I don't know what to say."

"You don't have to say anything. I'm just glad we got it right." His gaze is penetrating as if he is trying to figure this all out. I concentrate on eating the cake and completely avoid looking at him. For all the reasons I do not want to name.

CHAPTER 16

catalyst

Isla Ryder

"Perfect" - Ed Sheeran
"Catalyst" - Anna Malick
"Sin x Secret" - Charlotte Lawrence
"Love Is A Wild Thing" - Kacey Musgraves
"Fresh Laundry" - Allie X
"Landslide" - Fleetwood Mac
"Wild Side" - Laurel

Early Friday Morning, 2:30 a.m.

FINALLY, I SAY, "HAPPY BIRTHDAY, ROMAN." The words come out softer than I intend, still deliberately focusing on the cake before me because looking at him right now feels dangerous.

I can't afford to look at him—not when I'm thinking about how unexpectedly sweet, he is, how he just spent an hour in my kitchen starting at one in the morning recreating his mother's birthday cake because he wanted to. It's messing with my carefully constructed boundaries, blurring the lines between client and strategist until those personas feel like distant memories.

Ed Sheeran's "Perfect" drifts through the sound system, a seductive song contributing intimacy to this surreal scene. Roman turned the music down after we stopped dancing and started cutting the cake, but it still plays like an unexpected serenade, weaving through the space between us with dangerous hints of intimacy.

He leans closer, his voice dropping to that low whisper that sends heat racing along my spine. "I'm sorry for the things I said to you at the beach. I realize you're just trying to help me, and I overstepped with what I said and I'm sorry for upsetting you like that."

An apology from a guy, I already know, doesn't apologize.

For anything.

His sincerity hits me full force. It plays with all of my emotions. Yes, I'm right. This is a guy who doesn't apologize. I know this just by how he is looking at me, as if the entire concept of apologizing is entirely foreign to him and he's unsure how to deal with it.

I feel defenseless as my carefully maintained emotional walls continue to sway, threatening to fall down entirely under the weight of his genuine remorse. This isn't the practiced charm of Hollywood's heartthrob, Roman Lysander. This is something else. It is real, sincere, and even heartfelt, and it terrifies me how much I want to believe him.

My chest tightens with a mixture of relief and something far more dangerous—hope. The kind of hope I've trained myself not to feel, the kind that leads to devastating loss.

But here, in the soft glow of my living room at half-past two in the morning, with the taste of his mother's recipe for his birthday cake on my tongue and his quiet apology hanging between us, I feel my defenses cracking like ice on a lake in spring when the temperature warms up.

I set down my fork, finally allowing myself to fully meet his gaze. His blue eyes hold mine with an intensity that makes the rest of the world fade away.

"Every year for a long while, my birthday has been a sad affair—parties like what you just witnessed tonight," he says. "No gifts. Just the cake, lit candles, well wishes from people who don't give a fuck about me. But then earlier in the day, I literally run into this beautiful, amazing, brilliant girl on the beach, who accidentally slices her knee open, and turns out to be the only one sincere enough to talk to me all evening, share my birthday cake and champagne, and recognizes and shares in my love for music. And then, you make me a cake using my mom's recipe, and it tastes just like the ones she would make me every year. That's the best gift I've ever gotten. And I so appreciate it, Isla Ryder."

"I'm sorry I got so angry with you," I whisper, staring down at my half-eaten cake.

"I'm sorry I made you so angry," he says. "I said a lot of things that were out of line. I don't know you. I was wrong in making assumptions about you personally." He grimaces. "I didn't mean to hurt your feelings or imply anything about you or your family or your life. I'm sorry." Roman looks at me intently now. "I would just like to understand why you got so angry, what set you off, when you're ready... to tell me."

He gazes out through the darkened windows at the ocean as if intent on giving me space and time to answer without the added pressure of his stare.

My defenses shatter all at once. The vulnerability in his voice is disarming, a stark contrast to the confident swagger he usually projects. A pang of something unexpected—empathy, maybe—takes hold. I feel exposed, but unrestrained.

"I know what it's like to feel lost, to feel like you're playing a part, even if my performance is, normally, usually, pretty much always, except for that meltdown a few hours ago, one of absolute control and focused ambition, and not somewhat reckless charm like yours." My words are weighted with meaning.

"The thing is, what you do, like so many of my clients... it's a heavy price to pay for fame." The honesty surprises even me. "It's probably why I stay in the background, crafting someone else's narrative, trying to help them better navigate their famous world, and effectively hide from my own."

He nods slowly, still gazing out at the water and not at me. "Yeah. Fame is heavy. And lonely." Then, he turns back, his gaze searching my face, as if looking for a way into my soul. "What about you, Isla? Are you performing now? Or is this... *the real you?*"

The question is direct. My carefully constructed walls seem to sway with the intensity of the question and just the way he is looking at me.

The earthquake is coming. For me.

Am I performing? Always. Usually.

It's how I've survived on my own for almost the last decade. It's how I succeed professionally. But here, in the semi-darkness of this

Malibu beach house with champagne still thrumming through my veins, the lines feel blurred.

"Not performing. What you glimpsed earlier is the darkness I carry. There's just something so devastating in realizing I am all alone in this world, no matter how much I fill it up with strategies and tactics and plans. The aloneness of it all—the grief—still finds me. *Reminds me.*" I sigh big. "Oh my God, I'm just giving it all away."

And he's just sitting there, staring at me, taking it all in.

I stop talking and take a swig of champagne. And set my cake plate aside.

Stalling.

Need to.

"So yes, I think we all perform, to some extent, Roman, to try to outrun the broken parts. As a way of coping. Because, maybe, if we run fast enough, we won't feel the emptiness that is always so profound and stark, ready and waiting. But it's there. That's the truth. Grief is always trying to take hold of you and pull you into the abyss in the darkest of moments." I tap my fingers against the edge of the couch, a nervous habit I thought I'd outgrown. "The simple truth is, I'm just trying to hold on. And not drown."

My heart races. My mouth goes dry. "Public relations—my job—is my way of navigating the world. Surviving as best I can, which is perfectly executed most of the time, except for what you witnessed happen to me earlier on the beach. Sometimes, the grief catches up to me. For the most part, I think we just present the version of ourselves we want or allow people to see as a way to survive."

He leans in closer. The space between us shrinks to an alarming six inches of space. I can feel his breath on my lips. And surely, he already knows I'm holding mine now.

The air arcs between us like two currents meeting up, filled with unspoken tension, and this amazing magnetic pull I feel all the way to my core. This recurrent feeling of the commingling of selves and the transference of feelings between us happens all over again.

"But what about the version we don't allow people to see?" he murmurs, his voice low, intimate. "The one we keep hidden. The one that's... actually *real*?" His blue eyes search mine, intense and unwavering.

My breath catches. He's pushing, getting closer to the guarded parts of me I keep locked away. Parts I haven't shown anyone in years. Parts I certainly don't intend to show Roman Lysander.

But the champagne, the haven of this space, and the unexpected honesty in his gaze unravel me as if he's pulling the ribbon and undoing the bow.

It dawns on me, all at once, that resisting him, *this*, whatever this is between us, is futile.

"Maybe." My voice is barely audible above the waves outside the sliding glass doors. "Sometimes, the realest parts of ourselves are the ones we keep hidden, sometimes even from ourselves."

He leans in still further and inevitably reaches out. His fingers brush my forearm, a feather-light touch that sends heat racing through me, an undeniable visceral reaction.

My focus narrows still further to that single point of contact. The surrounding world fades away completely. There's just Roman and his touch.

"Or maybe... sometimes, we just need someone to help us find them. To actually *see* them," Roman says.

His eyes drop to my mouth. The unspoken question hangs between us, heavy and electric.

The sound of the ocean waves amplifies. The moonlight streaming through the tall windows intensifies in this particular moment.

It's just the two of us. No audience. No voyeurs watching us.

We're stripped bare of our public personas.

It's just us. Hollywood and Manhattan are facing something unexpected, something real, and something undeniable.

The champagne-fueled intimacy is intoxicating, dangerous, and startlingly romantic.

In the semi-darkness, his blue eyes grow more intense. He reaches out and gently traces the contours of my face. Just his touch sends a shiver through me, a deep tremor that has nothing to do with the cool night air flowing through the open sliding glass doors.

"Isla." My name is a husky whisper on his lips, heavy with want. His thumb strokes the side of my face, the touch sending sparks dancing across my skin.

Silence stretches, thick with anticipation, and charged with a longing that seems to spiral out of control. I lean into his touch.

And then he kisses me.

It's not gentle, not tentative, but an intense and powerful claim. I taste cake and champagne and something uniquely him.

For a moment, I'm frozen. I'm caught between pulling away and pulling him closer.

Then something breaks loose inside of me, and I kiss him back. Hard. Desperate.

My hands hold his face and then travel to his hair where I run my fingers through it, like I've wanted to all night. Then they drift down and feel the solid steel and warmth of his shoulders. He feels safe. He feels real.

The grief I carry recedes as this desire for him becomes all-consuming, where being this close to him fills up the emptiness inside of me. If just for a little while.

However temporary it might be, it is something I need from him. Something I must have.

His lips crash against mine with a force that steals my breath away. He is passionate and demanding, and my carefully constructed composure shatters like crystal thrown against granite stone.

Client.

Danger.

Mistake.

The alarms shriek in my head, useless against the tidal wave of adrenaline and something that terrifyingly feels like genuine desire. I respond instinctively, meeting his urgency, my hands finding the hard planes of his chest as if they have a will of their own.

This is madness.

This is professional suicide.

This is the baseball player all over again but amplified.

These raging thoughts flash, sharp and painful—the memory of Chad's betrayal, of losing control and having my vulnerability exploited, rushes back at me. It's the same reckless abandonment that destroyed my career momentum before.

No. But the protest dies unspoken and almost unacknowledged.

The champagne, the moonlight, the intense honesty he offered on the beach and while we were making his cake—*about being real*—the sheer, magnetic pull of him… it's a potent cocktail I haven't built enough immunity to. The fortress walls inside me, meticulously constructed from nine years of grief and the ashes of everyone I've ever lost, fractures under the pressure.

Mom. Dad. Tommy.

Everyone leaves. Everyone dies.

Or they betray you.

So why do I let him in?

Roman's hands are undoing my braid and running his fingers through the long strands of my hair, pulling me ever closer to him. His kiss deepens. It's possessive, demanding entry, and I grant it, acknowledging the surrender. My body ignites. Heat sears through my clothes like wildfire. His hand finds the small of my back, arching me against him, the undeniable proof of his arousal a stark reality against my stomach.

It's not detached analysis; it's pure, reckless impulse. The same impulse that got me into trouble with the baseball player, except this feels different. *Deeper. More dangerous.* He groans against my mouth, a low, feral sound that bypasses thought and goes straight to my nerve endings.

His mouth leaves mine, trailing fire down my neck. He pushes me back onto the soft leather of the sofa, his body a heavy, intoxicating weight. His hands slide to my hips, grinding against me. My body betrays me, warmth pooling ever lower. It's a traitorous response my brain cannot veto. His lips find mine again, swallowing my gasps for air.

He pulls back slightly, his breath ragged, his blue eyes stormy in the dim light.

"Isla," he whispers my name, rough with need. "Tell me to stop."

The words are there. *Stop. This is wrong. I can't.* But they catch in my throat. Looking at him, the unconcealed vulnerability warring with the desire on his face, mirrors something I keep locked so deep inside myself—the part that died with my family, the part that's been buried for nine years—that saying 'no' feels like I'm reinforcing the emotional walls I suddenly, desperately, want to tear down, if just for a little while.

Just once.

Just tonight.

Just him.

"Don't stop," I say, the words barely audible. It's surrender. It's permission. It's the most honest thing I've said in years.

He nods, a sharp, decisive movement, then cups my face, his gaze intense. He kisses me again, softer this time, yet somehow even more consuming.

Time dissolves. No past, no future, just the electric present.

His hands explore me further, finding the button of my leather jeans, the back zipper. His fingers brush my skin, tracing downwards with reverent precision. I moan when he finds the wet heat between my legs, moving rhythmically until an intense, involuntary orgasm rips through me like lightning splitting the night sky.

He pulls back, a bemused, almost awed smile touching his lips. He then strips off my leather jeans, tossing them aside. He adjusts my injured knee gently, the unexpected tenderness a sharp contrast to the storm of desire consuming both of us. The gesture is so careful, so protective, that my heart clenches painfully.

When was the last time someone took care of me?

When was the last time I let them?

We kiss again. His fingers find the edge of my lace underwear. He pauses, seeking permission as his gaze meets mine. I nod, a tiny betrayal of every rule I live by. He slips his fingers beneath the lace, exploring with a surprising gentleness that makes my heart ache. This isn't just physical. It's exposure. *Dangerous and terrifying.* He moves from me, shedding his shirt, his pants, and his dark boxer briefs.

He stops. "Condom." He curses under his breath. "Damn it."

"Taken care of," I whisper, the practical precaution a stark contrast to the emotional chaos.

Always prepared.

Always in control.

Except I'm not in control of anything right now.

He grins, that devastating Roman Lysander smile, now stripped of all artifice. This isn't the Hollywood heartthrob. This is just Roman, being open and real in wanting me. "Isla. I want you." He returns to me, sculpted muscle gleaming in the moonlight filtering through the glass doors. A fallen god. And I want him with a desperation that scares me. He lies partially on top of me and gently slides off my lace panties. His lips find my neck as his hand strokes my wetness, my legs parting instinctively as he enters me, slow at first, then building a rhythm that's both mesmerizing and demanding. I meet his thrusts. My body arches and begins chasing sensation, chasing ecstasy, chasing bliss, chasing joy.

This is what I've been running from. This connection. This feeling of being truly alive.

His eyes lock on mine, watching my reactions, absorbing every involuntary utterance, his own expression a mixture of fierce concentration and something achingly vulnerable. Our climax hits simultaneously, becoming a shattering wave that leaves us clinging to each other, breathless and gasping for air.

I feel him everywhere. In my skin, in my bones, in the hollow places where grief lives.

After. Silence descends, somewhat uncertain, laden with questions not uttered aloud. We lie intertwined, sharing the same erratic heartbeats that seem to synchronize as they slow down to a more natural rhythm. The intimacy between us is breached, openly shared, and having been answered.

The air remains charged with the unspoken enormity of what just transpired between us. Lost in thought, hope, even amazement that this thing we shared was so explosive, so intimate. *There are no words…*

Maybe that's the thing.

There are no words.

Eventually, Roman retrieves the bottle of Taittinger, pours two glasses, his movements economical even now.

He pulls me up and kisses me gently. "Upstairs," he murmurs, his voice husky.

He carefully leads me upstairs, holding me close as we ascend the long set of stairs to the master bedroom. Moonlight bathes the room in silver slats of light, while the lace curtains billow with the night's ocean breeze.

It looks like a scene from a movie I'd dissect, not star in. But here I am, the leading lady in my own destruction.

"Look at that view," I whisper, a pathetic attempt at distraction. "It's like something out of a film."

"The most beautiful view is right here," he says, his eyes never leaving my face.

I laugh a little. "That's such *a line.*"

He laughs, too. The sound is warm and genuine. "Maybe. But I *mean* it."

God help me, I believe him.

He sets the champagne flutes aside. His hands immediately find me again. He pulls me close, kissing me deeply before pulling back, his blue eyes dark with desire, still searching, still waiting, seeking permission, maybe even contemplating the idea of trust.

Trust. The word I've forgotten how to spell.

He pulls my Free People pearly top over my head and deftly unclasps my bra and drapes them over the chair by the dresser. I stand naked before him, feeling stripped bare in more ways than just one. Yet strangely empowered by the reverence I see in his gaze as he takes in every inch of me. No one has looked at me like this... *since never.*

He guides me to the bed with a reverence that makes my breath catch. His hands are gentle as he lays me down, the soft linens cool against my fevered skin. The moonlight streaming through the billowing curtains bathes both of us in silver, transforming this moment into something ethereal, almost dreamlike. His kisses are slow, deep, and languid. His hands roam, tracing curves. I follow with my own exploration of his amazing body.

His mouth finds mine again, and this time his kisses are different—slower, deeper, languid explorations that speak of worship rather than urgency. There's no rush now, no desperate hunger driving us forward. Instead, there's this deliberate savoring, as if he wants to memorize every sensation, every response. His hands begin their own careful exploration, tracing the curves of my body with the patience of an artist studying his masterpiece.

I follow his lead, my fingers mapping the sculpted planes of his chest, the defined ridges of his abdomen, marveling at the way his muscles respond to my touch. Every inch of him is perfectly crafted, like he was carved from marble by some Renaissance master.

Eventually, the sparks between us ignite slowly this time, building with the steady intensity of a fire that knows it has all night to burn. The hard length of him presses against my thigh, recovered and insistent evidence of his desire that sends heat pooling low in my belly. He moves lower, his mouth worshiping my breasts with a devotion that makes me arch against him. His tongue teases, drawing gasps from my lips that seem to echo in the moonlit room. His hand slips between my thighs, fingers stroking with that same reverent precision, building tension until I'm arching against him all over again, my body a live wire of sensation. My body responds, now insistent for fulfillment and the heady relief that comes with this amazing connection to him as he enters me again that we already discovered before, but feels deeper somehow, more profound at a soul level now.

We find that same hypnotic rhythm. His eyes remain locked on mine, witnessing my unraveling with an intensity that strips away every defense I've ever built. This isn't just sex—it's something far more dangerous. It's a connection forged with such reverence and intimacy that it seems to shake us both at a core level as we find release together, as we seemingly touch places at a soul level for us both.

Our hands find each other, fingers interlacing, and remain clasped as we move together. Our breaths are jagged as we both gasp for air, but they match in some peculiar synchronicity, and then even as our breaths slow down, they match in time. We find release together once more. It arrives with a completeness that leaves me breathless and wondering if this is what it means to feel truly alive again.

Serendipity.

I wonder if it would always be like this with him. And if a lifetime of such fulfilled wonder would ever be enough. Our coming together has this rightness to it I've never experienced before. I get lost in his ocean blue eyes that study me now in this quiet, introspective way.

What is he thinking?

He gazes at me for a long while with this shuttered look that doesn't quite reveal his feelings.

Is he in shock? Maybe. So am I. But then, he finally smiles.

He kisses my forehead with such reverence. It is its own brand of intimacy.

How it is possible that for a few precious suspended moments of time in being with him in this way that the hollowed-out space inside of me that grief normally creates and continually excavates with its massive emptiness suddenly feels infinitely whole and filled up? At least for a little while. How can that be?

This must be what it feels like to just let go and just be.

This is what I've been afraid of feeling my entire adult life...

This kind of bliss. So all-consuming. So massive. So joyful.

The loss of it is going to be catastrophic...

On some level, I'm already planning for that because it feels inevitable.

He pulls my body into his, laying claim, and folds his arms around me. His body spoons mine. He kisses the side of face and whispers my name with such reverence that it brings tears to my eyes. His breathing deepens. His arms relax but still hold on to me. Soon, exhaustion claims him. His breathing evens out behind me.

Sleep offers him escape.

It offers me... *nothing.*

I'm suspended in the in-between state of sleep and consciousness, but then I hear the mantle clock downstairs chime four times. Suddenly, I'm fully awake as reality crashes in on me. My head pounds. My knee throbs. My carefully constructed world lies in ruins all around me, just like the wreckage of that plane nine years ago.

What. Have. I. Done?

The familiar void opens beneath me, the same black hole that swallowed my family, which swallowed my former life, which threatens to swallow everything I care about now and have worked so hard to keep and maintain. *Powers & Winston. Kimberley. Vendetta. Ryder & Harper. My life. All compromised. For this.*

For him.

Roman sleeps right behind me, his leg possessively draped over my left hip, breathing softly against my hair. *Zeus in repose.*

Utterly magnificent.

My body aches—a dull reminder of a recklessness I haven't allowed myself in years. Not since the baseball player. Not since I learned that mixing business with pleasure has the potential to destroy everything you've worked for. For a moment, I feel nothing at all. The numbness is a welcome respite. It won't be long before the familiar recrimination floods in, cold and sharp, painting reality in all the vivid colors that final judgment wields.

This is how it starts. This is how you lose everything. Again.

Self-doubt settles in on me like fog rolling in from the ocean. I'm ready for the long-ass review of self-recrimination and the thorough root-cause-analysis of *'how do we fix this, so it doesn't happen again?'* scenario.

Go ahead, fix this, Isla.

Control this.

Like you controlled your parents' plane from crashing.

Like you controlled Chad from cheating.

Like you control anything that matters.

I'm walking a tightrope over the same abyss that claimed my family, and I've just cut my own safety line. One wrong step and the fall below will destroy everything I've built from the ashes of my former life.

I ease away from him, silent as a thief, and escape to the bathroom. The mirror reflects my disgrace: swollen lips, flushed skin, and green eyes wide with panic.

This isn't a random hookup.

This is Roman Lysander.

My client's son.

My project.

The walking personification of everything I swore *to manage*, not get involved with and literally detonate.

I rip off the bandage at my knee, welcoming the pain that comes with it. *Physical pain is easier. Physical pain makes sense.*

I shower, scrubbing my skin, a futile attempt to wash away the evidence of his exploring hands and sensuous mouth. But I can't wash away the way he looked at me, the way he said my name, the way he made me feel *seen* for the first time in a long while. And truth be told, since we're here, looking in the mirror... No guy has ever seen me the way Roman Lysander just did.

And that's the real danger.

I apply Neosporin and a new set of bandages with clinical precision. Teeth brushed. Hair finger combed. I find my black silk robe, tie the belt extra tight, ruefully acknowledge it's a flimsy shield against the fallout that is coming. For me.

Back in the bedroom, my stealthiness is pointless.

He's awake, propped on an elbow, watching me. Those blue eyes, dark and intense, hold a question. Curiosity? Assessment? He's impossible to read, and that terrifies me more than his charm ever could.

"You're awake," I say, my voice tight. "Sorry. Didn't mean to wake you." *Lame. So, lame.*

The abyss of my teenage grief yawns open, threatening to pull me back into that hollow place where nothing matters, where everyone you love disappears without warning, where survival means never getting close enough to lose someone again.

The abyss will come for me, anyway. It's only a matter of time. Ironic.

Playtime. Respite. Whatever this was. Is over.

Clearly.

"Isla?" His voice is low, questioning. "Are you okay? You seem... distant."

Distant. Like the space between here and heaven, where my family lives without me.

"I'm fine." Cool. Collected. The professional mask snaps back into place, however fractured. I avoid his gaze, focusing on the rumpled sheets, the damning evidence everywhere. "Just fine."

He sits up, his movements fluid, drawing my eyes to the bare expanse of his chest.

Distraction. Dangerous.

"You don't *look fine*." The hint of amusement I *cannot* tolerate right now touches his voice and his features.

"Well, I am. Fine. Perfectly fine. Absolutely, one hundred percent fine." I'm babbling now, the words tumbling out in a nervous cascade that betray me completely. "Why wouldn't I be fine? It's all *fine*."

He raises an eyebrow, clearly not buying it. "That's a lot of 'fines' for someone who's actually *fine*."

Time to deploy the strategy.

Containment.

Denial.

Survival.

"This." I gesture vaguely between us, the words clipped and sharp. "This *cannot happen again. Ever.* In fact, *it didn't happen.* That's the story we're going with. That's the narrative."

He raises an eyebrow. "Didn't *happen*? Isla, I'm pretty sure it did. *Twice.*"

Logic.

Damn him.

"It was the party. The champagne. Your… birthday." I tick the points off in an attempt to minimize and trivialize them. "You walked me home. We made the cake. End of story. That's how we play it." My tone aims for finality, for the control I no longer possess. "We're good, right?" Casual. Nonchalant. Another meaningless Hollywood hookup kind of tone. *As if they just sell those. As if I know how those actually work.*

He's so much more dangerous than the baseball player.

To me.

"Right," he echoes slowly. "It happens." His gaze is direct. Pointed. Relentless. Steady. Introspective even. Then, smirky. Playful. Charming. The prince of Hollywood is pleased. He had a great time.

So, did I. But *that* is beside the point.

He doesn't get it.

How could he?

He's Roman Lysander. Life is grand. Full of riches and fun. Sex with a stranger is as common as choosing ice cream flavors. Did you want some for breakfast? What a golden day. Another golden day for a golden boy. Hollywood's finest and best. 'The Sexiest Man Alive,' three years running. You can have whatever you want, whatever your heart desires, whenever you want it. Lots of ever's...

He's never lost everything that mattered. Well, his mom, but he still has his dad. He has family. I have no one.

He's never had to rebuild himself from nothing.

He's never had to learn that love is just another way for eventual loss.

I force myself to meet his eyes. "Look, Roman." Calling him Mr. Lysander feels like all kinds of ridiculousness now. "Whatever this was, it was a lapse. For both of us. Let's just forget it. And move on. Professionally."

A slow, knowing smile spreads across his face. *Arrogance.*

Infuriating.

And deeply unsettling.

"*Forget it,* Isla?" His voice drops, laced with something darker than sarcasm. "I don't think I'll be *forgetting this* anytime soon."

He gets out of bed, graceful, and entirely too comfortable being naked in my personal and private space, and heads to the en suite bathroom. Soon enough, I hear the shower running.

I sit on the bed and contemplate the wreckage. Recrimination settles in, practically announcing aloud how wrong this encounter was. The judgment is direct and harsh. Just how reckless and irresponsible can one actually be? New lows have been reached. So much worse than the baseball player.

Isla. Really?

After everything, you've learned about mixing business with pleasure.

After everything, you've learned about letting people in.

"Great job, Isla," I mutter to myself, running a hand through my tangled hair. "Spectacular work. Truly brilliant strategy. Sleep with the client. That always ends well."

The bitter sarcasm tastes like ashes in my mouth, but it's a familiar defense mechanism, one I've relied on since I was seventeen and had to learn to face the world alone. If I can mock myself first, maybe it won't hurt so much when others do it.

But no one has ever made me feel the way he just did.

No one has ever seen through me like that.

No one has ever...

I cut off the thought before it can fully form. That path leads to madness.

Twenty minutes later, he emerges, toweling his hair, water droplets clinging to his skin. The naked god surveys his conquest. *Me.*

"Nice shampoo," he comments, tossing the towel aside.

Naked, undeterred, comfortable with his amazing body.

He heads down the stairs while I gingerly follow. He gathers his clothes from the living room floor, all the remnants of our first encounter. I silently mirror him, collecting my own discarded items—leather, sequins, lace—accusations in fabric and silver strappy sandals.

We return to the master bedroom. He dresses unhurriedly, while my heart hammers against my ribs. Regret wars with the acknowledgement of the uncontrollable exhilaration of profound feelings that terrify me on so many levels that I've lost count.

It must be how you feel when you're actually falling; those precious seconds in the air where there is not a fucking thing you can do about it, anyway. Fait accompli.

Meanwhile, on the Isla-must-outwardly-garner-complete-control front, I realize two things:

He hasn't agreed to my terms.

He probably never agrees to anything.

"Thank you for walking me home." I aim for the polite dismissal and diplomacy like we're working out a peace agreement between two warring factions. "I probably would have stumbled into the ocean on my own." A rueful half-smile touches my lips.

"Yeah, the ocean's dangerous." Roman buttons up his white linen shirt. He looks up, his intense gaze pinning me. "Maybe other things are, too." He looks directly at me and shakes his head from side to side. "Anyway. Thanks for making me... the birthday cake, Isla Ryder."

The charm is back but edged with something else.

Anger? Resentment? Hurt?

"It's best this way," I say with diplomatic insistence. But desperation creeps in, too. "Pretending it didn't happen. It's the only way."

"*Pretending* it didn't happen," he repeats flatly. His jaw tightens, his eyes narrow. "That's your *best strategy*? That's all this was?"

I wrap my arms around myself, building back up my emotional walls as we talk this through. "It's not like that. It was more than that. I..."

The realization hits me like a physical blow.

I *care* about him.

Actually, care. About him.

More than I've cared about anyone since my family died.

That's the real danger here.

"Roman. We cannot be... The world doesn't work that way," I finally say. "I am not... I can't do both. It's best this way."

For whom? For you? For the scared 17-year-old girl who's been hiding inside you for nine years too afraid to love anyone?

"Right. Whatever you say. You're the image maker. I'm just the project," he says without heat, but it stings like a slap.

He runs his hand through his damp hair. That famous smile suddenly appears. It's dazzling, practiced, and completely hollow. "Don't worry, Ms. Isla Ryder. Your professional reputation remains intact. Wouldn't want to tarnish the company brand of Ryder & Harper Communications LA right out of the gate."

"This isn't..." I start but stop myself. *It's best he thinks that. That's easier.*

It's about survival. It's about not losing anyone else.

It's about the fact that everyone I've ever loved has left me.

"I get it. Last night was just another Hollywood hookup. It happens." He shrugs with practiced nonchalance. His own emotional armor slides back into place like the chamber to a lock.

But the way his eyes avoid mine tells a different story.

And he's not used to being the one dismissed or sent home.

Neither of us is being honest right now.

We're both retreating to our separate corners, intent on caring for our open emotional wounds incurred from this encounter.

Convincing ourselves that it didn't happen. Well, me anyway.

We go downstairs again. I box up his cake in a plastic container and put it in the black bag he brought. "You should have the cake. It's your birthday present. From me." I shrug with nonchalance.

He gets this stormy look as he gazes at me. I'm not sure if he is angry or insulted by my gesture.

"How thoughtful," he says, his voice dripping with sarcasm. "A cake and a memory we're pretending never happened. Best birthday *ever.*"

I flinch at the acid in his tone. "Roman, I—"

"Save it," he cuts me off. "I get the message, loud and clear." He heads for the sliding doors to the beach. "Paparazzi," Roman explains curtly at my questioning look. "They're everywhere. All the fucking time. You think you know everything about me? About my life? Try living under the microscope." He shakes his head again. A flash of anger and frustration crosses his beautiful features. "Forget it. You don't get it."

I don't get it? I don't get having your life dissected by strangers? Having every mistake broadcast for the world to see?

Try losing your entire family and having the media turn it into entertainment for the nightly news reel.

Try rebuilding your life while everyone watches and waits for you to fail.

"I understand more than you think," I say, the words slipping out before I can stop them. "About having your life torn apart in public. About being a spectacle for others to consume."

He pauses, something shifting in his expression. For a moment, I think he might ask what I mean, might want to know more. The possibility terrifies and validates me in equal measure.

But the moment passes, and his mask slips back into place.

He pauses at the door, turning back. The intensity in his eyes is startling. "See you around, Isla Ryder." His words are an alarming challenge, a gauntlet he's thrown down. "And don't worry." The ghost of that arrogant smile returns. "I won't forget a thing."

And then he's gone, leaving only the sound of ocean waves and the faint scent of his expensive cologne.

The silence slams into me like a physical force. The weight of it—the recklessness, the unexpected gift of pleasure, and the utter catastrophe of our intimate encounter—crashes down on me.

He's a disaster. A walking, talking, devastatingly attractive PR nightmare I just slept with.

But I'm a disaster, too.

And he saw it. He saw the hairline fractures beneath the control. He saw the scared 17-year-old girl hiding behind the polished professional. *He knows.*

The realization is alarming. This wasn't just champagne, cake, and chemistry. It felt... *real.*

More real than anything I've felt since my family died.

More real than anything I've allowed myself to feel. Ever.

I can feel myself unraveling in real time as the cognizance surfaces. I care about him on a level I have never felt before—not even with the baseball player, not even with the few men I've allowed close enough to me in the distant past.

Oh no.

And it has irrevocably complicated everything.

My mission. My boundaries. My carefully guarded heart.

Roman Lysander isn't just a project anymore. He's a threat. A challenge. And something else I cannot name but feel deep inside.

The real Roman could make me forget why I build these walls in the first place.

The real Roman could make me believe in forever again.

The real Roman could destroy me completely when he leaves.

Because they always leave.

I pick up the remnants of our impromptu celebration—the cake plates and the champagne flutes—my hands shaking slightly as I move through the motions of cleaning up. It's what I've always done after chaos: restore order, erase evidence, rebuild walls.

But as I wash the dishes, the water scalding my hands; I know this time is different. The game, I realize with sickening clarity that invades all of me, has changed irrevocably. And I have absolutely no idea how to play it now.

Control is gone.

The emotional walls I've built are not holding.

There are fractures everywhere.

Because, like he said.

It happened.

And nothing—not denial, not professional boundaries, not even my well-honed survival instincts—can change that fundamental truth.

I've spent nine years learning how to exist without truly living, how to function without feeling. Roman Lysander just showed me what I've been missing, and I'm terrified I'll never be able to go back to the carefully constructed emptiness I've called a life.

I press my forehead against the cool glass of the window, watching as the first hints of dawn appear on the horizon. The world keeps turning, indifferent to my personal cataclysm. In a few days, probably by Monday, I'll have to face him again—this man who's seen through every defense I uphold, who scaled all of my emotional walls and got through and touched parts of me I thought were dead and buried.

And I have no idea how to survive it.

CHAPTER 17

love, save the empty

Isla Ryder

"Love, Save The Empty" - Erin McCarley
"Borrowed Time" - A Fine Frenzy
"Hurricane" – MS MR
"Fresh Laundry" – Allie X

Early Friday Morning 6:00 a.m.

I'M JARRED AWAKE BY THE CALIFORNIA SUNSHINE. Beams of light slice across my face with cruel precision, and I cry out with a groan that is ripped from somewhere deep inside of me. I forgot to close the drapes along the East wall of the master bedroom. Draping an arm across my forehead shields my eyes, but consciousness drags me up to the surface, anyway. The digital clock on the nightstand glows an accusatory 6:30 a.m. and 9:30 a.m. in New York.

My body can't decide which time zone it belongs to anymore.

My mind is shattered, too. Oh yeah, we lost that completely. My mind is stuck in the Roman Alexander Lysander time zone.

He dominates every waking moment of every thought I have.

My head throbs—a dull, persistent ache that radiates from my temples outward. The price of Taittinger champagne, French 75 cocktails, and catastrophically poor judgment.

"No, no, no," I whisper into the empty room, rolling onto my side and burying my face in the pillow that still smells faintly of him. I scream into it, the sound muffled but satisfying in its primal outburst.

The ocean waves roar outside, indifferent to my personal, emotional crisis.

I slept with Roman Lysander.

The thought hits me with an almost physical force.

I, Isla Ryder—the calculated, composed, utterly professional PR strategist—succumbed to champagne and charm and those devastatingly blue eyes.

And the potent honesty from him. At least on the beach.

Until things went sideways. My nuclear rage.

His ignoring of it altogether? That, too.

And then, with the cake and champagne picnic in my living room, what's a girl supposed to do?

It's Roman Lysander. Would any girl in that situation actually say 'no' to him?

Me.

But I gave in to the very type of man I've sworn to avoid. The notorious Hollywood 'bad boy'. My client's son. My project.

"What is exactly wrong with me?" The question hangs in the air, unanswered even when I ask it aloud.

Everything. The waves whisper back.

Yeah, thanks.

I push myself upright, wincing as my body registers various complaints. My knee throbs beneath the bandage. My muscles ache in places I'd forgotten existed. My head hurts with this vice-like headache that seems without end. And my heart hurts because it seems to be involved in a new and unexpected way than ever before.

I'm still wearing the black silk robe I vaguely remember putting on after my middle-of-the-night shower—my futile attempt to wash away evidence that cannot be erased.

The sheets tangle around my thighs, and I yank them away with sudden violence, standing too quickly. The room tilts. I steady myself against the bedpost, waiting for equilibrium to return.

Quick assessment: running on fumes. Three hours of sleep, maybe four in total in the last 76 hours. Not enough food—when did I last eat something substantial? The sandwich Roman gave me yesterday. The cake at his party? The slice of cake he gave me later, his eyes impossibly soft in the dim light of my living room after my tirade against him. And obviously, entirely too much Roman Lysander altogether. *A given.*

"This can't be happening," I whisper, pressing my palms against my temples.

My heart races erratically beneath my ribs. The panicked bird, again, trapped in a cage, desperate to get out and fly away.

The PR strategist in me immediately calculates the professional damage—reputation decimated, credibility shattered, career potentially ruined. But another part, a part I've kept carefully buried, remembers the way his fingers traced my collarbone, how he whispered my name like a prayer.

"Stop it," I hiss aloud. "He's a client. The client's son. Your *project.*"

My stomach lurches unexpectedly. *Perfect.* A headache, a racing pulse, and now nausea. I can't afford to be sick. Not with Samantha flying in this morning, the office setup pending, and the entire Lysander rehabilitation project hanging in the balance.

And yet, his voice echoes in my memory: *"I see you, Isla. Not the image maker. You."*

And that terrifies me more than any professional consequence ever could.

Roman.

His name alone sends an electric current through me—part dread, and part something else I refuse to name. His face materializes in my mind: that devastating smile, those beautiful blue eyes that saw too much, and the vulnerability that flashed beneath his practiced charm.

Stop thinking about him.

Order given.

We're not able to follow.

I make my way downstairs, the smooth travertine stairs cold beneath my bare feet. I focus on that sensation, grounding myself in the physical world instead of the emotional chaos threatening to overwhelm me.

Coffee. I need coffee, more than I need oxygen, right now.

The kitchen reveals salvation: a gleaming Nespresso machine with a steamer attachment. Soon, a steaming latte warms my hands, its rich aroma a small comfort in a morning that already feels almost impossible to navigate.

I lean against the counter, looking out at the Pacific. The waves roll in, ceaseless and hypnotic. There's something reassuring in their constancy. The ocean remains unchanged and timeless, while my carefully constructed world has effectively shattered.

Last night wasn't a dream. It wasn't a nightmare, either, if I'm being brutally honest with myself. It was real—visceral, and electric, and frighteningly authentic.

"Stop it." I press my fingertips against my temples. "Just stop."

I'm the strategist. The level-headed one. The fixer. The *image maker*, as Roman called me last night. Always in control. Except when I'm not. Except when I'm throwing caution and professional ethics to the wind for a few hours of reckless pleasure with a client.

Client's son, my mind corrects automatically. As if that makes all the difference.

Other titles now clamor in my head, an unwelcome chorus: *Fool. Amateur. Nonprofessional. Heiress.*

The last one stings. I've spent my adult life outrunning that label —*heiress*—the poor little rich girl who lost her family and inherited a fortune. The girl who doesn't need to work but chooses to anyway, playing at careers while the safety net of family money always waits in the wings in nicely diversified investment accounts.

Like money solves everything.

But it doesn't buy a family. Or replace one.

It doesn't buy love of any kind.

They don't know how hard I've worked. How I've earned every client, every success. How I've built my reputation, year after year. How I've pushed away the grief and channeled everything into my career.

And now I've risked it all for what? One night with Roman Lysander?

"It was one night," I say aloud, testing the words. "A mistake. It happens." The justification sounds hollow, even to me.

It wasn't just the champagne or his undeniable charm. It was something more insistent—a loneliness I keep buried, a yearning for connection I rarely acknowledge and never allow myself to feel or want. For a few stolen hours, I let myself feel something real. And that terrifies me more than any professional fallout.

Because what if it isn't temporary? What if Roman has created some kind of permanence inside me? Like a spell or a curse. What if now that I know that feeling of being wanted, being needed, being... desired? *Loved? No.*

And now I can't change back?

Oh...

"And that's a problem," I whisper to the empty kitchen.

I finish my coffee in mechanical sips, staring out at the Pacific. The rhythmic roar of waves gradually works its magic, calming the storm inside of me.

The world didn't end.

The ocean keeps rolling in, rolling out.

I can fix this. I will fix this.

Equilibrium seeps back in, pushing back against the malaise of regret and exhaustion.

"Another shower," I decide aloud. A warm, sanity-restoring shower to wash away the mental fog.

I climb the stairs slowly, my knee protesting with each step. In the bathroom, I turn the water on hot, strip off the robe, being careful not to get the bandage wet.

The warmth relaxes my tense muscles, clearing away some of the mental haze. But his scent lingers in the misty air and in my memory—that expensive cologne mixed with something uniquely him. I close my eyes, seeking respite, but his smile flashes behind my eyelids, bright, burning, and knowing.

I open my eyes, half-expecting to see him standing there, like a hologram. He does seem imprinted on me somehow, inescapable.

"Oh my God," I breathe, leaning my forehead against the cool tile. "Isla, get it together."

I scrub my skin as if I can erase the memory of his touch.

It doesn't work.

Back in the bedroom, I dry off quickly. I swallow a double dose of Advil to alleviate the headache and the throbbing pain from the cut. It's definitely more painful today. I attribute it to our... activities. The thought brings an unwelcome flush to my cheeks.

Damage control.

That's the mantra now.

Professionally, personally, in every way possible. Damage control.

Compartmentalize. Separate last night from today.

The professional mission, the image rehabilitation plan, must take precedence.

I apply my makeup with practiced precision. Foundation to even out my complexion. Concealer to hide the shadows beginning to form under my eyes because I really haven't slept all that much since Tuesday. And now, it's Friday.

A subtle contour to sharpen my cheekbones. Neutral eyeshadow, mascara, a touch of blush, and a matte rose lipstick. Armor, layer by layer.

My hair is next—brushed smooth and pulled back into a severe chignon. The *I-mean-business* look. Professional. Controlled. The opposite of the disheveled, passionate woman who came undone in Roman Lysander's arms last night.

I stare at my reflection, searching for traces of that woman. She's hidden now, buried beneath carefully applied cosmetics and disciplined hair. *Good.*

I stand before the closet, staring blankly at my meticulously arranged wardrobe. What does one wear after career suicide? Something that says, "I definitely didn't sleep with Roman Lysander last night?" I touch fabric after fabric, rejecting options with increasing desperation.

As I dress, I imagine rebuilding the walls around my heart, brick by brick, until last night becomes just another mistake locked safely away.

I settle on white lingerie—a silent rebellion against the darkness of last night's choices—and the delicate pink lace camisole that carries a hint of softness beneath the steel. The crème-colored power pantsuit from Happy Isles, my favorite vintage haunt in Manhattan, completes the look. I add white patent stilettos that click authoritatively against the travertine floor.

Standing before the mirror, I examine the effect. The pastel pink camisole adds a delicate touch, but the suit and shoes scream power. Control. A small smile finally touches my lips.

"Okay," I say to my reflection. "You've got this."

But do I?

The question lingers as I descend the stairs again, each step a reminder from my body of last night's extracurricular activities. In the kitchen, I make another latte, stronger this time, and force myself to eat a piece of toast. My stomach rebels, but I persist. I need some kind of fuel for the day ahead. I climb the stairs again, deciding I should pack an overnight bag and plan on staying in town at The Harland apartments.

Then, contemplation arrives. Should I tell Samantha? About Roman? About what followed?

Samantha knows me better than anyone. She'll see through any pretense and sense the shift in me. And yet, the thought of admitting what happened—of saying it aloud—makes my chest constrict painfully.

No, I decide. Not yet. Maybe not ever. Some secrets need to stay buried.

I lean against the bathroom counter and stare in the mirror, suddenly overwhelmed by the magnitude of the day ahead. Meeting up with Samantha. Setting up our new office. Beginning the real work with Roman. *After* sleeping with him.

Thoughts of Roman consume me on a whole new level. So, I allow myself five minutes. Just five minutes to *feel* it all.

The way his hands cradled my face like I was something precious to behold and care for. The way his fingers gently traced the contours of my body and the way his hands spanned my waist from each side where his fingers touched, as if memorizing the shape of me for later.

The way he slowed down when I experienced sudden pain from the cut, his fingers tracing the bandage on my knee with a tenderness that made my breath catch. *"Tell me if this hurts,"* he murmured, and I did—because for the first time in my life, someone actually *wanted* to know.

Five minutes to remember how he watched me—not just with hunger, but with *reverence*, as if I were the only woman in the world. The way his breath hitched when I arched beneath him, his voice rough with wonder when he whispered, *"You're incredible."* As if *I* were the only one who'd ever bewitched him in that way.

Five minutes to admit that I've never felt anything like it—the way he *moved*, slow and deliberate, like he was savoring every second, every gasp, and every shiver he engendered within me. The way he kissed me like he was drowning, and I was the air he needed. The way he *held* me afterward, his heart beating wildly against my skin, his fingers tangled in my hair as if he never wanted to let me go.

Five minutes to acknowledge that I *liked* it. No—I *loved* it. The way he made me feel *alive*, like every nerve ending was lit up as if burning from the inside out. The way he laughed when I teased him, the way his eyes darkened when I bit my lip to keep from crying out, the way he *saw* me—not as the PR strategist, not as the heiress, but as the woman at the beach who shared a love for the movie, *Pride and Prejudice,* who had raged at him, and yet, he didn't hold it against me.

Five minutes to remember the way he said my name—not like a question, not like a demand, but like a *promise*. As if I was something he'd been waiting for.

Five minutes to admit that maybe, just maybe, Samantha was right at The Ophelia Lounge when she told me to *"loosen up and have fun."*

Because for the first time in my life, I *did*. And it was *glorious*.

The timer in my head goes off.

Five minutes are up.

I straighten my shoulders, smooth imaginary wrinkles from my suit, and tuck the memories away. They go into a mental box labeled "Never Again," sealed tight and pushed to the darkest recesses of my mind.

Because nothing good can come of this. Because I've spent nine years building walls around my heart for a reason. Because everyone I've ever loved has left me, one way or another. And I have to prepare for that. Like always.

I check my appearance one final time in the bathroom mirror. The professional mask is firmly in place now. Isla Ryder, PR strategist. Image maker. Not the woman who came undone in Roman Lysander's arms last night.

"Today is day one," I tell my reflection firmly. "Last night never happened."

The lie settles uncomfortably in my chest, but I ignore it. I need to develop a clear strategy for working with Roman professionally after what happened. We'll need boundaries—explicit, unbreakable ones. Perhaps I should limit our one-on-one meetings, insist on Samantha's presence whenever possible. I'll need to craft talking points for our first post-encounter meeting, maintain professionalism without revealing awkwardness.

"You've got this," I tell myself firmly. "You are Isla Ryder. You fix impossible situations for a living."

But a small, traitorous voice whispers from that locked mental box:

But who will fix you?

CHAPTER 18

la di die

Isla Ryder

"la di die" - Nessa Barrett, jxdn (feat. Jaden Hossler)
"Paper Love" - Allie X
"Cornflake Girl" - Tori Amos
"Blood In The Cut"- K. Flay
"Pretty When You Cry" - Lana Del Rey

Friday Morning 7:30 a.m.

I SLOWLY MAKE MY WAY DOWN THE STAIRS, dragging the roller bag carefully behind me, vaguely thinking I should have heard from Samantha by now. Her plane landed a few hours ago.

Where's my iPhone?

I race through the entire house looking for my iPhone and my black sequined clutch as impending doom begins to set in.

Upstairs. Downstairs.

Twice.

My *find-my-phone* app on my iWatch is not working because my iPhone is *not here.*

I sit on my stairs in complete defeat, the morning light casting long shadows across the entryway. After a moment's reflection, it dawns on me where my iPhone, my passport ID, my favorite lipstick, and my black sequined clutch are right this minute. The clutch containing all my lifelines is on the fireplace mantle at Roman Lysander's beach house.

This is a problem.

Why?

I wasn't planning on seeing him today. I was going to stay at The Harland apartment in West Hollywood all weekend and practice avoidance and figure out my strategy with all of this. My rollaway suitcase sits in the entryway, already packed for that promised weekend of restoration, where my standard operating procedure is to figure this all out and finesse my way through it.

That's the plan.

But I need my iPhone to do all of that.

Oh, I am so off my game again today.

The quiet ticking of the wall clock seems to mock me. I press my fingertips against my temples, trying to massage away the headache that still plagues me that seems to be without end.

What do I do now?

A subtle knock at my front door takes me out of my reverie and instantly restores a semblance of *actual joy*. Awesome. Samantha's here. She probably tried calling me from the airport and made the thirty-six-mile drive to check on me. She would do something like that. Commandeer transportation and head on out.

"Yay, you're here!" I yank open the front door with a gleeful smile for Samantha Harper, my best friend and wingman. "Samantha, thank God!"

And there he is.

Roman Lysander holds two steaming cups of Starbucks' finest coffee with my black sequined clutch slung over one of his still extremely attractive shoulders. *Cute.*

"Not Samantha." Roman laughs. An easy laugh. A guy without a care in the world. *Apparently.*

He steps into my entryway.

"But I love the enthusiastic greeting that you save for your wingman, but not for me," he teases. "She called your iPhone, which I answered, and she told me you love lattes. Here's yours: a grande latte, double shot espresso, 2% milk, extra hot, a dash of cinnamon, and a touch of vanilla. Just the way you like it, according to Samantha Harper." He hands me mine with that damn winning smile of his.

I pause, taking a moment to absorb this unexpected development. The scent of fresh coffee rises between us, momentarily grounding me.

"Thank you?" I faintly ask in question form. I take the hot cup of coffee from him, silently appreciative of the coffee sleeve because it is so damn hot.

"And here's your purse." Roman grins as he slips it off his left shoulder and carefully arranges it onto mine. "You left it on the fireplace mantel at my place."

A grand gesture.

Completely unexpected.

Completely not a part of the *'nothing happened'* plan that I came up with earlier.

And he never agreed to, actually.

"Thank you," I say demurely.

Coffee is exactly what my pounding head needs more of. But the delivery method by Roman Lysander himself? It completely throws me off balance. I blink, momentarily stunned, and fall silent.

Is this some kind of Hollywood power play of his?

Some alpha male dominance display disguised as a grand gesture?

What *is* he playing at?

Nothing happened.

That's still the game plan…

Unsure how to handle this surprising move by him, I step back, stand to one side, and let him in all the way. My publicist brain automatically kicks into gear. I quickly scan the street beyond his broad shoulders, instinctively looking for paparazzi and their cameras lurking in the bushes, but there are none. *Surprisingly.*

Maybe he's not as reckless as I thought. Or maybe he's just playing it very, very smart. *With me.*

"I walked the beach," he says, as if reading my mind. "You know, carrying lattes and a woman's forgotten purse with her most precious items. Her iPhone, especially. You really need a better password, Isla. 6-5-4-3-2-1 is too easy even for a thief who is not very good at math or at counting backwards to figure out." He laughs at his own joke, while I am busy calculating what all he may have seen on my phone.

My whole life is on there.

Take your pick.

Like Austen's Elizabeth Bennet discovering Darcy's letter, I feel exposed—my digital life potentially laid bare. If he had taken some time, and okayed snooping in that somewhat entitled mind of his, he would have seen everything I care about, including things I don't any longer.

Chad Jameson, for one. Photos of him I kept and shouldn't have.

He steps through my dining room and then on into my living room and glances around with a casual air that probably takes hours to cultivate.

"Don't worry, I only came to the front door because I didn't want to scare you by just showing up beachside at your sliding glass doors. But no one saw me."

"What a peach." My voice drips with as much sarcasm as I can muster, which, admittedly, isn't much this early.

I draw a slow breath, reconsidering my tone. "Sorry," I start again. "Thanks for the coffee and for bringing my clutch back and all my stuff inside," I say, because manners, even with Hollywood 'bad boys', still matter. "Not really a morning person. Still on East Coast time. And, uh, I didn't sleep very well."

Understatement of the year.

"That's a lot of information for a non-morning person." He rewards me with that infuriatingly charming white smile. *Again.*

He sets the empty cardboard coffee tray down on my glass dining table after retrieving his own latte. His blue eyes are fixed on me. A hint of amusement dances within their depths.

He takes a few steps closer to me, and I reflexively raise a hand, not quite ready to smack him, but ready to ward that smile off of his handsome face, still alarmingly beautiful to gaze upon, even at half past seven in the morning.

He's quick, though, having already set down his coffee next to mine, which I placed on the kitchen island. He steps back, holding up his hands in mock surrender.

"Careful, princess," he teases. That husky voice of his is a low rumble that vibrates right through me. "I'm trying to be nice here, with the grand gesture and all, in returning your lifelines, including your iPhone, and I'm guessing here, your *favorite* black sequined clutch."

I consider his words, grab the coffee again, feeling the warmth of the coffee cup against my palm. The sensation grounds me.

"Yes, to all of that. Grand gesture though, that's a bit of stretch, no? You didn't leave here on the best of terms. *With me.* Change of heart? What brought that on?" I cop an attitude for no reason at all.

I am playing with fire.

I can see it by the way he is looking at me, first in surprise, but then this angry glint returns to his baby blues.

"Like I said, trying to be *nice* here, and I figured you'd be in a panic by now over your missing iPhone. It's been ringing so much I had to put it on *silent.*"

I feel my face flush, which extinguishes my cool factor play all at once. "True. I was in a bit of a panic about five minutes ago." I affect a smile. "Sorry, I'm cranky. Got up early, and the self-talk about all of this hasn't been working on me. Like at all."

I bite my lip just so I'll stop over sharing with him. I try again. "To what do I owe this grand gesture, Roman?" I force another smile. "I mean, aside from the obvious coffee delivery and my iPhone and clutch purse delivery, of course."

"Your passport ID, too. Don't forget that."

My smile fades. "Wait a minute. What *exactly* did you say to Samantha?"

"I told her you'd left your phone and your purse at my place. I told her I was going to drop it off at Julia Winston's since I live so close," he teases. "And I asked her how you take your coffee since I was at the Starbucks drive-through. She told me. And that's it. That's all I said, although she had to repeat your coffee order so I could write it all down. I'm not implying you are high maintenance or anything." He gets this wide smile again and then shrugs with nonchalance.

"Imply away."

"I think I'll leave it there," he says, winking at me.

I finally pick up the coffee he's brought me again, blow on it because it's still steaming hot, and take a tentative sip. I instantly feel the warmth of it, a welcome sensation in my suddenly cold and clammy hands. And he just watches me do it.

"Thank you. This tastes great. Just the way I like it."

"You're welcome." He's got a different glint going on in his eyes now, as if he is busy making plans to pick up where we left off last night and start again. The sexual tension rises between us without either of us having to say anything.

This will not do…

I need to steer this conversation, wrench back control of it, before he runs with this whole *grand gesture* charade and turns it into some twisted morning-after rom-com scene.

We need to decide, right here, right now, how we are going to play this morning-after encounter, before things get out of hand. Because ignoring it? It is not an option with Roman Lysander standing in my kitchen, radiating charm like it is his goddamn superpower.

"How do you want to play this?" I invoke the softest tone I can come up with.

"Play what?" Roman asks, looking confused. "I just brought you coffee, your iPhone, your lipstick, your passport ID, and your purse, Isla. It's a grand gesture, not a marriage proposal."

"I didn't say it was, and I'm not looking for any of that." Somehow, I sound like every girl who has ever had her heart broken by a guy in high school. I set my coffee down and turn away from him, unconsciously hugging my sides as if I can piece myself back together under his scrutiny after what he just said.

Because truth be told, I am so fucking tired, overwrought, not feeling well, and overthinking absolutely everything. And this guy is dominating my every waking thought and still my body is aching for the feel of his touch all over again.

He comes up behind me and whispers, "I'm sorry. I really didn't mean it like that. I didn't intend to make you feel bad. I'm sorry."

I cannot turn around because he's got his arms tightly wrapped around me now. I'm trembling for no reason at all, and I know he feels it.

He puts his chin on my shoulder and whispers, "I'm sorry, Isla."

The warmth of his embrace seeps through all my defenses. I close my eyes, breathing in the scent of his cologne that mixes with the fresh ocean air coming through one of the open windows.

"You didn't do anything," I say tiredly. "I'm being stupid. Not enough sleep. I've got this big meeting with your dad, my biggest client, next Wednesday, and I'm seriously off my game again today." I try to wipe at my face with my left arm, but I'm encased in his embrace from behind. He reaches up to my face with one hand and wipes the tear away and still holds me firmly with the other.

"I'm sorry for every guy that has ever hurt you. I'm sorry for being an asshole and leaving you in the middle of the night like what we did together meant nothing to me. After you made me that cake. I don't want to be that guy. Anymore. I'm sorry."

"Can you please just stop? It's not you. It's not even what we did. It's what we have ahead of us. You cannot do grand gestures like this anymore, Roman. It gives the wrong impression because we're going with the 'nothing happened' play, remember?" I turn in his arms because he still won't let me go.

Mistake.

Now, I'm inches from his chest and I look up at him as he bends his face towards mine.

"We'll be friends," I say in desperation.

He is entirely too close.

"I don't want to fight with you, Isla. I want to *know* you. All of you." He sighs big. His grip gets even tighter around me. Then he leans in and presses his lips to my forehead.

I'm too stunned by his unexpected, sweet gesture to even move, and a part of me, a bigger part of me, doesn't want to. For just a few minutes, it feels like I'm not all alone in this world. That I belong. With him.

I languish in the bubble of being wanted, desired even, and not alone. Somehow, I'm caught up in the tranquility of it all in being this close to him and feeling safe within his orbit. His heart beats against the palms of my hands that rest upon his chest and I just savor it.

It feels like we've ascended to a whole new level of intimacy in this simple moment. *Unexpected.* And I realize we cannot change back.

He lifts his head from my forehead. And we gaze at each other. We are connected somehow. It's unacknowledged out loud. We don't say a word.

"We'll be friends," I finally whisper, without any kind of real conviction.

"*Good friends.*" He laughs.

He already knows he's winning.

And then he lets go of me and steps back. He studies my face more intently now. "It's going to be okay."

"Not so sure about that," I say wanly, "but thank you for saying so. And thank you for the coffee, Roman Lysander."

"Thank you for opening the door, Isla Ryder."

"You should go." I strive for a smile while subtly wiping another stray tear from my face.

"I should most definitely go before I do something I will *not* regret and definitely won't forget." Roman rewards me with another winning smile and saunters through my living room over to my sliding glass doors. He unlocks them, then looks back at me, and sighs. "Taking the beach back. Better that way."

I watch him leave in this schoolgirl stupor.

What is wrong with me?

A grand gesture of $9 Starbucks latte and he has me wanting him all over again. I rush over to the sliding glass doors, and there he is with his Starbucks coffee in his right hand subtly running down the beach toward his place.

His utter charm is going to be a fucking problem.

For me.

I finish the latte. It's good.

He's thoughtful.

It's not an asset that's working for me.

His thoughtfulness is decidedly working against me.

My defenses are down. In fact, I cannot even locate them.

It's a good thing he left because I want him all over again.

And this is going to be a problem of epic proportions.

I check my makeup one last time in the downstairs bathroom mirror. The reflection shows dark circles I've tried my best to conceal with concealer. I grab my precious iPhone and my MacBook and slide them into my laptop bag. Then I empty the contents of the treasured clutch back into my regular handbag and sling it over my shoulder.

I secretly laugh to myself, remembering Roman carrying the clutch over his shoulder. He is this charming distraction on so many levels I've lost count.

I grab my rollaway from the front entry, intent on keeping my plans for The Harland apartment this weekend because clearly there needs to be some distance and boundaries between Roman Lysander and me. At least, until Monday.

Then I head towards the beautiful metallic grey Porsche 911 parked in the garage that Kimberley told me about four days ago. I load up the suitcase in the front trunk compartment after a quick Google search tells me how. I slide into the driver's seat, find the keys under the driver's car mat, just like Kimberley said they'd be, and after another Google search confirms the ignition is oddly on the left side, I put the key in.

I'm finally ready, intent on starting up the car... And that's when I look down and realize it's a manual transmission. A stick-shift with seven speeds according to Porsche's website when I do one last, despairing web search.

Bully for them.

But I don't know how to drive a 7-speed stick-shift transmission. I barely drive at all. Truth be told, I don't drive, but I figure how hard can it be? Driving the Pacific Coast Highway *has* a certain appeal. It *is* a challenge I *am* willing to consider... *or was* until this 7-speed manual transmission revelation.

'Barely been driven,' Kimberley said.

'It's a classic,' she said.

'Great condition,' she said.

'It's fast. So fun. You're going to love it,' she said.

But I can't drive a stick shift, Aunt Kimmy...

I don't actually drive at all, but how hard can it really be?

The Porsche mocks me with its sleek lines and its impossible gearshift. Like something from a Fitzgerald novel—beautiful but inaccessible to those without the right background.

Oh...

God is not working with me today, and we all know why.

I get out of the car with all my stuff, looking like a passenger stranded unexpectedly at the airport. My phone vibrates from within my handbag where I put it twenty minutes before. Just now, remembering Roman told me he put it on silent because it was ringing so much.

I race to grab and answer it before it goes to voicemail, while noting I have five missed calls from Kimberley and ten from Samantha. It's half-past eight. I am woefully behind.

"Isla Ryder," I say breathlessly.

"Hey, girlfriend. Are you on your way? The phones are already ringing off the hook with meeting requests and Trent Lysander's assistant just called. Get this. She said 'he wants to meet *today* and not wait until next Wednesday' like we planned. I told her we set up everything for next Wednesday, but she said he's insistent about meeting *today* and has already rearranged his schedule for a one o'clock lunch meeting at The Ivy in West Hollywood with you, me, Roman, and Brandon Chase. Welcome to Hollywood, huh?"

I lean against the open garage door frame and try to take it all in, feeling the cool metal press against my right shoulder blade.

"Are you fucking kidding me?"

"I wish I was. This is… seriously, I don't know. To me, it feels like an abuse of power. How could we possibly be ready when we just got the account *four days ago*? Who does that?" Samantha asks.

I sigh big. "It's a set-up. It's a way to trip me up, *us* up, right from the get-go. Geez, Kimberley wasn't kidding when she said these Hollywood people play a serious game. Goddamnit." I pause, gathering my thoughts. "Let me think. Let me think…" I hold the bridge of my nose as if some exceptional wisdom is forthcoming. My heart races. I pace the driveway. Pacing always helps me think, especially when it's about strategy.

"There's no way we're going to present a 'strat' plan today," Samantha says.

"No way. Trent Lysander is probably the type that will just look for the gaps and pee all over it, anyway." We both laugh.

Laughter momentarily lightens the proverbial tension I already feel coiling up inside of me, like a spring under constant pressure.

"No. No to the strat plan. I've already got a working draft going so we can finish that up this weekend. We'll hold to our Wednesday meeting for that piece of it. Goddamnit. I just hate the overt manipulation going on here." I sigh big. Samantha mirrors me.

"Okay, here's how we play it. We'll just go with an introductory pitch expounding on our vast experience with difficult—no *challenging* —situations with high-profile clients. Trent Lysander doesn't need to hear this; he already knows the challenges we're facing with… Roman." I trip on his name. Hopefully, Samantha doesn't hear it.

"But we'll start there. We'll keep it high level—no personal examples of 'bad boy' behavior with Roman Lysander, in particular, just general scenarios we've been able to help previous clients with—*not* the fuckboy karaoke scene from earlier this week though. Too much."

"Yeah, but you handled *that* beautifully. And he's already calling my cell this morning, begging us to take him on as a client with our new gig. Kimberley resigned him and sent him our way."

"What? Wow! Okay, we'll talk about the wayward singer later. He's probably a walk in the park compared to what we're dealing with out here in LA. We'll *think* about it. *This weekend.*" I sigh. My mind races while this pervasive tiredness tries to overtake me at the same time.

"So, the lunch at The Ivy. What are you thinking?" Her prompting makes me smile. Samantha Harper keeps to the tactical side of things. This is exactly why we are such an amazing team.

"Right. Well, we want to keep it high level and not specific because Roman is going to be there. And I don't want him to feel like he's being attacked. And his best buddy, Brandon Chase, will also be there. And after what I saw last night at his birthday party, I need to better understand the dynamics between him and Roman. To say nothing of the dynamics going on between Trent Lysander and his son. There's tension all around. It's not just the financial aspects tied to *Vendetta*, but with Roman's career and the personal relationship between all three men. Fuck! I did not *need* this today. And that is exactly why Trent Lysander is pressing for a meeting. A *lunch* meeting. In a *public place*. At a swanky restaurant. *The Ivy*, you said?"

"Yep. The Ivy—a 'see and be seen' a place in West Hollywood," Samantha says. I can hear her typing on the keyboard, getting all the background intel as we speak.

"Damnit! It's a fucking power play! And I think I know what's he going to do. To me. *To us.*"

I casually raise my hand in an acknowledgment type of wave at a neighbor. The older man is looking at me with open curiosity.

Who paces their driveway in white patent stilettos, swearing away like a sailor?

Nobody in Malibu. Apparently.

"What exactly do you think Trent Lysander is up to, Isla?" Samantha sounds uncertain. "And how *was* Roman's party? You said, *birthday party*. Geez, I got so rattled by the phone call from Trent Lysander's assistant in moving up the meeting I forgot to ask about the party. Tell me *everything*. What happened? Who was there?"

I sigh big. "Roman's birthday party. Oh, Sammy girl, that's an Ophelia Lounge discussion. Please, please find us a new bar where we can go over the big stuff, like that party, with cocktails. *Tonight*. Right now, I must think this through. And on top of everything else, I just loaded up everything into Julia's Porsche, a classic from 2015 almost a decade ago. In perfect condition, but stay with me, only to discover it's a 7-speed stick shift transmission—a *manual* transmission. Imagine that," I say dryly.

"Oh shit. When's the last time you've driven one?" Samantha asks.

I sigh big. Samantha doesn't know I don't drive exactly. It was easy to hide my lack of driving ability at Penn and even easier in Manhattan with taxis, Uber rides, and subways. Aloud I say, "I have never driven a stick-shift car in my life, like *never*. So, I'm without a car and I— "

"Kimberley's calling me on *my* cell. I guess she couldn't get a hold of you," Samantha says in a rush.

"Okay, take her call. *Stall her.* My phone's about to die. Tell her I'll call her in thirty minutes. I'm going to have to charge my phone. Samantha? Can you hear me?"

No.

Because my phone is officially dead.

I stalk back into the house through the open garage. My heels tapping double time on the travertine floors with every step.

"Really? Really? This is how this day is going to go?" I yell at the walls, trying to get my bearings while searching through my laptop bag for the phone charger.

"Why are you doing this to me?"

The walls do not answer.

But we all know why.

The morning light casts long shadows across the floor, reminding me that time, like my patience, is running out.

sit still, look pretty

Isla Ryder

"Sit Still, Look Pretty" – Daya

Friday Morning 9:30 a.m.

MY CELL PHONE'S GONE DEAD, and Samantha's panicked energy lingers all around me. I let a few minutes tick by, staring out the window at the unfamiliar, sun-drenched landscape of Malibu. But then a plan sparks, laser-focused and necessary. It takes shape and hardens in my mind. It's not just about Roman's PR anymore or even launching Ryder & Harper Communications LA.

It's all about control.

Somehow, some way, the hidden clause about casting approval is being bandied about by someone. It's the only explanation I can come up with. This isn't just about public relations strategies or a retainer for them. It's about power. *My* power as the screenwriter with casting approval. Somebody knows that Ashley Thomas is really Isla Ryder. Now, it all makes perfect sense.

And that somebody starts with Trent Lysander because Roman certainly doesn't know. There is no doubt about that in my mind.

However, Trent Lysander is under a non-disclosure agreement, an NDA. So why such a hard push to meet today, and not wait until Wednesday? He's not the welcoming committee. He can't even carve out time for his only son's 28th birthday party.

It has to be a power play.

Against me.

Trent Lysander thinks he's bought access. Bought *me*. A hundred thousand dollars a month isn't just a retainer; it's a leash. He's banking on that sum in addition to working with Roman on rebranding his image to ensure my compliance, not necessarily around a public relations strategy plan, but around the casting decisions with *Vendetta*.

A million dollars a year isn't an investment in public relations expertise, especially for a brand-new boutique firm like ours. No. It's insurance. Insurance that I, the screenwriter with the unusual clause for casting approval, will ultimately cast Roman Lysander for the coveted role of Steven Stryker, which could net Trent Lysander's empire north of $300 million. My sole right to casting decisions, my PR strategies—none of that matters to Trent Lysander. This is exactly why he so readily agreed to Kimberley's pitch that I handle Roman's rebranding strategy. He just needs me locked down, beholden to him and his power. *Owned.*

And I walked right into it. Less than 27 hours in town, and I'm already involved in the Lysander family dynamics, tabloid speculation, and a professional compromise. I can feel it all settle around me like a dense fog. The French 75s, the champagne, the cut knee still painful, the Advil... flimsy excuses for tumbling into bed with Roman. But maybe that was partly by design, too. Roman's undeniable charm becomes a convenient complication.

Oh God, I sound paranoid.

But am I? Morgan Grant's poison-pen piece this morning feels targeted when I scanned my news updates and emails on my laptop. We were careful last night, aware of all those pairs of eyes watching us interact even in the relaxed atmosphere of Roman's beach house. Yet the "mysterious brunette" angle was played up, as if Morgan was fed the information directly. How? Probably doesn't matter.

Who benefits from painting Roman as unchanged, still caught up in fleeting encounters, *and* potentially compromises me as his new PR strategist? Brandon Chase, maybe wanting to keep his friend down? Or Trent Lysander, adding another layer of pressure, another angle to exploit? With me at the helm, so to speak.

Why is this still happening, Ms. Ryder?
Is this you, the mysterious brunette?
How does this help Roman?
What are you playing at, Ms. Ryder?

My money's on dear old dad. He's the one with three hundred million reasons to ensure I tow the line.

I pull a fresh legal pad from my laptop bag, the crisp yellow a stark contrast to the swirling uncertainty. Time for some serious math. Losing a $100k monthly anchor client is significant. It wipes us out before we even launch. Now, we definitely have to consider taking on the wayward singer, Robbie Anton. Replacing the Lysander Entertainment retainer means hustle. Ten smaller clients? Too many. Too fast. It dilutes the brand before it's even established.

But five? Five carefully selected clients at $20k a month? *Achievable.* More than achievable if we build the right reputation. *Exclusive. Selective.* Known for integrity. *Principled.* A reputation built around achieving *results*, and for *not* playing the Hollywood game.

We'll turn away the bad fits—the clients who won't commit to the strategy. And like *Hitch's* black calling card in the hit film, our reputation will precede us with word-of-mouth recommendations.

Resigning Lysander Entertainment wouldn't just be cutting a tie; it would be our founding statement.

There's no walking this back. Trent Lysander will not appreciate losing control and his perceived advantage. I'll make a powerful enemy on day one in this town. However, in this town, audacity gets noticed.

Our cachet—*selective, exclusive, principled*—could be cemented by this single defiant act.

Resign Lysander Entertainment.

This changes everything with Roman. *Everything.*

Professionally. *Obviously.* He'll side with his dad.

Personally. *Almost certainly.*

Sleeping with him was a mistake fueled by proximity and chemistry, but continuing under these circumstances? *Impossible.*

Because if I'm going to do this. *I need clean lines.*

Clean lines.
No compromises.
No dependencies.
No leverage.
Not from anyone.
A good strategy plan can fix just about anything.

I know what needs to happen.
Do you now, girl?
Your heart is beating at a rate of a hundred beats per minute.
We're just going to ignore all the feels from this morning; aren't we?
And move on to strategy.
Strategy. The message of the day.
Strategy. Strategy. Strategy.
See? If you think it often enough, the focus will come. Surely.

First, the practicalities.

I call Ivan Steinberg, my financial manager, back in New York. He picks up on the second ring, a note of pleasant surprise in his voice.

"Ms. Ryder! An unexpected pleasure. What can I do for you today?"

"Ivan, hello. I need some information regarding liquidity. I'm launching my own public relations firm here in Los Angeles, separate from Kimberley's." Time to rip off the proverbial band-aid. "I need to know how much cash I can access readily, specifically from the *Vendetta* novel proceeds account, without disrupting the overall investment strategy."

A pause, the faint clicking of keys. "Certainly. Let's see… the account holding the initial sale funds and subsequent royalties currently sits at just over fourteen million dollars. It's in a high-yield cash account, earning about four percent annually. Very liquid, as you requested for potential ventures like this. The annual interest alone is approximately five hundred and sixty thousand dollars. You haven't touched any of it since the initial deposit."

Relief washes over me, cool and clean. "Okay. That's perfect. I'm thinking of drawing down that annual profit—the five-sixty. Would that significantly impact the portfolio's momentum?"

"For a venture you're passionate about? Not at all, Ms. Ryder," Ivan says reassuringly. "It's profit generated, not principal. Consider it seed money. We can revisit if you need further funding down the line, but this initial withdrawal is easily absorbed. Remember, that account is separate from your main inheritance portfolio, which continues to perform well, and doesn't factor in the potential backend percentage from the *Vendetta* film adaptation." He mentions the 2% gross clause, the potential $7 million payout based on studio projections, almost as an afterthought, reinforcing the point without dwelling on the staggering numbers. Money isn't the issue. Control is.

"Right. Good," I say, feeling lighter. "So, withdrawing the $560,000 will work."

"It's your money, Ms. Ryder. I think investing in your own firm is an excellent use of your 'fun money,' as you once called it. Just provide the account details for the transfer."

I dig through the folder Kimberley gave me, locating the information for the new business account she'd preemptively set up. I read the numbers off to Ivan.

"Excellent. I'll initiate the transfer immediately; you should see it reflected shortly. I'll send a confirmation text." He pauses. "May I ask the name of the new firm?"

"It's Ryder & Harper Communications LA. I'm bringing my colleague, Samantha Harper, in as my full partner."

"Ryder & Harper Communications LA," he repeats. "A strong name. Sounds formidable. Congratulations, Ms. Ryder. On this, and all your successes. Your dad would be so proud of you. Your mother, too. Please don't hesitate to call if any other financial matters arise."

"Thank you, Ivan. You're a lifesaver."

"Always happy to assist. Take care."

I hang up, scribbling "$560,000" on the legal pad. Six months. That gives us a cushion, enough time to land those first five clients, to build our foundation without compromise. Samantha and I ran the numbers for expenses and salaries with our preliminary business plan analysis. The $560,000 should give us enough breathing room to build our client base with the right clients without undue financial pressure. We're good. A weight has lifted. At least, one of them.

***

Next call: Kimberley.

She answers with her usual brisk efficiency. "Kimberley Powers."

The sound of her voice is grounding. "Hi there, Aunt Kimmy."

"Isla, sweetie. Good timing. Samantha's been... expressive. And I'm hearing whispers from the Lysander camp. Talk to me."

"What are the whispers? I'm guessing questions about the legality of the NDA surrounding the casting clause?"

"Yes, exactly. Legal called this morning, relaying a query from Lysander Entertainment's legal office," Kimberley confirms. "What are you thinking? What's your strategy?"

"The strategy is I need to know I have your full backing before I potentially detonate things." I keep my voice even.

"Always. You *know* that. What's happening?"

"Priorities are shifting," I say with bravado. "First, Samantha will be a full partner in Ryder & Harper Communications LA, like we planned, but *I'm funding* it. The initial seed money is already transferred." I take a breath. "Meaning we are *not* dependent on Lysander Entertainment as an anchor client. I appreciate you landing the account. The million-dollar billing is huge, I get it. But Trent Lysander is already making power plays. He moved the meeting planned for next Wednesday to *today* at some swanky restaurant called The Ivy—a 'see and be seen' type of place, popular with the power hitters of West Hollywood."

I pause, letting that sink in. "He wants me pinned down before I've even unpacked. There's no purpose for that this early in taking over the account, *and* he's invited Roman and Brandon Chase to the meeting, in addition to me and Samantha. I think we both know where this is going. Yeah?"

"Whoa," Kimberley breathes. "He didn't waste any time moving that meeting *and* adding Roman and Brandon, did he? That's aggressive, even for Trent." Her voice sharpens with understanding.

"Yes. To me, it confirms the retainer was always about the casting clause, not PR strategy—especially since he was *still* pushing Melody Parker on us earlier this week on that conference call. He thinks he can control us because of the money. The retainer."

A wicked laugh escapes her. "Oh, my goodness, don't you just love it when men like this underestimate you?"

"Yeah. I see it as a queen takes knight move leading to checkmate of the king if he plays it out," I reply coolly. "You good with that?"

"It's not up to me. It's your firm. Your play," she says, the amusement clear in her voice. "Isla, you've got this. If you've already secured your own funding and that's temporary because you'll make up the revenue shortfall in no time. You can work with Roman directly. He can afford your services. And I sent the singer, Robbie Anton, your way. He should stay clean for a while. I scared him straight and so did you. You can get out from underneath Trent Lysander's quest for power and launch however you want."

I hesitate, then press on. "Kimberley... can I ask you about the NDA? The non-disclosure agreement Trent signed about the casting clause. I just want to confirm things."

"Yes, of course." Her tone sharpens, serious but confident. "Remember, the NDA is a critical legal safeguard. If Trent breaches it, Lysander Entertainment loses the film rights to *Vendetta* immediately."

I exhale; relief mixed with tension. "Does he remember that? So, if he violates the NDA and leaks my pen name as the writer of *Vendetta*—that Isla Ryder is Ashley Thomas. The film rights revert?"

"Yes. I personally went over it with him and his legal team, two weeks ago. And Powers Media—the production company we have in place—that's not just a side project. You, me, Samantha, and Julia Winston are partners. True girl power, when needed. We're prepared to step in to secure independent financial backing to protect the integrity of *Vendetta* and the creative control you rightfully hold. And that financing can be initiated within hours of a breach. It's all set up. Ready to go if needed."

Her voice softens a little with reassurance. "You're not alone in this. The legal and financial muscle is ready. Trent might think he's playing hardball, but we have the tools and the team players in place to call his bluff if he steps out of line and violates the NDA."

"Good. Because if he pushes that angle, we're done playing his game."

"Exactly. But Isla, you must be ready for the fallout of all of that. Because if Trent loses self-control, and loses face, he won't take it well. He's a scorched earth kind of guy, used to getting his way with everything. But you have the leverage if you need it, Isla. The *real* leverage."

"Okay. I understand. I'll remind him of the terms of the NDA more than once." I nod to myself, even though Kimberley can't see it. "Thanks. This means everything."

"I'm proud of you, Isla. You're setting boundaries, taking control, and ethically structuring it all out."

Sure. In control. Except for what took place about six hours ago.

"Thanks." One word syllables work. If I say more now, I'm going to lose it.

"Damn, I wish I could be there to see Trent Lysander's face if you end up laying all this out with him."

"Wish you were here, too." My anxiety rises like a sudden change in temperature settings. I sigh big. "Kimberley, I don't want to do this. Like I said, I'll remind him about the NDA in place, more than once, if he goes there." I inhale and let it out slowly and then say, "maybe I'm being overly cautious and it's just a meet and greet type meeting. But I don't think so. Samantha already pushed back about meeting today and his secretary was insistent about keeping the lunch with Trent today at The Ivy. She cleared his entire schedule for this meeting. *Today.* At the very least, I must be prepared for the possibility of his play for power, his play for leverage."

"You're right to be ready. Not sure why he would do this right away. Except maybe to intimidate you right out of the gate and obtain your compliance."

I freeze, with notable clarity and fear all at once. Suddenly, I understand exactly *why* he is doing this today. Because someone saw and knows about me and Roman. And Trent Lysander knows. Morgan Grant? Maybe. Either way, that's the *why* of today. The play Trent's going for—my compliance because he knows I'm compromised already. *Fuck.*

"Sounds like drinks will be in order after this lunch meeting, regardless," Kimberley says with a laugh.

"Yeah, Samantha's already scouting bars for post-meeting decompression tonight. Ophelia Lounge vibes required."

"Perfect. Sounds fun. But like I said earlier though, watch your back, Isla. Trent plays hardball."

"Got it. Thanks for having mine, like always. I'll text you later with details." I end the call, feeling the weight of what's coming settle like steel in my spine while this other part of me laments the spiraling loss of Roman on the other side of this move.

Breathe.

Slow down.

Keep it together.

One of those.

Ten minutes go by. I dial the new office number Samantha texted earlier.

"Ryder & Harper Communications LA, Samantha speaking." Her voice is bright, professional.

"Hey now," I tease. "Shouldn't the service be catching that? Save your voice for charming potential clients?"

"Isla! Thank God. Did you talk to Kimberley? Is the sky falling?"

"Sky is clear, funding secured, partnership confirmed. Update the voicemail and any signage protocols immediately: We are officially Ryder & Harper Communications LA."

A beat of silence, then, "Funding secured? What's up?"

"We're getting maneuvered into a power play, and we ain't playin'," I explain succinctly. "So, I moved some funds over into the account so we can launch this gig the way we want. Our tagline will be *exclusive, selective, principled*. More on that later. Right now, logistics. I need a car that doesn't require a degree in mechanical engineering to get into the city. I need to hit the actual office, assess the space, so we can still make this ridiculous one o'clock lunch at The Ivy with Trent Lysander."

"Car is handled," Samantha says, sounding slightly breathless, but I know she has everything under control. "I had to coordinate with Trent's assistant about the lunch details. *Don't ask.* Anyway, I heard from Roman regarding the lunch meeting and learned he's still out there in Malibu. When I mentioned you were stranded with a stick shift you couldn't drive, he offered to have his driver, Manny, bring you into town. Said he was heading in any way. They should be there in about fifteen minutes."

Roman. Driving me into the city. An hour trapped in a car with the man whose father I'm about to professionally torpedo, and whose career I might be handling pro bono after sleeping with him. *Perfect.*

"Oh... no, no, no. That's not... ideal," I manage, trying to keep the apprehension out of my voice. "Well, it's... efficient."

"Isla," Samantha sighs dramatically. "He was *so nice* about it. Offered immediately. You get an hour with Roman Lysander in the back of a luxury car. Some people would pay for that privilege! How are you *not* thrilled?"

"You're killin' me, Sammy girl," I mutter, borrowing the Sandlot line. "There are layers upon layers to this." I groan. "Okay. We'll discuss them over very strong drinks later. Speaking of which, bar status?"

"Reservation made. Post-Ivy debrief is locked and loaded. Are you staying in town tonight?"

"Abso-fucking-lutely," I confirm, using her favorite emphasis. "Okay, office intel. Give it to me straight. Does it suck?"

"It's… functional," she says diplomatically. "Good bones, decent view, but sparse. Needs art, personality, maybe some vintage finds. Definitely more style. And honestly? A higher floor would make the view even more spectacular. The landlord's been hovering—nice guy, already asked me out."

"Naturally." I laugh a little.

She giggles. "Politely declined for professional reasons. But he seems amenable. Do you want me to inquire about higher floors? Maybe a slightly larger suite with a proper conference room and two real offices? Because my current cubicle situation is not befitting a partner, just saying."

"Yes, do your magic. We want the upgrade. Corner suite, if possible, two offices, at least, conference room. Highest floor. Penthouse suite with a private elevator would be the absolute. Only the best for Ryder & Harper Communications LA. Statements will be made today."

I glance towards the hallway, hearing the crunch of tires on the driveway. The front door and garage are still wide open from my earlier frantic attempts with the cursed Porsche.

"Looks like my ride might be here. I should be there in about an hour, traffic willing. Plenty of time to see the space before heading to The Ivy. And Sammy girl? Switch the calls to the service. Your priority now is scouting bigger, better office space, and preparing for our first major clients."

"You got it. I'll see about the top floor. Oh my God, Isla, that would be amazing. Woo hoo!" Her excitement races through the phone.

I laugh and then look up and over, a sixth sense telling me he's here. My breath catches. Leaning against the doorframe of the office, silhouetted against the bright California sun, is Roman Lysander. He has an expression of amused surprise, clearly having overheard Samantha's celebratory squeal and witnessing my own answering laugh.

My elation diminishes. It's instantly tempered by the weight of the conversation we need to have. Decisions I've just made that will inevitably affect him. But I manage a small wave. Roman returns it with that easy, magnetic smile that makes ignoring him so impossible.

"Got to go," I say into the phone, my eyes still on Roman. "My ride's here."

"See you soon!" Samantha says with an easy laugh. "Drinks immediately after the meeting. I'm already anticipating the stories."

"See you soon, Samantha Harper." I end the call.

The air sparks with so many unspoken things. *Clean lines.* Our connection that's about to be undone, the cash transfer is already complete, and the leverage I'm determined to dismantle, even as its most charming embodiment, stands waiting to drive me into the heart of the battle.

CHAPTER 20

wreck of the day

Isla Ryder

> "Wreck of the Day" - Anna Malick
> "Complicated" – Avril Lavigne
> "Delicate Weapon" - Grimes, Lizzy Wizzy
> "Flowers" – Miley Cyrus
> "Cornflake Girl" - Tori Amos
> "Stupid Girl" – Garbage

Friday Morning 10:00 a.m.

"KICKING ASS, TAKING NAMES, I SEE. And I hear you don't drive a 2015 Porsche 911 Carrera S with a 7-speed stick shift. Damn it all to hell with a manual transmission, yeah?" Roman leans against the doorframe, his charm as effortless as the California sun.

"Exactly. Something like that, yes." I manage a small, grateful smile, snapping my laptop shut. "But I refrained from kicking the tires. White patent leather, you know. Didn't want to scuff them. I appreciate the ride, though. You have no idea."

The scent of his cologne—woody and expensive—drifts across the room, triggering an immediate and unwelcome flutter in my stomach. I inhale deeply, steadying myself against the wave of attraction that threatens my composure.

"Happy to help," he says, his blue eyes crinkling at the corners, but concern shadows his features. "But I also hear my dad is making a power play. Moving a meeting scheduled for next Wednesday to today, Friday afternoon at The Ivy. Classic move. Sorry about that." His brow furrows. "Not sure what he's up to, Isla. But you're going to have to be very careful."

"Yes, I think so." My hands move automatically, packing the laptop into my bag, coiling the charger, grabbing my iPhone. I check my purse —wallet, passport ID, cash. Files secure. My mind races ahead in calculating angles and anticipating confrontations.

The cool leather of my laptop bag grounds me momentarily, its familiar texture a small comfort against the rising tide of anxiety. The sound of my heartbeat seems unnaturally loud in my ears, a persistent drumming that reminds me of what's at stake.

I look up to find him watching me with a touch of amusement. He follows me around as I hit the remote on the garage wall, the garage door gliding down with a soft whir. I frown at the Porsche and head back inside and Roman trails after me like an ever-curious shadow. I grab the suitcase waiting by the front door.

He stops, surprise replacing amusement. "Are you moving out? Already?"

"No." I adjust the strap of my laptop bag. "Just staying in town for the weekend. I think I told you that Kimberley landed me a place at The Harland in West Hollywood for weekdays. I figure I'll work on the strat plan there this weekend."

"The Harland. Nice." He nods, impressed. Curiosity sparks in his eyes. "What's a strat plan?"

"Strategic plan," I reply, keeping it brief. "Rebranding… changing the narrative. PR lingo. That's it."

"A strat plan. Okay." He glances at his watch, his easygoing manner replaced by subtle urgency. "We should get moving. Traffic gets unbearable if we leave much later than this."

"That's fine." I take a breath.

This is it. The point of no return.

"But Roman, I have some things to talk to you about as we head into the city if your driver can just drop me off in West Hollywood so I can meet up with Samantha at the new office, and before lunch at The Ivy.

But the thing is, do you trust your driver? I have some things to tell you about that aren't for public consumption."

He gives me a curious look, and his head tilts ever so slightly. "Yes. Manny's the best. He's saved my ass more times than I can count. He can be trusted with my life. He doubles as security when needed. And he respects my privacy and knows anything discussed is confidential."

"Okay. That's good." A fraction of relief surfaces. It's not enough to assuage the anxiety taking hold of me, but enough to at least appear outwardly calm. "That works." I manage a tight smile and follow him out to the waiting SUV.

Roman's Escalade gleams all shiny black under the California sun, looking like it rolled straight off a movie set—tinted windows, chrome accents, undoubtedly loaded with every conceivable feature one can imagine. Inside, the contrast is stark: pristine white leather seats with subtle grey piping. 'Manny' turns out to be a mountain of a man in a perfectly tailored charcoal grey suit. His dark eyes and wide smile are both warm and genuine as he takes my suitcase and loads it into the back of the SUV. I insist on keeping my laptop bag with me.

"I'll sit in the back with Isla," Roman says to Manny after introducing me. Manny is already opening the rear passenger door for me. "She has some stuff she needs to brief me on. You good?"

Manny nods. His expression is professionally neutral, but I catch a flicker of curiosity in his eyes via the rearview mirror as he settles behind the wheel.

Roman slides into the seat opposite me, the space suddenly feeling charged and intimate. Manny pulls the SUV smoothly out of the driveway. The quiet hum of the engine is a stark contrast to the tension building steadily inside of me. We turn towards the Pacific Coast Highway, the vast expanse of the ocean momentarily distracting.

I'm holding my breath again, clasping and unclasping my hands, and looking out the window, away from him, trying to find some semblance of calm, which is slipping away from me at an accelerated rate.

Get it together, Isla.

The leather seat creaks softly beneath me as I shift my weight. The scent of the new car leather mingles with Roman's cologne and the faint trace of coffee lingering in the air. Outside, the ocean glitters like scattered diamonds under the morning sun, a beauty so vast and indifferent to the turmoil churning inside me, I experience true envy.

"You look all mysterious," Roman observes, his gaze sharp, analytical now as I turn to look at him. "Is this good news or bad news?"

"Some good. Some bad." My voice sounds steadier than I feel. "A bit of both, I think. Depending on one's perspective."

Roman laughs, a low, rumbling sound I've come to appreciate. "She talks in riddles like my last therapist," he remarks to Manny, who grins back in the rearview mirror at us. Their easy camaraderie is a world away from the calculated moves and hidden agendas I'm navigating now.

Roman turns his full attention back to me. "We come prepared because we're thirty-six miles out from home. Would you like coffee, water, or something stronger? A sandwich? Birthday cake? Because I already know you haven't eaten today, aside from that latte."

He grimaces slightly. "Lunch with my father is going to be a war game. You won't be eating much of the fancy food at The Ivy because you'll be playing defense about whatever he's decided needs to be addressed, changed, or eliminated completely, and you'll be trying not to drink too much, while he does his absolute best to put you on edge about all of it."

"Well, okay then. Thanks for the heads-up." His bluntness is oddly reassuring. "This might actually make things clearer for you then. Birthday cake is tempting, but not right now. Yes, to the sandwich, water, and coffee. Hold the alcohol, although a French 75 right about now would feel practically medicinal," I say wistfully. I force a smile wider than usual, trying to project a confidence I don't entirely feel. "I'm having drinks with Samantha after the fireworks show, though. So, I'm good."

He studies my face, his blue eyes searching as if trying to decode the signals I'm sending. Then, he turns, reaching into a sleek cooler integrated into the console near the third row. He retrieves a sandwich wrapped in cellophane, unwraps it with surprising dexterity, and places it on a heavy, designer glass plate before handing it to me.

"Last night's birthday party special," he says. "Turkey, cranberry sauce, cream cheese, and avocado on sourdough bread. Apparently, that's how they like 'em in Manhattan."

I express surprise at his warmth. "Somebody's done some homework. On me?" I raise an eyebrow. "I'm touched."

He hands me a chilled bottle of water and then pours coffee from a silver thermos into a thick ceramic mug. The aroma fills the small space, rich and comforting, momentarily distracting me from the impending conversation.

"You're in the wrong line of work." I take the coffee mug.

He rolls his eyes, a hint of his usual playfulness returning. "I'm not saying or implying you're high maintenance or anything."

"As I told you before." I meet his gaze and attempt to smile. "Imply away."

He laughs, a genuine sound this time, and my stomach clenches. I feel this dull ache of faraway pain that I instinctively know is coming for me. What I have to say next could extinguish that laughter and could shatter whatever fragile connection is forming between us.

A sigh escapes me, heavier than intended. He hears it. His laughter fades, replaced by that intense and concerned look of his again. "Tell me what's going on, Isla."

Breathe.

Start at the beginning.

The *real* beginning.

"Well… first things first." I shift slightly in the plush leather seat. "Before I explain the *'why'* behind everything, including my apparent and growing paranoia about your father's meeting… I need to tell you something about myself." My voice is no more than a whisper as, almost subconsciously, I prepare to share a secret no one else knows.

The SUV's tires hum against the asphalt, creating a rhythmic backdrop to my confession. Sunlight filters through the tinted windows, casting shifting patterns across Roman's face as he waits.

"Nine years ago. My dad, my mom, and Tommy were flying in from the States for Christmas to spend the holidays with me in Switzerland. I was attending The American School In Switzerland. TASIS. The Swiss, not so clever with naming their schools. My parents wanted me to have a broad educational experience." I frown while this unbearable sadness overtakes me. It takes a few minutes to recover.

Finally, I say, looking over at Roman, "I was not happy about those plans. I just wanted to be home for Christmas and not spend it in Switzerland. But it had turned into this big getaway vacation my dad had all planned out. I'd just talked to them ten hours before. They'd taken a private Lear jet. Due to arrive. Never came. Swiss police at my dorm room door with the news. 'No survivors. So sorry.' Your world just… *ends*." I shake my head from side to side, feeling the disbelief and shock all over again.

The memory of that night floods back—the sharp knock on my dorm room door, the stoic faces of the police officers, the words that didn't make sense at first, then crashed down on me like an avalanche. The cold stone floor beneath my knees when I collapsed. The taste of salt from tears I didn't realize were streaming down my face.

"Kimberley comes to Switzerland, but she's going through her own stuff. What do you do? Nobody knows what to do for a seventeen-year-old girl who just lost her entire family. And the media coverage back home in the States was insane. Joshua Ryder, famous playwright, dead at 45 in a plane crash with his family. The only surviving heir is the young 17-year-old Isla Ryder, all alone. What will she do? What will she *fucking* do?" I look down, feeling the squeeze of Roman's hand on mine.

"So, your dad is Joshua Ryder? The famous playwright? We went to Manhattan to see one of his plays on Broadway once. My mom and me. She loved the theater. She knew your dad, I think," Roman says softly.

"Sometimes, the world is very small, yeah? I wish they were here."

"Me, too," he says.

I withdraw my hand from his, suddenly feeling self-conscious. Still attempting to create boundaries.

He frowns, studying me intently, probably confused by the mixed signals I'm giving off. "You said *Kimberley*. I don't understand the connection. How did she—?"

I nod. "Kimberley Powers… she's more than my boss and mentor. She's my aunt. My mom, Ashley Powers Ryder, was her older sister. Kimberley became my guardian for that year until I turned eighteen. She wanted to protect me from all of that as best she could. And I made it easy for her. After… the funerals. So, so many people were there. I never returned… *home*. I just insisted I was fine returning and finishing school. Where was I going to go? Back to a high school I'd never attended in Connecticut. So, even *more* strangers could stare at me, not knowing what to say or do. No, it was just easier to lie, to say I was fine, and return to school. Kimberley stayed a few days with me and then she left me there."

Roman waits. His attention is fully focused on me now.

The sandwich sits untouched on my lap, the scent of sourdough and cranberry sauce wafting up, suddenly nauseating. My fingers trace the cool edge of the ceramic mug, seeking an anchor in the physical world as I dive deeper into memories I've kept submerged for years.

"The truth was, I was a mess, Roman. I hated it there, but I didn't tell anyone. It was a very dark time for me. The few friends I had made there—well, no one knows what to say to the girl who's lost everything and everyone. I finished the school year that spring and spent the summer in Manhattan because Kimberley had moved back to the States by then, and she had met Brad. Dr. Bradley Stevenson, who keeps us all grounded, especially Kimberley." I smile, thinking of my uncle.

"And then I started at Penn that next fall, where I met Samantha Harper. We were… fast friends. I think I told you, Samantha is from Austin, Texas. Raised on a ranch. Has five older brothers. She is sunlight itself. She literally saved my life. I was in a very dark place, and she pulled me back from the ledge more than once. Also, freshman year, I had a lit professor, who put together who I was, and, as part of his class, he encouraged me to journal and write, so I did."

I close my eyes for a moment, trying to catch my breath and slow down. When I open them, Roman is watching me even more closely.

"My dad always talked about character motivation being the absolute for a story to work, whether it was a play, a film, or a novel. He told me often that it's the development of an amazing character with motivation that drives a story, and it's absolutely necessary in order to write a good one. He always emphasized focusing on strong character development. Believability. Authenticity. We talked about it all the time. He was teaching me, preparing me for a writing career. That was his plan and mine."

I take a deep breath and hold it for a few seconds. "So, we were working on a story together. A thriller, of course. And the motivation for the story came from the character's love for his wife. It was just an idea.

A premise. Just the beginning of one. Then Dad... they... everyone was *just... gone.*" I wipe a tear from my face.

"It took years to write, partly because of my lack of skill, but then that got better with practice and the lit professor's encouragement. Still. It was just emotionally hard for me to write the novel. Without my dad. We had all these plans to write it together. And he wasn't here. Anymore." I stop and take in air and exhale slowly.

I already know the next part is going to be the beginning of what changes everything between us.

I can feel Roman's gaze on me, intense and unwavering. The air in the SUV feels charged, heavy with the weight of my confession. Outside, the coastal landscape rushes by in a blur of blues and greens, a stark contrast to the darkness of my memories.

I look over at Roman.

"So, I finally finished the novel three years ago. The publisher wanted to leverage my father's name—Joshua Ryder—the famous playwright, but I refused. So, I used a pen name because I wanted the anonymity. I wasn't after fame. It was an homage to my dad's love for thrillers, his writing legacy, the deep love he had for my mother, and our shared quest for this story I felt I needed to finish. For him. And for me." My voice trembles slightly at the last words. "And then, somehow, it became a bestseller." I take a beat to somehow gather myself.

"That bestselling novel is *Vendetta.* I wrote *Vendetta.*" The words feel strange, heavy in the air after years of silence. I risk a glance at Roman. His expression is unreadable—surprise, skepticism, maybe something else.

"So..." he says slowly, processing. "Ashley Thomas. The bestselling author of *Vendetta.* That's *you.* Ashley Thomas. Your mom's first name is Ashley and Thomas, your little brother."

I nod slowly. "Yes."

He looks genuinely stunned, but there's a glimpse of something else. Respect?

"I read *Vendetta* when it first came out. And recently again. It's good, Isla." He meets my surprised look with a slightly defensive edge. "Don't look so shocked. I read a lot—books, scripts, plays. I do my homework for my craft, just like you do for yours."

"Thanks for reading my work," I say softly, shaking my head. "I... I misjudged you... before we met, before spending time with you. I apologize for that. I should always try to remember people aren't always who they seem to be. It's that trust thing, again." I sigh, trying to maintain focus even though my heart is racing.

The memory of my earlier dismissive thoughts about him stings now. It's a sharp reminder of how easily I'd categorized him without truly knowing him. The irony isn't lost on me—I, who guard my own depths so fiercely, denied Roman the same complexity and consideration.

"Anyway, I never touched the royalty money for *Vendetta*. I had a trust fund from my parents. I've never touched that either, except for the separate trust fund money I received when I turned 25 and bought the Brownstone with. The Ryder estate is still in Darien, Connecticut. The Whitakers live there, not in the main house. They have their own home on the property and take care of the estate. I haven't been back... not since... I was seventeen."

I can still picture the Darien house perfectly—the sprawling lawn where Tommy and I played, the library and study where Dad worked, Mom's garden with its riot of colors in summer. The memories are preserved like insects in amber, beautiful and untouchable. The thought of returning there is its own kind of heartbreak.

"Like I said, I stayed and finished school in Switzerland, then stayed briefly in Manhattan that summer and then started at Penn in the fall and met Samantha there. Graduated. Interns at Powers & Winston. Promotions. Manhattan." My gaze drops to my hands.

"Most of the people working at Powers & Winston don't even know that Kimberley and I are related. It's just better that way. It's been the best way for me to cope, to keep the past—*my past*—locked down in order to survive and live a somewhat normal life." I shrug my shoulders, trying for nonchalance, but I tremble anyway.

I glance over at Roman. "Like you guessed already, the pen name, Ashley Thomas, is a way to honor my mom and my little brother." The admission hangs in the air, intense and painful. "I'm sorry. I know this is a lot. Talking about them, my life before... It's hard for me. I never do. But I think it's important for you to understand why I hid my identity as it relates to *Vendetta*, and why I still do." I look at him, allowing him to see some of the pain and grief I carry. "It is why *Vendetta* is so *personal* to me." I sigh.

"After *Vendetta* hit big, film production companies, like your dad's, started reaching out with interest. Kimberley convinced me to write the screenplay in order to retain control if the film rights were ever picked up."

"I think I understand," Roman says, his voice softer now, the defensiveness gone. He seems to be connecting the dots. "The anonymity, the connection to your family..." he pauses, but then his brow furrows again. "What I still don't get is... why the urgency now? Why the cloak-and-dagger routine? And what does it have to do with this lunch my dad has called for at The Ivy? And why does any of this mean you can't just keep working for my dad and handle my public relations?"

"Because," I say, the word sharp, cutting through the quiet intimacy, "your father's power play isn't about controlling my public relations strategy with you, even if it just turns out he's attempting to wield power in threatening to pull the retainer from our new gig, Ryder & Harper Communications LA. And I've already taken care of that piece. *No.* His intention is all about controlling *Vendetta.* That's the power play and the leverage he's going for."

"I don't understand. What do you mean?"

"Powers Media, Kimberley's production company, in which the four of us are partners—Kimberley, Julia Winston, Samantha, and me—sold the film rights for *Vendetta* to your dad's company, Lysander Entertainment, two years ago." My voice gets lower and even more intense. "Kimberley handled the negotiations. Part of the legal contract, as the screenwriter includes the *unusual two percent* payout on the film's gross sales. I didn't care about the money, but Kimberley insisted we needed this for leverage, and I agreed. We wanted ironclad terms upfront so that only serious investors would make an offer for film rights because, above all else, retaining control of the creative direction of the film was an *absolute. For me.*"

Breathe.

Here we go.

"But there's another clause. The crucial one. *For me.* The only reason I was willing to sell the film rights to *Vendetta* in the first place. As part of the deal, to protect the creative integrity of the screenplay, because it's *my work* and *my vision* and *my dad's,* I have the final say on the casting of the lead roles, including the lead role of Steven Stryker for *Vendetta.*"

Silence.
Absolute silence.

The silence stretches between us, thick and heavy, like fog descending inside the Escalade. The air conditioning hums quietly, but it feels like even the mechanical sounds are holding their breath. Roman's face goes completely still, his blue eyes are fixed on me with an intensity that makes my chest tighten. The casual ease he'd shown a half hour before—the playful banter, the gentle teasing—evaporates entirely.

I watch him process what I've just revealed, see the exact moment when true understanding dawns. His jaw clenches almost imperceptibly, and something shifts behind his eyes. Not anger, exactly. Something deeper. More complex. The same look I've seen in photographs from his early career—that flash of vulnerability he usually keeps buried beneath layers of practiced charm.

The leather seat creaks softly as he leans back, putting distance between us without actually moving away. His hands, which had been relaxed on his knees, slowly curl into loose fists. The transformation is subtle but unmistakable—his emotional walls going up in real time.

"Final say," he repeats, his voice carefully neutral. Each word measured, controlled. "On casting. For *Vendetta.*"

It's not a question. It's him working through the implications, the power dynamics, the reality of what I've just laid bare. The silence that follows feels dangerous, charged with the weight of everything unsaid.

CHAPTER 21

white horse

Isla Ryder

"White Horse" - Taylor Swift
"Wreck of the Day" - Anna Malick
"Complicated" – Avril Lavigne
"Delicate Weapon" - Grimes, Lizzy Wizzy
"Flowers" – Miley Cyrus
"Cornflake Girl" - Tori Amos
"Stupid Girl" – Garbage

Friday Morning 11:00 a.m.

THE AIR BECOMES SUFFOCATING, all at once, charged with unspoken accusations. Even the sound of tires on asphalt seems muted, as if the world itself is holding its collective breath, just waiting for the proverbial fallout.

Because it's coming.

A bead of sweat trickles down my spine, cold and insistent. I meet his gaze directly. He just stares at me, his blue eyes wide with surprise, then they narrow with notable suspicion. The warmth radiating from him earlier vanishes completely. It's replaced by a dawning chill of fresh understanding and open contempt.

The air between us electrifies with unspoken condemnation.

"This..." he starts, then stops, searching for words. "This... from the girl who swears she doesn't care about *money*." His tone is rich with irony. "Negotiating two percent gross is impressive for a *screenwriter*. It's unheard of. But the *final say on casting?* On the *leads? Wow.*" His voice drops, suddenly laced with a sharp bitterness. "That's *true power*. You're good, Isla. Very good."

"Kimberley wanted to ensure my rights are protected," I whisper, feeling both defensive and exposed. "She knows how important the story and the characters are to me. What it represents to me. And my family, especially my dad."

Roman turns away from me. He stares out the window at the coastline. His profile is rigid. His jaw clenches with notable tension.

The connection between us feels like taut steel wires spanning a chasm, but now they are structurally failing one by one under the strain and pressure. Metaphorically, I feel the sickening lurch. I'm losing my grip and already expecting the inevitable fall into the abyss below.

I am falling.

There's no coming back from this.

The realization feels catastrophic.

The sandwich sits forgotten on my lap. The idea of food is even more nauseating. The coffee grows cold in my hands.

Outside, the ocean stretches endlessly, indifferent to the human drama unfolding in this small, enclosed space. The contrast is almost cruel—the beauty of the world continuing while something precious shatters between us.

Finally, he speaks. His voice is low and strained, directed at the window. "I don't know what to say to you right now." Then he turns back to me. His blue eyes are cold and distant. "Who *are* you, Isla Ryder?"

Pain lances through me. Piercing and abrupt but somewhat expected.

"I'm the stranger you helped on the beach yesterday. The same girl you asked to your party, the one you baked a cake with, and were...

with last night," I whisper, my voice barely audible. "The one you brought coffee to this morning." My throat tightens. "It feels like you've done more for me in the last twenty hours than anyone else I've met here. And you're this famous actor... and I'm just the anonymous writer of *Vendetta*, just this ace PR strategist, trying to stay off the proverbial stage."

I take a shaky breath and look straight ahead because looking at Roman now is too difficult.

Heartbreaking even.

Oh no.

Complete understanding of all the feelings I have for him dawns on me, all at once.

In desperation, I say, "I need you to understand the dynamics. What I believe is about to happen at this lunch. Your father thinks he has leverage over me because of his PR retainer with Ryder & Harper Communications LA, but *he is* tying that to my casting authority over *Vendetta*. He moved the meeting up to force my hand before we can establish anything in relation to your branding strategy."

I glance over. He's still looking at me with that unnerving stillness.

My mind races with how to mitigate what's happening here. All at once, I'm convinced I can turn this right around with an innovative approach.

"Do you have any cash on you? A dollar, ten, twenty... even a hundred?" My voice gains a sliver of firmness.

He looks utterly bewildered. His anger is momentarily overshadowed by confusion. "Isla..."

"*Money*, Roman. Just a bill. Any bill." My urgency mirrors his earlier impatience. This feels vital. It's a necessary severing.

He reaches into his pocket and pulls out a sleek silver money clip, which holds a surprisingly thick roll of $100 bills. He thumbs through them. "How much do you need?" The question is flat, devoid of its earlier teasing warmth.

"You really shouldn't carry that much cash." It's a pointless deflection born of nerves.

"Isla." His voice is tight with discernible frustration. "*How much?*"

"Just the smallest one you've got. A hundred-dollar bill is fine." I sigh big. "This is... symbolic. A symbolic transaction."

He lets out a short, humorless laugh. "You hear this, Manny? A symbolic transaction. She gets more mysterious by the hour." He pulls a crisp $100 bill from his money clip. "I just follow along. For reasons I cannot yet define." There's no amusement in his voice now, only weariness and suspicion.

"I appreciate that about you, Mr. Lysander." The formality is intentional because I suddenly need to create distance between us. "Money. Pay up." I hold out my hand.

He hesitates for a fraction of a second, then places the bill into my palm. The crispness of the bill paper and his light touch feel strangely significant.

A severing.

I can feel it coming.

It's not the one I was planning.

I place the bill carefully on the plush carpet between us. "Okay then. That's done. This represents our agreement. You are now *my* client. *Our* client with Ryder & Harper Communications LA. Samantha's and mine. This $100 bill seals it until we draw up a formal contract with you. Any work we do for you, your rebranding, the strategy plan… it will be pro bono. It will be completely separate from Lysander Entertainment. Separate from *Vendetta*." I look him straight in the eye. "We're severing the tie to your father's contract, Roman. Right now. No middleman. No leverage."

He stares at the bill I've placed on the carpeted floor between us, then back at me. His expression hardens into something unreadable and infinitely more dangerous. "Okay," he says, the word drawn out, heavy with implication. "Why? My dad can be ruthless—severely destructive —when crossed, Isla. And this? This *will* cross him. And I'm being nice here," he adds, glancing towards the front, "because Manny has issues with my swearing."

"Good to know, but I can swear, too, as you well know." My tone is light, but something I don't actually feel. "Manny will find out about my own swearing habit soon enough. Especially the f-word. Ask my Malibu neighbor about the Porsche this morning. Sorry in advance, Manny." I catch Manny's brief, sympathetic smile in the rearview mirror.

It's a fleeting moment of shared humanity before the storm breaks wide open.

Roman ignores the attempt at levity. A humorless, almost cruel smile touches his lips. "Eat your sandwich, Isla Ryder." He gestures towards the plate still on my lap. "Because if you think *I* make you nervous, just wait. You're about to see my father's temper in full swing. But I guess I'm just not understanding the *why* yet. Why go through all of this?"

His cell phone rings, shrill in the tense silence. My stomach plummets.

"It's my dad." He shows me the caller ID. His expression is grim.

"Can you... *not take* it?" My throat feels like sandpaper.

The doubt I've been suppressing surges.

Did I just make a colossal mistake?

I watch him silence the call, sending it to voicemail. Seconds later, it rings again. Brandon Chase.

"Don't take his call either," I plead, leaning forward slightly. "Not yet. Just give me five minutes. Let me finish explaining. Then I think you'll understand why they're both calling you now."

He hesitates, then silences Brandon's call, too. He stares out the window again, his jaw working overtime as he clenches and unclenches it. The phone vibrates intermittently on the seat beside him— presumably texts now. The air in the Escalade is thick with distrust and unspoken accusations. It's suffocating.

The vibration of his phone against the leather seat creates a persistent, anxious rhythm. Each buzz feels like another nail in the coffin of whatever connection we had built. The taste of copper fills my mouth—I've been biting the inside of my cheek without realizing it.

"After spending time with you, it's clear to me that your father hasn't told you about the casting clause and he actually can't. He's bound by a very strict non-disclosure agreement, an NDA, which prevents him from sharing that information with you or anyone else. But I believe he's about to pressure me anyway and try to control me through the casting clause."

I pause, searching his face. "I know it sounds paranoid, and maybe it's nothing, but the NDA is very clear: if your dad violates it, Lysander Entertainment immediately loses the film rights to *Vendetta*. He should *know* that already, and I want you to be aware of what's truly at stake for him if he goes there. You need to warn him."

I swallow hard. "This morning, when Samantha called and told me he had moved the meeting up, that's when I knew. And then, I called Kimberley, and she told me that the attorneys at Lysander Entertainment were already calling her office this morning and inquiring about the parameters of the NDA with her attorneys. So… *we know* he's trying to force my hand—ignore the contract *and* the NDA, use his money, his power, and his influence to push the casting he wants by leveraging the PR retainer with Ryder & Harper over my proverbial head."

I gesture toward the hundred-dollar bill between us. "I just want what's best for *Vendetta*." I look him squarely in the eye. "And for my first official client. I will help you with your rebranding. I'm really good at it. You'll see." Then softly, "And we'll keep it pro bono. Clean lines. *See?*"

He finally looks at me, a thin, bitter smile tugging at the corner of his mouth. "Yeah, I *see*," he says quietly, the word heavy with reluctant understanding. "But that's not the point, is it? You help me with rebranding? How? You also decide who gets the lead role of *Vendetta*? How does that work, *exactly*, Isla? How were you going to play that out?"

"Keep them separate. Focus on your rebranding and then—"

"So secretly watch everything I do and see if I'm good enough to play your precious Steven Stryker? Yeah. I get it now. You hold the power to make or break my film career, Isla. The role of a lifetime." His eyes lock onto mine, sharp and cold, but shadowed with a gleam of something deeper—distress and disappointment, maybe even rage. "This isn't just about me. It's about my dad, too. Trent Lysander is going to go ballistic when he realizes too late what's at stake. He'll probably burn everything down, ignoring the fact that the odds are already stacked against him." He exhales slowly, the bitterness in his voice giving way to grim acceptance. "Thanks for warning me. I guess this fight is bigger than either of us."

"Roman, just know, Samantha and I remain committed to your rebranding." But desperation creeps in on me. "We *will* transform your image. Position you for serious roles. Roles like Steven Stryker and—"

"Yeah, that's the catch, though, isn't it?" He cuts me off, his voice rising slightly, sharp with anger now. "*You decide*. It's *your* decision. Not my dad's. Not Everest Bishop's. Not a casting director's. Certainly not mine. It's *yours*. You hold all the power over my fucking film career."

He leans toward me; his intensity pins me against the seat. "So how do I ever know? If I even get the part of Steven Stryker, how do I know if it's because I earned it because of talent? Or is it because you feel sorry for me? Or because we hooked up one night and you feel you owe me something? Or because my father leverages you in some other way I don't even know about yet?"

He shakes his head. This look of profound disillusionment washes over his features. "*See?* The one thing you are right about is the conflicts of interest. But it starts with *you*, Isla."

His gaze sweeps over me, dismissive, damning. "You've *known*. You've known from the moment we met on that beach what the conflicts were. Take it from me; someone who lives under the tabloid microscope: somehow, some way, they *will* all find out. Your secrets. Our connection. Truth or not, it won't matter. And you think I'll just be okay with all of that?" He scoffs. "Who would be? Believe it or not, I *do* have a moral compass. *Do you*, Isla? Suddenly, I'm not so sure. Look, I don't know what game you've been playing with me, but— "

"I'm *not* playing a game with you!" The denial bursts out of me, vehemently defensive.

I'm in shock.

After all, I've just shared with him?

And he is talking to me this way?

"Isla, your entire career as an ace PR strategist is *built* on playing games. Setting up narratives—true or not—to influence perception. That's the *definition* of the job!" His voice is laced with open contempt. He throws his hands up in exasperation, then lets them fall heavily onto his knees. He looks away, his profile etched with anger and hurt. "I think we're done here, Isla. I don't know what to think. I don't know what's *real* with you anymore." His voice drops again, low and venomous. "And I don't need your *fucking charity*."

He looks utterly devastated.

And I mirror him as I can feel myself shatter.

His words crush me. Each one driving deeper than the last. His anger—piercing, almost metallic—fills the space between us.

I debate telling Roman about Morgan Grant's article. The publicist in me knows I should tell him. But the personal part of me is too devastated by Roman's hostility to bring up exactly why his father has chosen today to meet. Yes, someone saw and knows about me and Roman. That's the play Trent Lysander is going for—insuring my compliance because he knows I'm compromised with his son already. But now, I'm not sure Roman even wants to hear it and somehow it will be one more thing he blames me for. So, I stay silent. *I embrace the silence.*

Outside, the landscape has changed; we're moving through the city now, buildings rising around us like indifferent sentinels. The sunlight that filters through the windows feels harsh, exposing every crack in my carefully constructed façade.

The Escalade slows, pulling smoothly to the curb in front of the sleek, modern lines of the executive office suites where Ryder & Harper Communications LA is located. Manny shifts the SUV into park. The sudden silence amplifies the wreckage that's taken over the space in the last half hour.

It's over.

"I believe this is your stop, Ms. Ryder," Manny says, his professional tone unwavering, though I sense pity in his eyes as they meet mine briefly in the rearview mirror. "I'll get your suitcase." He exits the SUV and heads towards the rear of the vehicle.

Numbly, I open the car door, dump out the coffee onto the street and set the empty mug next to the sandwich and place both on the floor next to his $100 bill. I grab my laptop bag. My movements are stiff. Robotic.

I finally dare to look at Roman. He stares straight ahead, avoiding even looking at me. Then he finally turns to me. His face is an impenetrable mask. The charming actor is completely replaced; he's a stranger now with cold, stormy blue eyes who doesn't even seem to see me. His smile is wicked with a deliberate imitation of warmth. It doesn't reach his eyes at all. The animosity radiating from him feels physical. It's like a blade piercing through all the layers of my carefully constructed defenses and straight into my soul.

"I'm sorry," I whisper. My words are inadequate. Pathetic. "I'm sorry for not telling you sooner. I didn't know how. My ability to be open… it's absolute shit. As you well know by now." The apology feels hollow even to me. "I'm sorry, Roman."

"See you at lunch," he says. The fake smile is firmly in place. His voice is chillingly pleasant. *Actor engaged.* "The Ivy. Should be quite the performance. I, for one, cannot wait." He pauses. "Good luck."

I can only nod. My throat is too tight to form actual words.

Manny appears at the open car door. I practically fall out of the SUV, scrambling for composure, desperate to escape the suffocating atmosphere of betrayal and accusations that radiate from him now.

By telling the truth and sharing my past, he dismissed all of it over the coveted role of Steven Stryker. There's no getting past this for either one of us. Any trust between us is irrevocably gone now. Set afire by both of us. Equally destroyed.

And I have no idea how to even begin fixing it.

There is no fix for this.

"See you at The Ivy then. You should warn your dad about the ramifications of the NDA and ensure he doesn't go there." I aim for indifference, hoping it masks the devastation threatening to engulf me as I land on the sidewalk.

Indifference. It's all I have left. It's the emotional armor I pull around myself as Manny sets my suitcase on the sidewalk beside me.

It's what propels me away from his Escalade without looking back.

It's all that sustains me now.

Awe, the catch.

His words echo in my mind, sharp and cruel. *'You have the power to make or break my film career, Isla. I see that now.'*

The catch.

Our ending.

All too soon.

I stand frozen on the sidewalk. The bustling sounds of West Hollywood fade into that familiar dull roar. The sun feels too bright, the air too thin. I stare unseeing at the elegant entrance of the office suite, and then numbly stare up at the tower.

I am so utterly broken by his words, by the hatred I saw in his eyes, that tears won't even form. My body feels hollowed out. Only the shell of me on the outside is left.

I've been holding my breath. My lungs ache for air. A choked gasp escapes.

Losing his trust, severing that tentative, fragile connection we formed in a matter of hours. It's more than just a physical ache. It's a confirmation of my deepest fear. The gaping hole inside of me opens even further. The very void I've spent years trying to protect, trying to pretend doesn't exist, is suddenly vast, wide, and all-consuming.

This. This is why.

Why I build walls.

Why I keep secrets.

Why I run.

'What are you so afraid of, Isla?' he asked me, just last night. His voice

was soft and endearing in the moonlight as he looked at me and wanted so desperately to know what I am always always always so afraid of.

This. This crushing weight of loss.

This feeling of being utterly, irrevocably alone because nothing lasts.

I recall my conversation with Kimberley just days ago, when I said, 'I don't care about the money.'

'Yes, *but everyone else does.* Just be aware of that. Power and money and fame—the three things that rule the world of the rich and famous.'

Oh God. It's true. That's all they care about. Even Roman.

That's all they care about.

And now, our connection is destroyed because of those very things.

Everyone leaves.

Everyone dies.

Everyone betrays you in some way.

The concrete beneath my feet feels unsteady. A passing businessman brushes against me, muttering an apology I barely register. The scent of coffee from a nearby café mingles with exhaust fumes and the subtle tang of jasmine from planters lining the sidewalk. These sensory details register distantly, as if through a thick fog that separates me from the world.

This never-ending agony of so much profound loss that tears at my very soul is the *why* of me.

The internal devastation from his outright rejection and recognizable hatred rushes through me like a silent tsunami, where the momentous force destroys everything in its wake. This incredible heartbreak engulfs all of me in a matter of minutes.

I look up and over just in time to catch the last of Roman Lysander's black Escalade disappear into the relentless flow of late Friday morning traffic in West Hollywood.

I am left standing on the edge of my new life.

I am set utterly adrift by the hatred I saw in his eyes.

Alone again, naturally.

A taxi honks nearby, the sound jarring me back to reality. I blink, realizing I've been standing motionless for minutes. My hand trembles as I reach for my suitcase handle. The world continues its relentless pace around me—people rushing past, cars flowing by. Life continuing, while I stand frozen in the aftermath of emotional devastation.

With mechanical movements, I walk toward the building entrance. Each step requires conscious effort, as if I'm relearning how to move through the world. The security guard nods as I approach, his casual greeting washing over me without penetrating the numbness.

In the elevator, I catch my reflection in the polished metal doors—a woman I barely recognize. Composed on the outside, shattered within. The perfect metaphor for my entire existence.

As the elevator rises, carrying me toward Samantha and our new beginning, I force myself to take deep breaths.

To rebuild the walls. To reset the mask.

By the time the doors open on our floor, I've constructed a semblance of professional composure. It's fragile, but it will have to do. Because in less than two hours, I'll be facing Trent Lysander across a dining table at The Ivy.

And Roman will be there, watching with those cold, contemptuous eyes that as recently as this morning looked at me with warmth and desire and the possibility of more.

The thought sends a fresh wave of pain through me, but I push it down, locking it away with all the other losses I've survived.

One step at a time.

One breath at a time.

Survival is what I do best.

But this feels different.

This feels catastrophic. I'm not sure about survival at this point.

love, where is your fire?

> *"Love isn't something you find.*
> *Love is something that finds you."*
>
> —Loretta Young

> *"The world breaks everyone*
> *and afterward many are strong*
> *at the broken places."*
>
> —Ernest Hemingway, *A Farewell to Arms*

CHAPTER 22

gold dust woman

Roman Lysander

"Gold Dust Woman" - Fleetwood Mac
"Ghosts of You" – 5 Seconds of Summer
"Everybody's Changing" – Keane
"Bitter Sweet Symphony" - The Verve

Late Friday Morning

THE AIR IN BRANDON CHASE'S OFFICE doesn't just smell expensive; it smells sanitized, scrubbed clean of anything resembling genuine human emotion. Brandon is a man of structure and plans and order. It's how he survives.

It's late Friday morning, pushing towards eleven, and the Beverly Hills sunlight battering the panoramic windows feels less like illumination and more like an interrogation lamp. It bounces off the stark white walls, the glass desk, the chrome accents, and somehow manages to highlight the aggressive sterility of the place. It feels offensively pristine. A stark contrast to the wreckage piling up inside my head.

I'm running on fumes—not the usual post-bender exhaustion, but something else entirely.

Isla Ryder fumes.

The lingering scent of her perfume in the Escalade, the phantom weight of her gaze, and the echo of her words slicing through the carefully constructed bullshit I call my life.

"I wrote the novel, Vendetta."

"I have final say on the casting of the lead roles, including the lead role of Steven Stryker for the film, Vendetta."

And my response. *"I get it now. You hold the power to make or break my film career, Isla. The role of a lifetime."*

Her voice. My voice.

Now it's on a nauseatingly constant loop in my mind. The $100 bill still lays symbolically on the floor of the SUV along with her untouched sandwich, like an incendiary device set to go off at an undetermined time only she knows. *Pro bono. Charity.* From the woman holding the goddamn keys to my future.

I walk in, still feeling the electrically charged atmosphere of that car ride that ended less than thirty minutes ago. The bitter aftertaste of betrayal —hers, mine, the universe's.

It feels like the worst kind of cut. The kind that doesn't bleed right away, but when it does, it doesn't stop.

It's a low-grade hum beneath my skin. A dissonant frequency, disrupting the usual practiced calm I project. I try to shove it down. I try to bury it under layers of indifference perfected over years under the Hollywood microscope. But it persists—stubborn, relentless.

It's like a lightning strike that lingers.

The kind that changes you from the inside, even if it doesn't kill you.

At first.

Brandon paces, like a director trapped in a screening room watching his passion project tank with test audiences. He looks crisp, sharp, and impatient in a dark suit that probably cost more than my first car, offset by a bold silk tie the color of arterial blood. He nods curtly; a gesture aimed somewhere in my general vicinity. All business. No charm wasted. Not today.

My skin radiates with awareness. This isn't a casual check-in. This isn't a "Happy late Birthday, how'd the party go?" kind of meeting. This is damage control. This is the pre-game sermon before the main event— the lunch meeting from hell my father apparently orchestrated with the woman who just detonated a bomb in the middle of my life.

Isla. Ryder.

He gestures vaguely towards the plush white couch, an island of intimidating softness in the corner. But I remain standing. Restless energy vibrates through me, making sitting feel like another type of surrender, like passive acceptance of whatever strategic maneuvering he's about to deploy.

Predictably, Brandon launches straight in. No preamble.

"Okay, Roman, we need to talk strategy. Seriously." He stops pacing and finally faces me, his expression etched with professional concern. Maybe a hint of frustration. "The studio's getting even more twitchy. Everest Bishop called this morning. Apparently, Morgan Grant's latest piece ruffled some feathers."

Ah, Morgan Grant. The perpetually circling vulture of LA gossip, always ready to feast on the slightest misstep. I force a casual note into my tone, though my jaw tightens. "Morgan Grant? What's she peddling now? Last I checked, a little mystery keeps people interested."

Brandon waves a dismissive hand, though his eyes remain laser sharp. "Mystery is one thing, Roman. Unpredictability linked to an eight-figure film investment is another. This piece..." He taps his tablet, angled so I can't see the screen. "...it's got hints. Whispers about a 'sophisticated brunette,' a late-night beach walk after your birthday party. It's vague, but it's enough to make the suits nervous. They connect dots faster than editors splice together a trailer from a film that isn't even shot yet. They see Roman Lysander's 'Bad Boy' persona potentially derailing their golden goose, *Vendetta*."

My stomach drops. *Sophisticated brunette.*

Isla.

So, someone *did* talk. Or someone *saw*.

I feel the weight of countless lenses, invisible but omnipresent. Hollywood has eyes everywhere. More cameras than a surveillance state.

And my father, he has the means. He knows how to plant seeds, and how to twist the narratives. The timing feels too convenient, hitting just as Isla Ryder arrives from New York, and just as this lunch meeting is suddenly sprung on all of us.

"It was nothing," I lie. The words feel thin and dishonest on impact.

Like delivering a line I don't believe in. "Met someone at my birthday party, staying nearby, walked them home. End of story. Grant's *reaching*."

Brandon gives me a look that says he doesn't entirely buy it, but he doesn't press—not on that specific detail, anyway. His focus is broader today.

"Reaching or not, it lands at a bad time, and it goes against the set-up narrative tying you to sparkly clean Melody Parker that your dad seems to be engineering personally at this point. You already know that Everest is sensitive about optics. He wants his Steven Stryker focused and committed. Not generating tabloid fodder the week before pre-production discussions intensify."

He sighs, running a hand through his perfectly styled hair. "Look, the 'bad boy' thing? It's served its purpose. Got you noticed. But it's a liability now, especially in connection with *Vendetta* while trying to land the lead role. We need to actively shift the narrative. Show them the actor, not the headline."

He starts pacing again, energized now, outlining *his* plan. "I've been working on it. We lean into craft. Arrange that interview with *Actors on Actors*. Set up a meeting with that indie director you admire, show them you're serious about diverse roles. We highlight your prep work for Stryker, maybe leak some controlled, positive behind-the-scenes stuff about your dedication. We build a narrative of focus, maturity, and artistic commitment. I'm sure those are some of the same strategies that Isla Ryder has in mind for you. We'll work together on it. For you."

He's outlining a solid strategy. The kind of careful, deliberate image recalibration that actually works long term. It's smart. It's targeted. It's exactly the kind of thing Isla Ryder was supposedly hired to do and would agree with, I'm sure. If that was her intention, but is it? *I don't know anymore.*

But my mind snags on the irony. While Brandon lays out a plan to build a perception of seriousness, I'm reeling from the knowledge that my shot at the role hinges not on my talent or dedication, but on the whim of a woman I just met, a woman whose motives are suddenly shrouded in suspicion, and a woman my father is clearly trying to manipulate.

"Sounds great, Brandon," I say, the words hollow. "Serious actor. Got it."

My lack of enthusiasm, the discordant note in my voice, finally seems to register with my best friend. Brandon stops pacing and finally studies me. "You seem… *off*. More than usual. What's really going on? Is it Grant's column?"

Before I can formulate a response, deflect, or confess, Brandon's phone buzzes insistently on his massive, impeccably polished glass desk. He glances at the caller ID, and a flicker of annoyance crosses his face. He hesitates, then answers. His voice shifting back into smooth talent manager mode.

"Mr. Lysander…Trent. Yes… Yes, I'm with Roman now. Concerns? About the optics? Yes, Morgan Grant's piece, I saw it… Absolutely, we're addressing it. I have a comprehensive strategy. Melody Parker?" Brandon's eyebrows shoot up. He turns slightly away from me, lowering his voice, but I can still hear the edge of disbelief and his pushback.

"With all due respect, sir, I think that's a reactive and somewhat superficial fix. My strategy focuses on substance. I understand the studio's anxiety, but a manufactured relationship feels counterproductive in demonstrating seriousness. Yes, I understand *Vendetta* is the priority. Stability. Right." He listens for another long moment, his jaw tightening almost imperceptibly. "Okay. Let me discuss it with Roman. Yes. See you at The Ivy then. Right. Goodbye."

He ends the call, placing the phone back on the desk with a quiet thud that resonates loudly in the suddenly tense silence. He looks at me. His expression is a mixture of frustration and weary resignation.

"Obviously, that was your dad," he states unnecessarily. "Apparently, he and certain elements at the studio have their own ideas about 'image stabilization.' They think pairing you publicly with Melody Parker will project the 'stability' they need to see. He's pressing hard for it now." He shakes his head, scoffing. "A strategic girlfriend. That's their brilliant counter to another gossip columnist's whisper. Ignore the long game and just throw some glitter on it. Classic studio panic moves, like slapping on a voice-over to fix a third-act problem."

Melody Parker. Of course. The human equivalent of a press release—bright, shiny, and utterly devoid of substance. The perfect Hollywood cliché. And my father's preferred method of control—manipulation disguised as assistance. Dad procures and buys me a girlfriend, however manufactured or plastic she might be and feel, so I have the stability, however designated, for the studio and the director. Never mind, my feelings about any of it.

Feelings. What are those?

A fresh wave of fury washes over me because it's not just about Morgan Grant's column. This seems to directly tie to Isla Ryder. This *is* about the casting clause. My father knows. Isla told me about her ties to it. The NDA he's under with Kimberley Powers' company. What was the name of it? Powers Media? Isla already told me this.

And now… this Melody Parker bullshit. It all makes sense. It's a preemptive strike. A way to muddy the waters, to create a public narrative that boxes Isla Ryder into the narrative of my father's choosing. Maybe even further creates leverage *against* her personally, if she's seen as interfering with my 'stable' relationship with Melody Parker. Or, if Isla is even seen with me. It's a power play aimed squarely at the woman who holds the key to casting.

And Brandon… Brandon's caught in the crossfire, pushing back against my father's interference, trying to implement *his* actual strategy.

He's not the enemy here.

He's just another pawn in one of my father's endless games.

The realization clarifies things and sharpens the anger raging away inside. The betrayal I feel from the car—Isla's perceived betrayal—is still raw and still confusing. *It stings.* But beneath that anger lies something deeper, more devastating–a crushing despair that threatens to swallow me whole.

It feels like every other connection that's inevitably soured under the glare of my life. But this, my father's calculated maneuvering, using Brandon, even the Melody Parker thing, in trying to control the *Vendetta* outcome through smoke and mirrors… It is a cold, yet familiar fury that I've dealt with before.

"He certainly knows, doesn't he?" I ask, my voice low, dangerous. "My father. He knows about Isla."

Brandon looks startled, then wary. "Knows what, specifically? He knows she's the PR strategist Kimberley Powers sent, the one tasked with your rebranding. He seemed intensely interested in having Isla handle your rebranding strategy."

"He didn't *tell* you?" The pieces click into place, ugly and razor-sharp. "Brandon," I finally say, my voice unnervingly steady despite the chaos inside me. "Isla Ryder is Ashley Thomas."

His confusion is immediate. "What? The author of *Vendetta*? That's not possible."

"There's more." I'm so bitter I cannot even form words. I take a beat, feeling the weight of this revelation sitting heavy in my chest like a goddamn stone. "He didn't tell you that Isla Ryder—writing as Ashley Thomas—*wrote Vendetta* and the goddamn screenplay. And that Kimberley Powers, queen of Powers & Winston, is her aunt, and with some side company, Powers Media, negotiated a clause giving Isla Ryder final fucking approval on casting the lead roles for *Vendetta*. Including Steven Stryker."

I watch Brandon's face as the information lands. Shock. Disbelief. Followed by a wave of dawning comprehension, then pure, unadulterated rage—directed not at me, but outwards.

"Final *say*?" he breathes, the color red rising in his neck. "*What*? And your dad *knows this*? Your dad knows she holds that kind of power, and he doesn't tell *us*? He just feeds us lines about 'optics' and 'studio nerves' and constantly *pressures* us about your image?"

He slams his hand down on the glass desk, making the pens rattle. "No wonder he's pushing this Melody Parker idiocy. It's not just about stabilizing your image for the studio; it's about controlling the narrative in and around *Isla Ryder*, too. Creating a public distraction, maybe trying to pressure her indirectly about casting. Jesus Christ! He sets us up, feeds us bullshit talking points while knowing the real stakes are completely different!"

He turns to me, his eyes blazing now with shared indignation. "He's playing *everyone*, Roman. Using the studio's anxiety, using Morgan Grant, trying to leverage you against Isla, trying to leverage *her* contract through public perception. This Melody Parker thing isn't just an idiotic ploy. It may be a calculated weapon in *his* game against *Isla Ryder*."

Brandon stops pacing suddenly. His brow furrows as something clicks for him. "Wait. How did you even find out about this casting clause? Your father obviously didn't tell you."

I hesitate, caught in the headlights of his direct questioning. The beach. The party. Last night. It all flashes through my mind in a chaotic montage.

"I met her. Isla Ryder. Before today."

Brandon's eyes widen. "You *met* her? *When? Where?*"

"On the beach. Yesterday. She was running. We literally collided into one another. She cut her knee when she fell on some broken glass at the beach, and I helped bandage her up."

I pause. Swallow hard. The memory of her blood on my hands is suddenly vivid and intense. The warmth of it. The strange intimacy of that moment with her when we first met. "I didn't know who she was right away," I say with feigned indifference, though my fingers flex involuntarily at the memory of it all and her. "Then I invited her to my birthday party last night, and she came. And then, she told me herself. In the car ride on the way here. Just now." I laugh, but it's hollow, devoid of humor. "And yes, she has final say on casting. Written into her screenwriter's contract. She controls whether I get the role of Steven Stryker." The words are torn from me. Each one burns my throat as I say them. "It's all separate from the whole retainer agreement with the public relations firm she and Samantha Harper have formed with Ryder & Harper Communications LA, where they're on retainer to Dad's company."

Brandon freezes, his expression shifting from confusion to shock to betrayal in rapid succession.

"That's... *Jesus Christ.*" He collapses into his chair. "Your father... He must *know.*"

"Of course he knows." The bitterness in my voice is unmistakable. "It's the same playbook he used during *Olympus Rising.* Remember? When he leaked those 'candid' photos of me and Cassandra to distract from the script rewrites? Manufactured drama to control the narrative."

Understanding dawns with my best friend. "The mysterious brunette from Morgan's column. That was *her.* That's who Morgan is hinting at? Isla Ryder?" He lets out a low whistle and studies my face for a few moments. "Jesus, Roman. Did you two...?"

"It wasn't a hook-up. It was... more than that." The defensive tone and hints of despair in my voice betray more than I intend.

I'm assailed with memories of her vulnerability, her tears, her easy laugh on the beach later when I walked her back home that first time. How I was enamored with the passion in her voice when she spoke about her work, and the film, *"Pride and Prejudice"*, and how she quietly spoke with such honesty about grief with the loss of her entire family.

The way her emerald green eyes caught the glimmering lights at my birthday party, the way she tilted her head when she was figuring out my playlist, the way she listened so intently to the songs I'd chosen for her, the thoughtful way she made me a birthday cake at one in the morning, the way our night together and the intimacy we shared in ways I've never felt before seemed real, the way she looked as she told me her most deeply personal revelations during the car ride an hour ago—it all comes flooding back to me in the form of a proverbial tsunami wave of too much emotion, too much angst, too much of everything.

There's no coming back from this.

Aloud to Brandon, I say, "We talked. About real things. She seemed... different. *She seemed real.* Until she wasn't."

I turn away, staring out at the Los Angeles skyline, a sprawling testament to beautiful facades hiding structural rot. The sun catches on glass and steel, creating a dazzling illusion of perfection that mirrors everything about this town.

"I brought her a latte this morning because she left her clutch with her passport and iPhone on the fireplace mantel at my place last night. Then, she needed a ride because she doesn't drive a manual transmission, so Manny and I gave her a ride." The words tumble out, each one carrying the weight of what I thought was a genuine connection. "And she's upset about the lunch meeting and already questioning why Trent is demanding that they meet today and not next Wednesday like she and her business partner, Samantha Harper, had planned. So, she tells me this whole story about writing *Vendetta* and having a final say on casting. She told me *everything* in the Escalade on the way here, right before this lunch takes place with Trent. In less than an hour."

I run a hand through my hair. "I feel like I'm in some twisted version of *Chinatown* where I'm both the detective and the mark." I shake my head. "But I don't know what to believe. Anymore."

Brandon studies me with newfound understanding. "And you don't know what to believe about *her*, either."

"Right. I don't know what to believe about *anything* anymore," I admit, the words scraping my throat raw. "Or, it's like that scene in *Heat* where Pacino and De Niro finally sit down across from each other, and you realize they're the same person on opposite sides of the law. Every word is both true and a potential lie."

I run my hands through my hair again, feeling the weight of history repeating itself. My fingers are cold, but my scalp burns with frustration. "I thought Isla was different. When we met on the beach... when we talked at the party... it felt real. For once in this fucking town, I thought I'd found someone genuine."

My voice cracks slightly, revealing the emotional wound beneath.

"She *saw* me, Brandon. Not Roman Lysander, Hollywood's favorite fuckup. Just… me. And I let myself believe it. *Believe her.*"

I stare out the window again, unseeing.

"And now? Now I find out she's been holding my career in her hands this entire time since we first met. That everything—every moment, every conversation, every touch—was probably just a part of her assessment of me. Was I good enough? Was I redeemable enough? Was I *worthy* enough to play her precious role of Steven Stryker in her film, *Vendetta*?"

The devastation hits in waves, each one stronger than the last. I press my palm against the cool glass of the window, needing something solid to ground me.

"I've spent my entire life being judged, evaluated, and found wanting. By my father. By critics. By fans. But this… feels like someone reached inside and pulled out whatever small part of me still believed in something real and effectively stopped my heart from beating."

I turn and look at him. Hoping for some kind of answer that will make this insurmountable pain expanding inside of me just go away.

I watch something shift in Brandon's expression. He's known me long enough to recognize when something's different. When something's gotten past the carefully constructed emotional barriers, I've built around myself.

Brandon watches me closely now, concern etched across his features. He's seen me through breakups, scandals, and career setbacks, but this is different. This isn't just professional disappointment or wounded pride.

This is something breaking at my core.

"You *like* her," he says quietly. Not a question.

I don't answer immediately. The truth is both simpler and more complicated than his statement. I stare at my hand against the glass, watching my breath create a small circle of fog that expands and contracts with each exhale.

"She got to me," I finally say. The admission feels like a surrender. "We made a connection. Before any of this clusterfuck. She just… saw through the bullshit. Called me on it. No agenda. At least, that's what I thought." My tone is bitter. Now I find out she's not just connected to *Vendetta*—she *created* it. She has the power to decide if I get the role that could change everything for me. And she's been hired to fix my image. It's the most twisted conflict of interest I've ever heard of."

Brandon's expression softens slightly. "Or she's *arming* you."

"What?"

"Think about it. She tells you about her role in casting *before* this lunch. Before your father could use it against you or manipulate the situation. She gave you information that changes how you'll approach this meeting." He leans against his desk, thoughtful. "Maybe she wasn't setting you up. Maybe she was giving you a fighting chance."

The idea catches me off guard. I haven't considered this angle. It doesn't erase the sting of discovering the power imbalance, but it casts her actions in a different light. I remember the tension in her shoulders as she spoke, the way her voice had wavered between professional detachment and something more vulnerable.

"Or maybe she's the most brilliant player in this game," I say, unable to fully surrender my suspicion. "Maybe telling me was just another move on the proverbial chess board."

Brandon shrugs. "Maybe. But from what you've said, she doesn't sound like someone who plays by Hollywood's rules. And you were with her last night. Did she seem like the type of girl that would risk everything just to be with you?"

"No. It wasn't like that." I turn from the window, remembering the way she'd looked at me on the beach, in the moonlight. The way she'd challenged me, questioned me, and seen me. "She's next level. She made me feel alive in ways I never thought I could feel with someone else. But I don't want to talk about her. I can't."

"Well, do you trust her?"

The question hangs in the air between us. I close my eyes briefly, seeing her face, hearing her voice. The quiet intensity when she talked about writing the novel, *Vendetta*, just an hour ago. The way she'd looked at me last night when I admitted my fears about pretty much everything.

"I don't know... I want to, though. That's the problem. I want to." The admission costs me something, but it feels necessary. Like lancing a wound.

"I'm not sure that's your most pressing problem, Ro. It might be that if you *don't* trust her... Well, it seems to me based on what I know about her from her file and what you've said. Isla Ryder doesn't strike me as someone who tolerates fools or cowards. Like *at all*."

"That's what makes her so dangerous. To me," I mutter, but the conviction in my voice wavers. The memory of her hurt expression in the SUV rises unbidden—the flash of pain in her eyes before she'd masked it with all that cool professionalism of hers. *Had that been real? Or just another performance?*

"I don't know what to tell you. I need to meet this girl to get a bead on her."

"Well, there's lunch in less than an hour. You'll meet her soon enough. Then, you can tell me what you think I should do, beyond staying as far away from her as possible. *My current plan.*" Even as I say it, I'm not sure if it's what I want. Or if it's even something I can actually do.

My father's manipulation is clear and unambiguous and utterly infuriating. He's treating *Vendetta*, this role, Isla, me, even Brandon, like chess pieces on his personal board.

And Brandon, my best friend and manager, he's not the betrayer. He was kept in the dark, just like I was, fed a line, expected to execute a play without knowing the real objective. His loyalty, unlike Isla's suddenly questionable position, feels solid, a known quantity in a sea of uncertainty. And in this town, in my life, that kind of loyalty is rarer than an honest film executive. It's something I value, something I need.

"Alright," I say, the restless energy consolidating into cold resolve. "Forget Melody Parker. We tell Trent that's not happening. At lunch, we tell him his strategic distraction is dead on arrival. That's *not* happening."

Brandon nods sharply, already shifting back into manager mode, but with a new, harder edge. "Consider it done. He wants to play games. Fine. But he's not playing them through me or you, not on this. Wow! With Isla having final say on casting… that changes the entire landscape of everything." He looks at me closely, assessing me. "This lunch meeting at The Ivy… it's not just a meet-and-greet. It's the main event. Round one."

"Looks like it," I say grimly. The thought of facing my father across a table, with Isla sitting right there, knowing what I now know, knowing the power she holds, and the game he's playing… it's going to be a performance, alright. Just not the one my father anticipates.

"What's your play?" Brandon asks.

I shake my head. The intense anger from the car ride has cooled into something more controlled but no less potent. The sting of Isla's revelation, the unmitigated feeling of betrayal by her I just can't shake, and the feeling of being manipulated by her, even if unintentionally, is still there.

"I don't trust her. Not fully. Maybe not at all. Maybe never. The conflicts she outlined seem insurmountable. How can I ever know if I earn the role if *she's* the one casting? How can *she* make that decision without bias after... *everything*? *It's a complete mindfuck*. My play?" I echo, a humorless smile twisting my lips. "My play is to show up. See what hand everyone reveals."

I think of Isla's earnest explanation, her vulnerability mixed with that core of steel, and all her talk of contracts and leverage. Then I think of her final words in the car, the hurt and despair I saw in her eyes, despite the indifferent sound of her voice when she said, *'See you at The Ivy then.'*

And yet her eyes mirrored the same destruction I feel now.

I don't know what to think.

'I don't know what's real or what isn't with you right now. And I don't need your fucking charity.'

My words. Harsh. And maybe true.

Maybe she isn't playing a game. Maybe she's just as caught up in this as I am. Or maybe she's the most skilled player of them all. The ambiguity is maddening, a familiar echo of fleeting connections promising something real before dissolving into headlines or misunderstandings.

Isla *felt* different. Until she wasn't. Until her revelation of the film rights contract, the casting clause, the goddamn conflicts of interest becomes the only thing I can see.

"Roman," Brandon calls after me as I turn towards the door, his voice serious. "We need to be *careful* at this lunch. You know your dad doesn't enjoy losing control. And Isla Ryder, she sounds like she knows how to protect her interests. You're walking into the middle of something extremely complex and potentially dangerous for your career, and even personally."

"Tell me about it." I step out into the hallway, heading to the private elevators. "See you there."

***

The world tilts. Everything is definitely unreliable. My father, the manipulator. Brandon, the surprising ally. And Isla... the beautiful, brilliant PR strategist, and now mysterious writer, who holds my career in her hands, who sparked something real in me before dousing it with the revelation of the ice-cold reality of contract clauses and conflicts of interest.

The woman who just might be, despite everything, the only one telling me the truth, even if it's a truth I don't want to hear.

I'm tempted to call her. Just to hear her say to me one more time, *'I have casting power,'* as if masochism is something I need practice on.

I call Manny instead. "Manny, change of plans," I say, my voice tight. "We won't head to The Ivy just yet. I need… I need a detour. Find me a quiet spot with a view. Somewhere I can think before walking into the goddamn lion's den."

The betrayal I feel from Isla is a fresh wound, definitely personal, and feels almost fatal. It echoes past hurts and betrayals and manipulations of everyone I've encountered in my life previously and just reinforces the emotional walls I keep meticulously maintained.

But my father's actions… that's a different betrayal altogether. Older, deeper, and colder. A calculated undermining that feels like the foundation of my entire existence.

As the elevator descends, I catch my reflection in the polished doors. I look the same, but I don't feel the same. Something has shifted. Something fundamental has changed.

One feels like a tragedy.

The other feels like war.

But both are almost interchangeable.

And the battle is about to begin.

CHAPTER 23

i remember everything

Roman Lysander

"I Remember Everything" - Zach Bryan, Kacey Musgraves
"Somewhere Only We Know" - Keane
"Creep"– Radiohead

Friday Afternoon 12:25 p.m.

THE DETOUR MANNY FINDS—a serpentine road climbing into the hills overlooking the Pacific—offers a spectacular view. Endless azure ocean dissolving into the cerulean void above. Usually, it centers me.

Today, the vastness just mirrors the chaotic emptiness churning inside of me. My skin feels too tight, like it's barely able to contain something so volatile and this dangerous. The quiet isolation does nothing to silence the loop playing in my head: Isla's confession, her justification, my accusation, her hurt, my anger, the goddamn $100 bill still on the floor of the Escalade like a miniature plutonium core, silent but catastrophically potent.

Pro bono. The words taste like ash. Like pity. Charity from the woman who holds my entire future in her hands. It scrapes against my emotionally raw nerves like sandpaper being run across an open flesh wound.

Just for fun.

Or directed torture.

My fingers drum against my thigh as memories flood unbidden—my father and me at the chessboard when I was ten, his voice cold as he captured my queen: *"You telegraphed your move, Roman. Never let them see what you're planning."* Not a lesson in strategy, but in deception. I wonder if Isla learned the same lesson from her father, or something entirely different.

The ocean blurs before me. I close my eyes, but the emptiness persists. A hollow ache spreads from my chest outward. Like a poison in my bloodstream. I feel worse.

Manny pulls up to The Ivy an hour later, dropping me off street side. The black Escalade glides away with the quiet efficiency of a getaway car. Stepping out of the cool, controlled environment into the sun-drenched sidewalk feels like walking onto a brightly lit stage just as the curtain rises on a particularly nasty drama.

Fame is a currency here, but today it feels like counterfeit bills—flashy but ultimately worthless in the face of the real power plays unfolding inside.

I pause just inside the entrance. The maître d', who appears to have been waiting for me, escorts me to the back patio where the richest creatures of Hollywood preside. If they could buy ambient sunshine, they would. I scan the patio where filtered sun with a modicum of Monstera greenery is allowed to live, creating the perfect union between man and nature. Hollywood Style.

The Ivy in West Hollywood isn't just a restaurant. It's a stage.

Sunlight, aggressively cheerful and weaponized by the California climate, bounces off pristine white tablecloths and the expertly applied veneers of the lunchtime crowd. Every clink of silverware, every murmured conversation, feels amplified.

The air carries the mingled scents of money—expensive perfumes, freshly pressed linen, and the particular aroma of entitlement that costs more than most people's monthly rent.

It's part of a performance where deals are sealed, careers are made or broken, and reputations are meticulously curated or casually destroyed over $40 salads. The kind of place where the air itself seems thick with ambition, smelling faintly of expensive perfume, desperation, and lemon-infused water.

The restaurant with its white picket fence, overflowing flower boxes, and patio buzzing with the low hum of privileged conversation, usually feels like quintessential LA charm. Today, it feels offensively cheerful. A technicolor façade slapped over something rotting from the inside out.

I'm deliberately late. Not fashionably, just enough to make a point.

Let them wait. Let them wonder.

Let him—*my father*—stew in the perfectly arranged power dynamics he's undoubtedly established at the table.

Let Brandon wonder, knowing the ground has shifted beneath his Gucci loafers.

Let Isla… *Oh… fuck.* Thinking about her sends a jolt through me. Leftover heat from last night mixed with this expanded, confusing cocktail of anger and betrayal that started during our shared car ride a little over two hours ago.

There they are.

A tableau of Hollywood tension.

My father, Trent Lysander, holds court at the prime table, radiating the effortless authority that comes with controlling a media empire. He looks relaxed, tanned, wearing a crisp white shirt open at the collar— the *no tie; it's Friday* look—the picture of casual power. Like a king surveying his domain, a faint predatory smile plays on his lips.

I am an exact replica of him, except for the eyes and his always intense Type A personality. His eyes run grey more than the deep blue like mine, Mom's genetic contribution, along with her more sunny, somewhat empathetic disposition, except for the last three hours and whenever I face a crisis or a betrayal that's when Dad appears in my demeanor, like the inherent flaws in character you cannot truly hide from forever. *Am I a product of my environment or genetics?*

You study it. You tell me.

• • •

Across from him, Isla sits poised and composed, a study in professional cool. She wears the tailored cream pantsuit that screams Manhattan competence, with her pink camisole that adds just enough confusion to her power—probably intentional. Her dark hair is pulled back sleekly.

Sophistication radiates from her like an extra superpower. Her face is a carefully constructed mask of neutrality, but I saw behind that mask this morning. I saw the flash of vulnerability, the guardedness, the sharp intelligence, and the devastating power she wields—the power she hid until the last possible moment.

It grates.

Her composure.

Her seemingly effortless control when I feel like I'm being shredded inside by conflicting impulses. Is it genuine strength, or the practiced calm of someone who knows exactly what cards they hold?

Beside her, Samantha Harper—her partner, is that *in crime?*—acts as a silent sentinel. Her blue-eyed gaze is watchful. Protective energy emanates from her. Samantha is the polar opposite of her best friend, Isla Ryder. She's the blonde bombshell to Isla's dark mahogany looks. Beautiful. Sophisticated. Intelligent. Ethereal like Isla. Just in the blonde version, instead of the brunette one. They look like a united front, an island of calm defiance in the face of the Trent Lysander empire.

Seeing Isla hits me like a sucker punch to the gut. The anger from our confrontation in the Escalade is still volatile, like an undelivered poison; deadly but harmless until deployed. You're going to die from it, but the timing is still unknown.

The question still echoes: *Who is she?* The bestselling author of *Vendetta*. The screenwriter with final casting approval. The woman who holds my career aspirations in her hands. Or the woman I spent hours with, talking, connecting, touching... only to find out she was holding the ultimate trump card. *Which one is she really?*

All I know is the feeling of being played again.

It cuts deep.

Too fucking deep.

Then there's Brandon. He looks like he's two seconds from bolting. The usual smooth confidence is gone, replaced by tension that radiates off of him in waves. He's reeling from the bombshells I dropped in his office more than an hour ago.

Ashley Thomas, the *Vendetta* author and screenwriter, is actually Isla Ryder with final casting approval.

He knows now how thoroughly my father played him, feeding him curated bullshit about optics and studio nerves while hiding the real stakes—her power. The realization that he's just a pawn has him completely off-balance.

His focus keeps drifting across the table to the beautiful blonde, Samantha Harper. There's a glimmer of unguarded interest there. He's latching onto her presence as a momentary escape because this calm, stylish, blue-eyed blonde from Manhattan is a world away from the Lysander family drama.

It's a dangerous distraction, ignoring the apex predator at the table, but I see why he's doing it. He's looking for solid ground in a situation that has just turned into quicksand. Samantha is an unexpected, maybe even refreshing, focal point amidst the chaos.

My ally looks lost, and that's a problem.

Taking a breath, I plaster on the Roman Lysander smile—the one I reserve for cameras and uncomfortable situations. It feels stiff, alien on my face.

Time for the performance to begin.

I walk towards the table, the low hum of conversation momentarily dipping as heads turn. My father looks up, his expression unreadable but with discernible hints of impatience. Brandon offers a strained smile that doesn't reach his eyes.

I look at him. *Calm down, bro. Let's play this out.* He nods somewhat subtly.

Samantha's gaze is wary.

And Isla.

Isla.

She looks up. Her emerald green eyes are darker, telegraphing animosity or defiance. They meet mine. There's a shimmer of something behind the professional façade. Outrage? Indignation? But for a split second, the air electrically charges with the memory of our night together but then is simultaneously erased in the next with the fresh memory of this morning's hostile confrontation.

You mad, baby?

I'm not the one who lied about everything.

"Roman. Glad you could *finally* join us," my father says, his tone smooth but edged with steel. He gestures to the empty chair beside Brandon at the round table for six. The seat of the compliant son.

I ignore it. Instead, I pull out the empty chair beside Isla, deliberately positioning myself across from my father and Brandon. A minor act of defiance, but the shift in energy around the table is immediate. Brandon's unease intensifies. My father's eyes narrow almost imperceptibly.

Isla glances at me, a fleeting, unreadable expression crossing her face before the mask slips back into place. Samantha subtly shifts in her seat, her posture still protective of Isla, but perhaps a fraction less tense now that I'm not so aligned with the opposition.

"Sorry I'm late," I say, settling into the chair. "Traffic was brutal."

A standard LA excuse.

Meaningless.

A waiter appears instantly, hovering. "Can I get you something to drink, Mr. Lysander?"

"Just water for now." My eyes briefly meet Isla's again. She looks away, focusing on the menu as if it contains state secrets.

The small talk begins, strained and brittle. My father inquires about Isla and Samantha's flights, their initial impressions of LA, all delivered with the practiced charm of a man used to controlling every room he enters. Brandon chimes in with forced enthusiasm, praising their reputation and acumen, showing notable interest in their boutique public relations firm as if we're all going to be good friends.

He doesn't yet know about all the undercurrents between Isla and me, just some of them, so he's looking for cues from me which aren't exactly forthcoming.

It's all bullshit, a carefully choreographed dance around the real issues simmering beneath the surface.

I stay mostly silent, observing. Watching the way my father subtly steers the conversation, the way Brandon seems preoccupied with Samantha Harper, and the way Isla responds to my dad's inquisition with polite, measured professionalism. She gives nothing away.

Samantha remains quiet except for covert glances at my best friend, probably wondering if he's an ally or foe to Isla. She barely glances in my direction. She's been briefed. *About me.* Her presence here is to serve as a steady, grounding force for Isla.

The troops are assembled.

Which side are we all going to take?

My father leans forward, his fingers in that familiar steeple—a signal for the conversational shift that's coming. The motion triggers a flash of memory: him, sitting across from me at the chessboard, fingers steepled exactly the same way before he'd take my rook, my knight, and my hope of winning. The muscle memory of those childhood defeats tightens inside my chest like a fist.

"So, *Vendetta.* An exciting project. Everest Bishop is thrilled with the script. Ashley Thomas' work is truly exceptional." He smiles benignly, but his eyes are laser focused.

"And of course, we're all incredibly excited about Roman taking on Steven Stryker. He was born to play that role," he says. It's casually stated, as if it's a done deal. A foregone conclusion. Classic Trent Lysander. State your desired outcome as fact and dare anyone to contradict you.

I watch Isla. Her expression remains neutral, but I see the slight tightening around her beautiful mouth, the careful stillness in her posture. She doesn't take the bait. She simply offers a noncommittal nod. "It's a complex role. It requires a specific kind of depth."

Her voice is calm and professional, but the implication hangs in the air. *Depth.* The one quality the tabloids—and perhaps even my own father—seem determined to deny I possess.

My father waves a dismissive hand. "Roman has the depth. He just needs the right vehicle. *Vendetta* is *that vehicle.* It'll solidify him as a serious actor, put all this... *noise*... behind him." He glances at me, a look that's both paternalistic and proprietary.

The 'noise' he's referring to is the carefully cultivated 'bad boy' image, the scandals happily fueled by Morgan Grant and her posse. The image Isla is supposedly here to fix.

Brandon, seeing his cue, jumps in. "Speaking of changing the narrative, Trent, after your phone call earlier, Roman and I discussed the Melody Parker situation, and we want to go in a different direction. We'll work directly with Isla and Samantha and focus on highlighting

Roman's craft." He smiles, looking between my father and me, then at Isla and Samantha. "Roman wants to move away from all of that. Miss Parker would be more of a distraction than an asset at this juncture."

Ah, the Melody bomb. Dropped precisely as planned.

My father shakes his head in disapproval. "But Melody is a lovely girl. Stable. Good for his image. The studio is pleased. It shows maturity. Roman, you need to reconsider."

Maturity. As if dating America's sweetheart, a woman whose personality seems largely manufactured for public consumption, is the benchmark for emotional growth.

Here's my moment. The chance to shut this down and move forward with the plan Brandon and I already agreed upon. *The smart play.*

Instead, I lean forward, voice low but carrying. "You think so, Dad? You actually approve of Melody Parker?"

My words drip with something darker than sarcasm. Dad's eyes gleam with surprise, maybe even satisfaction. He thinks I'm coming around to his way of thinking.

"Yes, Roman. I think she's perfect for you." Dad smiles. The predator in him pleased. "Exactly. Stability sells. Stability wins."

I deliberately turn my gaze to Isla, watching for her reaction. This is the moment. This is the test. Her professional mask wavers for just an instant, and I catch something almost painful shimmering behind those beautiful eyes of hers.

Why am I doing this? We already decided. Brandon and I already fucking decided.

But I can't stop myself. The need to hurt her, to make her feel even a fraction of what I felt during that car ride this morning, overrides everything else.

"Is that what you want, Roman?" Isla's voice cuts through the ambient restaurant chatter like a blade. Her emerald green eyes bore into mine with an intensity that makes the rest of the table fade away. "A *relationship* with Melody Parker?"

The question hits me like acid at my throat. There's something desperate in her tone, carefully controlled but unmistakably there. She's asking about more than just a publicity stunt, and we both know it.

I should say *no.* I should stick to the plan.

Instead, I twist the knife.

"Would that *bother* you?" My voice carries just enough of an edge to draw blood.

Her composure fractures slightly. "I'm simply asking as your publicist. Samantha and I would never manage that kind of... arrangement." The words come out strained, professional veneer barely intact.

"Arrangement," I say, letting the word hang between us like a blade. "That's what we're calling relationships now?"

"Roman—" she starts, but I cut her off.

"What's wrong? Afraid your idea of a perfect Steven Stryker can't handle dating America's sweetheart?" The cruelty in my tone surprises even me.

She flinches as if I've struck her. For a moment, her mask slips completely, and I see it—the depth of her pain, undisguised and unguarded. It's not just professional disappointment or strategic concern. It's personal. Devastatingly personal.

The sight stops me cold. This isn't the calculated response of someone playing games. This is someone who's been gutted and is trying desperately not to bleed out in public.

What the hell am I doing?

"I see," she whispers, her voice barely audible. She looks down at her hands resting on the table, and I watch her rebuild her walls in real time, brick by emotional brick.

The surrounding table has gone silent. Brandon looks uncomfortable. Samantha looks overly protective and angry, as if ready to strike out at me if the signal from Isla is given. My father seems intrigued by the undercurrents he's witnessing but doesn't yet fully understand all the dynamics, but it won't take him long.

Fuck. Fuck. Fuck.

Without thinking, I reach across the table and touch her hand. She looks up, completely startled. *Still wounded by me. Clearly.*

"I'm not starting anything with Melody Parker," I say firmly, my voice carrying across the table to my father as much as to her. "That's not happening."

Her eyes search mine, looking for the lie, the manipulation, the angle. But there isn't one. Not about this.

"That kind of publicity stunt isn't something we'd manage anyway." Samantha's interjection is delivered with such a cooling effect, I am left to wonder if she can control the weather, too. "Our firm doesn't deal in manufactured relationships."

My father's expression darkens. "Roman, you're making a mistake."

"No," I say, my hand still covering Isla's. "I'm making a choice. The Melody Parker thing is dead. Find another way to sell stability."

Isla carefully pulls her hand away. The professional mask slides back into place, but something has shifted between us. The anger is still there, the betrayal still fresh, but underneath it all is something far more complex, far more fragile.

Something that might be worth salvaging, if we can both stop trying to destroy each other long enough to figure out what it is.

Brandon shifts uncomfortably, shooting me a look that clearly asks, *'bro, what the fuck are you doing?'*

I don't know what I'm doing. I'm hurting her on purpose in these subtle ways to make some kind of point. *But what point, exactly?*

You hurt Roman Lysander; you pay for what you've done.

It's not working.

Neither one of us is winning. What are we fighting for?

I want to hate her. That would be so much easier. But the pull is still there, magnetic and undeniable.

It's like I've imprinted on her, and I can't get her out of my head.

And I'm drowning here.

Clearly.

My father watches me closely now, confused by the turn of events, wondering what I'm playing at and why I'm not falling in line like I always do. Like I have for the past twelve years since Mom died.

His eyes narrow, studying the interaction between Isla and me with the calculating intensity of someone who's just realized his opponents might not be playing the game he thought they were. The silence stretches, heavy with unspoken questions and barely contained tensions.

"Well," he says finally, his voice deceptively light, "It seems there are some... dynamics... at play here that I wasn't aware of." His gaze shifts between Isla and me, and I can practically see the gears turning. "Perhaps we should discuss the actual business at hand. Isla, I understand you have some thoughts about Roman's rebranding strategy?"

She straightens. The professional mask is firmly back in place with practiced ease. But I catch the slight tremor in her hands before she clasps them in her lap below the table.

"Yes," she says, her voice steady now. "Samantha and I have reviewed Roman's current public profile extensively. The current persona has served its purpose in terms of generating interest and maintaining relevance, but it's become a liability for more serious roles."

"Such as Steven Stryker," my father prompts, that predatory smile returning.

"Such as any role that requires the audience to see his depth and vulnerability," she says smoothly. "The goal is to establish and then expand his versatility—to establish Roman as a versatile actor capable of carrying complex, meaningful projects."

Brandon leans forward, finally finding his footing again. "That aligns perfectly with our long-term strategy. We want to highlight Roman's commitment to craft, his preparation process, and his range—"

"His *stability*," my father interjects, shooting me a pointed look. "Which brings us back to the Melody Parker situation."

The temperature at the table drops by several degrees. I feel Isla tense up beside me, though her expression remains neutral.

"With all due respect, Mr. Lysander," Samantha speaks up, her voice crisp and professional, "manufactured relationships are antithetical to authentic rebranding. They create more problems than they solve, particularly when the goal is to establish genuine credibility."

"Genuine credibility." My father's tone suggests he finds the concept quaint. "In Hollywood?"

"Especially in Hollywood," Isla says quietly. "Audiences are more sophisticated than they used to be. They can discern a publicity stunt from miles away. If the goal is to position Roman as a serious actor, then every aspect of his public persona needs to support that narrative authentically."

I watch her as she speaks, noting the passion that creeps into her voice when she talks about authenticity, about truth in storytelling. It's the same intensity I heard when she talked about *Pride and Prejudice* on the beach, the same fire and depth that drew me to her in the first place.

Before I knew for certain who she was. Before, everything got so fucking complicated.

"And what would you suggest instead?" my father asks, his tone suggesting he's humoring her.

"Focus on the work," she says simply. "Document his preparation process for auditions. Showcase his collaboration with respected directors and acting coaches. Highlight his interest in challenging material, not just commercial successes."

"Boring," my father says, dismissing all of her ideas out of hand.

"The public wants romance, drama, something to invest in emotionally."

"They want authenticity," Isla counters, a flash of steel in her voice. "They want to believe in the person behind the performance."

The fucking irony. She's talking about authenticity while hiding the biggest lie of all—her power over my career, her true identity, the conflicts of interest that makes this entire conversation a farce.

"And what about personal relationships?" I ask, my voice deliberately casual. "Where do those fit into this authentic rebranding?"

Isla meets my gaze directly, and for a moment, the professional mask slips again. I see the hurt there, the confusion, the same intense vulnerability I felt during the car ride this morning before everything effectively blew up between us.

"Personal relationships should be personal," she says quietly. "They shouldn't be commodified or weaponized for public consumption."

The words hit like a gut punch. Because that's exactly what we're doing, isn't it? Commodifying whatever this is between us, weaponizing it against each other in this twisted game of power and betrayal.

My father laughs, a sound devoid of warmth. "How refreshingly *naïve*. In this business, everything is for public consumption. Everything is a commodity."

"Not everything," Isla says, her voice barely above a whisper, but her eyes are locked on mine.

The waiter appears, breaking the tension momentarily as we order—salads and entrees that none of us will probably touch. Props in this elaborate performance we're all giving.

As soon as he leaves, my father leans back, fingers steepled again. "Let me be frank," he says, his voice taking on the tone he uses in boardrooms when he's about to destroy someone's career. "Roman *needs* *Vendetta*. This role could change everything for him. And while I appreciate your... theoretical approach to public relations, the practical reality is that studios want guarantees. They want stability. They want assurance that their investment won't be derailed by another scandal or another Morgan Grant exposé."

He pauses, letting that sink in. "Melody Parker represents that assurance. She's charming, she's popular, and she photographs well with Roman. It's a smart business decision."

"It's also completely hollow," I find myself saying, the words tumbling out before I can stop them. "You want me to fake a relationship with someone I barely know to convince a studio I'm stable enough to play a role that requires emotional honesty?"

"Welcome to Hollywood, son," he says dryly.

"No." The word comes out harder than I intended. "I'm not doing it. Find another way."

The silence that follows is deafening. My father's expression shifts from surprise to something darker, more dangerous.

"Roman," he says, his voice low and warning. "You're not thinking clearly."

"Maybe I'm thinking clearly for the first time in years."

Brandon shifts uncomfortably, caught between loyalty to me and years of working within my father's system. Samantha watches the exchange with sharp eyes, protective of Isla, but clearly fascinated by the family dynamics playing out in front of her.

And Isla... Isla looks like she's watching something break in real time and isn't sure whether to try to fix it or just get out of the way of the falling pieces.

"Perhaps," Isla says carefully, "we could explore some alternative approaches. Ways to demonstrate stability without manufactured relationships."

My father's smile is razor sharp. "I'm listening."

But I can see it in his eyes—he's not really listening. He's calculating, and planning his next move in this game, where apparently everyone else is a chess piece, except him.

The food arrives, providing another momentary reprieve. But I can feel the tension building, the careful politeness starting to fracture under the weight of all the things we're not saying.

The casting clause.

The power Isla holds.

The fact that she could end this entire conversation with six words: "Roman won't be playing Steven Stryker."

But she doesn't. She sits there, outwardly professionally composed, letting my father think he has the upper hand while she clearly holds all the cards.

I can't tell if she's on my side or about to destroy me.

I don't know if that makes her my ally or the most dangerous player at this table.

Maybe both.

The game just got messier. And I'm still not sure who's playing whom.

But one thing's becoming clear—Isla Ryder is a fucking warrior, and I've been treating her like just another Hollywood player since our shared car ride.

And that might be my biggest mistake yet.

CHAPTER 24

hold back the river

Roman Lysander

"Hold Back The River" - James Bay
"When Doves Cry" - Prince
"Cold Heart" – Elton John, Dua Lipa, PNAU
"Save Your Tears" - The Weeknd, Ariana Grande

Friday Afternoon 3:00 p.m.

THE FOOD SITS UNTOUCHED, growing cold, as the tension at our table reaches a breaking point. My father's patience—never his strongest virtue—wears thin like expensive fabric fraying at the edges. I catch the subtle shift in his posture, the way his shoulders square, and his jaw sets.

Game time.

"Roman." His voice carries that familiar edge of authority that used to make me fall in line immediately. "Let's cut through the philosophical debates about authenticity and focus on reality. You want the Stryker role? Then you need to demonstrate the kind of judgment that makes studios comfortable investing eight figures in you."

He leans forward, and I catch a whiff of his cologne—the same expensive scent that filled his study during all those childhood lectures about responsibility and family legacy. The smell triggers muscle memory: ten years old, standing before his desk while he explained why I'd disappointed him again. My stomach clenches involuntarily.

"Melody Parker isn't just a suggestion. It's a strategic necessity. The studio executives need to see stability, maturity, and commitment. They need to see that you can maintain a relationship with someone who enhances rather than threatens their investment."

Enhances rather than threatens.

His gaze lands briefly on Isla. The implication slams into me like a sledgehammer. He's not just talking about Melody anymore. He's talking about the "sophisticated brunette" from Morgan Grant's column. The woman sitting beside me who holds more power over my career than he does. A fact that clearly infuriates him.

Isla's composure never wavers, but I see her clasped hands in her lap tighten almost imperceptibly. She knows exactly what game is being played here. *We all do.*

"And what if I refuse?" I ask, my voice steady despite the adrenaline coursing through my veins.

My father's smile turns cold, then calculating. His dark blue eyes get that mean glint, the one where the punishment was meted out shortly thereafter when I was a kid. "Then you'll discover just how difficult it can be to get meetings in this town. How quickly projects can fall through. How easily an actor can find himself... in between opportunities."

The threat is naked.

Undisguised.

Fall in line or watch me systematically dismantle your career using every connection, every favor, and every piece of leverage I've accumulated over decades in this business.

Thanks, Dad.

Brandon looks like he wants to crawl under the table.

Samantha's protective instincts kick in as she watches Isla, probably calculating whether they need to abort this entire mission.

And Isla...

Isla sits perfectly still, but I feel the energy radiating off her like heat from a forge. She's watching this power play unfold, seeing exactly how my father operates. How he uses threats and manipulation disguised as paternal concern.

She's cataloguing every move.

"Enhance rather than threaten. That's an interesting perspective, Mr.

Lysander," she says quietly, her voice cutting through the tension like a Japanese Katana sword cuts through silk. "But I think you're operating under some false assumptions about Melody Parker."

The shift in her tone makes everyone at the table lean in slightly. There's something in the sound of her voice, just a slight hint of controlled fury that promises devastation.

"She's certainly… *visible*," Isla says, "but she's volatile. I saw it in real time at Roman's birthday party. Melody Parker is her own set of problems." The faintest hint of disdain enters her tone. "She didn't know who I was. Roman invited me to his birthday party as a courtesy, having helped me earlier in the day with a mishap at the beach during a run. Ms. Parker came up to me and made a point of making me feel unwelcome in her sphere, without knowing exactly who I was. It's a dangerous thing… for a *serious* actress to do."

Here we go.

"What did she do, Isla?" Samantha asks, clearly ready to defend her best friend.

"She just made an offhanded comment about what I was wearing."

"What did she *say, exactly*?"

"It's not important."

"It *is* important." I weigh in for reasons I can't fully explain. Suddenly, I need to know exactly what Melody said to her. The protective instinct kicks in, surprising even me.

"It's nothing, really." Isla attempts to laugh, but it sounds hollow.

My dad watches her intently, filing away every word she utters.

Isla shrugs nonchalantly. "She said, 'you'll learn'. It was just a backhanded comment. No harm, no foul, but I would say that since she didn't *know* who I was, it was careless—"

"It's just a bitchy thing to say," Samantha interrupts fiercely. "Your Free People top with the black leather jeans and the Iggy Crystals slingbacks? Chef's kiss. Dressed to the nines. Oh my God, what is *wrong* with these people?"

"Everything," I say with a tired smile. For just a moment, the tension breaks slightly at the table. "You looked fantastic. Ethereal."

Her lips part as if to smile, but she doesn't. Instead, she touches Samantha's hand, just for a moment. "Sammy girl, let's stay on track," Isla says softly, but shares a grateful look with her friend.

"I'm with Sammy girl," Brandon says with a laugh. He's clearly enraptured with this woman who would go to the mat to defend her friend even in front of Trent Lysander. "I realize I saw you talking to the caterer Julie before my birthday speech to Roman, Isla. You looked great."

"Thanks, Brandon. Traded some recipes with Julie," Isla says quietly.

"Isla's a fabulous baker," Samantha says with enthusiasm. Isla subtly shakes her head at her.

"She is." The words are stolen from me. I don't know what made me say them out loud. Isla gives me this warning look. Telegraphing clearly, *'Don't,* Roman.'

Still.

New alliances are forming in real time.

It's all whipsawing past my father, who seems to be seething at the interruption, and more determined than ever to get things back on track for whatever mass destruction he has planned.

"Regardless," Isla says, picking up the thread of the conversation. "The point is not about fashion or even her throwaway comment. It's just that kind of volatility, and carelessness in not knowing who the players are, that could get her into trouble, which would just add an extra burden to what we're trying to accomplish with Roman. And Ryder & Harper Communications LA *will not* manage someone like that," Isla says with a subtle shrug of her slim shoulders.

She lays the last comment out there as if she's just set a bomb in the middle of the table to be detonated later. And then, she smiles at my dad ever so sweetly.

Holy fuck.

Melody Parker will not be cast in the role of Evelyn Stryker in the film, Vendetta.

"In any case," Isla says softly, "as I said, Melody Parker represents her own set of problems. A fake relationship like that has a significant downside. If the public gets any sense that it's fabricated, then all momentum is lost and irrecoverable, as Samantha has clearly stated *twice* now. Exactly the opposite of what we're trying to accomplish here."

She looks directly at my father again. The smile vanquished as if it never was. "I guess you have to ask yourself—is a fake relationship even remotely something that Steven Stryker's character would ever consider in order to be taken seriously? I think not. At least, that's the measurement of character that I would use. Would the character of Steven Stryker ever consider a fake relationship in order to fool the public into how *serious* he might be? Would that actually ever make it into a film?" Her laugh is brittle. *Cutting.*

My dad's eyes flash dark blue. "I don't think you need to be insulting Roman."

"I'm not insulting anyone. It's a dangerous plan. Brandon told you they are no longer considering it. And Roman..." Her gaze lands on me, and I catch this imperceptible question crossing her features—if I weren't looking for it, I would have missed it. "Roman backed his play."

She tears her gaze away from mine. Her hand trembles slightly, and she quickly hides it beneath the table. It's the only indication that things are not quite right with Isla Ryder. I seem to be the only one who notices.

I watch her armor up again in real time—shoulders straightening, mask sliding into place, and her emotional walls rebuilding.

She's protecting herself.

From all of us.

From me.

"A manufactured, fake relationship is not something Samantha and I would ever manage. *Like ever.*" Her voice grows stronger. "So, there's that. We don't work that way. Our goal is to work with clients who are interested in embracing positive change, controlling the narrative, yes, but striving for honest communications. We're selective. With the goal of effectively vetting every client we take on, ensuring that the relationship is based on trust and honesty. No more, no less than that. And in this town, we think Ryder & Harper Communications LA can make a tremendous impact with a few select clients who agree with our philosophy."

Trust and honesty. The words hit me hard. After this morning's car ride, after all the accusations I hurled at her, the irony cuts deep.

"Well, what exactly are you bringing to the table, then, Ms. Ryder?" My father practically hisses. "I haven't heard any of your great ideas or been presented with your strategic plan."

"Well, let's see." Her voice takes on a dangerous edge. "It's Friday afternoon. The markets just closed where I'm from. I just got off a plane from the East Coast yesterday, Samantha arrived early this morning, and you want a strategic plan from Ryder &

Harper Communications LA within hours of our arrival here? Life just doesn't work that way, Mr. Lysander. And I appreciate lunch at The Ivy, but I'm just wondering—what is *your objective*, exactly? What did you hope to accomplish before our first weekend in town?"

She's turning the tables. Putting him on the defensive.

"Well, at a hundred-thousand-dollar clip a month, I would expect you to have something concrete to present to me since I'm paying you such an exorbitant retainer," he says. "You should be working 24/7 on Roman's rehabilitation strategy plan. That's why I'm paying you so much."

The shift in Isla is subtle, but I see it. The final piece of armor slides into place.

She sets down her water glass with a sharp thwack—hard enough that I think it might shatter. The sound cuts through the ambient restaurant chatter like a gunshot. Other diners glance around because of the noise. She doesn't even blink.

Here we go.

"Well, this is all very fascinating," she says coolly, her tone polite but firm, reclaiming control of the conversation. "I think it's important that we establish some ground rules going forward."

She straightens in her chair, and despite everything—the hurt, the anger, the sense of betrayal between us—I can't help but admire the way she commands the room. There's a quiet strength in her that's impossible to ignore.

She's magnificent.

"First," she says, "Roman's personal life is off-limits. No manufactured relationships, no strategic dating arrangements, and no publicity stunts designed to project stability. If he chooses to date someone, that's his decision, not a marketing strategy."

My father's expression darkens, but he doesn't interrupt.

"Second, any rebranding efforts will focus on his craft, his preparation, and his commitment to the work. We'll document his process, showcase his range, and highlight his growth as an actor. But it will be authentic, not manufactured."

She pauses, her eyes finding mine briefly before returning to my father. "And third, there will be no interference, no threats, and no attempts to control or manipulate the casting process. Roman shall be considered for the role of Steven Stryker based on his merit as an actor, nothing more, nothing less."

She's drawing battle lines.

"But perhaps we should address the primary reason we are here, Mr. Lysander." Her voice grows deadly quiet. "Go ahead. Tell us. And I shall remind you that you and your company, Lysander Entertainment, are under a non-disclosure agreement with Powers Media. Kimberley Powers sends her regards, by the way. And I will reiterate one last time that you are under an NDA. If you want to discuss Roman's branding strategy, *great*. Everything else is *off the table*."

Dad raises an eyebrow, unused to being interrupted or called out so directly. He recovers though, and a slow, dangerous smile spreads across his face. The kind of smile that precedes imminent destruction.

The king preparing his killing blow.

"I believe we *should* address the conflicts of interest that *do exist*. I would like your absolute assurance that there aren't any, Ms. Ryder."

"There aren't any. Everything is under control. I've briefly met with Roman. We're encouraged that we can make this work."

"But perhaps... a change in strategy is going to be necessary, Ms. Ryder?" Dad asks. His contempt for her becomes obvious. I can't figure out what his real axe to grind with Isla is.

"Trent," she says deliberately, using his first name like a weapon. "Don't do it. You're being ridiculous. There's no need for this hostility. And I will remind you one last time that you are under a non-disclosure agreement with Powers Media and that is tied directly to *Vendetta*. Take it offline with Kimberley Powers. She'll be here early next week." She pauses for a moment in an attempt to slow things down, I think.

"Better yet. Pick up your cell and *call her*. *Right now*. We can wait. You don't want to do this. You know what the terms are of the NDA you're under. Let's discuss Roman's branding strategy from a high level. That's fine. Everything else is off limits. Do you *understand* me?"

"I believe we should address the conflicts of interest that exist, Ms. Ryder. Or should I say... Ms. Thomas?"

And there it is.

He leans forward, his voice dropping to a conspiratorial whisper, clearly intending this to be the killing blow, the revelation that will expose her, isolate her, and drive a wedge between us.

"You see, Roman, your talented PR strategist here is also the brilliant author, with the pen name of Ashley Thomas, who wrote the novel *Vendetta* and the screenplay. And, thanks to some rather aggressive negotiating by her aunt, Kimberley Powers, she holds final approval over casting. Specifically, the casting of Steven Stryker."

He looks at me, expecting shock, anger, betrayal. Expecting me to turn on her. He nods, not waiting for my reply. "Quite the conflict of interest, wouldn't you say? Having the woman rebuilding your image also holding the key to the role that could define your career?"

This is the leverage my father planned on. Expose Isla, make her position seem compromised, force her hand, and make me distrust her completely so he can control her. And normally, it's a strategy that would work, but this NDA and this casting clause are not normal. They're highly unusual contractual terms.

I let the silence hang for a beat, feeling all eyes on me. Isla's gaze is steady, waiting. My father looks triumphant. Brandon looks shocked, even though he already knows.

Time to choose a side.

I meet my father's gaze directly. "I know about it. Isla told me this morning."

Checkmate.

"I'm not under the NDA, Trent. I can tell whoever I want, but you can't. I *warned* you, more than once," Isla says quietly, but I can tell she is seething, almost meteoric at this point.

The shift in the atmosphere is immediate and noticeable to everyone in the restaurant. The air pressure drops suddenly, like an airplane losing altitude in mid-flight.

Grab your oxygen mask, you're gonna need it.

My father's triumphant expression dissolves into stunned confusion.

Brandon nods, reinforcing the play. "Roman told me this earlier today, Trent. We're aware of Ms. Ryder's connection to the film and her final say about casting."

My dad clearly thought this was his ace in the hole, the secret weapon to control both Isla and me. And I've just defused it.

"She *told* you?" Trent repeats, thrown off balance.

"She did." I turn towards Isla. There's a fleeting look of surprise in her eyes now, maybe even grudging respect. "And I respect her right as the creator of this story, as the screenwriter, to make casting decisions based on who is best for the role. Based on *merit*. Not manipulation." The last word is pointed, aimed squarely at my father.

I've chosen a side. Not necessarily her side completely—the trust issues between us are still there, almost too complex to navigate.

But I am definitively not on his side.

My father's face darkens. His favorable mask is completely gone, replaced by cold fury and dangerous power. "Merit? Don't be naïve, Roman. This is Hollywood. Everything is manipulation. And Ms. Ryder here seems to be playing a very dangerous game. One that could end her public relations career and her fledgling PR firm, Ryder & Harper Communications LA, before it even launches here."

The threat is naked. Undisguised.

"Mr. Lysander... Trent, do you play chess?" Isla asks with barely veiled rage.

The question cuts deep. *Chess.* The game my father used to teach me that winning means sacrificing everything—even integrity. I feel my jaw tighten involuntarily.

"I do. It's been years. Kelly and I used to play," he says in exasperation. "Roman plays, too. Why, exactly?"

"My father taught me when I was nine. The thing is in chess you have to plan your moves and look ahead. That's how you play to win. It's calculated. It takes years of practice to be really good at it. Patience. Calculated moves. Understand your opponent. Good skills to have." She nods and looks at him in clear defiance. "I have all of those."

She leans across the table and looks straight at my dad. "At the age of seventeen, I lost everything and everyone who ever meant anything to me. And I could have turned inward and jumped into the abyss." She half smiles, and it's terrifying. "That would have been easier, but I didn't. No, instead I channeled my pain into strategy, looking ahead, calculating moves, and anticipating the opponents' moves, too. Like chess, just the way my famous dad taught me to. And I'm very good at it. Deadly good at it. Now I'm—"

"This is all so very fascinating, Ms. Ryder. Do you have a point?" My father says, interrupting her.

Wrong move, Dad.

"I'm not finished!" Her closed fist pounds the table, rattling the silverware. The sharp crack echoes through the restaurant like a gunshot all over again. "Far from it. You just violated an NDA regarding my identity. You'll be hearing from our legal team at Powers Media and Kimberley Powers herself regarding that. Did it put you in jeopardy for retaining the film rights to my screenplay? *Read your fucking contract, Trent.* The move is queen and knight to king. Checkmate."

Holy shit.

"Ms. Ryder, you don't know who you are dealing with— "

"Oh, I believe I do. Let me go further. I think you continually tip off Morgan Grant to cause chaos and exert control—the only way you know how—for and often against your only son as it relates to his 'bad boy' persona. Feed the beast as it were, however, you see fit. Because for you and your kind, it's all about control. I think I was expected to be the pawn that would be blamed for those continual woes. That way you could leverage your power over me as it relates to PR strategy, but what you are truly after is my power over casting as it relates to *Vendetta*. And there are three hundred million reasons why you would do this." She shakes her head in disbelief and fury.

She's dissecting his entire strategy in real time.

"Like I said, *read your contract*. You are in clear violation of those terms. And the three other people at this table just saw you do it. I only need two of them to back me up. Roman, here, can do whatever the fuck he wants. I realize this means I'm off your Christmas list this year, Trent, but I honestly don't fucking care."

She looks directly at my father, her gaze steady. "Samantha and I have briefly discussed our objectives with clients with Ryder & Harper Communications LA. They do not align with yours... And for the record and pretty much everyone else in this restaurant and the gossip that seems to spread like wildfire in this town, as if directly related to a *Game of Thrones* episode, I just want to make it perfectly clear, I will not be bought, bullied, or intimidated by the likes of you and Lysander Entertainment.

"And with final say in casting for the lead roles in *Vendetta*, because I *wrote* the screenplay, I intend to eliminate any confusion or questions regarding the conflicts of interest. So, in light of those, Ryder & Harper Communications LA is resigning the Lysander Entertainment account, effective immediately, as in, right now," she says softly. "That's the play: checkmate the king with queen and knight."

She's walking away from the million-dollar retainer. She told me she was thinking of this, but I wasn't sure she would actually do it.

She's walking away from the empire with nothing.

She continues, her voice unwavering. "We believe there are significant conflicts of interest that make a continued professional relationship untenable under the current structure." She glances briefly over at me, then back to my father. "However, as I discussed with Roman earlier, Samantha and I remain committed to assisting him personally with his image rehabilitation and strategic career guidance. We'll be doing so pro bono."

Pro bono.

Charity. There's that word again. It burns me up, reigniting the rage I felt during our car ride. She's cutting my father out completely, severing the financial ties, but keeping me on as a client—*on her terms.* The implications are massive. She's drawing a line in the sand, declaring independence from Lysander Entertainment's influence, aligning herself solely with me, and yet she retains the power inherent in managing my narrative. *And power over me.*

Before my father can even respond, Samantha says, "Our firm operates on principles of mutual trust, transparency, and professional courtesy, Mr. Lysander. This environment," Samantha gestures vaguely at the tense tableau, "is untenable. Isla's decision is final, and it has my full and unequivocal backing." Samantha has instantly reinforced the move, her voice precise, professional, leaving no room for argument.

Silence.

Absolute, stunned silence descends on the table. Even the background chatter of The Ivy seems to momentarily pause. Everyone in the place is intent on listening to what is transpiring at table number one.

My father stares at Isla. His face is a mask of disbelief that morphs into incandescent rage. He's been publicly fired by the woman he just tried to destroy, by a firm that just officially launched less than four days ago.

Folks, the show is ending now.

Tip your waiters.

I watch Isla. She met my father's attack head-on, weathered the storm, and then delivered the killing blow with surgical precision. A strange, conflicting mix of emotions swirls inside me. Grudging admiration for her sheer, unadulterated guts. Yet, I still carry this untenable rage at being caught squarely in the crossfire of her meticulously planned counter-offensive. And a grim, undeniable satisfaction at seeing my father, for perhaps the first time, face a consequence he absolutely cannot control or spin.

He's been stripped of his leverage.

And may have just lost his film rights to *Vendetta*.

His power play has been exposed and neutralized in front of me and his top talent manager.

I make eye contact with Brandon. He looks momentarily stunned by the speed and finality of the resignation, but there's also a dawning understanding in his eyes as he glances from Isla, to Samantha, to me. He's processing all the dynamics that just played out and my earlier intervention.

He's putting the pieces together.

The resignation hangs there, irrevocable.

"Yes. I believe we're done here." Isla pushes back her chair, her movements fluid and precise. "Lunch is paid for. By all means, stay and enjoy yourself, Trent. Gentlemen." Samantha rises with her, a silent statement of solidarity.

Brandon and I exchange another brief, loaded look. Then, almost in unison, we stand up, too.

The four of us—a fractured, complicated group, bound by circumstance and conflicting loyalties, but momentarily united in this single action. We turn our backs on the one and only Trent Lysander, my father, leaving him sitting alone at the table, a solitary figure surrounded by the wreckage of his own making, his face contorted in impotent fury.

The king dethroned.

Outside on the bustling West Hollywood sidewalk, the temporary alliance evaporates instantaneously. The merciless California sunshine assaults my eyes after the shaded patio—too bright, too cheerful for the devastation we've just witnessed.

The city doesn't care what just imploded at table number one inside The Ivy. It just keeps roaring.

The fallout charges the air, electrifying every breath with unspoken words and unresolved tensions.

"I already texted Danny. He should be here momentarily," Isla says to Samantha.

I overhear her and can't stop myself. "What, you're poaching my people now, too? *Danny?*"

She looks at me with eyes devoid of any warmth or connection. Any trace of the woman who baked a cake for me, who opened up to me with the intimacy shared between us last night and even this morning before the car ride has been extinguished. "Danny, yes. We're fast friends. I needed a ride because in this God-forsaken town, transportation is apparently another currency. Do you *really* want to do this here, *now, Roman,* on the open sidewalk with everyone watching?"

Her cell rings. She answers it, along with a dismissive wave of her hand at me. "Kimberley. Yeah. Broke it. Warned him. Couldn't help himself. Teaching me a lesson was more important. Okay. I'll tell Samantha. Yeah. Not the way I wanted it to go down, but... Yes, I know. Love you, too."

She turns to Samantha. "Kimberley's sending you the link. Get it up on the website. We're good to go."

She looks drained of the adrenaline from what just transpired with my dad, but her expression is resolute. She avoids looking at me altogether now, instead offering Brandon a curt, professional nod and then a firm handshake.

"Nice to meet you," she says with veiled irony. Her armor is firmly back in place, stronger than ever before. "You might be interested in getting in on this action. Sammy girl, give Mr. Brandon Chase a business card. Text him the password codes. *Only him.* You'll want to check out the website. Give it about twenty minutes. A link will be up there shortly." She smiles, but it doesn't reach her eyes.

"Isla," I say, anger bleeding through my voice. "We need to talk. About what just happened in there." I point at the entrance to The Ivy.

"No, Roman. No more *talking.* I was just effectively lanced by your father in there. And you just sat there, and *fucking watched.*" She nods and then bitterly smiles at me. "Like you said, 'Isla, I don't even know who you are.' So true. You *don't.*" Her smile ends.

Her words slice through me like a sword, finding the exact spot where my defenses are weakest. I want to defend myself, to point out that I backed her play, that I chose her side over my father's, but the words stick in my throat. The intense rage in her voice—however briefly revealed—silences any protest I might have made.

She's right. I did just watch. I let her take the full force of his attack.

She turns to Brandon. "The pro bono offer stands if you can talk your best buddy Roman here into it. Reach out to Samantha, and she'll set it up."

She looks past me and gives a little wave. "Danny's here," she says to Samantha, completely ignoring me.

Samantha steps forward, positioning herself slightly in front of Isla, a subtle but clear act of shielding. "Right," she says, her voice deliberately bright. Samantha glances between Brandon and me.

"Danny, for a ride back to The Harland, where some of us clearly need to regroup. Decompress." She turns pointedly towards Brandon, lowering her voice slightly. "Catch LA, later on. I made reservations for 8:00 p.m. We'll start there. Explore a bit? Definitely need to blow off some steam after those... fireworks."

She turns to me, and her expression shifts to something akin to disappointment. "I was looking so forward to meeting you." She hesitates. "Isla doesn't just open up to anyone. You should know that. But you hurt her, more than the baseball player ever could. She doesn't trust easily if ever, and you as much told her you don't trust her. It's killing her. You just lost out on the best thing to ever happen to you, Roman Lysander. Maybe you'll figure that out. I don't know."

The baseball player. Chad Jameson. I'm worse.

Samantha's words land like body blows, each one finding its mark with devastating accuracy. The rest—about trust, about Isla opening up —creates a maelstrom of confusion inside me. My chest constricts painfully.

"Sammy girl, let's go. You're wasting your time. Let's go!" Isla calls out to her best friend from the curb.

Samantha turns away from us, already pulling out her phone. The message is crystal clear: They are a unit. They have a plan. And it doesn't include us. Samantha creates distance, draws a boundary, and manages the exit with the same strategic precision Isla displayed inside.

They move in unison as a team, arm-in-arm, off the sidewalk toward a black sedan. Samantha takes shotgun. Danny quickly exits the car and helps Isla into the back seat, holding her hand like she's royalty.

Queen and knight to king.

Checkmate.

"Hey Roman," Danny says easily to me as I stand there on the sidewalk. "Isla called me about three hours ago. Needed a ride. She said it would be like a getaway scene, like *The Italian Job*. Guess so. Isn't she something?" He laughs, closes her passenger door, and slides into the driver's seat. Within thirty seconds, Danny's black sedan slips into the traffic, leaving Brandon and me standing there in front of The Ivy like awkward bystanders watching them go.

Through the car's tinted windows, I see Isla is already on her phone again, and so is Samantha. The mix of emotions inside me intensifies into a gut-wrenching knot. Anger at her deliberate distance. The way she shut me out after dropping that bomb in the SUV earlier, then executing this power play with such precision—*like a nuclear strike, that's irrecoverable*—and affects us all.

Jealousy? Maybe. Of what, exactly? Her self-possession? Her bond with Samantha? The ease with which she just walked away from me —*fucking drove away*—with *Danny*, the waiter and B-list actor. *My guy? What the absolute fuck is that?*

Confusion reigns.

The sting of her rejection, both implicit and explicit just now, feels staggeringly sharp, almost fatal.

But even now, the pull of her remains—infuriating and undeniable. The mystery, the steel beneath her grace. She cut through my father like she was wielding a sword and left me bleeding because I was partially in the fucking way.

I pull out my phone, needing to do something, anything, other than stand here feeling like a truck has just run over me. I dial Manny.

"Yeah, Manny. Meet us out front."

Beside me, Brandon lets out a low whistle. He claps a hand on my shoulder, a gesture of camaraderie, but his eyes are shrewd, observant. He watched the entire exchange: my defense of Isla against my father's attack, however qualified, my lack of shock at Trent's revelation, and my equal lack of surprise at the resignation. The charged words vibrating between Isla and me, and probably even the way my gaze tracked her departure down the street with Danny driving the fucking getaway car.

"That was spectacularly rough and brilliant. I don't even know *what* that was," he says, his tone carefully neutral. But his eyes hold a new depth of understanding. He sees it now. *He finally gets it.*

"This isn't just business. This isn't a casual fling, or a calculated PR move. And you're not just pissed about the casting clause," Brandon says quietly. "You *care* about *her*."

I don't answer. Words die in my throat, strangled by the truth Brandon just called out.

Maybe I don't want to trust anyone.
Maybe that's easier.
Maybe that's safer.

But when she looked at me at the table—hell, I still wanted to trust her.

Why?

Why is that?

"Why does it seem like I just watched my life walk away—*drive away*—from me? What the actual fuck is wrong with me?" I ask aloud.

Brandon looks over at me with unspoken understanding and notable empathy.

He seems to be putting it all together.

Maybe he can fill me in.

"Let's go talk this out. Manny's on his way, yeah? *You* can decompress at my place." The guy grins like he's got a secret, slipping one of the white square business cards in his pocket that Samantha tossed to him as they left.

I nod mutely, unable to summon a response. I feel completely whipsawed. *Ambushed. By her. The loss is incalculable.*

Standing up to my father, watching him get taken out—that should feel like a victory of some kind. And in a way, it does. A small, bitter one. Isla Ryder executed her plan brilliantly, severing all the ties to my father, taking control of her own narrative and, by extension, a significant piece of mine.

It both infuriates and impresses me on a level I cannot help but acknowledge and admire.

Manny pulls the Escalade smoothly to the curb. He's already jumped out opening the rear passenger door for me, offering me escape.

But escape to where?

She played queen to my father's king and slammed the board shut. And I'm just the pawn left wondering what game we were playing. She walked away from my father. *And from me.*

And I remain rooted to the sidewalk, abandoned, with nothing but the fallout.

And the emptiness.

Alone again, naturally.

This pattern—this circular return to isolation—feels like the only constant in my life. The temporary connections, the brief moments of genuine feeling, all inevitably dissolve into this familiar emptiness. It's happened with every relationship, every friendship that threatened to matter.

Yet something about this time feels different. *Worse.* Like losing something I never fully had but desperately needed. Isla, with her sharp mind and vulnerable heart, her chess metaphors and fierce loyalty, cut through my defenses in a way no one else has managed.

And now she's gone, taking with her the possibility of something I can't even name.

I climb into the Escalade, the silence inside the vehicle a stark contrast to the chaos in my mind. As we pull away from The Ivy, I glimpse my father emerging onto the sidewalk, his face a thundercloud of rage and humiliation. For once, I feel nothing at the sight of him. *The victory is hollow without someone to share it with.*

Brandon's words echo in my head: *You care about her.*

The truth of it aches like a physical wound. *I do care.* And that terrifies me more than any power play my father could ever devise.

Brandon shifts uncomfortably but says nothing.

The game is over. And I lost.

We all lost.

Except maybe her.

CHAPTER 25

something in the orange

Roman Lysander

"Something In The Orange" – Zach Bryan
"Alrighty Aphrodite"– Peach Pit
"Do It Again" – Steely Dan

Late Friday Afternoon

THE SILENCE INSIDE THE ESCALADE is a physical entity, thick and suffocating, pressing in on me from all sides. My chest feels like it's wrapped in barbed wire, each breath scraping against something raw, bloody, and exposed. The leather seat beneath me might as well be broken glass—everything hurts. Everything burns.

It's heavier than the usual post-argument quiet. It is the vacuum left after a detonation, the air still crackling with residual energy, smelling faintly of ozone and scorched earth—like the aftermath shots we filmed for *Retribution*, when the entire set was rigged to implode.

I am the imploded set.

Not just damaged. Completely demolished from the inside out, structure compromised, nothing left but smoking ruins where something solid once stood. The façade might look intact from certain angles, but one strong wind and the whole thing will collapse.

Manny navigates West Hollywood traffic with his usual calm, but his eyes find mine in the rearview mirror more than usual. He's assessing the emotional wreckage in the back seat, and whatever he sees there tells him I look exactly as destroyed as I feel.

Brandon sits beside me, staring out the window with the coiled tension of a man who just watched the rulebook get shredded and set ablaze. He's in absolute awe of what he witnessed.

Meanwhile, I'm burning in my own private hell.

My throat feels like I've been swallowing sand. Samantha Harper's words ricochet around my skull like bullets in an empty chamber.

'…You hurt her more than the baseball player ever could. She doesn't trust easily, if ever, and you as much told her you don't trust her. It's killing her. You just lost out on the best thing to ever happen to you…'

Did I get this all wrong?

My stomach drops at the thought. The city lights blur into streaks of indifferent color, each one a tiny pinprick in the promise of gathering darkness. *If I was wrong…* The implication is a chasm opening at my feet, deep and bottomless, with no visible way across.

We left my father sitting alone at The Ivy. A king on a rapidly shrinking island of his own making. Isla Ryder—Ashley Thomas—whatever name she chooses to conquer under, walked away. Not just from him, but from me. The finality of it leaves a ringing in my ears, like standing too close to the pyrotechnics on set because the safety coordinator forgot to warn you.

Checkmate.

Her word…

Delivered with the cool precision of an assassin. She didn't just outmaneuver my father; she dismantled him, piece by calculated piece, using his own arrogance against him. She exposed his violation of the NDA in front of his star son and his top manager. Then she resigned. She walked away from a million-dollar-a-year retainer like it was pocket change. And then offered to take me on *pro bono*.

The words hits me again. My jaw clenches so hard I taste copper. My hands curl into fists against my thighs until my knuckles turn white. It's a brand seared into my ego, hotter than stage lights.

Pro bono. Charity.

A power play disguised as generosity…

Or… something else entirely?

I don't know what it is anymore, but it feels like another layer of manipulation, another way for her to maintain control while pretending she's relinquished it. Severing the ties to my father, yes, but binding me to her with invisible threads of obligation and… *what? Gratitude?* It's like watching the third act twist in a psychological thriller where you suddenly realize the victim has been the puppet master all along.

But even as I think about it, the words feel hollow. Even forced. Like I'm reading lines that I don't believe anymore. It's the knee-jerk cynicism, the ingrained defense mechanism of a guy who's seen too many masks and worn too many himself.

I'm still playing my father's game, even now. Even after watching her break free of it.

My stomach churns like I've been drinking on an empty stomach for hours. Her parting shots to me echo as sharply as the confrontation itself. *'No, Roman. No more talking. I was just effectively lanced by your father in there. And you just sat there, and fucking watched.'*

Her voice, tight with fury and disdain, rings in my ears like feedback from a badly positioned microphone. Followed by that bitter smile: *'Like you said, 'Isla, I don't even know who you are.' So true. You don't.'*

My chest constricts, the imploded set of my interior crumbling further with each remembered word. She wasn't entirely wrong, was she? In that specific moment, when Dad went for the kill, violating the NDA he *knew* was in place, did I leap to her defense?

No.

I'd already defused his initial leverage by confirming I knew her identity. But when he doubled down, launching that direct, hostile attack, I hesitated. The residual anger and suspicion from our confrontation in the Escalade still swirled—the feeling of being played, the revelation of her casting power, still raw and visceral.

Maybe it was the sheer speed of it all, the whiplash from her bombshells to Dad's ambush. Or maybe, deep down, a part of me just… watched because I was momentarily paralyzed by the collision course, seeing her formidable strength and wondering if she even needed saving. Her green eyes, usually so vibrant, had gone flat, like ancient sea glass, reflecting nothing but the storm she was weathering.

It was like watching a stunt coordinator walk through fire without a flame-retardant suit—you know you should intervene, but you're mesmerized by the audacity of it all.

Part of me, the part that's seen too much Hollywood bullshit, even admired the cold precision of her counter-attack. But another part, a newer part I don't quite recognize, felt like I'd failed some unspoken test.

And she saw it as abandonment.

The realization hits me like a physical blow to the solar plexus. I lean forward, pressing my palms against my chest, where it feels like something vital is tearing. Another wall of the imploded set collapsing inward, crushing what remains.

Abandonment. By me. Of her.

After she'd just told me about losing her entire family. After she'd revealed her heart and shown me the most wounded parts of herself. After she'd trusted me with her vulnerability on a level I can't even comprehend. And what did I do? I made it about me. About my career. About my feelings of betrayal over a contract clause.

Geez. What kind of monster am I?

The image of her getting into Danny's car—*my guy, Danny*—burns behind my eyelids like staring at stage lights too long. The easy familiarity between them, the way he held her hand like she was something precious. My fingers curl tighter against my thighs until my nails bite into the fabric. The spike of possessiveness, of intense jealousy, cuts through like a shard of glass has lodged between my ribs.

It's a feeling so intense, so unfamiliar in its sharpness, that it terrifies me. It's not just about a role, or an image. This is something else entirely.

'You care about her.' Brandon's words, spoken quietly on the sidewalk, hang in the air like smoke that won't dissipate.

He saw it. He saw through the anger and the defensive walls I threw up like a child building a fort. He saw the raw nerve Isla touched—the one I try so hard to pretend doesn't exist. It's like he's pulled back the fourth wall and spotted the *real story* beneath the performance.

I risk a glance at my best friend. He's still looking out the window, but there's a faint smile playing on his lips. Not amusement, exactly. More like... stunned appreciation. Like he just watched someone pull off an impossible stunt without breaking a sweat.

"Spectacular," he murmurs, almost to himself. "Absolutely fucking spectacular."

I grunt noncommittally, turning my gaze back to the blur of storefronts and palm trees. My reflection in the window looks hollowed out, like I've just come off a three-day bender or a particularly grueling night shoot. Like someone who's forgotten how to sleep.

"I mean, Roman." Brandon turns to me now, his eyes alight with something I haven't seen in them before—pure, unadulterated awe mixed with the adrenaline of a near-miss explosion. "Did you *see* that? The way she just... *handled* Trent? No fear. Just facts, strategy, and ice-cold nerve. She walked in there, let him make his play, exposed his flank, and then just... *checkmate.*"

He shakes his head, a breathless laugh escaping him. "Called him out right in front of us. In front of half the power players lunching at The Ivy." He leans forward, energized like he's just mainlined espresso. "I've known your father my whole adult life. I've seen him dismantle careers, crush competitors, and bend studio heads to his will. *No one* stands up to Trent Lysander like that. *No one.* And she did it without breaking a sweat."

"She blindsided me, Brandon," I say, as the anger flares hot in my chest. My voice comes out rougher than I intended, like I've been screaming. "The casting clause, the NDA... she knew *exactly* what she was going to do. She used me to set the stage."

"*Used* you? Or *warned* you?" Brandon's gaze sharpens. "She told you everything *before* the meeting. Gave you the heads-up about the NDA, which you forgot to tell me about, by the way. She told you about her power over casting, she told you about what your father was likely planning. She could have kept you in the dark. She could have let you get ambushed alongside me. But she didn't."

His voice gains momentum, like he's working through a complex equation in real time. "She laid her cards on the table, Roman. Yours, mine, and Trent's. She knew he'd violate the NDA because he couldn't resist the power play. He couldn't stand not controlling the narrative. She anticipated his move. That's not *using* you, Ro. That's *trusting* you enough to show you the game board before the first piece is even moved."

"*Trusting me.*" The words feel foreign in my mouth, like speaking a language I've never learned. I'm the guy people manage, manipulate, or try to get something from. *Trust?* That's for other people. Not Roman Lysander. "Oh, God. I said some things to her I'm not proud of."

"What *things*?"

The words burn coming out. "Something along the lines of, 'your entire career as an ace PR strategist is built on playing games' and 'I don't know what's real with you anymore.' And… 'I don't need your fucking charity.'"

The remorse burns hot, spreading through my chest. The imploded set of my emotional landscape collapses further, dust and debris clouding everything.

What kind of asshole reduces someone's life's work to manipulation?

"Oh… shit." Brandon's face falls. "No wonder she's so pissed at you. That's fucking cold, man. That's like telling Scorsese his entire career is built on playing with cameras. It's reductive as hell."

"Not helping." My neck flushes red with embarrassment. The burn of shame and regret spreads through all of me. My dress shirt suddenly feels too tight.

"And she still holds all the casting power over *Vendetta*." I sound like a petulant child actor who just learned his scene got cut. The whining makes me hate myself a little more. "Final casting approval. How is that not a conflict? How do I ever know if I get the part of Steven Stryker because I earned it?"

Brandon studies me with those sharp eyes that see through my bullshit for a living. When he speaks, his voice is gentler than I expect.

"Maybe she just created the only scenario where you *can* earn it. By taking Trent's money completely off the table, she removed the biggest conflict of all. Now, if she casts you, it can't be because her firm is getting paid a fortune by Lysander Entertainment to rebrand your image. It has to be about the work." He pauses, letting that sink in. "She neutralized Trent, Roman. And maybe, just maybe, she did it to give you a clean shot."

A clean shot.

The concept hangs there, tantalizing and terrifying. A shot based purely on merit, on talent. The very thing I've craved my entire fucking career. The legitimacy I've chased through years of headlines and self-sabotage.

It's like being offered the lead in a Nolan film after a career of superhero franchises—the validation every serious actor secretly hungers for.

Could Isla Ryder, the woman I just accused of playing games, actually be the only one offering me the clearest path to it?

My entire body feels like I'm in free fall, plummeting through the wreckage of that imploded set with nothing to grab onto.

The Escalade slows, turning into the private underground garage of The Harland—a sleek, exclusive residence building known for its luxury suites and discretion.

"Your place? *Here?* At The Harland?" I stare at him, my paranoia detector starting to ping like a metal detector at airport security. "Since when? Like *Isla? She's staying here*, too."

"About six months now," he shrugs, opening his door. "Needed a base closer to the studios, easier for late nights. Malibu's great, but the commute's a bitch sometimes. Besides," he says, a glint in his eye as he steps out, "the amenities aren't bad. Come on up. We need to debrief properly. And maybe crack open something expensive."

Manny opens my door, his expression professionally blank, but I sense his awareness of the shifting dynamics. The man sees everything. "Will you be needing me further, Mr. Lysander?"

"No, Manny, thanks. I'll call you if…" My voice trails off. *If what? If I figure out what the hell I'm doing with my life?* "I'll call you. Appreciate you handling… everything."

"Always, sir." Manny gives a slight nod, acknowledging the unspoken chaos of the day, before sliding back behind the wheel.

The Escalade glides away, leaving Brandon and me standing in the cool, quiet concrete of the garage.

I follow Brandon towards a private elevator, my mind still racing. Brandon having a place here, the same place Isla's staying… it feels like another piece clicking into a puzzle I don't fully grasp yet. Like finding out the key grip on your new film is your ex's brother. Or maybe it's just this town, a tangled web of connections where everyone orbits everyone else, whether they realize it or not. The thought that Isla is somewhere in this very apartment building sends a strange current through me. It's a mix of apprehension and a pull I can't quite define.

Is there anything in this town that isn't connected to everything else?

The elevator opens directly into a stunning penthouse suite. Floor-to-ceiling windows offer a panoramic sweep of the city, from the

Hollywood Hills to the hazy sprawl stretching towards the ocean. The décor is minimalist chic—charcoal grey sofas, chrome and glass tables, abstract art on the walls. It's stylish, expensive, and feels distinctly… unoccupied. More like a high-end hotel suite than a home. Like a perfectly dressed set waiting for the actors to bring it to life.

"Nice digs," I concede, walking towards the window.

The view is undeniably impressive. A God's eye perspective on the city where fortunes are made and destroyed with dizzying speed. *Like today.*

The sun is just beginning its descent toward the horizon, painting the sky in bruised yellows and fiery oranges, that "Something In The Orange" shade Zach Bryan sings about, the kind that makes you feel like everything good is either gone or just out of reach. It stabs at something in my chest, marking the passing of the 24th hour of knowing her.

The song hits differently now, a haunting echo of possibility and loss wrapped in that burning sunset glow. Twenty-four hours since we collided on the beach. Twenty-four hours of discovery, connection, and now devastation. The orange light catches on the glass buildings, transforming them into burning towers, beautiful and terrible, like the wreckage of what I've just destroyed with Isla.

Brandon heads straight for a sleek built-in bar. He pulls out a bottle of what looks like very old Macallan and grabs two heavy crystal tumblers. "Drink?"

"Yeah. Definitely." My voice sounds like I've been gargling gravel. The aftermath of emotional warfare. Few words form, but the thoughts race and will not stop, while my mind seems to melt all the way down.

He pours generous measures of the expensive scotch, the amber liquid catching the fading light like liquid gold. He hands me a glass, the crystal cool against my palm. The weight of it is grounding, substantial—something real to hold on to when everything else feels like it's dissolving into chaos.

"To Isla Ryder," Brandon says, raising his glass. "And Samantha Harper. The giant slayers."

I hesitate, the glass halfway to my lips. The toast feels wrong somehow, like celebrating after a funeral. Then I think about what I just witnessed—Isla's surgical dismantling of my father, her refusal to be intimidated or bought. The sheer fucking courage of it. The way she'd looked, not triumphant, but... resolute, like a warrior who'd won a battle she never wanted to fight.

I clink my glass against his. "To... surviving the fallout."

The scotch smells like caramel and smoke and expensive regrets. It burns a welcome path down my throat, momentarily searing away the knot of conflicting emotions. It hits my empty stomach like liquid fire, a sensation I welcome for its clarity.

Brandon swirls the amber liquid—scotch, neat, mirroring my father's preference, though Brandon lacks the same predatory stillness when he drinks it. He takes a sip, his gaze fixed on the sprawling panorama of Los Angeles laid out beyond the floor-to-ceiling windows of his apartment.

It's aggressively modern, aggressively minimalist, all sharp lines, chrome, glass, and shades of white and grey. Impersonal. Expensive. A high-tech fishbowl suspended above the city's frantic energy. It feels less like a home and more like a staging area for a life lived elsewhere.

Which is usually Malibu. Like mine.

I'm pacing back and forth across the gleaming white floor, the restless energy that propelled me out of The Ivy still thrumming through all of me, a frantic counterpoint to the apartment's sterile calm. The confrontation at lunch replays in my head—my father's predictable, explosive rage, Isla's chillingly quiet resignation, Samantha's immediate backup, Brandon's stunned-then-knowing silence, the four of us standing, leaving Trent sputtering in the wreckage.

A win? *Maybe.* Seeing my father publicly dismantled felt satisfying, in a dark, complicated way, like watching a particularly deserving villain finally get his on-screen comeuppance. But the victory is overshadowed by the intense, churning mess Isla left me stewing in after our conversation in the Escalade.

'Who are you, Isla Ryder?'

'You have all the power over my fucking career.'

'I don't need your fucking charity.'

My words. Her face. The flicker of genuine devastation in her eyes before the mask slammed down, impenetrable.

Then the $100 bill exchange.

Pro bono. The words still sting, a barb coated in something that feels suspiciously like pity disguised as professional maneuvering. A way to sever ties with my father, yes, but also a way to keep *me* tethered to *her*, indebted, under her control, in a way that feels even more insidious than Trent's financial leverage. It's a classic Hollywood move—make someone owe you, then they're yours. Except… Isla doesn't feel classic Hollywood. She feels… different. Which makes it all the more confusing.

"Your dad really lost his shit back there," Brandon says finally, breaking the silence. He turns from the window, leaning against the sill. "Classic Trent Lysander. When the script deviates, burn the set down." He shakes his head, a wry twist to his lips. "But Isla… man, she didn't even flinch. Just cut him loose. Cold."

"She had it planned," I mutter, stopping my pacing to stare out at the hazy cityscape. The orange in the sky is fading to a deep, bruised purple. "The whole thing. The hundred-dollar bill in the car, the 'pro bono' declaration… that was the setup. Severing the tie so she could resign without breaching *her* contract if he pushed too hard. Calculated."

I'm clinging to this interpretation, to the idea that she's a master strategist, because the alternative—that she was genuinely hurt, that *I* hurt her—is too fucking uncomfortable to acknowledge directly. Not yet.

"Calculated? Maybe," Brandon concedes, swirling his drink again. "But walking away from an annual million-dollar retainer? That's not just calculation, Roman. That's a fucking statement. She didn't just neutralize Trent; she bought her freedom. Maybe yours too, if you think about it. No more Trent Lysander trying to pull your strings through the PR contract he was bankrolling."

His words hit a nerve. Freedom. It's a tempting concept, especially where my father is concerned. But the idea that Isla's move somehow benefits me feels complicated. Tainted by the power imbalance, she revealed, the one that now hangs between us like a guillotine blade.

"Freedom?" I scoff, turning back to face him. "She traded one form of leverage for another. Now, instead of my father holding the purse strings, I find out she holds the casting vote on *Vendetta*. My entire shot at playing Steven Stryker, in *Vendetta*, rests on her whim. How is that freedom?" The frustration bubbles up again, hot and bitter. "It's the same old story, isn't it? Different puppet master, same fucking strings. And that pro bono stunt? Still feels like charity."

Brandon studies me. His expression becomes thoughtful. "Look, I get why you're pissed. The casting clause… yeah, that's a mindfuck. And finding out like that a few hours before? Rough. But the pro bono thing. Are you sure you're seeing it clearly?"

He pushes off the windowsill, walking towards me. "Think about it. She takes Trent's money, she's compromised. The tabloids would have a field day— 'Million-Dollar Payoff? Star's PR Guru Holds Casting Power!' By cutting the financial tie, by making it pro bono, she removes that conflict. It protects her integrity, but it also protects *you*."

His logic is annoyingly plausible. It chips away at the anger, leaving the confusion and hurt more exposed.

Did I misread it?

My father raised me in a world where everyone *has* an angle. Trust is a liability. It's a hard habit to break, even when something inside me silently screams that Isla isn't part of that same cynical script.

Brandon walks over to a leather armchair, sinking into it with a sigh. He loosens his tie. The picture of a man unwinding after a battle won— even if he was mostly a shocked observer.

"Seriously, Roman. I'm still reeling." He swirls the scotch in his glass and that look of awed disbelief returns. "The *way* she just dismantled him... the sheer nerve. I've never seen anything like it. She's playing chess while everyone else is playing checkers. Your father thought he had her cornered... and she just turned it right back on him. Called his bluff. And then she just walked away."

"And took the money right off the table," I say. The grudging admiration surfaces again. I unconsciously smile. This is new for me, this grudging respect for someone who's also thrown my world into chaos. Usually, I just want to crush them or dismiss them.

"Exactly. And the pro bono offer? *Genius*. It keeps her connected to you, keeps her involved in the narrative shaping, but completely removes Trent's financial leverage. He can't pull the funding. He can't threaten her firm. And now, he can't even threaten her casting power. She's *firewalled* herself."

Brandon pulls something from his pocket. The business card Samantha gave him. Sleek, minimalist, heavy cardstock. White, embossed in gold with a Gordian Knot graphic. No names, no titles, no address. Just a QR code in the same embossed gold on the back.

"Check this out. Pure class. Understated. Confident. Just like them. Samantha slipped this to me as they were leaving. Said the website link was on the back. Reminds me of that move from *Hitch*, remember? The black calling card? No info, just intrigue. These women... they're next level." He looks genuinely impressed, almost starstruck, which is a rare sight. Brandon's seen it all in this town.

I stare at the card in his hand. A QR code. Modern. Impersonal. Efficient. So... Isla. And Samantha. My fingers itch to take it, to scan it, to see what secrets it unlocks. But my pride, or maybe just sheer stubbornness, keeps me rooted.

What am I expecting to find?

An apology?

An explanation?

Or just more proof that she's ten steps ahead of everyone, including me.

"So, are you going to scan it?" I ask, trying to sound casual, like it's just another piece of Hollywood ephemera.

Brandon grins, already pulling out his phone. "Hell yeah, I am. Curiosity, and professional interest, you know? Ryder & Harper Communications LA. They just made the boldest launch statement this town has seen in years. I definitely want to see what their digital footprint looks like." He fumbles with his phone for a moment, angling it over the card. "Password protected, of course. Samantha texted it to me. 'Just me,' she said."

I watch him scan the code, a knot tightening in my stomach. Password protected. Exclusive. *Just him.*

The jealousy stirs again—irrational but undeniable. He's my manager, my best friend. But Isla... Isla feels like she should be *my* puzzle to solve, not something Brandon gets a sneak peek at.

"What does it say?" I finally ask, the words tight.

Brandon's eyebrows shoot up as he scrolls. "Whoa. Okay. This isn't just a PR firm website, Ro. This is... a goddamn manifesto." He looks up at me, his expression a mix of shock and dawning respect. "It's about 'truth in narrative,' 'authentic engagement,' 'strategic partnerships built on mutual integrity.' There are case studies—anonymized, but clearly high-level. Political campaigns, crisis management for Fortune 500s, artist rebranding. These women aren't playing in the minor leagues. They're heavy hitters."

"Truth in narrative," I repeat, the words feeling like ash in my mouth. My own cynical dismissal of her career— *'your entire career... is built on playing games'*—comes roaring back. The remorse is a fresh burn.

"And there's this section," Brandon continues. "'The Ryder & Harper Protocol: A Commitment to Uncompromised Counsel.' It outlines their policy on client selection, conflicts of interest... They'll walk away from any situation that compromises their ability to give honest, unfettered advice. Even if it means walking away from... well, like a million-dollar retainer from Trent Lysander." He looks at me pointedly. "She wasn't kidding, Roman. This is who they are."

My legs feel unsteady. I sink onto the edge of one of the charcoal grey sofas. *This is who they are.* Not a game. Not a manipulation. A fucking *protocol.* A code.

And I basically spat on it.

"She really meant it," I whisper. The realization is a slow, agonizing admission. Like I'm watching a film in reverse, seeing all the clues I'd missed, all the moments I'd misinterpreted through my own jaded filter.

Her vulnerability on the beach, her quiet passion for *Pride and Prejudice*, her insistence on the truth even in the Escalade when she laid out the whole ugly mess. It hadn't been a performance. It had been... *Isla.*

"Yeah, Ro. I think she did." Brandon's voice is softer now. He puts his phone down. "And that pro bono thing? After reading this, it feels like a lifeline. Maybe she sees something in you worth fighting for, even if you make it hard as hell."

Something worth fighting for. No one's ever said that about me. Not really. Not in a way that felt clean, untainted by my father's ambition or Hollywood's endless hunger for more.

They always want more.

My chest aches—a deep, hollow ache. The pain of profound misjudgment. The sickening realization that I might have just destroyed the one genuine thing to walk into my life in years.

The image of Isla's face when I'd hurled those accusations at her in the car flashes in my mind. The shock, the hurt, and then the way her eyes shuttered with the emotional armor of steel sliding back into place. I'd done that. I'd put that look there.

'You hurt her more than the baseball player ever could...' Samantha's words. They make sense now, in a way that twists my gut into a tighter knot. That asshole had probably just been a garden-variety cheater or user. I'd attacked Isla's core, her integrity, her very identity as a professional.

"I fucked up," I say, the honest admission torn from somewhere deep inside. "I really, really fucked this up."

Brandon nods slowly. "Yeah. Maybe you did." He doesn't rub it in. He doesn't need to. The evidence is spread out before me like the wreckage of a car crash.

"So, what now?" I ask, desperate for an answer, a solution, a rewind button. "How do I fix this?"

The question feels pathetic, childish. I'm Roman Lysander. I don't *fix* things like this. I move on. I get a new PR team. I find another role. But the thought of moving on from Isla, from this, whatever this is between us… it feels like I'm cutting out a vital organ.

Brandon considers me for a long moment. I already discern the sympathy radiating off of him. "I don't know if you *can* fix it, easily. Trust, once it's broken like that… it's hard to rebuild. Especially with someone like her. She strikes me as someone who values loyalty, integrity, above all else. You questioned her integrity, her core identity."

The truth is a cold weight in my stomach. The Gordian Knot on their card. It's a puzzle that can't be untied, only cut. Have I just severed something irreparable?

"But you could try," Brandon continues. "You could *apologize*. For real. No bullshit, no spin. Just own it."

Apologize. It sounds so simple. And yet, for me, it feels like scaling Everest in my fucking underwear. When was the last time I genuinely apologized for anything without an ulterior motive, without my father or a publicist scripting it for me?

Although I did apologize to her last night for the terrible things I said to her at the beach. How many more apologies would I have to make? When will I stop hurting her and actually recognize her truth, so I no longer have to apologize to her?

"And then what? Even if she accepts my apology, what about *Vendetta*? The casting? It's still a mess."

"One thing at a time, Ro. First, figure out if you can get back in the same room with her without spontaneous combustion. The *Vendetta* thing comes later. But right now? You're bleeding out from a self-inflicted wound. Stop the bleeding before you worry about winning the Oscar."

He's right. My mind races, trying to find an angle, a strategy. It's how I'm wired. How Trent wired me.

There has to be a way to leverage this…

The thought dies within seconds of thinking that way. That's the old Roman. The Roman who got me into this mess.

What would Isla do?

She'd analyze the situation based upon the truth. She'd make a bold, direct move.

The silence stretches, filled only by the distant hum of the city. The orange in the sky is almost gone, replaced by purples and blues and the first tentative stars and the cold glow of electric light.

I walk back to the window, staring out at the sprawling, glittering beast that is Los Angeles. A city built on dreams and deception, where truth is rare. Isla Ryder felt like the truth itself.

And I treated her like just another part of the deception.

I press my palm against the cool glass, feeling the barrier between myself and the vast city below. The orange has almost completely faded from the sky now, leaving only a thin line of gold at the horizon—a reminder of what's been lost, what's slipping away.

The song loops again in my head, haunting lyrics that feel like both a warning and a promise. The thin line of gold at the horizon seems to pulse with it.

"You know," Brandon says quietly, coming to stand beside me at the window, "when you walked into my office this morning, you were pissed about being manipulated. About being a pawn in someone else's game. But after what I just saw today—what Isla did at The Ivy—I think maybe you've had it backwards this entire time."

I turn to look at him, questioning.

"Your father's been playing you your whole life, Roman. Using you as an extension of himself, a vessel for his ambitions. But Isla? She just showed you what it looks like when someone fights *for* you, not against you. When someone values the truth enough to walk away from a million dollars to preserve it, and maybe, just maybe, she did that for both of you."

His words hit me hard. The imploded set of my emotional landscape shifts again, but this time, it feels less like collapse and more like... reconstruction. A tentative rebuilding from the ruins.

"So, what do I do?" I ask again, my voice barely audible.

Brandon smiles slightly. "You stop playing by Trent Lysander's rules. You start playing by your own. Or maybe," he adds with a knowing look, "by Isla Ryder's. Truth in narrative, authentic engagement, mutual integrity. Doesn't sound like a bad place to start."

I nod slowly, feeling something settle within me. A decision. A direction.

The fight isn't over. Maybe it's just beginning. Maybe I need to fight for something other than a role or an image. Maybe I need to fight for her.

For us.

For the truth.

The orange is gone from the sky now, but its afterglow lingers in my memory, in the possibility of what might still be salvaged from the wreckage.

Something tells me we're not done…

CHAPTER 26

nothing in my way

Roman Lysander

"Nothing In My Way"—Keane
"Do It Again"—Steely Dan
"I Remember Everything"—Zach Bryan, Kacey Musgraves

Friday Evening - 6 :00 p.m.

BRANDON PULLS OUT HIS PHONE again, reading from a text he's just received. "Samantha. She says there's a backdoor. She told me to go click on it." He looks over at me with a sheepish grin. "I just sent her a text complimenting them on the cool website." He shrugs. Nonchalant.

Why can't I ever be nonchalant?

Why does everything connected to me have to be so fucking complicated?

"What? We already saw the website."

"She says there's more," Brandon says. He scans the QR code on the back of the white cardstock again. Their website loads up again. I watch over his shoulder, curious despite the emotional hurricane still raging in my chest. The landing page is as minimalist as the card—just the firm's name against a clean background. Professional. Elegant. But then Brandon taps a discreet icon, almost hidden in the corner, and enters a password Samantha texted him.

The screen changes. The sleek corporate façade dissolves, replaced by something entirely different.

My breath catches. The hairs on my arms stand up like I've just walked onto a set where the air conditioning is set to arctic. My heart hammers against my ribs like it's trying to escape.

VENDETTA - PRIVATE PLACEMENT PORTAL
Target: $100,000,000.00
Current: *$62,500,000.00*

"Holy shit," Brandon breathes, scrolling down. His finger trembles slightly on the screen as he scrolls.

The page details the offering. Minimum investment: $500,000. Open only to accredited investors via direct invitation. It outlines the production entity—a newly formed LLC, clearly firewalled from Powers Media and Lysander Entertainment. It lists key attachments: Everest Bishop confirmed as Director. A target premiere at the Cannes Film Festival next spring. A major independent distribution house already attached for North American theatrical release, contingent on final funding and delivery.

"She wasn't kidding," I say aloud, my voice barely above a whisper. "This isn't just talk. This is a fully formed, high-stakes independent production, launched in real-time, bypassing the entire studio system. It's like watching someone build an entire studio back lot overnight while the executives were sleeping."

While I was questioning her motives.

Brandon keeps scrolling, his eyes widening with each new detail. "Yes. Look at this. The structure… it's revolutionary. Tiered investment riders offering up to 10% ROI based on box office performance benchmarks. And a guarantee…" His voice drops to almost a whisper. "Holy Christ… secured against Isla Ryder's personal assets derived from the original *Vendetta* novel proceeds and her inheritance."

He looks up at me, his expression a mixture of shock and profound respect. "She's putting everything on the line, Roman. Her entire fortune. She's personally guaranteeing the investors' money back if this doesn't happen. That's… unheard of. That's insane courage."

Shame courses through me at my arrogance. *She's put everything on the line.* Isla's betting her entire fortune and future on this vision, while I was accusing her of playing games.

She's betting on me, potentially.

Brandon points to a section listing initial anchor investors. The names are anonymized— "Investor Alpha," "Investor Beta"—but the amounts are staggering. $5 million here, $10 million there.

"Wait," Brandon says, tapping on a footnote link. A separate, password-protected page opens, presumably for those already granted higher access. He must have gotten that password from Samantha, too. This page isn't anonymous.

"Jesus Christ," he whispers, holding the phone out so I can see. My heart pounds against my ribcage like it's trying to escape through my throat.

Heavy hitters. A-list actors, directors, producers, even tech money. People with serious clout and deep pockets, all lining up behind Isla Ryder. This isn't just a film. It's a movement. A quiet rebellion against the established order, orchestrated by a woman my father tried to crush less than three hours ago.

It's like the ending of *Spartacus*, where everyone stands up and declares their allegiance: "I am *Vendetta*."

"They're going for a hundred million," Brandon says, disbelief coloring his voice. "This isn't indie, Roman. This is a full-blown, independently financed blockbuster. She's taking the fight directly to the studios. To your father. And she's *winning*. This thing is going to close and reach its funding goal before midnight. Easily."

She's winning.

She was building an empire, while I was sulking about casting clauses.

Brandon sets his scotch down, eyes blazing with newfound purpose. He starts tapping rapidly on his phone, navigating to his banking app.

"What are you *doing*?" I ask, bewildered.

"I'm in," he says without looking up. "I've got some liquid cash. Two million. Liquid cash. The riders offer 10% return—better than decent. But fuck the return." He looks at me, deadly serious. "This is a chance to be part of something real, Roman. To change how this industry works."

He shakes his head, a humorless laugh escaping him. "The

guarantee… she's bankrolling the risk herself. The woman has guts I've never seen before. She believes in this enough to bet everything. How can you not back that?"

He completes the transfer, confirmation flashing. He leans back, looking exhilarated and slightly terrified. "Done. I'm officially an investor in *Vendetta*."

Reality crashes down on me like a collapsing set piece. Isla's bold move. The massive independent production. A-list backers. Brandon's investment. Everyone's moving forward, taking sides, placing bets.

It's like being in the middle of a high-octane third act. All the players are making their final moves, and I'm still stuck in the second act, paralyzed by indecision and wounded pride.

"But where does that leave me?" The question escapes me, sulky and uncertain. My voice cracks, like I'm thirteen again. I drain my scotch, the burn not enough to mask the vulnerability that bleeds through all of me.

Brandon studies me, the adrenaline fading to familial concern. "Where do you *want* it to leave you, Roman?"

He leans forward. "I saw the way she looked at you at The Ivy. After your father's attack, when you backed her play about merit. There was relief in her eyes. Surprise. But definitely relief."

He pauses, swirling his scotch. "And when she walked away, yeah, she was pissed. Hurt. Maybe devastated. But now, hearing what you said to her in the SUV." He nods. "I see *her side* of things. Like I said before, earlier. This girl probably doesn't trust anyone, *ever*, except her wingman, Samantha Harper. But she trusted you, Ro. With *everything*. Including stuff about her family and the fact that your dad was under an NDA. If he disclosed who she was, he loses his film rights. She *told* you to warn him. She told you *everything*. I mean, what *more* do you *want* from her?"

My throat constricts. The scotch sits heavy in my stomach. I can't even talk. Devastation swirls.

I did this.

"But I saw something else, too." His voice is now more earnest. "She *cares* about you, Roman. More than she lets on. More than maybe she even realizes." He looks at me directly and grimaces. "But the baiting bit about Melody Parker—what the fuck was that? But then, you salvaged it when you held her hand, told her you weren't taking up with Melody. Your father was oblivious at that point, but you *know* that won't last, and she'll be a target for him now."

He takes a sip of his scotch, letting his words sink in. The ice clinks in his glass, the only sound in the vast room. "But Roman, she'll put up walls thicker than Fort Knox after what happened today, especially after what you told me you said to her in the Escalade. But they're not impenetrable. Not yet, anyway."

Outside, the city lights begin to twinkle as dusk settles and fades to a purple sky of lit stars.

Before I can process it further, Brandon glances at his watch. "Shit, it's after six. Need to shower and change before we head out."

I frown. "Head out *where*?"

"Catch LA? Samantha Harper? She practically invited us on the sidewalk." He grins with genuine enthusiasm. "Definitely need to follow up on *that* connection."

Catch LA. The 'see and be seen' rooftop restaurant in West Hollywood.

"You're kidding," I mutter, running a hand through my hair.

"Why? What's the big deal?" Brandon asks, then comprehension dawns. "Oh. Right. Isla." He lets out a low whistle. "Even more reason for you to go. Smooth things over with her."

"No," I say, recoiling. "No fucking way, Brandon. Run into *her* tonight? After everything? I'm not putting myself through that." The image of her cool composure flashes in my mind. "What? She holds my career in her hands and expects me to just hang out?"

"Okay, first," Brandon says patiently, "she didn't invite *you*. Samantha invited *me*. Second, what are you going to *do*—avoid Isla Ryder forever? You're tied to her through *Vendetta*. That casting clause isn't going away just because you plan on hiding out and sulking in Malibu." He steps closer, lowering his voice slightly. "And third… I saw you two at lunch. Even with the fireworks all around you two, there was something there. The way you looked at her when she walked out. That wasn't about a hookup. Maybe figure out what is going on between the two of you instead of just defaulting to anger."

His words land uncomfortably accurate. It wasn't just a hookup. Last night felt different. *Real.* Until the contracts and the clauses and the goddamn weight of my life crashed down on all of it.

"It's complicated, Brandon."

"Everything with you is *complicated*," he shoots back without heat.

"But maybe this is worth figuring out. She stood up to Trent Lysander. *Your dad.* Walked away from serious money—a million-dollar annual retainer. *Why* Roman? She could have just played along for a while and collected his cash. She didn't. Because she doesn't operate that way. She seems loyal as hell to Samantha. Maybe she's not the enemy here. Maybe she's just as caught up in the Hollywood bullshit as you are. And it's only her second day here. Maybe, this was the only play she could make for you and for her."

He claps me on the shoulder. "Look, I'm *going*. Samantha's cool, and I'm not letting Trent's meltdown ruin my Friday night. You can sit here and stew in your existential angst or come have a drink and see what happens. Maybe clear the air. Maybe *apologize to her*. Something you *never* do. It's your call."

He disappears towards the master bedroom, leaving me alone with the echo of his words and all the angst about Isla churns through me. He's right. Avoiding her is futile. *Vendetta* looms, tying us together in the most fucked-up way imaginable.

And personally… I'm a goddamn mess. The anger is still there, the suspicion, the feeling of being manipulated. But underneath it, buried beneath layers of defense mechanisms, is the undeniable attraction I felt towards her on the beach, under the stars, and then during our intimate night together. The glimpse of her vulnerability behind the armor. I cannot get her out of my mind.

Oh my God, this girl.

A half hour later, Brandon emerges from his bedroom. Dressed to the nines for an evening out, wearing a dark dress shirt in a charcoal grey, with tan dress pants, and Italian loafers. I recognize as Brunello Cucinelli. *Expensive. Understated. Cool.* His cologne wafts straight towards me. He smiles wide.

Samantha Harper has no chance. Brandon Chase will impress.

"Fine," I say, cutting him off before he can even ask what my plan is going to be. "I'll *go*. But I'm not promising anything. And if she looks at me like I'm something she's just scraped off the red sole of her Louboutins, I'm *out*."

Brandon grins, triumphant. "*Progress.* Go shower. Guest bedroom has everything. You can borrow some clothes and stay over. You look like you wrestled a bear and lost."

The hot shower water washes away some tension that's been building all afternoon inside of me, though it does nothing for the anxiety and turmoil roiling in my gut now.

I slip into one of Brandon's shirts—black, fitted, expensive. Close enough to my size. As I button up the dress shirt, reality settles back in like fog rolling off the Pacific.

Seeing her tonight.

The prospect terrifies and electrifies me equally. After today's spectacular implosion, after the things I said in the Escalade, after watching her walk away with that devastating composure... facing her across a crowded bar feels like stepping onto a stage without knowing whether I'm playing hero or villain.

"She's probably going to turn me down even if I try to talk to her," I say, reentering the living room. The admission tastes bitter, but honest. "After what I said, after accusing her of manipulation, after making her pain about my own wounded pride... why would she give me the time of day?"

Brandon looks up from his phone, smiling. "Told Samantha we were coming. She texted me back and told me it's a private party. Security and everything."

The look of pure terror on my face causes his expression to shift. The triumphant anticipation he exhibits slightly fades, replaced by something more serious. More brotherly.

He sets his phone down and sighs—not with frustration, but with the weight of someone about to deliver hard truths.

"Okay, Ro. You have a choice here," he says quietly. "You can stay pissed about the casting clause, nurse the grudge. You're *good* at that particular play. You can feel sorry for yourself because you feel manipulated somehow. No matter how many times I've pointed out, that isn't the case here with Isla Ryder. You can let your pride or fear of being vulnerable keep you on the sidelines while she builds this empire without you. Because she *will*... she's already doing it."

He pauses, holding my gaze while I struggle mightily with the uncomfortable truth.

"If you do nothing. If you let her walk away after today, you lose her. *For good.* Because this isn't about public relations or a casual relationship or a hookup. This is next level. And you *know* it is. She knows it, too. But if you walk away from her now, without resolving anything with her? *That's it.* There's no going back with a girl like this. She's high stakes. Or," he says, the word carrying the weight of possibility, "you can do something different. Something unexpected."

He leans forward, scotch forgotten. "For once in your life… Roman… maybe make it about somebody else besides yourself."

The harsh words land hard, knocking the air from my lungs. I can barely breathe.

My chest constricts with recognition—the uncomfortable, searing kind that comes when someone forces you to see what you've become.

It's like watching a playback of your worst take and realizing you've been phoning it in for months.

"Think about what *she* just went through," he continues, passion bleeding through his manager façade. "What she *risked*. What she *sacrificed*. She stood up to your father—*Trent fucking Lysander*—in front of half the industry, knowing it could destroy her career and her newly formed PR firm and walked away from a million-dollar retainer. And then, as if that wasn't enough to fill her day, this girl, Isla Ryder, just put her entire fortune on the line as collateral for her film, *Vendetta*."

He gestures with his glass, ice clinking softly. "And she did it all while you sat there at lunch questioning her motives. After she'd already trusted you with everything. Her backstory, her ties to *Vendetta*, her family history, her vulnerabilities. Things she probably hasn't shared with anyone except Samantha."

My throat feels raw, like I've been swallowing broken glass. The shame burns hotter than the scotch.

Having it pointed out to me about what she just went through is its own kind of torture.

I replay the scene at The Ivy—not from my wounded perspective, but from hers. The calculated cruelty in my father's voice as he violated the NDA. She'd sat there, spine straight, absorbing each verbal blow with stoic grace. But I'd seen the microscopic flinch when he mentioned the conflicts of interest and attacked her integrity. The implication. It cut her deeply, showing the fissures of hurt in the way her fingers tightened around her water glass.

She'd been hurt. Genuinely hurt. Hurt by the implications.

And I'd just… watched.

Like a fucking spectator.

She hadn't been playing games. She'd been fighting for her life, her reputation, and her future. And when she needed me to have her back, when she needed me to stand with her against the man who raised me to be exactly like him, I hesitated.

I'd chosen my father's playbook over her trust.

The scotch seems to turn to acid in my stomach. I set the glass down with shaking hands, crystal meeting table with a sharp clink.

Guilty as charged.

"Jesus," I whisper, pressing palms against my eyes until I see stars. The pressure doesn't relieve the ache building behind my temples. "I fucked this up with her."

"Yeah, man. You did. But the question isn't whether you screwed up —it's whether you're going to do something about it or sit here feeling sorry for yourself while she changes the industry without you, and you lose her altogether because you did *nothing*. Isla Ryder is not someone you win back if all you're offering her is indifference. You'd actually have to fight for her."

He gestures toward the window, toward the sprawling city where Isla is likely regrouping, planning her next move. "A *grand gesture* might be warranted here, Roman. Something that shows her you understand what she's trying to accomplish. Something that proves you're not just another guy who's going to let her down. Something that says you're willing to trust her, even when it's complicated as hell."

Grand gesture.

The words hang heavy with possibility and risk. My mind flashes back to the beach—the easy connection, the shared vulnerability. Her blood was on my hands as I cleaned her cut. My birthday party, the charged moments, the intimacy between us that on the surface would appear to be reckless but the reality was far different, deeper, moving. One could go as far to say life changing. And the way she looked at me when she talked about her dreams.

Then to the car, the intense confrontation, bitterness on both sides. The pain in her voice when she told me about losing her family. How I'd turned that into something about *me*.

What kind of person does that?

Finally, to The Ivy. The defiance, the power, the dismissal. The way she'd looked at me when she walked away—like I was just another disappointment in a life that had already given her too many.

Who is Isla Ryder?

She's everything.

To me.

Brandon's right. Maybe the only way to bridge the chasm between us isn't to demand answers or fight for control, but to offer something else entirely.

Trust. Support. A leap of faith into the unknown, right alongside her.

It's terrifying. It goes against every survival instinct I've honed to a fine art in this town. Letting my guard down, being vulnerable, putting someone else's needs ahead of my own. It feels like career suicide. Emotional suicide. But the alternative... letting her walk away, letting this fragile, infuriating, undeniable connection wither because I was too proud or scared to fight for it... feels infinitely worse. Like watching dailies of the best scene I've ever filmed, only to discover the camera malfunctioned and nothing was captured.

I feel a shift inside me, like tectonic plates realigning. My heartbeat steadies. My breath deepens. For the first time since this morning's car ride, clarity washes over me like perfect lighting on a crucial scene—sudden, revealing, and transformative.

I know what I need to do.

I know who I want to be.

For her. For me. For both of us.

"Brandon," I say, my voice steady for the first time all day. "That grand gesture you mentioned?"

He looks up, understanding flashes in his features. He smiles.

"I think I know what it needs to be."

CHAPTER 27

looking for water

Isla Ryder

"Looking for Water" - Alex Parks
"Born Without A Heart" - Faouzia
"Vampire" – Olivia Rodrigo
"Leave The Pieces" – The Wreckers
"Uninvited" – Alanis Morissette
"Flowers"- Miley Cyrus
"High By The Beach" - Lana Del Rey

Friday Evening 6:30 p.m.

THE SILENCE IN THE HARLAND penthouse apartment isn't peaceful. It's the ringing quiet after a bomb blast, the air still thick with ozone and the phantom echo of detonation.

Three hours ago.

I'm losing time.

It's standing still.

As am I.

The actual explosion took place a mile away at The Ivy, but the aftershocks reverberate through every corner of this pristine space. We're back—Samantha and I—having dumped my single suitcase here hours ago before racing out to face Trent Lysander's ambush disguised as a lunch meeting.

An ambush I just turned back on the hunter.

And his prodigal son.

My reflection stares back from the floor-to-ceiling windows overlooking the sprawl of Los Angeles, a city I barely know, bathed now in the hazy gold of late afternoon. The woman looking back seems... different. *Harder.*

The adrenaline still courses through my veins like liquid fire, a high-frequency hum that blurs the edges of exhaustion and makes everything feel hyperreal.

But beneath my outward calm, something else has crystallized inside me. Pure, unadulterated fury at Roman Lysander. This absolute rage that I'm having trouble controlling and makes my hands tremble when I think about how he weaponized my own vulnerability against me with the whole Melody Parker thing at The Ivy and his cold dismissal in the SUV earlier.

'I don't know what's real with you anymore.' His words still burn like acid.

And then his silence.

His fucking silence when his father went in for the kill and missed.

The sharp throb in my right knee punctuates every step I take, a persistent reminder of my collision with Roman—both literal and metaphorical. The bandage is damp with something that might be blood or might be the antiseptic ointment I applied this morning. The cut hurts worse today than yesterday.

Yesterday. A lifetime ago.

The pain has intensified throughout the day, a dull ache that spikes with movement, but I push it down. Physical pain is manageable. Treatable.

Emotional devastation is another matter entirely.

For a fleeting moment, I'm reminded of the opening scene in *Vendetta* where Evelyn Stryker walks through her empty house after her husband leaves for work, sensing something is wrong but unable to identify it yet. That eerie stillness before catastrophe strikes.

I shake the thought away. *This isn't fiction.*

This is my life unraveling in real time.

Again.

The shock of Trent's blatant NDA violation, the cold fury it ignited, the calculated risk of resigning—it's all coalesced into this razor-edged clarity. We drew the line. We walked away.

Now comes the real battle: proving we didn't just sever ties but that we seized control.

Samantha paces the sleek, minimalist living area, her phone pressed to her ear, the cord of her headset snaking down her pristine white blazer paired with a cerulean blue lace top beneath. She's a whirlwind of focused energy, confirming details, her voice crisp and efficient. Every few minutes, she shoots me a look—assessing, protective, and worried. I know she sees the cracks in my emotional armor, the way I favor my right knee, and the tight line of my mouth that has nothing to do with professional stress.

No, that's pain, physical and emotional, equally.

She knows what Roman said to me in the SUV. I told her everything as soon as I hit the office after the unceremonious drop-off at the curb by Roman and his driver, Manny, and even more during the Uber ride to The Ivy.

I told her everything that happened at his birthday party, our fight on the beach last night after the party, baking Roman the birthday cake at one in the morning at the beach house which then led to our intimate encounter, the grand gesture latte this morning. But then, the cruelty of his accusations during the car ride into town when I told him everything—opening up about my family, about *Vendetta*, the casting clause, and the conflicts of interest, including what I thought his father had planned for me. The way Roman reduced my entire career to manipulation and game-playing. How he dismissed my vulnerability about losing my family as if it were just another PR strategy.

"Your entire career as an ace PR strategist is built on playing games."

"I don't know what's real with you anymore."

"I don't need your fucking charity."

Each word served as a sharp edge of a knife, precisely aimed at the softest parts of me. The parts I'd foolishly exposed to him in that goddamn SUV, thinking he might understand. Thinking he might be different.

Thinking I could trust him.

"Yes, secure video conference line... Patching in Kimberley now... Julia's confirmed as well." Samantha gives me a fierce grin and a thumbs-up, but her eyes linger on my face, searching. "We're good to go."

Are we?

Showtime. Act Two.

I take a careful breath, smoothing down the silk camisole I wore to lunch—a deliberate choice, armor in shades of cream and pink that now feels like a costume from another life. My hands look steady, but my stomach churns with notable anxiety and nausea. There's the undeniable rush from our strategic victory over Trent Lysander. Satisfaction in watching his smug confidence crumble in real time.

But underneath it all, the wounds Roman has inflicted hurt far worse than the cut on my knee. That will heal. Other parts of me, vital parts, seem like the pain is without end.

The way he looked at me when I revealed my identity as the writer, Ashley Thomas, of the bestselling novel, *Vendetta*. Like I'd betrayed him personally. Like sharing the most vulnerable parts of my story—my family's deaths, my father's influence on my writing, the way I channeled grief into *Vendetta*—was just another manipulation tactic.

And then, when his father attacked, Roman just... watched.

He watched Trent violate the NDA, watched him try to destroy my credibility, my very identity, and offered me no defense whatsoever.

No shield for me. Absolutely nothing offered to me.

His silence was worse than any accusation. It confirmed every fear I've harbored about trusting anyone, about being left exposed and utterly alone when the attack comes.

You can't trust anyone. Ever.

As Jane Austen wrote in Pride and Prejudice:

"My good opinion, once lost, is lost forever."

How ironic that I'd always found that line excessively harsh when I studied it in college. Now it feels like a necessary truth, a shield against further harm.

"Isla?" Samantha's voice cuts through my spiraling thoughts. "You still with me?"

I blink, refocusing on the present. The sleek monitor dominates one side of the room, ready for our video conference about to go live. The

Vendetta Private Placement Portal—our declaration of independence, our weapon—already live.

"I'm here." My voice sounds faraway, even to me.

Samantha studies me with those sharp eyes that see through everything. "Your knee's getting worse, isn't it?"

"It's fine." The lie comes automatically, practiced. I've been telling it all day.

"Really? That's what you're going with? With me? No." Her tone is gentle but firm. "You've been favoring it since we left The Ivy. And you took more Advil twenty minutes ago."

Of course, she noticed. Samantha notices everything. It's what makes her brilliant at this job, and what makes her such a fierce friend.

"It's manageable," I amend, which is closer to the truth. "I'll deal with it tomorrow."

She nods, but I can tell she's filing this information away, probably already planning to drag me to urgent care whether I want to go or not.

"Okay, they're both on. Kimberley? Julia? Can you see us? Audio good?"

"We see you both and we hear you, loud and clear. Isla. Samantha." Kimberley's voice, even filtered through the speaker, is pure command. No nonsense, all strategy. The sound of her voice steadies me. This is familiar territory.

"Crystal clear, darlings," Julia adds, her tone warmer, laced with the familiar sophisticated drawl that always makes me think of expensive perfume and boardroom steel. "Ready for the update."

Samantha clicks the mouse, bringing the portal landing page into focus. It's stunning. Sleek obsidian background, minimalist design, the *Vendetta* title treatment stark and compelling in simple black lettering. Below it, a secure login and a discreet tagline:

Powers Media, LLC Presents:
Vendetta - A Private Placement Offering

My name. Samantha's name. Julia Winston. Kimberley Powers. Our creation.

A defiant flag planted firmly in hostile territory. Seeing it live, active, sends a jolt through me—terror and fierce pride intertwined. The validation I've craved my entire career, built on my own terms.

We're real.

"Portal went live precisely three hours ago, timed with our exit from

The Ivy," Samantha reports, her eyes scanning the real-time dashboard. "The first wave of pre-commits hit exactly as planned. Confirmed wire instructions sent."

She starts reading from the screen, a litany of power players Kimberley and Julia had quietly courted for weeks.

The A-list of names washes over me like a benediction. Hollywood royalty. Titans. They're not just investing; they're making a statement. Backing the narrative. Backing *us*. Against Trent Lysander. Against the old guard.

Against Roman, if it comes to that.

The thought hits me harder than expected, a fresh wave of pain that has nothing to do with my knee. Despite everything—his accusations, his silence, his cold dismissal—part of me had hoped… what? That he'd come around? That he'd see past his wounded pride to understand what I was trying to accomplish?

Foolish. Naïve.

Exactly the kind of thinking that gets you hurt.

And invariably has.

Foolish girl.

"Excellent," Kimberley says, satisfaction clear in her voice. "Phase one executed. Now, The Ivy. Walk me through it again. Trent really self-destructed?"

I stay stoic and silent. Samantha gives me a questioning look, and I indicate to her that she should go ahead.

So, Samantha launches into the story, her eyes occasionally glancing at me with concern as she recounts the lunch meeting while I remain ever silent. I listen with only half of my attention. The other half is focused on managing the increasing discomfort in my right knee and the emotional chaos Roman's betrayal has unleashed inside of me.

"And Isla calmly informs him she'd *already told* Roman everything," Samantha continues, her voice rising with relish. "Then Roman backs her up. He says, '*She told me this morning.*' Brandon Chase confirms it too. Trent's face…" She laughs, but it's edged with protective fury. "He looked like he'd swallowed his own fancy silk tie."

Roman backed her up.

The words echo strangely. Yes, he'd confirmed he knew about my identity, about the casting clause. But when Trent launched his real attack, which was personal, vicious, and designed to isolate and destroy me, Roman remained silent.

Passive.

Watching.

"And the resignation?" Kimberley asks.

"Flawless," Samantha beams, though she's still glancing at me, imploring me to jump in. "Isla announces Ryder & Harper resigns Lysander Entertainment, effective immediately. But—and this was brilliant—offers to take Roman on pro bono, which effectively removes any conflicts of interest Trent was trying to manufacture."

Pro bono. The words taste bitter now. I'd meant it as a clean break, a way to neutralize Trent's leverage while maintaining professional integrity. But Roman perceives it as charity.

'I don't need your fucking charity.'

The memory makes my chest tighten. I reach for my water glass, needing something to do with my hands, and notice the slight tremor I can't quite suppress.

"Good," Kimberley states flatly. "He needed that arrogance checked. *Severely.*"

"Publicly," Julia adds, velvet-gloved ruthlessness in her tone. "Even better."

"Okay, updates coming in," Samantha says, her attention snapping back to the monitor. "Hold on... another wire transfer notification just cleared." Her fingers fly across the keyboard. "Brandon Chase..." She pauses, eyebrows shooting up. "Two million dollars."

Two million. From Brandon. The amount surprises me—it's substantial, meaningful. It signals his break from Trent's orbit, his recognition of where the real power lies now. Smart money, following smart strategy.

At least someone understands what we're building here.

"Smart money," Kimberley murmurs, echoing my thoughts. "He knows a sinking ship when he sees one."

"Definitely choosing sides," Julia agrees.

We have gone over the finer details of the offering. Divided up some of the action items, and reviewed the secondary tier of private investor invitations to be sent to potential investors, including the hedge fund contacts that Julia still has connections to and a few more of my clients over the years.

Then Samantha refreshes the screen again and goes very still. The energy in the room shifts and becomes electric with tension. "And...

wow." Her voice drops to almost a whisper. "Okay. Um…" She shoots me a questioning glance. Something like shock registers on her pretty face.

"What is it, Samantha?" Kimberley asks, her tone sharpening.

Samantha swallows hard, then reads slowly, carefully, as if the words might disappear if she says them too fast. "Incoming wire transfer confirmed. Source: Roman Lysander Personal Trust." She takes a breath, meets my eyes across the room. "Amount… *twenty million dollars.*"

The air leaves my lungs in a silent rush. *Twenty. Million. Dollars.* The number hangs in the space between us, impossibly large, incomprehensible. It doesn't compute. Not after this morning. Not after his venom in the SUV, the accusations of manipulation, the betrayal etched on his features so clearly, and when I revealed my power over the role of Steven Stryker, he covets so openly. And certainly, not after he watched his father try to destroy me and *said nothing.*

My blood runs cold, then scalding hot. Twenty million. From his *personal* funds. Not Lysander Entertainment money. *His own.*

What game is this?

What kind of power play is he trying out now?

The pain in my knee spikes suddenly, forcing me to shift my weight. The movement sends a fresh wave of discomfort up my leg, and I grip the edge of the desk to steady myself. Samantha notices immediately, starting toward me, but I wave her off with what I hope is a reassuring smile.

I will not fall apart. Not now. Not over him.

The silence on the video conference stretches uncomfortably.

Then Kimberley breaks it with a little snarky laugh, dry as desert sand. "Well, Isla. It appears you have an undeniable way of inspiring… *generosity*… in Hollywood's leading men."

Heat floods my cheeks, threatening to expose my carefully maintained composure. The weight of those zeroes, the implications, the sheer audacity of the gesture—it's overwhelming and infuriating at the same time. I focus on my breathing, refusing to hyperventilate in front of the two most powerful women in public relations.

Control. Maintain control.

Julia joins in, her laughter lighter but carrying the same teasing weight. "First Brandon throws in a couple million. Now Roman drops a cool twenty? What *is* your secret, darling? Forget PR. Maybe you should just start a hedge fund."

My mouth opens, but no sound comes out. I feel cornered, exposed, my professional façade threatens to break wide open under the increasing pressure and that staggering number and their knowing amusement. The familiar panic rises—the feeling of being seen too clearly, of having my defenses stripped away.

This is why I don't let people in.

This is why I keep the walls up at all times. Most of the time.

This is exactly why.

"How *is* Roman?" Julia asks, her tone shifting to something gentler, more probing. "Beyond the... financial contribution." There's genuine concern in her voice now. "I've always had a soft spot for him, you know. Seeing past the headlines and that carefully cultivated 'bad boy' image, his father encouraged. He's a good guy, truly. Terribly misunderstood."

A good guy.

The words sit strangely with me. *Is he?*

Terribly misunderstood.

The misunderstood. His playlist. The homage for his birthday. 'Music is a glimpse into someone's soul,' he said.

The misunderstood.

Is Roman one of the misunderstood?

Oh.

Or, is he just another Hollywood prince who can't handle being challenged, who lashes out when his privilege is threatened?

"If he could just get out from under Trent's suffocating shadow, his life would be so much better," Julia says thoughtfully. "I suppose you've managed that for him now, haven't you, Isla? Severed that particular cord quite decisively today."

Severed the cord, yes. But at what cost to whatever fragile connection was forming between us.

"That whole rebellious act," Julia goes on, "mostly smoke and mirrors, fueled by his father's ambition and grief he never properly dealt with. He lost his mother, you know. Horrific circumstances, sudden and tragic. Trent just papered over it, pushed him back onto movie sets. Roman carries that weight of grief."

Grief. The word resonates uncomfortably. I know something about carrying that weight, about the ways loss can shape and twist you.

But Roman's knowing about grief and what it can do? It doesn't excuse his cruelty toward me this morning during the car ride. It doesn't erase the way he weaponized my own vulnerability against me with the whole Melody Parker thing at The Ivy.

That one just burns all the way through. I can't shake it.

"He's a charmer, yes, a heartbreaker even," Julia says softly, holding my gaze. "But there's depth there, Isla. Real sensitivity. He has more in common with you—with your own losses—than you might think."

More in common. The thought is unsettling, unwelcome. I don't want to find common ground with Roman Lysander. I don't want to be anywhere near his ground, common or otherwise. I want to stay angry. Anger is cleaner and simpler. It doesn't require forgiveness or understanding or the terrifying vulnerability of trust.

"He's..." I start, then stop, unsure how to finish. *Cruel? Selfish? Damaged?* All true, but somehow inadequate. "He's complicated," I say immediately cringing at how weak it sounds.

Complicated. Like that excuses everything.

Kimberley's voice cuts through my self-recrimination with laser precision. "Love," she declares with the finality of a judge's gavel, "works in mysterious ways."

A fresh wave of laughter ripples through the video conference— warm, conspiratorial, aimed squarely at my burning face. I manage a strangled sound that might be a laugh or might be a choke.

Love. The word hangs in the air like a challenge. Is that what this is? This maddening pull toward someone who can hurt me so precisely, so devastatingly. This need to understand him, even as I want to destroy him.

Love?

Love. *No.*

No, no.

No!

No. Absolutely not.

I don't do love.

I do strategy. I do control. I do survival.

Love is for people who can afford to be vulnerable.

I cannot afford that. Like ever. Never.

"Alright, team," Kimberley says, shifting back into business mode with the efficiency that shows us all just how she and Julia so successfully built their empire. "Next steps. Legal needs to finalize the transfer protocols, confirm E&O insurance is binding under the new production entity. Samantha, track every incoming wire, cross-reference with pledge commitments. Isla, keep your head clear. The narrative is shifting. Trent will retaliate, but we have the momentum."

"And the moral high ground," Julia adds firmly. "Don't forget that."

"We won't," I say, grateful to be back on familiar ground. My voice sounds steadier than I feel, which is something.

"Keep us posted on the… funding developments," Kimberley says, the teasing back in her tone. "Especially any more… *grand gestures.*"

"Will do," I say, aiming for breezy, landing somewhere near absolutely stressed out, my voice an octave too high.

They sign off with more encouragement and barely concealed laughter.

At my expense.

The connection ends. The room plunges straight back into that ringing silence.

The monitor still displays Roman's contribution. $20 million. The number of zeros and the amount pulses with its own malevolent energy, demanding acknowledgment, demanding… *what.*

Understanding? Forgiveness? Gratitude?

Fuck that. Fuck all of that.

"Okay," Samantha says slowly, turning from the screen to face me. Her blue eyes are wide, searching mine. "Twenty million dollars. Isla…" She takes a step closer, concern evident in every line of her lovely frame. "That's not just support. That's not just strategy. That's a *grand gesture.* Capital G *squared.* You can't just *ignore* it, Iz."

I take a beat. Then a breath. Then exhale. "Why not? Why can't I ignore it?" The words come out sharp, edged with the absolute fury I've been suppressing all day. "He didn't say *anything.* There are no words from him, just a moneyed request to get in on the action. *Twenty million dollars. What-the-fuck-ever.* I'm not *interested* in his money."

Money doesn't erase what he said.

Money doesn't fix the way he looked at me like I was the enemy.

I push away from the desk, needing movement, needing distance from that glowing screen and the twenty-million-dollar number that mocks me at a soul level. The sharp pain in my knee makes me stumble slightly, and Samantha's there instantly, steadying me.

"Easy," she says softly. "When's the last time you took anything for the pain?"

"An hour ago. I'm fine." Another automatic lie.

"No, you're not. You're hurt—physically and emotionally—and

you're trying to power through it like some kind of warrior goddess." Her voice is gentle but firm. "Which is very *you*, but also very stupid."

Despite everything, I almost smile. *Almost.*

"But a \$20 million investment," Samantha says carefully. "Maybe this is his way of taking back what he said. Of showing you he believes in the project. In you."

I shake my head. The movement sends another spike of pain racing through my skull. *God, I need sleep.* "It doesn't change what he said. How he looked at me. The Melody *fucking* Parker thing! The way he just... *watched* when his father went all in for the kill."

'Your entire career is built on playing games.'

'I don't know what's real with you anymore.'

The accusations still burn like acid.

"Hold his funding," I say suddenly. My decision crystallizes with painful and laser-sharp clarity. "I don't want his money. I'll pull funds from my *Vendetta* royalties before I take a *dime* of Roman Lysander's money."

Samantha blinks rapidly, clearly surprised. "Are you *sure*? That's a lot of money to turn away."

"I'm sure."

Surer than I've been about anything all goddamn day.

"We don't need him. We don't need his guilt money or his grand gestures or whatever psychological game this is supposed to be *this time* with Roman Lysander."

I especially don't need anything from Roman Lysander.

Absolutely nothing.

"You know," Samantha says carefully as she's reading a text on her phone, "Kimberley just sent a text. She's invited Trent Lysander to invest. She says it's her way of disarming him before he takes things further."

Of course she did. Kimberley always thinks ten moves ahead. Keep your enemies close, especially when they have something to lose.

"Should I tell her you want to put a hold on Roman's funding?" Samantha asks, ever the diplomat.

"Absolutely *not. No.*" The words come out fierce and final. "*You're* in charge of it. We'll deal with it this weekend. Like I said, I'll make up the difference. I don't want his money. I don't want *anything* from *him.*"

Nothing. Not his money, not his apologies.

Not his complicated grief that supposedly excuses everything he does.

"Okay, I understand." Samantha nods slowly, but she's watching me with that penetrating gaze that sees too much. "But Iz… you're not looking so good. You're pale. You're favoring that knee more than you were this morning, and you look like you haven't slept in days."

"I'm fine," I insist, but even I can hear how hollow it sounds. "I *haven't* slept in days." I force a smile at her.

"No, you're not. And that's okay. You don't have to be fine. Not with me." Her voice is soft, understanding. "He really got to you, didn't he? And what he said in the SUV? The Melody Parker thing? I don't even know what that was. A way to hurt you?"

Her direct questions break something loose inside me, threatening to fracture the carefully maintained walls, holding back everything I've been suppressing. I close my eyes, seeing Roman's face again—the cold fury, the sense of betrayal, the way he'd looked at me like I was the enemy.

Like I was just another manipulator in his life, full of manipulators.

"In the car. At The Ivy. Where should we start? He made me feel like…" I start, then stop, unsure how to finish.

Like I was exactly what everyone always assumes I am. Like my grief was just another strategy. Like opening up to him was the stupidest thing I've ever done.

"Like what?" Samantha prompts gently.

"Like I was exactly what he accused me of being," I whisper. "A manipulator. A game-player. Someone who uses people's vulnerabilities against them." The words taste bitter. "Samantha, I told him about my family. About losing them. About how that shaped *Vendetta*. And he turned it into something about him, about his career, about whether I'd cast him based on merit or pity."

As if my pain was just another chess piece to be moved around the board.

I think of the scene I wrote in *Vendetta* where Evelyn Stryker's journal is discovered—the raw, unfiltered grief poured onto those pages, only to be twisted and used against her husband by the very people who killed her. I wrote those pages sitting by my brother's grave, pouring my own grief into fiction because reality was too painful to face directly.

Samantha's expression darkens. "He said that?"

"He accused me of playing games and said that was the definition of my job. So everything I shared with him—every moment of vulnerability—he saw as manipulation. As if I was playing some long game to control him." I laugh, but it comes out broken. "Maybe I should have been. Maybe that would make it hurt less."

Maybe if I'd actually been the calculating bitch, he thinks I am, his words wouldn't have cut so deep.

"Oh, honey." Samantha pulls me into a fierce hug, careful of my injured leg. "He's an idiot. A scared, wounded idiot who's been manipulated by his father and the film industry his whole life and doesn't know how to recognize genuine emotion when he sees it."

She sighs big and gets this vexed look. "I mean, Trent Lysander threatened Roman's career if he didn't go along with the manufactured relationship bit. *His own son.* It was disturbing to watch the family dynamics play out right in front of us like that. Cringe-worthy even. I mean, oh my God! I'm not engendering extra sympathy for him. But at least you have me and Kimberley and Julia. Roman has Brandon, and that's pretty much it, yeah?"

"That was horrible to watch. It is its own kind of personal tragedy." I sigh heavily, feeling sadness. "The thing is, I just don't have the energy to deal with the implications of all of that right now, or *him*, tonight, Sammy girl. Please. Can we *not* talk about Roman Lysander the rest of the night?"

"Right. Sure. No more talk about Roman Lysander tonight. You got it."

She puts her arm around me, and I lean into her warmth, allowing myself this moment of weakness. She smells like her signature perfume and the faint scent of the expensive coffee we've been living on. Samantha is familiar. Safe.

Unlike the actor. No, Roman Lysander is *not* safe. Whatsoever.

This is why I keep people at arm's length.

This is why I don't trust anyone.

Because when you let someone in, when you show them your true self, they can destroy you with surgical precision.

Like Roman did today.

"Come on," Samantha says, pulling back to study my face. "Let's get out of here. Let's celebrate the win. The *real* win. *We* did this. *You* did this. We took back *Vendetta*. We launched the funding portal. We left Trent Lysander sputtering in our dust."

Her eyes sparkle with fierce pride, and I feel an answering spark of satisfaction. She's right. Whatever else happened today, we won. We seized control. We proved that we don't need the old boys' club or their approval or their money.

We especially don't need Roman Lysander.

"We earned a ridiculously expensive dinner and some champagne to celebrate," Samantha says. "Catch LA is all lined up. Reservations at eight." She gets this satisfied, secretive smile.

And I have to wonder what she's up to, but I cannot handle any more surprises, and I have to hope she doesn't have any lined up.

Catch LA. The rooftop 'see and be seen' hotspot. Normally, I'd avoid it like the plague, preferring quiet corners and anonymity.

But tonight... feels different. Tonight, maybe being seen is the point. A signal that Ryder & Harper Communications LA has arrived.

And we're not hiding.

We're proud of what we've accomplished, and we answer to no one.

A slow smile touches my lips—the first genuine one since Roman's cold dismissal this morning. "Okay. Catch LA it is. But we are *not* discussing Roman Lysander's inexplicable finances or the hold I've placed on them anymore tonight. I'll deal with that this weekend. We can work on his strat plan this weekend and work out the logistics with all of it with Brandon Chase next week."

"Deal." Samantha grins, though her eyes say she doesn't believe me for a second. "Now, what does one wear to announce to Hollywood that you've just seized control of its next potential blockbuster?"

We head toward the massive walk-in closet off the master suite, a space larger than my first New York apartment. The ritual of choosing an outfit feels like armor selection—each piece a deliberate choice in the message we're sending.

Tonight, our statement needs to be clear: We are here. We are powerful. We are in control.

Even if internally, I'm wrestling with the seismic aftershock of a twenty-million-dollar gesture from the one guy who has the power to complicate absolutely everything in my life.

"Something in black," I say, reaching for a dress that screams sophistication and power. "Queen power. Chess just saved our asses. Let's play it out."

Samantha nods approvingly. "I love it when you go full warrior goddess."

Warrior goddess. If only she knew how fragile I feel beneath the armor. And, on top of everything else, I think I'm getting sick. The flu or something. I'll have to up my intake of Advil.

And yet, the pain in my knee is nothing compared to the gaping emotional wounds Roman has inflicted with his words and actions on my emotional wellbeing today.

How every step forward feels like I'm walking across broken glass. *Barefoot.* And there's no mental trick to it to outrun or escape the pain that engulfs me now. It's like a roaring fire. But this isn't a drama series. I'm not 'Khaleesi' stepping into the pyre with the dead Khal Drogo, and dramatically reemerging unburned, changed, and all powerful.

No. I'm burning down.

Slowly.

But that's tomorrow's problem.

Tonight, we celebrate.

Tonight, we show Hollywood exactly who they're dealing with.

And if Roman Lysander wants to buy his way back into my good graces with his guilt money, he's going to learn that some things cannot be bought.

Some wounds don't heal with grand gestures.

I think of my father's favorite passage from Hemingway's A Farewell to Arms: *"The world breaks everyone and afterward many are strong at the broken places."*

I've been broken before—by the loss of my entire family, by the loneliness that followed. I survived. I rebuilt. I became strong at the broken places.

But this feels different. More intimate. More devastating.

Because I let Roman in. I showed him the fractures. And he used them against me.

Some trust, once broken, stays broken.

I take a long shower. Standing under the hot water spray temporarily restores me.

Afterwards, I apply Neosporin to the swollen cut, which is more painful and red than yesterday, and carefully re-bandage it with fresh bandages, gauze, and the black athletic tape Samantha miraculously procured for me to better camouflage my wound.

Now, I gingerly slip into the black lace outfit—a masterpiece of design. This ensemble manages to be both elegant and dangerous. Exactly what I need to be ready for tonight.

I catch my reflection in the full-length mirror. The woman looking back is polished, powerful, and untouchable.

Perfect.

Let him see what he threw away.

Let them all see.

The sharp pain in my knee as I adjust the fit reminds me that some battles leave scars. But scars are proof of survival. Proof that you fought and won.

And I've won this time.

Even if it cost me everything.

CHAPTER 28

uninvited

Roman Lysander

"Bitter Sweet Symphony" – The Verve
"Uninvited" – Alanis Morissette
"Cold Heart" – Elton John, Dua Lipa, PNAU
"Please Please Please" - Sabrina Carpenter
"Love Like Mine" - Stela Cole
"West Coast" - Lana Del Rey
"Vampire" – Olivia Rodrigo
"Wake Me Up When September Ends" – Green Day

Friday Night 8:30 p.m.

THE ASSAULT BEGINS THE MOMENT, Manny opens the passenger door of the Escalade. Not physical, nothing so clean. This is sensory. Catch LA on a Friday night isn't just a place. It's an event horizon that sucks light, sound, and breathable air into a vortex of manufactured cool.

Music thuds, a relentless bass line vibrating up through the soles of my Italian loafers and rattling my teeth. The air hangs thick with a cloying mix of expensive perfume, a slight film of cigarette smoke drifting from some unseen corner of the rooftop, and the vaguely oceanic tang of overpriced sushi. Flashing lights—strobes from the DJ booth and the incessant glow of phone screens held aloft like offerings—fracture the scene into chaotic, glittering shards. A prism.

Brandon claps me on the shoulder, leans in to shout over the din. "Showtime, Ro."

I barely register him. My eyes are already scanning, sweeping the packed rooftop bar, instinctively seeking her out. It's a reflex now, unwanted but undeniable.

Find Isla.

Assess the damage.

Gauge the temperature.

Survive the encounter.

The scene before me feels like the third act of a psychological thriller—where the protagonist realizes he's been in the wrong movie all along.

What am I even doing here?

What's my motivation in this scene?

And there she is.

Holding court. That's the only way to describe it. Not near the main bar, too pedestrian. She and Samantha Harper are positioned at a high-top table near the edge of the terrace. The glittering sprawl of West Hollywood serves as a backdrop that seems almost staged for their benefit.

Jesus, it's a feeding frenzy. And she's the main course.

I stop just inside the threshold, letting the river of bodies flow around me, using a potted palm and a gaggle of impossibly thin model types as cover. Brandon pauses a few steps ahead, glancing back, waiting for my cue. I give none. I need a moment to process the tableau.

Isla.

She's wearing this all-black ensemble, a lace bodysuit that drapes over her curves like water over smooth stones—expensive, deliberate, and devastating, with a long black skirt slit to her waistline showing off her left leg whenever she moves. Perfectly cinched at her small waist where my hands have been. Have spanned and touched. It clings and flows in all the right places, sophisticated yet simple, like someone who doesn't need to try. Her long, dark hair is swept back in a high ponytail that drapes down her back, held in place by a diamond clip that glitters under the ambient light.

She's the queen, the most powerful piece on the chessboard.

Fucking ethereal, all over again. Just like the first time I saw her properly, standing there in the chaos of my party, looking like she'd wandered in from a different, and definitely better, world.

Except tonight, she isn't adrift.

Tonight, she *is* the world.

At least, this glittering, treacherous corner of it.

I'm enchanted by her, just watching her face, her laugh, her gentle movements. The way her dark hair catches the light. The way her smile radiates with this amazing joy just because it's her.

But then, my thoughts are interrupted by the music playing, Alanis Morissette's "Uninvited". The haunting melody and lyrics about someone showing up where they don't belong feels almost too pointed to be coincidence. And yet, I actually know this song's true meaning. It's about internal conflict and emotional barriers where someone isn't allowed to see the deeper parts of the other person.

Is this a message? *Yes...*

To me? *Uncertain.*

Am I just being paranoid? *No.*

Then, an updated rendition of Elton John's "Cold Heart" with Dua Lipa plays. Then, Sabrina Carpenter's "Please Please Please" mocks the façade of someone who can't admit their flaws—an actor no less. Too on point to miss. "Love Like Mine" with Stela Cole follows that one, the defiant anthem of a woman who knows her worth. Then, Lana Del Rey sings "West Coast". It's like a ballad directed at me about a woman contemplating a complex relationship, unsure whether to pursue it or let it go.

It becomes painfully clear that this is a litany of songs directed straight at me. Did she select each one with surgical precision, knowing exactly how they'd land? *Yes.*

I'm dead. There may be no coming back from this.

Isla Ryder is leaning against the high-top table, one hand holding a drink the color of radioactive Kool-Aid—some lurid orange concoction in a tall glass and the other just resting there. Her head tilts as she listens intently to someone obscured by the crowd. Then she laughs, a genuine, throaty sound that somehow cuts through the music, and it hits me like a physical blow.

She is… *enjoying* this.

My mind flashes back—the vulnerability in her eyes after our collision on the beach, the shared grief whispered between us, the desperate, reckless heat of last night, the cold fury in the Escalade this morning, the icy dismissal outside The Ivy just hours ago. How can all those women be contained in this one laughing ethereal figure dressed in black lace and bathed in neon?

I watch her face, trying to decipher the code. Is the smile real? Or is it the expertly crafted armor of a PR strategist who's just staged a coup? Is the ease in her posture genuine, or a performance for the circling sharks?

She contains multitudes. And the whiplash is making me dizzy, but it doesn't matter. I want to know all of her parts now.

People orbit her like planets around a newly discovered star. I recognize faces—A-list actors I've worked with, powerful producers who usually wouldn't give the time of day to anyone without an eight-figure deal pending, agents whose calls Brandon usually has to chase for weeks.

Tonight, they flock to her. Not just polite nods or air kisses. These are genuine embraces, enthusiastic handshakes, wide smiles reflecting something more than obligatory industry schmoozing. They lean in close, congratulating her, congratulating Samantha. The energy around that table is electric. It's charged with the thrill of rebellion.

They're celebrating her coup. Celebrating my father's downfall.

And maybe mine.

The thought lands cold and heavy in my gut.

They are cheering the independent spirit of the young, beautiful woman who told Trent Lysander to shove his retainer and his control, and to basically, 'fuck off'. The gifted writer who reclaimed her story and is now funding it herself with the backing of Hollywood's quiet rebels. My father's enemies are legion, and tonight, Isla Ryder is their Joan of Arc. Christ, that's straight from a movie poster tagline, but it fits.

I see Reese Witherspoon break away from a conversation with another A-lister and make a beeline for Isla. They hug, then stand talking animatedly. Isla nods and listens intently with that unnerving focus she has; the kind that makes you feel like the only person in the universe. Even from across the room, I can see the respect in Reese's expression.

My fists clench at my sides. This should be my arena. My crowd. I am Roman Lysander, the heir apparent, the golden boy, the one whose name opens doors and parts crowds. But tonight, standing in the shadows, I feel like an interloper, a ghost at the feast.

The sensation is uncomfortably familiar—like walking onto a set where all the blocking has been changed without warning, and suddenly I'm the extra trying to find my mark while the real stars take center stage.

———

Then *he* appears.

Danny.

The waiter from my birthday party. The kid I'd specifically assigned to look after Isla and make sure her glass was never empty and shield her from the worst of the sycophants. *Danny*, who drove the goddamn getaway car from The Ivy earlier today, spiriting Isla and Samantha away while leaving me standing on the curb like a chump. *My guy. Danny.*

He moves through the throng with the effortless grace of a dancer, weaving around bodies toward her. No tray tonight. He isn't working. He reaches Isla's side, smoothly inserts himself between her and Reese Witherspoon, says something brief. Reese blinks, momentarily surprised at the interruption, but Danny doesn't seem to notice or care. He takes Isla's free hand.

What the actual fuck?

Isla looks at him, a flicker of surprise on her face, but then... she smiles. A small, almost private smile. And she lets him lead her away from the high-top table, away from Reese fucking Witherspoon in mid-sentence, towards the makeshift dance floor near the DJ booth. She doesn't even hesitate. Just hands her radioactive drink to Samantha and goes with him.

Who the fuck does he think he is? Since when does "the waiter" cut in on an Oscar winner to dance with the bestselling author of *Vendetta*— the PR strategist, *mine*—whatever the hell she is to me now?

Shock morphs into a white-hot surge of something ugly and possessive. Jealousy? It feels bigger, more primal than that. It feels like watching someone walk into my house and take something that belongs to me.

Except she doesn't belong to me. She's made that painfully clear.

And the fact that Danny, of all people, can command her attention when I can't... It's a humiliation sharper than anything I've ever felt before. *I did this.*

Is this a message?

A power play orchestrated by her?

Or does she simply not give a damn who asks her to dance, as long as it isn't me?

Miley Cyrus is singing *Flowers*. A song about moving on, about buying your own damn flowers and being better off alone.

Messages are being sent all over the place.

For me.

And she's dancing with *Danny*.

It's like watching someone else get cast in the role you were born to play.

My jaw tightens until my teeth ache. I watch them move together. Danny is a good dancer, fluid and confident. Isla moves with a natural grace, even in that ridiculous crush of bodies. She's laughing again, head thrown back. The diamond clip catches the light, sending blinding little sparks across the room.

Fuck this.

Brandon finally moves into the space, apparently deciding after fifteen minutes that I'm not going to spontaneously combust on the spot. Not yet anyway.

He heads straight toward their table, and says something to Samantha, and then gestures towards the dance floor. Samantha smiles, nods, and lets Brandon lead her out to join the fray.

Samantha's wearing a peach-colored dress, short enough to be dangerous. *Holy shit.* Samantha Harper is a bombshell, no question, but tonight she radiates a confidence that amplifies it tenfold. She and Brandon look good together, laughing easily as they find a space near Isla and Danny. Brandon can't stop smiling. He's looking utterly charmed by Isla's wingman, Samantha Harper.

Great.

Now Brandon's in on it, too.

The sense of isolation slams into me hard. It's *annihilation.*

I feel like the protagonist in one of those art house films where everyone else is in on some cosmic joke, except for him. The frame slowly pushing in on my face while the world spins merrily on without me.

Here I am, Roman Lysander, Hollywood's supposed heartthrob, lurking near the entrance like a goddamn stalker while my manager and my PR strategist's partner dance without a care in the world, and the woman currently occupying 99.99% of my brain space is *laughing* and *dancing* with *Danny*.

This is pathetic.

Humiliating.

Like watching myself get written out of my own movie.

The twenty million dollars that was in my bank account two hours ago—my latest attempt at a grand gesture—still sits in digital purgatory. I stare at the *Vendetta* portal on my phone, watching other investments flow seamlessly into Isla's project while mine remains frozen in unapproved status. Her name climbs toward full funding status, while my contribution sits rejected. Unwanted.

She won't even take my money.

My name, Roman Lysander, the cachet that normally opens every door in this town, might as well be scrawled on a bathroom wall for all the good it is doing me tonight.

My face plastered on magazine covers as *Sexiest Man Alive* for three consecutive years. *Irrelevant.*

The golden boy who could charm his way into any project, any party, any woman's bed. *Irrelevant.*

Next.

It is like being the star of *Sunset Boulevard* in reverse—instead of a forgotten relic clinging to past glory, I'm watching my current reign crumble in real time. Norma Desmond had her delusions. I have mine. It's the growing realization that none of it means shit when the one person you want to notice you has already written you out of the script.

Dethroned right alongside my father. The irony tastes like ashes, bitter and choking. We built our empire by controlling narratives, manipulating stories, and bending people to our will.

Tonight, Isla Ryder is the director, and I'm not even an extra in her scene.

Got to make a move or go home. This is fucking pathetic. The thought hammers at me. But what move? Stride out there and cut in?

Demand she talk to me? Drag her off the dance floor? Every scenario feels wrong. Aggressive. It's exactly the kind of entitled bullshit she probably expects from me now. The kind of bullshit I displayed in the Escalade this morning.

I've been off my game all goddamn day *since* that car ride.

Now, I'm mimicking her words…

Oh, this girl.

My eyes narrow, tracking Brandon and Samantha on the dance floor. They are talking, heads close together over the music. Brandon says something, then subtly, imperceptibly, tilts his head in my direction.

Oh, for fuck's sake. Now they're *running plays on me.* Annoyance wars with a grudging respect for their seamless teamwork. I could kill Brandon right now. He knows I'm watching. He knows I'm stewing.

This is intervention, LA-style.

It is like being the subject of one of those carefully orchestrated "spontaneous" scenes in a reality show. Everyone has their lines except me.

CHAPTER 29

save your tears

Roman Lysander

"Wake Me Up When September Ends" – Green Day
"Save Your Tears" The Weeknd, Ariana Grande
"A Sorta Fairytale" - Tori Amos

Friday Night 9:15 p.m.

TEN MORE MINUTES GO BY. Then Samantha expertly spins out of Brandon's hold with a laugh, pats his arm, and begins weaving her way back through the crowd. Straight towards me. She moves with purpose, her eyes locked onto mine across the pulsing sea of people.

I brace myself. Whatever is coming, it will not be sugar-coated or be pretty. Samantha Harper strikes me as the type who sharpens her words before even speaking.

She reaches my little pocket of shadow. The noise seems to dip momentarily as she stops beside me. Without preamble, she links her arm through mine, a gesture that feels both friendly and proprietary, like she is taking me into custody. Her perfume is something light and citrusy, a stark contrast to the heavy florals choking the air from the usual Hollywood stars.

She leans in, her voice low but clear, cutting through the thumping beat. "Okay, it's her playlist you're hearing. I'm a little afraid for you, Roman," she starts, no sugar-coating here. "She is beyond royally pissed at you."

Confirmation. Not that I needed it.

The image of her icy glare outside The Ivy is permanently burned into my retinas. Still, hearing it stated so boldly stings.

"Yeah." My single word is clipped, while I attempt to rein in the cascade of emotions assaulting me, knowing all my worst thoughts have just been confirmed.

"I think it's partly exhaustion." Samantha's head inclines towards Isla, who is now laughing at something Danny whispers in her ear.

"Seriously, she hasn't had a proper night's sleep since Monday because she got a phone call at two in the morning on Tuesday and had to immediately deal with the pop star fiasco back in New York, then packing all the next night Wednesday, and then the long red-eye flight, the move itself, and then *you*, the injury on the beach is still bothering her." She gets this worried look. "She's taking Advil like they're Skittles… Your dad. *You*. Already said that. Then, all of this…" She waves a vague hand, encompassing all the chaos of the past day, the drama with my father, the launch of their firm, *me*.

"But Roman…" Her tone shifts, losing the slight edge of excuse, becoming deadly serious. She turns her gaze back to me, sharp and appraising. "That only goes so far. I know you think you've met her halfway with the investment and showing up tonight, but you're going to have to go the *entire distance*. She ain't playin'."

Samantha sighs big. "You don't have a confirmation text on the twenty million dollars because she's having me put a hold on your funding. She doesn't want your money, Roman. She's talking about pulling funds, if need be, from her novel royalties account from *Vendetta*, and I quote, 'before she'll take a dime from Roman Lysander.' Sorry."

"So. You're saying she's extremely upset." The words come out flat, a statement rather than a question. My throat feels like I've been swallowing sand again.

"I've never seen her quite like this. Like *ever*. You want a chance at redemption? You are going to have to go the entire distance and meet her there." Samantha's gaze is penetrating, as if she's trying to excavate the answer from somewhere inside me. "What does she need, Roman? What is she asking of you? Think about it."

Echoes of Brandon's words about a 'grand gesture' ricochet in my skull. *What does that even mean?* What could possibly bridge the chasm I created with my accusations in the Escalade? How do you undo the damage of just silently watching while your father tries to destroy the woman sitting next to you at the table at The Ivy? How do you prove you're not just another entitled asshole who sees her as a means to an end—a role, a career boost, or another conquest?

But Samantha isn't finished. "Her walls are so high right now…" She pauses, searching for the right words. "Honestly? I think she put in a moat, too. Maybe some dragons. I've known her for years, Roman. I've seen her handle crises that make hardened CEOs weep. I've never seen her quite like this. Not even with the baseball player. This closed off. This… fortified."

Fortified. That is the word to describe her.

Isla on the dance floor doesn't look vulnerable; she looks like a citadel, beautiful and impenetrable.

"I know you two just met," Samantha acknowledges, her grip tightening slightly on my arm, as if to emphasize her point. "And yeah, the timing, the circumstances. It is all one gigantic fucking mess. But Roman, she's the real deal. What happened today? At The Ivy? That's her. Fierce, brilliant, and she doesn't back down. She is worth fighting for." Her gaze holds mine, intense and unwavering. "But your window? It is closing. *Fast.* You might have to break the glass."

Break the glass.

An emergency measure.

Desperate. Dangerous. Exactly how I feel.

Like, that moment in a disaster film when the protagonist has to shatter the safety barrier to reach the emergency controls. The point of no return.

My throat feels tight. I swallow, forcing out the words, trying to project a calm I don't remotely feel.

"I'm aware." It sounds lame even to my own ears. *Defensive. Helpless.* "Not sure what else I can do. Or, what I'm supposed to do."

The admission hangs in the air between us, open and honest. I think about what happened in the Escalade this morning—how I took her vulnerability, her grief over losing her family, and twisted it into something about me. About my career. About whether she'd cast me out of pity. I made her pain about me, when she was finally letting someone see the real Isla Ryder and her pain.

What kind of person does that?

The kind raised by Trent Lysander, where every emotion is a

weapon, and every connection is a strategic play. The kind who has spent so long playing the role of Roman Lysander, 'bad boy' heartthrob, that he's forgotten how to just be a real person and express true emotion with someone. To someone.

Isn't that what acting is supposed to be about at its core? Truth? Finding the authentic emotional connection that makes a performance real? How ironic that I've spent my entire career chasing that authenticity on screen while being utterly incapable of it in my actual life.

Samantha gives up a small, impatient sigh, like a teacher dealing with a particularly slow student. A hint of exasperation shows in her features. "Well," she says, her voice regaining its brisk, practical edge, "dance with me, for starters. Standing here brooding like Hamlet isn't helping anyone."

It isn't a suggestion. It is a command.

She tugs gently on my arm. "And I'll task Brandon with Isla."

Task Brandon? Right.

The phrase grates, reinforcing the feeling that I am being managed and maneuvered. But what choice do I have? Stay here and continue my pathetic vigil? Maybe Samantha is right. Maybe getting me out of the corner is step one. Maybe Brandon can run interference, test the waters, and soften the beachhead before I attempt a landing. Or maybe they are just trying to keep me from doing something monumentally stupid out of sheer frustration.

It feels like being a pawn in their game, Isla's game.

But a pawn has to move to stay on the board.

And isn't that what I've been my entire life? A pawn in my father's game? Am I always moving according to someone else's strategy, never claiming my own power?

I hesitate for only a beat, the internal battle raging—pride versus desperation. *Desperation wins.* It usually does, especially the past thirty-two hours. I give her a single curt nod.

"Alright," Samantha says, with notable approval in her eyes. She pulls me forward, out of the shadows and towards the swirling energy of the dance floor.

The music envelops me, louder now, inescapable. Bodies press close. Samantha finds a small space and starts moving easily to the rhythm, pulling me with her. I go through the motions, my feet moving automatically, but my attention is locked on Isla across the dance floor.

I look over and realize Danny is gone. Isla is now dancing near

Brandon. They aren't touching, maintaining a careful distance, but they are talking. Brandon leans in slightly to be heard, a serious expression on his face. Isla listens, her expression unreadable from this distance.

Is he *pleading* my case?

Running interference as tasked?

Or is he *just… talking*?

The song playing is *Vampire* with Olivia Rodrigo—about a brutal takedown of someone who takes and takes until there's nothing left.

Holy fuck. She hates me.

The lyrics slice through the ambient noise with surgical precision. Am I the vampire in her story? The one who drained her of trust, of vulnerability, of the fragile connection we'd built so quickly? But then, I just burned it all down?

My mind races, replaying Samantha's words. Royally pissed. Go the entire distance. Walls high. Moat. Dragons. Real deal. Window closing. Break the glass. What does she need from me? She wanted me to trust her. *Blew that.*

To *see* her.

I do. *Don't I?*

I see a woman who lost her entire family at seventeen. Who channeled that grief into writing a novel that became a bestseller. Who built a career out of shaping narratives, not because she enjoys manipulation, but because she understands the power of story. Who took on my father, the most powerful man in Hollywood, without flinching. Who trusted me with her vulnerability, and I threw it back in her face.

What do I know about that kind of courage? That kind of resilience? I've hidden behind my father's power my entire career, even while rebelling against it. I've never truly stood alone.

The 'grand gesture' Brandon spoke of earlier crashes back into my consciousness with the force of a tidal wave. What the hell does that look like? How do you demonstrate trust after shattering it so completely? How do you breach walls that Samantha, her closest friend, describes as fortified with illustrative moats and dragons?

Apologies feel inadequate. Words feel cheap, especially after the way I'd weaponized them earlier in the Escalade.

Flowers? *No.* Jewelry? *Like what exactly?* The usual bullshit peace offerings feel insultingly trivial given the stakes, given her. This isn't about placating a fleeting romantic interest. This is about… everything. *Vendetta.* My career. The chance to work on something meaningful, something hers. The chance to prove I am not just my father's son, a spoiled brat playing at being an actor. The chance to maybe, just maybe, earn back a fraction of the tentative connection we'd forged before I torched it so completely.

The pressure builds inside my chest—pressure from Samantha's urgent warning, pressure from the sight of Isla across the floor, so close, yet impossibly far, pressure from my own churning gut telling me this is a crossroads I cannot afford to navigate badly.

I need to do something decisive. Something that cuts through the noise and the bullshit. Something that shows her I understand. That I see her, not just the screenwriter or the PR guru or the woman who holds my career in her hands, but the person she is beneath the armor. Something that proves I am willing to risk... what? My pride? My carefully constructed public image? More than that. Something that requires a genuine leap of faith.

But what?

What the hell can be the grand gesture?

It's like being handed a script with my most important scene missing —just a note that says, *"Actor to improvise authentic emotional breakthrough here."*

I dance mechanically while Samantha serves as a warm, steady presence at my side. And yet, my mind is miles away, caught in a paralyzing loop of indecision and the terrifying, insistent urge to act. The music pounds, the lights flash, the crowd surges all around me, but all I see is Isla, a queen in her new court, and all I feel is the incredible weight of the closing window and the jagged edges of the glass I might have to break.

The question hangs heavy in the strobe-lit air, unanswered, and still terrifying.

What do I do now?

And do I have the guts to do it?

And then the DJ shifts gears, the thumping beat fading into something else entirely. A familiar guitar riff cuts through the noise, melancholic and instantly recognizable. Green Day's Wake Me Up When September Ends.

A wave of something sharp and bittersweet washes over me, pushing aside the jealousy and frustration for a moment. My mother's favorite song—because of course it would play now. Even in this plastic jungle of LA networking, the universe has a sense of humor only a screenwriter could appreciate.

It's too on-the-nose, hearing it now. *Here.* Almost like some cosmic director decided my life needed a soundtrack at this exact moment. I can practically hear my mother's laughter at the cliché of it all. And yet…

Her voice echoes in my head, clear as if she were standing beside me instead of Samantha. "Life's too short, Roman. Seize the day. Always." That's what she used to say to me, especially when I was hesitating, caught up in my own head, letting fear dictate my choices.

The song is about loss—Green Day's frontman wrote it about his father's death. About wanting to sleep through the pain until it's over, about the ache that lingers long after the leaves fall.

It speaks to me, resonating with a grief I've carried for too long, buried under layers of bullshit bravado demanded by my father and this town.

I always think of my mom when I hear it, think about the time I lost, the years spent running from the pain instead of facing it, the way I let her memory become a ghost instead of a guiding light.

Maybe she is telling me something vital right now. Seize the day. Stop lurking in the shadows, paralyzed by pride and hurt. Stop waiting for permission or the perfect moment that never comes. Samantha said I might have to break the glass. Brandon talks about a grand gesture. Maybe this is it. The universe, or my mom, or whatever force is at play, giving me a firm shove in the most Hollywood way possible—with the perfect music cue.

The window is closing. Fast. Hearing this song, Kelly Lysander's song, crystallizes the choice with painful clarity. Do something real, something decisive, or risk losing everything that might actually matter, letting another September fade into regret.

I look across the dance floor at Isla. She is still talking with Brandon. The song seems to have reached her too—there's a stillness in her now, a pause in her movements. She's listening. She knows this song. It means something to her.

My heartbeat syncs with the drumbeat. I'm still dancing with Samantha, but my body is on autopilot. My mind is racing ahead, assembling pieces, connecting dots, forming something that might be a plan, or might be the stupidest idea I've ever had.

But it's something.

It's real.

And it's mine.

It's like that moment in a scene when everything suddenly clicks—when the character's motivation becomes crystal clear and the performance shifts from technical to transcendent.

I lean down to Samantha's ear. "I need to go do something. Right now."

She pulls back, studies my face with narrow-eyed intensity. Whatever she sees there must satisfy her because she gives a single, decisive nod. "About damn time! So, you're going to tell her how you feel about her, yeah?" she asks, and releases my arm.

Her words hit me like a thunderbolt. *Tell her how I feel about her.* Not apologize. Not explain. Not justify. Not buy my way back with investments or projects or promises.

Tell her how I feel about her.

The simplicity of it staggers me. The honest vulnerability it demands terrifies me. This isn't about grand gestures in the Hollywood sense—expensive gifts or public spectacles. It's about the grandest gesture of all: truth. Honesty. Emotional nakedness.

I've spent my entire life hiding behind characters, behind my father's name, behind carefully constructed personas. But Isla deserves the real me, stripped of pretense and performance.

That's what she's been asking for from me all along.

"Yes," I say, my voice steady with newfound clarity.

I turn, pushing through the crowd, moving with a sense of purpose. Not toward Isla—not yet—but toward the DJ booth at the far end of the rooftop. The song is still playing, the melancholy guitar carrying over the murmur of the crowd, who have slowed their frenetic pace to match the change in tempo.

This might be career suicide. This might be emotional suicide. This might be the most un-Roman Lysander thing I've ever done.

But for once, I don't care. Because for once, I'm not doing it as Roman Lysander, son of Trent, heir to the throne, Hollywood's golden boy.

I'm doing it as just… me. The sixteen-year-old kid who lost his mom.

The guy who's trying and failing but still trying to be better than the legacy he inherited. The actor who wants to make something real.

And maybe, just maybe, the guy who's falling for the one woman in this town who sees through all the bullshit.

I reach the DJ booth, lean over the equipment, and begin to speak rapidly into the startled DJ's ear. His eyebrows shoot up.

Then he half yells back at me, shaking his head, "Hey man, she's already got the playlist set. There are like two hundred songs she's designated to be played. I believe they're directed your way, bro. 'Uninvited?' She told me to tee that one up as soon as you got here. But, if you got a list, I'll give you a fifteen-minute set. I know who you are. She said you might show up, and I am supposed to tell you, *'no.'*"

"Fuck me. She knows my moves." I groan, running a hand through my hair. Of course, she expected me to do something like this. She's ten steps ahead of me; she has been since the moment we met.

"Dude, she's the queen of the night tonight. She rented the whole place out and paid me quadruple what I normally charge. I'm just following her orders. But like I said, I'll give you fifteen minutes. 'She ain't playin'.' That's what I heard her say to her friend, the blonde? When they first got here."

The DJ leans closer, his expression shifting from professional detachment to genuine curiosity. "Look, man, I've been a DJ in this town for eight years. I've seen every kind of Hollywood drama play out on my dance floors. But this? This is next level. She walked in here like she owned the place—which, technically, she does tonight—and laid out a musical battle plan that would make Sun Tzu weep. Two hundred songs, all strategically selected." He shakes his head in admiration. "That's some serious psychological warfare, bro."

I can't help but let out a bitter laugh. "Yeah, she's... *thorough.*"

"Thorough? Dude, she handed me a playlist with timestamps, emotional arcs, and what she called 'narrative beats.' I thought I was getting hired to spin tracks, not orchestrate a three-act emotional opera. And the way she talked about you..." He trails off, studying my face with newfound sympathy. "She said, and I quote, 'If Roman Lysander shows up tonight, he's going to try to charm his way out of trouble. Don't let him.' But then she paused and added, 'Unless he actually surprises me.'"

He grins. "So, the question is, Roman Lysander—are you here to charm, or are you here to surprise her?"

It's like getting script notes from an unexpected source—sometimes the best insights come from the people who aren't caught up in the drama.

"Surprise her, most definitely. Okay. How much is this special request going to cost me?" The words come out sharper than intended, frustration bleeding through.

"Per song. A hundred bucks." Then, he laughs and shakes his head from side to side. "No man. You already have enough problems. *Clearly.* And a selected playlist isn't going to do it. *Sorry.* Hopefully, you've got more than that."

"I do," I say, the conviction in my voice surprising even me. Because suddenly, I know exactly what I need to do. It's been there all along, just beneath the surface of my confusion, hurt, and despair.

"Good. Good." He nods, leaning forward with obvious interest now. "Because honestly? I'm rooting for you. That woman over there? She is fierce as hell, but there's something about the way she said your name… Like she was trying to convince herself she didn't care. And in my experience, you don't put together a two-hundred-song-emotional manifesto for someone you're indifferent to."

"Right. Thanks for telling me that." I actually laugh. "What's your name, by the way?"

"Tom Landon." He grins and we do the bro handshake and kind of lean in.

I have a friend, maybe. That makes three. Brandon, Manny, and this guy, Tom.

"Okay, what do you have for a playlist?" Tom asks, grinning.

We work out the playlist, a carefully curated selection that might just say what I need to say through song. At least, it's another way to convey what I'm feeling and trying to say to her. In case, God forbid, I forget my lines.

I look at the DJ. *Tom.* He seems keenly interested in whether I'll be able to pull this off. "I need at least twenty minutes to set some things up. I'll swing by. That will be the signal to start playing the set, yeah?"

"Sounds good. Good luck. You're going to need it." He laughs again, but there's a hint of genuine encouragement in his eyes, like he's invested in seeing how this Hollywood fairy tale—or tragedy— plays out.

The window is all but closed.

But I'm about to throw a rock right through it.

Like a third-act twist that changes everything that came before, I finally see what needs to happen. The grand gesture isn't about money or apologies or even the role of Steven Stryker.

It's about showing her who I really am. About being as brave as she was when she shared her grief with me. About matching her vulnerability with my own.

About trusting her enough to see the real me—not the carefully curated 'bad boy' image, not the dutiful son, not the actor playing a part —but the flawed, fucked-up, genuine person underneath it all.

It's time to go off-script. To improvise the most important scene of my life.

CHAPTER 30

perfect

Roman Lysander

"Perfect" - Ed Sheeran
"You Learn" - Alanis Morissette
"I'm Good" - Bebe Rexha and David Guetta
"A Sorta Fairytale" - Tori Amos
"Watch Me Shine" - Joanna Pacitti
"Perfect Day" - Hoku
"Birds of a Feather" - Billie Eilish

Friday Night, 10:00 p.m.

I SLIP OUT OF CATCH LA with the music trailing behind me. Pat Benatar's powerful voice belting out, "Love Is A Battlefield" as the door swings shut, the lyrics following me like a taunt. I shake my head and actually laugh.

I'm so fucked with this girl. I really don't know what I'm doing.

Clearly.

Manny sees me immediately. There is a perk in being considered Hollywood's Heartthrob—a parking spot right out front. Apparently, I'm good for business.

He is already out of the SUV, posture alert, eyes scanning the perimeter with professional precision. "Sir. What do you need?"

"Well, Manny, I'm about to crash and burn again with the girl you met this morning. And I need to make a grand gesture, probably more than one."

"Thought so." A small grin breaks through his usually stoic expression—which, for Manny, is practically a smile. He reaches into the back of the SUV and hands me the cake from the cooler before I even ask.

"Thanks, Manny." I start to turn away, my mind already racing with what I'll say to Isla.

"Sir?"

I turn back. "You forgot this. I believe you're going to need this as well." He hands me the small red velvet jewelry box that he's kept for me for years in the glove box right next to his firearm in any of the SUVs he's driven for me. "I believe the emergency measure for the biggest grand gesture of them all has arrived, sir. Ms. Ryder appears to be *the one.*"

Manny has this big smile on his face now. He's very proud of himself. The guy has been with me since I turned sixteen. Right before my mom died. She'd insisted I have a driver to take me back and forth to auditions when she couldn't. And we knew Dad wouldn't have time. And she wasn't keen on me driving myself everywhere. So, she hired Manny. *'He's a good man, Roman, and I trust him completely.'*

It's like she knew that I would need someone like Manny, and I have —*needed Manny*—ever since my mom died. He's the one person I can talk to. The only one who knew how I was really feeling about my life even then. Now he's been through more than twelve years of stuff with me. Manny knows me as well as Brandon Chase. Probably even better.

I'm completely stunned. Manny—my driver, my security guy, my personal gladiator and friend—has figured it all out *before* me.

"Yes... She is *the one,*" I finally say.

"Go get her, sir."

I stand with him for a few minutes with the cake box in one hand and the red velvet box in the other. We just kind of bask in the silence. In the *knowing.*

Then, he says, "You can do this, sir. She's going to make you very happy. She's real. And everybody deserves that kind of love when they find it. You're scared, I know, but you can do this. And telling her you love her. That's all she needs to hear. Go on. Go *tell her*. You're just wasting time standing here with me."

I'm in a state of proverbial shock that might become permanent if I don't get it together, like right the fuck now. I nod. "Okay then. Thanks for the pep talk, Manny."

My mind swirls with questions.

How do I do this? How do I tell her I love her? I love her? *Yes. I do.* Manny just laid it all out for me. Is it that simple? What if she says no? She might. She's royally pissed. Oh my God. This is… insane. There's that. Okay.

What does she need from me? The girl who appears to have it all but doesn't have what she needs.

What does Isla need from me?

Support. Trust. Love.

From me.

Love.

Me.

It's been there all along. An answer to the simplest of questions. What does Isla need from me?

Love.

The realization hits me like a freight train derailing at full speed, scattering cargo across miles of track. Standing here on the sidewalk outside of Catch LA, I turn and nod one last time at Manny, too stunned to even smile as all the feelings wash over me.

I'm in love with her.

Not falling. Not developing feelings. Already there. Completely, irrevocably, catastrophically gone.

The thought should terrify me. Roman Lysander doesn't do love. Roman Lysander does casual, convenient, whatever keeps the demons at bay without requiring actual investment or vulnerability in someone else. Roman Lysander keeps things surface-level because depth means drowning, and I've been holding my breath underwater since my mom died.

Apparently, Roman Lysander is full of shit.

In a daze, I walk back inside Catch LA carrying the box of cake and the velvet jewelry box. I take my position by the potted palm once again, slip the jewelry box into my dress pants pocket like it's a secret weapon

—something I'll hold on to for now, while my mind and body catch up to the implications of what I'm *really* about to do.

'What does she need?' Samantha asked me not more than fifteen minutes ago. Did I answer? Can't remember. Because, as usual, I was making it all about myself. My money. Her rejection. Her playlist. Her messages through song lyrics. What does it all mean? Why can't I figure this out?

Well, Manny figured it out. Manny has a loving wife and three kids. He knows what life is all about. Apparently, I'm just figuring all of that out. *Now.*

The bass from Catch LA's sound system vibrates through the floor-to-ceiling windows, a relentless pulse that matches the hammering in my chest. Bebe Rexha and David Guetta's *"I'm Good"* plays, the message from the song hitting me with crystal clarity. Here, in this glittering chaos of Hollywood's finest, Isla Ryder is holding court like the queen she is.

And I'm here, hiding like a coward, paralyzed by the weight of what I've just realized about myself via Manny's directive. 'Go get her, sir.'

I love her. And the lady doesn't tolerate cowards.

'Only gladiators need apply.'

She told me this yesterday.

I love her.

I love her fierce intelligence, the way she dismantled my father with surgical precision. I love her vulnerability, hidden beneath all these layers of professional armor. I love her patience and kindness in baking me that birthday cake. I love the way she felt in my arms the first time we kissed, and the way she looked at me last night like I was worth saving. I love her strength, her absolute refusal to be bought or bullied or controlled.

And I destroyed it. All of it. With my suspicion, my accusations, and my inability to trust the one person who's been honest with me from the very start.

Brandon finds me at the entrance. Concern etched across his features. "You alright?" he asks, studying my face with the wariness of someone who's witnessed too many of my spectacular self-destructive scenes. "You look like you've seen a ghost."

Maybe I have. The ghost of who I used to be before a brunette with emerald green eyes and a steel spine walked into my life and detonated everything, I thought I knew about myself.

"*Roman.*" Brandon's voice cuts through the spiral. "Talk to me."

I turn from looking at the dance floor, still tracking Isla's every move, and run a hand through my hair—a nervous tell I've never been able to shake, one that would make my old acting coach cringe. "I've fucked up. Spectacularly."

"Yeah, we've covered that. Several times already. The question is, what are you going to do about it?"

The question hangs in the air like smoke from a cigarette you can't quite extinguish. What am I going to do? The usual Roman Lysander playbook feels pathetically inadequate. Flowers? *Please.* The investment gesture? *She just turned down my twenty million dollars.* A song? Like the DJ said, *the playlist isn't going to cut it.* It might buy me some time, though.

And no, this isn't one of my rom-coms where the leading man wins back the girl with a perfectly timed serenade.

But then it hits me, crystallizing with the kind of clarity that only comes in the third act when everything finally clicks into place.

Pride and Prejudice 2005. Her favorite movie. Darcy's proposal in the rain—raw, honest, pride stripped away like old paint. No games, no manipulation, just truth laid bare.

That's what she needs. What we both need.

The truth. Out loud.

"I need to get in there," I say, the words coming out rougher than intended. My throat feels like I've been chain-smoking for hours. "I need to tell her."

"Tell her what?"

"That I love her."

Brandon's eyebrows shoot up so fast they practically disappear into his perfectly styled hairline. "You *love* her? Roman, you've known her for like *a day.*"

"Thirty-two hours and counting. I should have told her yesterday at the beach."

"That probably would have appeared a little fast. But *this,* waiting until *after* the 24-hour mark, shows some real restraint, like you put some thought into it." Brandon's expression shifts from concern to something approaching awe, like he's witnessing a rare astronomical event. "Depends on how you look at it, I guess." He grins. "You've never said that about *anyone.* That you *love* them. *Ever.* Not even close."

He's right. The closest I've come to love was a series of convenient arrangements with women who understood the game, who wanted the association more than the man. Safe. Controllable. Emotionally vacant. Like the Melody Parker thing my father wanted. Exactly like that.

Nothing like the terrifying free fall of whatever this is...

Well, this is love in all of its forms—with Isla.

"She's going to think I'm insane." I pace the small alcove near the entrance. Me and the potted palm—a nervous duet. All around us, the restaurant is chaos—paparazzi lingering outside, fans trying to get past security, the usual circus that follows wherever Hollywood congregates. "She put a hold on my money, Brandon. She doesn't want anything to do with me. Not sure how to cross that chasm quite yet."

"Maybe she's protecting herself. Maybe she's as scared as you are."

The possibility stops me cold. I look at him hard. "Isla Ryder, *scared*? The woman who just took down Trent Lysander, my dad, in front of half the industry? Who seems to have built an empire in less than forty-eight hours?"

"She's human, Roman. You hurt her. *Badly*. This playlist is brutal, but what does that tell you? She took the time to put it together. Why? If she doesn't care about you at all... Why would she take the time to put together a playlist that sends you these 'on point' messages of how hurt she is by you in a thousand different ways? She's not indifferent. She's scared. That's my take. And I'm usually right about women—many things, of course—but women, most especially. Whereas, *you*? You've never stopped to study them long enough. Until now."

I remember the flash of vulnerability in her eyes when she told me about her family. The way she trembled when I touched her. The careful walls she's built around her heart, higher and stronger than anything my father ever constructed around his media empire.

True enough. She's not invincible. She's just better at hiding the hairline fractures than anyone else, including me.

"I need to do something," I say, the restless energy building to a crescendo. "Something that shows her I understand. That I *see* her."

"A grand gesture, then," Brandon says quietly. "Like we talked about all afternoon. Obviously, *not* the $20 million."

"A *real* one. Not Hollywood bullshit." I pause, the pieces clicking together like a perfectly edited sequence. "She loves that movie *Pride and Prejudice*. Darcy's proposal scene. The heavy rain."

Brandon stares at me. "You want to recreate a scene from a Jane

Austen-based romance film? In the middle of a rooftop party? With half of Hollywood watching?"

"Why not? She said I don't know who she *is*. Maybe it's time to *show her* I know *who she is*, and I do *see* her. Show her who I really am, too."

The plan forms in fragments, desperate and half-mad but somehow feeling right. More right than anything I've done in years.

"I need that rain sound effect from that shoot, three weeks ago," I tell Brandon, my voice gaining strength with each word. "The artificial rain we used for the crying scene."

"Roman—"

Brandon looks at me like I've completely lost my mind. Maybe I have. Maybe that's exactly what this situation requires.

"You realize this could backfire spectacularly," he says, already reaching for his phone. "I mean, I know I told you I think she's scared. And I still think that. But she's also very pissed. Really pissed. Samantha made that crystal clear. And I checked in with Isla, too. *Confirmed*. She ain't playin'. I'm *concerned*. For *you*."

"I know. I know." The admission tastes like copper pennies and regret. "But doing nothing... letting her walk away... that's worse than any public humiliation."

He studies my face for a long moment, then nods. "Alright. But if this goes south, don't blame me when you're trending on "X" Twitter and Instagram for all the wrong reasons."

Twenty minutes later, I'm standing outside the garden entrance to Catch LA, heart hammering against my ribs like it's trying to escape. The artificial rain sound system is positioned discretely around the rooftop's perimeter—Brandon's connections in the industry proving their worth once again. I'm still carrying the small white box containing the giant piece of the birthday cake Isla made me, somehow still perfect despite the chaos of this day.

It's ridiculous. Absurd. The most un-Roman Lysander thing I've ever contemplated.

But for once, I don't want to be Roman Lysander, Hollywood's golden boy with the tarnished reputation. I want to be the man who picks up the pieces when someone falls. The one who listens when she talks about her family. The one who sees past the emotional armor to the woman beneath.

It feels like I might be attending my own execution. My palms are sweating—actually sweating, like I'm a nervous teenager instead of a seasoned actor who's performed in front of millions. The small cake box feels impossibly heavy in my hands, weighted with significance beyond sugar and flour.

The doors open, and I'm immediately assaulted by the sensory overload of Catch LA in full swing. Music pounds, conversations blur into white noise, and the air hangs thick with ambition and expensive perfume. But my eyes find her immediately, like a compass needle swinging true north.

Isla.

She's back at her high-top table near the terrace edge, and she's... radiant. That's the only word for it. The black lace ensemble clings to her curves like it was designed specifically for her body, and the way the city lights catch the diamond clip in her hair makes her look like some sort of dark angel presiding over her newly conquered kingdom.

She's laughing at something Reese Witherspoon is saying, head thrown back, completely at ease. The sight should make me happy—she deserves this moment, this triumph—but instead, it feels like a knife between the ribs. She's moved on. Already. While I've been outside having emotional revelations, she's been here building her empire and apparently having a fantastic time doing it.

Tori Amos' song, *A Sorta Fairy Tale,* is playing. I know this song. It's about the journey a failed relationship takes that the two of them try to save. Instead of being wounded by the lyrics, it actually gives me hope because it tells me that Isla recognizes we have a relationship. Now I just need to try and save it.

Then Danny reappears at her table, two champagne flutes in hand.

The jealousy hits like a physical blow, doubling me over. It's irrational, possessive, everything I've despised about myself when it comes to relationships. But watching her with him, laughing at whatever he's whispering in her ear...

I want to tear him apart with my bare hands.

"Easy, tiger." Samantha Harper appears at my elbow like she materialized from thin air. "That's just Danny. He's harmless."

"Harmless?" I can barely get the word out through gritted teeth. My jaw aches from clenching it so hard. "He's got his hands all over her."

"He's *talking* to her. That's not a crime that I know of." Her blue eyes are sharp, assessing. "And even if he wasn't, what exactly do you plan to do about it? March over there and beat your chest like some caveman?"

The accuracy of the description sounds wanting. "Maybe."

"That'll go over well. Nothing says, 'I've changed' like a public brawl over a woman who's already told you she's done with you."

"Ouch. Wow. Thanks for the support there, Samantha."

"You'll recover. She won't. She isn't recovering, I mean. I've never seen this before."

I force myself to unclench my fists, to breathe through the surge of primitive rage. She's right. Charging over there like some testosterone-fueled idiot would only prove every terrible thing Isla thinks about me right now.

"I'm sorry. I'm trying to get this right. With her. But what the hell am I supposed to do?"

She studies me for a long moment, like she's trying to solve a particularly complex equation while coaching a first-grader. "I don't know, Roman. Let's think about it together. What does Isla Ryder need? *From you?* Money? *No. She's got plenty of that.* Status? *No.* She's had that her whole life, and you don't even know the half of it. Power? *No, she's* doing pretty well all on her own, as your dad can attest to, and half the people here who have invested in *Vendetta* in just the past six hours. So, if this isn't just about the role of Steven Stryker or your wounded ego or your dad's. What does she need? Really need? A friend? *No.* She's got me." Samantha sighs heavily.

"So, what's left in this girl's life? What's she missing, Roman? What if she needs someone who cares about her, has her back when the vultures come, and there are a lot of those in LA, yeah? If you really care about her, then you already know what she needs from you."

"I love her." The words come out honest, unfiltered. "I know that sounds insane after thirty-three hours, but I do. I love her."

Something shifts in Samantha's expression. The calculation drops away, replaced by something that might be considered sympathy. Or pity. I can't tell which is worse.

"Then prove it," she says simply. "Not with money. Prove it with honesty. With vulnerability. Show her the guy she glimpsed on that beach, just yesterday, who took such loving care of my running gazelle girl without hesitation or pretense. *Be that guy.* Not the Hollywood prince everyone expects you to be."

"Can you get the kitchen to plate this cake? Two forks, linen napkins, a candle? I need a minute to figure out what to say and how to say it."

"Fine. I'll *help* you. But Roman, cake will not do it. You already know that, right? The girl can buy her own white cake with Italian buttercream frosting every day of the fucking year. And she's an amazing baker. She can make that kind of cake all on her own. That's what she does when she's stressed out. *She bakes.* Amazing cakes. Cinnamon rolls. Bread. *From scratch. Did you know that?*" She laughs a little.

I give her a sheepish look. "She baked me a birthday cake at one in the morning last night. This is one of the last pieces of that cake."

She nods like she already knows. "Oh my God, Roman Lysander, my utterly handsome, hot, kind of maybe friend. Do you know how lucky you are? She made you a birthday cake. Still, you only know the parts of Isla Ryder she *lets* you *see.* And you should be grateful because, from what she's told me so far, she's let you in on a lot of things she doesn't share with anyone else, sometimes not even *me.* But, Roman, you are entirely too focused on *you* and *not her. Typical guy.*" She rolls her eyes at me.

I've been gut-punched by her best friend.

She knows it, too.

"Sorry. Harsh, but true." She smiles and then frowns a little. "Even so, I'm worried about you. Particularly, your general well-being and safety. Actually." She sighs deeply. "She might indeed turn you down. She can be stubborn like that. And we're leaving in like thirty minutes. She's running on fumes, and we're headed out to The Harland. Isla desperately needs some rest."

"Okay. *I got it,*" I say slowly. "Look, can you help me out with the cake? *Please,* Samantha. I know we just met this afternoon, but can you do this for me? I know what she needs. I got it. *I promise you.* I do. I know it's not about cake, per se." I feel for the jewelry box in my pocket as I hand Isla's best friend the cake box. "If you could just have the kitchen staff plate it up with two forks and two napkins and a candle? That would be great." I give her my winning smile. She rolls her eyes at me again.

Not winning. On any front whatsoever with Samantha Harper.

"Fine," she says with a huffy breath. "I'll *help* you. Be back in a few. Because, *Roman,* time is running short here. Go big or *go home.*"

She returns in three minutes. My mind is still blank. I haven't figured out what I'm going to say or how to say it.

Failure is mounting as a real possibility.

"Good luck." Samantha lights the candle and sends me off.

I make a long, winding turn toward Tom, the DJ. We nod at each other. The signal's been given. He segues in with my playlist set with a slight interruption and pause before launching into my set. Hoobastank's *"The Reason."* We're going with the truth right away.

I'm not a perfect person.

She already knows this. Especially now.

But the song is about finding a reason to change. And the reason for me is this formidable warrior goddess I've fallen in love with, standing just forty feet from me now.

The artificial rain begins as I make my way through the crowd, a gentle patter at first, that makes people look up in confusion before realizing it's not real weather. Conversations pause, phones come out, and I can practically feel the collective shift in attention. I protect the candle flame with one hand and carry the plate of cake with the other.

Perfect. An audience for my potential humiliation.

But at least this way they cannot rewrite the story.

I'm setting the narrative. For once.

This is my truth.

Isla and Danny have stopped talking, both looking around as the sound system fills with the unmistakable white noise of heavy rainfall. Her eyes find mine across the crowded floor, and I see recognition dawn in them.

Understanding? *Probably not.*

Grudging awareness. *Maybe.*

And something else I cannot quite read.

Anger? Resignation? Hope? Rage? *Maybe rage.*

It's not looking good for Roman Lysander.

I thread through the bodies separating us, the cake plate clutched in my hand like a talisman. More people are starting to notice—whispers follow in my wake.

"What's Roman Lysander doing?"

"Who's the cake for?"

Phones angle for better shots. By tomorrow, this will be all over social media, dissected, and analyzed. Turned into content. Hopefully, with the real story. Roman Lysander is in love with this emerald green-eyed goddess he ran into on the beach in Malibu.

Or they'll make something up. They always do.

I don't care.

For once in my life, I don't care about the optics or the headlines or what any of these people think. There's only Isla, standing at the tall table in her black lace ensemble of armor, watching me approach with those devastating emerald green eyes.

Danny melts away as I get closer—smart kid. *Way to read the room.*

Samantha appears at Isla's side, whispers something in her ear, then disappears into the crowd. Brandon materializes near the DJ booth, phone to his ear, coordinating the sound effects.

Everyone's playing their part in this elaborate production, except the two people it actually matters to.

CHAPTER 31

slide away

Isla Ryder

"Slide Away" - Miley Cyrus
"A Sorta Fairy Tale" - Tori Amos
"i hope ur miserable until ur dead" – Nessa Barrett
"Vampire" – Olivia Rodrigo
"You Learn" – Alanis Morissette
"Mariners Apartment Complex" - Lana Del Rey
"Watch Me Shine" – Joanna Pacitti
"The Reason" - Hoobastank

Friday Night, 10:00 p.m.

ROMAN IS NOWHERE to be found. A phantom limb, an ache where he should be, or perhaps, more accurately, where he shouldn't. My eyes, traitorous and insistent, keep trying to track him, a habit formed in the crucible of the last thirty-something hours. I've seen him, of course, in flashes—a golden head bent in earnest conversation with Brandon, a brief, almost conspiratorial exchange with Samantha.

Brandon even cornered me earlier, a forced casualness in his voice as we navigated a semi-dance, his words a clumsy attempt at something.

Reconnaissance? Mediation? *He's really torn up, Isla.* As if that excuses anything.

Later, I saw Roman himself dancing with Samantha, a polite, almost stiff pantomime of enjoyment. Each sighting is a fresh stab, a twist of the proverbial knife he plunged into my heart this afternoon.

My mind is a ravaged landscape, a battlefield strewn with the wreckage of his words, his betrayals. *I'm so angry at him for everything.* The fury is a living thing inside me, coiling and uncoiling like a viper, its venom seeping into every thought.

I wish he hadn't shown up at Catch LA. This was supposed to be *my* night, Samantha's night, a celebration of our audacious bravery, our victory. *Vendetta* is ours, wrestled free from the grasping hands of power-hungry men like his father.

So why does *he* consume my every waking thought?

I'm trying to keep it together, to paste on a smile for Samantha, for the parade of industry power players who now orbit our table. Reese Witherspoon is charming, effusive, her praise for Roman echoing Julia Winston's earlier sentiment *'such a great guy, so misunderstood'*. It's a chorus I'm beginning to find nauseating.

What is wrong with this town and these glittery people? Do they not see the darkness lurking beneath the polished veneer? Or do they simply choose to ignore it, blinded by the charisma, the fame, the *idea* of Roman Lysander?

The guy skewered my heart this afternoon. His words about Melody 'fucking' Parker, a deliberate, cruel incision designed to draw blood. And it did.

It nearly derailed me entirely, almost made me lose my entire focus during the high-stakes confrontation with his father. But I held on. I kept it together. I won.

Vendetta is mine, its financial future secured by a coalition of rebels, the very people willing to challenge the entrenched system his father represents. We'll hit our hundred-million-dollar target by midnight, a testament to the power of a story well told, and a vision fiercely protected.

So why, *why* am I wasting the precious energy of this triumph on Roman Lysander? Why does his absence, his presence, his very existence feel like a gaping wound in the fabric of this night?

Is it because I let him in?

Is it because, for a fleeting, foolish moment, I allowed myself to believe he might be different?

The vulnerability of that admission is a fresh wave of shame.

I'm just trying to survive this night, to maintain the illusion of control until the *Vendetta* funding portal officially closes, as a resounding success. But I feel awful, a creeping sickness that has nothing to do with the champagne Samantha keeps pressing into my hand. I'm burning up, a feverish heat that radiates from within, making my skin feel tight and my thoughts increasingly fractured. Each hour that passes, the malaise deepens, a heavy cloak settling over me. I'm not going to last much longer at this glittering charade.

And the playlist. My God, the playlist. Perhaps curating two hundred songs charting the anatomy of a broken heart, and the treachery of men like Roman Lysander, was... excessive. A touch dramatic, even for me. But the thought of walking across this crowded rooftop, through the gauntlet of curious eyes, to tell Tom, the DJ, to abandon my carefully constructed symphony of pain? It's an impossibility.

My knee throbs with a vengeance, each step a fresh agony. *I don't stop to question why that is. How sick am I?* The thought is a fleeting shadow, quickly dismissed. I can't afford to be sick. Not now.

No. I'm armored. I'm a fortress. Another couple of hours. That's all I need. Samantha promised. Then escape. Sleep.

Miley Cyrus is singing "Slide Away." I just love this song. It perfectly explains how I feel right now. We're not kids and whatever this is, or was, just needs to end. We need to just slide away. Go back to our lives.

It's been *a day* since I met him. A single day. Okay. Truly ridiculous, but all the feels are there.

It feels like a major loss of some kind.

So, yes, we just need to slide away, as it were.

Samantha can run point on Roman's public relations plan. I'll just be in the background endorsing the strategy for his public relations.

Just not out front. Nowhere near him. In fact.

Point of fact. *Doable.*

Maybe if I sleep long enough, for a decade or two, I'll forget the devastating pull of Roman Lysander's orbit and forget the brief, searing moment he meant something to me.

Only I could fall in love with someone in less than 24 hours.

It's ironic, really… pathetic, even.

And I *will* get past this. *I will.*

The admission is a bitter pill, swallowed down with another sip of champagne that tastes like sweet poison.

God, please make it stop.

This hollow ache.

This relentless haunting.

Nessa Barrett's "I hope ur miserable until you're dead" begins to throb through the speakers, and a perverse satisfaction courses through me. I don't even feel a shred of guilt. I hope Roman is somewhere within earshot. The lyrics are a direct hit.

Message received? Hope so.

Don't fucking bring up Melody Parker to me ever again. Got it?

If I'm going down as a psycho bitch in his mind, then let's lean into it.

Let's go there right the fuck now.

Danny Vazzano, a charming distraction, materializes at my side, offering a hand. "Dance?"

Perfect. Why the hell not? Leaving Reese Witherspoon mid-anecdote is undoubtedly a faux pas, but my capacity to care about social niceties has been thoroughly depleted.

My priority now is telegraphing my rage to Roman Lysander, using every weapon at my disposal—song lyrics, indifference, the casual company of another guy. Danny, bless his oblivious heart, serves that purpose beautifully.

Front and fucking center. Watch me, Roman. Watch me not care.

The song shifts. Olivia Rodrigo's "Vampire." *Ouch. Too close to home, even for me.* The lyrics are a soft, brutal evisceration. *A goddamn vampire.* Is that what he is? Is that what *I* am, for using this music to flay him open? The thought is unsettling. I loved you truly. You got to laugh at the stupidity. Yes. My stupidity. For believing, for even a second. *Yeah, me. All fucking day long… believing in fairy tales.*

Twenty minutes, or maybe an eternity, later, I spy him. My breath catches, a painful hitch in my chest. Roman. Standing near the garden entrance, a small white box clutched in his hand.

What the hell is he up to now? Why can't he just leave?

This party, this victory, it isn't about him. For once. The *'Sexiest Man Alive'* three years running looks utterly out of place tonight, a discordant note in my carefully orchestrated symphony of success.

How is that possible? He owns every room he enters.

"Hey, you doing, okay?" Samantha's voice, laced with concern, cuts through the haze. She materializes at my side, her gaze sharp, missing nothing. I grip the tall table, trying to project an aura of unbothered triumph. *Not working.*

"I'm great. This is fun. Thanks for putting it together." My smile feels stretched, artificial, like a poorly applied mask. I'm afraid it might crack and reveal the intense, festering emotional wound beneath.

I'll look like Heath Ledger in Batman as the Joker for the rest of my days.

"Roman's here." Samantha states the obvious, her eyes tracking him.

I'm aware. Painfully aware. "Saw you dancing with Brandon Chase. How's that working out?" I deflect, needing to shift the focus, even for a moment.

"He's very nice. Pretty stoked about his investment in *Vendetta.*"

"Uh-huh. Asking about his buddy Roman's investment too, I'm sure." The bitterness in my voice is undeniable.

"A little." Samantha's gaze softens, turning back to me. "I'm worried about you." She scrutinizes me, her internal medical advisor clearly on high alert. The silent handoff from one Roman Lysander to my best friend, it seems.

"Yeah. I know. Appreciate it, Sammy girl." My voice is tight. "I just need a little break. A good night's sleep, and I'll be right as rain." I grimace internally at using Roman's cliché metaphor he said at his party. It instantly conjures up fresh images of Roman and all these foolish, romantic notions that I have no business entertaining.

Not now. Maybe not ever. After today.

I give Samantha a tight smile, conveying that I'm just relaxing and enjoying myself. The expression feels stretched across my face like a mask that might crack at any moment, but I force it to hold.

I take a deliberate sip of my cocktail—something fruity and far too sweet that tastes like artificial paradise—just to make the point that I'm having fun. The liquid burns slightly going down, or maybe that's just the effort of maintaining this charade.

"Hmmm... so good," I murmur, letting a hint of theatrical pleasure color my voice. The lie tastes worse than the drink.

Samantha's worried expression softens slightly, and she gives me a smile in return, seemingly satisfied with my playful party efforts. The concern doesn't entirely leave her eyes—she knows me too well for that —but she appears willing to accept my performance at face value, at least for now.

"Good," she says, though her tone suggests she's not entirely convinced. "Just… pace yourself, okay? And if you need anything—"

"I'm fine, Sammy girl. Really." I wave her off with what I hope passes for breezy confidence. "Go have fun. Dance with Brandon. I saw the way he was looking at you earlier."

That does the trick. A genuine flush creeps up her neck, and her smile becomes less clinical, more real. She eventually moves off in the direction of the dance floor again, her peach dress catching the ambient light as she weaves through the crowd. Probably seeking out Brandon Chase as I suggested. They seemed to have made a connection tonight— one of the few bright spots in this glittering disaster of an evening.

I watch her go, noting the easy confidence in her stride, the way conversations pause as she passes. Samantha Harper in her element, collecting allies and building bridges while I stand here like a wounded general surveying a battlefield that I'm unsure if I've won or lost.

The moment she's out of sight, my carefully constructed façade threatens to disintegrate. The cocktail glass trembles slightly in my hand, and I set it down on the nearest surface before anyone notices. My knee throbs with renewed vengeance, and the fever that's been building all day seems to pulse behind my eyes like a warning light I can no longer ignore.

Still, I do.

Tori Amos' "A Sorta Fairy Tale" weaves its melancholic magic through the speakers. *Oh, God. This song.* It's about the haunting beauty of a failed love, the desperate attempts to salvage something from the wreckage. A little too on point, perhaps, but when I curated this playlist, a small, traitorous part of me wanted him to know that I factored love into the disastrous equation of us. Since he understands music so intimately, let the melody convey what words cannot.

You lost, buddy. You lost me. And I ain't playin'. Anymore.

Danny returns, a fresh flute of champagne in hand. I drain it in one go. The bubbly champagne is a fleeting distraction. He offers his hand again, and I take it. Dancing is an anesthetic, a way to numb the relentless throb of my knee and the sharper ache in my soul. Danny makes me laugh, a genuine sound that feels foreign and surprising. He's friend-zoned, thoroughly and unequivocally, but his easy company is a temporary balm to my wounded soul.

Across the room, Samantha is talking to Roman again. A fresh wave of irritation washes over me.

This cannot be salvaged. There is nothing he can say or do that will turn this around.

Well, almost nothing. The thought, absurd and unwelcome, surfaces at the edge of my consciousness before I ruthlessly extinguish it.

My cut is a fierce, throbbing pulse now, the pain radiating up my leg. I lean more heavily on Danny as he escorts me back to the table.

Another drink. Yes.

Cocktails and champagne, the elixirs of denial.

Then I hear it—the distinct, unmistakable sound of heavy rain. Not the gentle patter of a California shower, but a downpour, insistent and immersive. It takes a moment for my fevered brain to register its artificiality. The sound piped through the rooftop speakers, enveloping us.

Like a set. In a… movie.

No. No. No.

Oh my God.

This guy will not stop.

Now, what.

My heart executes a painful, betraying flutter. *Pride and Prejudice.* Darcy's rain-soaked confession. It's exactly the kind of grand, cinematic gesture Roman Lysander would orchestrate. He has the depth, the romantic soul, to remember our conversation on the beach, to understand its significance.

And I gave him a lot to work with that day. *Yesterday.*

The thought is a fresh stab of pain. It was only yesterday, yet it feels like a lifetime ago, a different world, before the betrayals, before the armor slammed back into place.

Oh, Roman. Really? Here? In front of all these people? Why? Why would you do this?

His own words echo back: *'You have no idea what it's like under the microscope. They make up stories about me that aren't even true.'*

That's exactly why he would do something like this.

To reclaim his own narrative. With me.

And then, I see him. Roman Lysander, always a beautiful sight no matter how much I try to hate him, in dark, expensive designer clothes, moving across the dance floor, a path parting before him as if by magic.

The crowned prince of Hollywood approaches the outcast cinder girl. *Me.*

He carries a small cake plate, a single lit candle flickering precariously, its flame a fragile beacon in the artificial storm. He's protecting it with one hand, like it's the last ember of hope in a dying world.

Kind of like our… relationship… *that we don't have.*

The thought is a whisper of despair. *But we do,* argues another, more insistent voice, from some hidden recess of my heart.

I bite my lip to keep from smiling. He looks… adorable. Earnest. And utterly terrified.

He makes a detour toward the DJ booth. Tom. There's a slight interruption, a pause in the downpour of sound, then Hoobastank's "The Reason" fills the air.

What is he doing?

I cross my arms, a defensive posture, as Samantha materializes at my side, her voice a low murmur against the music. "He has something to say, and he won't be deterred. Just go with it. I'll rescue you in a few if it all goes south."

I shoot her a questioning look but find myself nodding. My own body betraying my resolve. "What could he possibly say to make up for what he's done?" I whisper to her. The words sound like a desperate plea even to me.

Samantha gets that whimsical, secretive look again, the one that makes my stomach clench with a mixture of dread and anticipation. My heart executes another painful somersault.

Damn it all to hell. I've had a day. A day and a half of emotional whiplash.

Can't a girl catch a break?

Does all of Hollywood have to witness whatever madness Roman Lysander is about to unleash?

Conversations have ceased. All eyes, all phones, are now trained on Roman Lysander. He continues his slow, deliberate approach, the pathetic little cake plate clutched like a sacred offering. The crowd, animated and hungry for drama, watches the prince of Hollywood make his pilgrimage to the wounded girl in the corner.

This will be viral by morning. Another weekend spent in damage control, trying to spin the narrative that he seems determined to shatter.

Danny, bless his prescient soul, gives me an apologetic look and melts into the crowd. I stand straighter, bracing for impact, as Roman crosses the halfway point across the dance floor and approaches me.

Brandon Chase hovers near Tom's DJ booth, phone pressed to his ear, no doubt coordinating this theatrical downpour.

Is everyone in on this elaborate, painful charade?

CHAPTER 32

the reason

Roman Lysander

"The Reason" - Hoobastank
"Chasing Cars" - Snow Patrol
"Every Breath You Take" - The Police
"Just What I Needed" - The Cars
"I Want To Know What Love Is" - Foreigner
"Perfect" - Ed Sheeran
"Ordinary World" - Duran Duran
"Perfect Day" – Hoku
"Birds of a Feather" – Billie Eilish
"Waiting For A Girl Like You" - Foreigner

Friday Night

MY HEAD IS SPINNING. Not from booze. Not this time.

It's Isla. The sheer force of her—that takedown at The Ivy, the way she built this empire brick by digital brick while everyone underestimated her. The way she's looking at me right now with that mix of fury and something else I cannot name.

Until now. *Despair.*

Yeah, *despair I caused.*

My stomach clenches. Acid churning. What if this doesn't work? What if I'm about to make the biggest fool of myself in front of half of Hollywood? What if Isla just walks away from me?

The thought makes my knees weak. And not in the good way.

But the alternative—doing nothing, letting her slip away—feels far worse than any public humiliation. I've survived box office bombs and tabloid takedowns.

I can survive this.

Maybe.

I move through the crowd at Catch LA, the transition from planning to execution a blur of nervous energy. Brandon's tech team has created the illusion of heavy rain, the sound enveloping the space with cinematic precision. The lights dim slightly, creating an intimate atmosphere despite the packed venue.

A-listers mill about, suddenly confused by the atmospheric shift. I catch snippets of conversation:

"Is this some kind of immersive experience?"

"New marketing stunt for that *Noah's Ark* reboot?"

"God, I hope the roof isn't actually leaking. My Louboutins..."

The artificial downpour drums against invisible windows as my playlist begins with Hoobastank's "The Reason." The crowd parts, murmuring in confusion and anticipation. I notice several celebrities exchanging glances, leaning in to whisper to each other.

Hollywood loves drama. Especially when it's unscripted.

By morning, this will be on every gossip site from TMZ to Perez Hilton. Another Roman Lysander meltdown for the highlight reel. Except this time, I'm not melting down, and I don't give a fuck.

The crowd's eyes follow my every move as I make my way through them, clutching a plate with one of the last pieces of my birthday cake she made for me. The piece with extra frosting. The best piece. Two forks rest beside it. The single candle flickers, defying the odds to stay lit amidst the heightened atmosphere.

My heart thuds in my chest. The rhythm of the manufactured rain is a frantic counterpoint to the soothing cadence of the simulated storm. Each step feels monumental, echoing with the weight of what I'm about to do. My mouth is desert-dry, tongue sticking to the roof. I should have grabbed a drink first. Dutch courage.

But no. This needs to be clear-headed. Sober Roman is making a sober choice.

I move deliberately across the crowded floor. Heads turn as I pass. Of course they do. The wax drips onto the frosting—minutes feeling like hours as I navigate toward the only person in the room who matters.

My palm sweats against the cool ceramic plate. This giant piece of cake is my ridiculous yet sincere offering. Something real from yesterday that changed everything between us. In a town where authenticity is the rarest currency of all.

From across the room, I see Samantha saying something to Isla, who just nods and closely watches me now as I approach her. She's standing by the high-top table again. The music shifts subtly. "Chasing Cars" with Snow Patrol now plays beneath the sound of rain. A song about the relentless pursuit of love. About one guy chasing a girl like a dog chases cars—always a little out of reach, but it still doesn't stop him.

And it won't stop me.

It's about love in this twisted, weird way, and I have to hope she gets the reference.

And then there she is. Just five feet in front of me. Isla, the woman who's consumed my every thought for the past day and a half. She stands out in her black lace ensemble, like a queen amidst her people. Her eyes narrow as I approach. There's a flash of confusion, disbelief, and anger, all vying for dominance.

"Roman? What is this?" Her voice cuts through the artificial storm, sharp as a blade. "What are you *doing*?"

I step toward her, protecting the flame of the candle with one hand while my pulse hammers in my throat. "I need to talk to you."

"*Talk* to me?" She laughs, but it's hollow, edged with hurt. "You had your chance to talk to me at The Ivy. You had your chance to talk to me in the Escalade. Instead, you decided to believe the worst about me without even asking more questions. You made *assumptions*. The wrong ones. And now you want to stage some... What? A Hollywood moment? With an audience?" She gestures around us at the gathering crowd. "This is *exactly* what I *don't* want, Roman."

Her words are direct, and my courage plummets at hearing them. She's right. Of course, she's right.

My throat tightens. I feel sweat beading at my hairline. The cake plate trembles slightly in my hand.

"I know." My voice barely carries over the rain sounds. "I know I screwed up. I've been doing it my whole life—hiding behind roles, behind the Lysander name, behind the image. But this isn't that. This isn't staged. I'm not acting."

"Aren't you?" Her green eyes flash. Her chin lifts, challenging me. "Because it looks like a scene from a movie to me. Complete with sound effects and an audience."

I swallow hard. "The rain... it's from *Pride and Prejudice*. I wanted to—"

"I know what it's from," she says. "I remember our conversation. But Darcy's first proposal was a disaster precisely because he didn't truly see Elizabeth. He was so caught up in his own world, his own assumptions. And I told you this. *Yesterday*." Her voice drops, intimate despite our audience. "And it's just the same as that. Because you don't see me either."

Something in her words cuts through me. Sharper than any director's criticism I've ever received. She's not just angry—she's disappointed. And somehow that's worse. My chest constricts, like someone's tightening a vise around my lungs. It's hard to even breathe, knowing I've disappointed her so much.

"You're right." My voice shakes. My hand trembles. I almost lose my grip on the plate of cake again. "I didn't see you. I saw what I expected to see—another industry player making calculated moves. But I was wrong, Isla. So wrong. I'm so sorry." The admission hangs heavy in the air in conjunction with the ever-steady sound of heavy rain all around us.

The music shifts to The Police singing "Every Breath You Take" creating the perfect backdrop for what I'm about to do. The crowd has fallen silent, rapt. I notice several celebrities watching intently, their expressions a mix of curiosity and growing investment in the drama unfolding. A hundred phone cameras are probably already recording this. It will be everywhere by morning. Potentially impacting *Vendetta*, my career, and everything we've both worked for.

Fuck it. Some things matter more than a carefully crafted public image.

"The truth is..." I stop, running my free hand through my hair. "I watched it. After our conversation yesterday afternoon. I watched that particular scene between them seven times, actually, trying to understand exactly what you meant about Darcy getting it wrong."

"You watched that scene seven times?" she asks, looking uncertain. She takes in this fact and seems to tabulate it in that beautiful brain of hers. Her lips part ever so slightly.

I'll take it. It's a break in the armored posture.

"I did." I look at her with renewed hope. At least she's listening to me.

"Well, what did you think of it? The scene?" she asks, still sounding mad but curious at the same time.

I sigh and cast about for time and the right words. "I understand why Darcy's first proposal failed. He made it about himself, about what he wanted, without ever considering Elizabeth's feelings. Just like I did with you earlier today. I was wrong. You were right. And I'm so sorry."

Silence.

She shakes her head in disbelief. "And what are you *sorry for* specifically?" The cool girl façade fades entirely, and she just gazes at me with newfound fury. "Sorry for accusing me of playing games? Sorry for questioning my integrity? Sorry for bringing up the idea of dating Melody *'fucking'* Parker, as if last night was just an *illusion* for us both? Or are you sorry for sitting there like a gargoyle statue while your father attacked me?" She extends her arm like Vanna White, showcasing my failures, while a bitter smile touches her lips. "There's so much to *choose* from, Roman. Which thing are you *most sorry* for?"

I visibly wince at the 'gargoyle' reference. "Ouch." The word escapes before I can censor myself.

I take an unsteady breath, the cake plate nearly slipping from my grip for a third time. "I'm sorry for all of it. For lashing out at you by bringing up Melody Parker—it was juvenile, wrong, and hurtful. I knew it even as I was doing it. I'm sorry for every fucking word I said during that car ride this morning. Every second I hesitated when my dad went after you. Every time I made you defend yourself to me when you were the *only one* being honest with me the entire time."

"You know what the worst part is?" She lowers her voice to an intimate level intended just for me. "It isn't the accusations. It isn't even the distrust. It's realizing that you think so little of me that you believe I'm capable of manipulating you. That everything between us is just another PR strategy. *To you.* When all I want to do is help you." She looks defiant as she lifts her chin and stares up at me. "I'm really good at what I do, Roman, and you dismissed my expertise as if it's worthless. Meaningless. The truth is half of the people investing in *Vendetta* are my *clients.* That should tell you *something.*"

"Isla—" I'm wounded by her stark honesty and being called out by her.

"Do you have any idea what it takes for me to tell you about my family?" Her voice cracks. Unshed tears gather at her lashes. "I never talk about them *at all*. To anyone. But I shared them with you. And you..." A jagged sigh escapes her. She wipes at her eyes with the back of her hand.

Then she winces in sudden pain. I watch as she grips the table behind her for balance.

"Are you okay?" I ask in earnest.

"I'm fine. No concern of yours," she says coolly.

And we're back to square one. She's icing me out.

She sighs. "I told you about the casting clause in relation to my family. I told you why it was important to me. And you... I don't *trust* people, Roman. I don't let them *in*. But *I let you in*, and you threw it back in my face the moment things got complicated." The last words are a broken whisper.

The accusation is a fresh wave of agony that steals my breath away.

"I know." My voice is hoarse with emotion and barely audible over the artificial rain. "I know, and I'm sorry. I'm sorry for making you feel like you had to defend your motives to me. I'm sorry for not having your back when my father attacked you. I'm sorry for being so fucking scared of what I was feeling that I convinced myself you were the problem."

A single tear streams down her face.

The music changes yet again. The Cars singing "Just What I Needed" about finally finding the right person, but it doesn't seem to resonate with her at all.

It's been ten minutes and I'm not getting anywhere fast with Isla Jane Ryder. She keeps her arms tightly crossed across her chest. She's armored up, as it were. If she had a weapon, it would be pointed straight at me.

Nothing I am saying is working. The candle is getting dangerously close to the frosting. Next, they'll be calling the fire department.

'Hollywood Star Sets Place On Fire' will be the headline.

"Isla..." I try again, forcing the words out. "Look, I know how this seems." The words tumble out now. "Roman Lysander, making a scene. Another public spectacle. But you have to understand—I've never *felt* this way before. *Never*. And it terrifies me. That's why I lashed out. Because the way you make me feel... it's like someone ripped out my script and I'm standing here without any lines, completely exposed."

"Roman, please." Her voice softens slightly but is still firm. "This isn't the place. *Everyone* is watching."

"Let them," I say, surprising myself with the conviction in my voice. "I don't care anymore. I've spent my entire life performing for an audience. This is the first time I'm being real and all I care about is you."

Something crosses her features—doubt or the faintest glimmer of hope.

I frown, all at once, realizing this is not going the way I thought it would at all.

The silence between us stretches, taut and unbearable. She is just standing there in a complete, but silent panic, willing me to stop.

She takes an unsteady breath, gently smiles at me as if I am a child that is going to be disappointed with what she has to say next.

"Let's take a beat, Roman," she says softly. "We'll be *friends*. Good friends. That is the best solution. Logical. Safer, for both of us." She actually smiles at me, then whispers urgently, "You need to stop this madness right now. It's irrecoverable. Let's talk offline. I'll help you manage the fallout. We'll work on damage control this weekend. Together, I promise. We can be friends. Okay?"

"Are you seriously trying to friend-zone me right now, Isla Jane?" I shake my head, smiling ever so slightly. But then, courage materializes for me from out of nowhere. "*No,*" I say in defiance. "That's not what I want. That's actually not what you want either."

"Yes, it is. We'll be friends. That's it." She gives me this imploring look. "We can *fix* this. If you *stop*, right now."

"I don't want to *fix this*. I want to *live this*." The words come out fierce. Determined. "Yes, I'm aware. I *know* it sounds crazy. I *know* it's been just thirty-three hours." I glance down at my watch and check the time. "But I can't... I don't want to go back to my life without you in it."

"Why should I believe you?" It's a challenge, but the anger has drained from her voice, replaced by something more vulnerable. "How do I know this isn't just another role you're playing?"

"Because I'm *terrified*." The words feel like they're being torn from somewhere deep inside me. "I'm standing here, in front of everyone, without a script, without a character to hide behind. Just me. Roman. Terrified that you will say *no*, that I've ruined everything before it even had a chance to really begin. But I'm still here, still trying, because the thought of not having you in my life is by far worse than any rejection."

The candle burns lower, dangerously close to the pristine white frosting. I get this wry smile. "This is part of my grand gesture. Dual promises. One of the last pieces of cake from the cake you made for me last night and the grand gesture of cake corners for the rest of your life." I hold out the plate with the cake and the lit candle towards her. "This felt like the last real moment between us, before everything became so complicated." My hand shakes visibly, betraying the calm I'm trying to project. "The last piece of the cake you made. Lots of frosting. The best part."

She doesn't take it.

"Well, that is a grand gesture. Coming from you," she says softly. But then, she shakes her head from side to side with discernible sadness. "You think this is about cake?" There's an edge to her voice I haven't heard before. "Or about your twenty million dollars? I don't need your money, Roman. I don't need a grand gesture or a public declaration. What I need is someone real. Someone who sees me—*really sees me*—and chooses to stay, anyway."

She looks up at me again with these sad green eyes. "Cake isn't going to save us, Roman. But I appreciate the gesture all the same." She takes the plate from my outstretched hand, closes her eyes, seems to make a wish, blows out the candle, turns, and sets it on the table behind her.

Next.

The muscles in my jaw tighten. My skin feels too hot, too tight. I take a deep breath and sigh big.

"I do *see* you, Isla," I finally say, my voice rough with emotion. "I see how hard you've worked. How much you've sacrificed. I see how you protect Samantha, how you're building this PR firm from nothing but your convictions, your philosophy, and your principles. I'm in *awe* of you." I swallow hard. "I see the way you tilt your head when you're thinking, and how your eyes light up when you talk about your work. I see you, Isla. The creative, brilliant, beautiful woman that you are, despite all you've lost. How you endure. How you love. I want to be in your world with you. I *need* to be with you. If you'll have me. If you'll choose me."

"I Want To Know What Love Is" by Foreigner begins playing.

Something shifts in her expression—a softening around the eyes, a slight parting of her lips.

I take a deep breath, the sound of the rain a frantic counterpoint to my pounding heart. "The truth is, I love you, Isla Jane Ryder, most ardently." My voice cracks on the last words. "And not because it's convenient, or good PR, or because you're brilliant at what you do— though you are. I love you because…"

Words suddenly fail me. My carefully rehearsed speech disintegrates, and all I'm left with is the raw, unfiltered truth.

"—because when I'm with you, I don't have to pretend. For the first time in years, I can just… *be*." The admission costs me, leaves me feeling flayed wide open. Vulnerable. "I love how you call me out, demanding I be real with you. Honest. I love how you see through the Roman Lysander brand straight to the mess underneath, and somehow you don't run away screaming."

Her eyes shimmer with unshed tears, but her posture still remains guarded. "Roman, we barely know each other. This is—"

"I know it sounds crazy," I interrupt. "One and a half days. Thirty-three hours and fifteen minutes since we crashed into each other." I check my watch again. "It's insane." I run my hand through my hair and try to smile. "But I've found something with you I've never experienced before, Isla. And I can't… I don't want to go back. I want to wake up and see your face first thing in the morning. I want to be the guy who gets to hear about your day. The good, the bad, all of it."

I take an unsteady breath and continue, reaching into my pants pocket, feeling for the ring box.

"I know I hurt you," I say, each word deliberate and heartfelt. My voice sounds foreign to my own ears—intense, unfiltered, without the polish of a carefully crafted performance. "I know I didn't trust you when I should have. I let fear dictate my actions instead of listening to what I was feeling."

I sigh deep. "I cannot… imagine my life without you. The thought of losing you is worse than anything my father could ever do to my career. Worse than losing the role of *Vendetta*. Worse than anything." I swallow hard. "Worse than losing my mom. That's a hard truth to say out loud, but it *is* the truth. I cannot lose you, Isla."

I step closer, lowering my voice so she knows it's meant just for her, despite our audience. "And just so you know, I didn't invest in *Vendetta* because I want something from you. I did it because I believe in you— your vision, your talent, your integrity. All of it. I'm all in."

The bass of the music pulses through the floor, vibrating up through my legs, matching the rhythm of my racing heart. My skin buzzes with it, like I'm about to jump out of myself.

I smile softly, remembering our second meeting. "I'm sorry I didn't offer you the corner piece of my birthday cake at my party. I'm sorry I left you in the middle of the night because I was too terrified of how quickly you broke through every emotional wall I've spent years building."

"This is something I should have done the moment I realized what you mean to me. *Yesterday, Isla.*" I drop to one knee and hold up the red velvet ring box.

"Something real. Something honest. Something that has nothing to do with PR or publicity or any of the bullshit that usually defines my life."

Isla stumbles backward, colliding with the waiter who has been hovering for the last twenty minutes, probably wondering if we're going to order or burn the place down. "Roman, *what* are you *doing?*" she asks. It is a strangled plea.

The crowd surges closer, like a hungry beast devouring the spectacle. Phones flash—a thousand tiny suns illuminating my upturned face and hers.

I can hear livestreams starting: *"We're at Catch LA tonight, and you're not going to believe what's happening..."*

"Isla Jane Ryder," I say, my voice cracking with emotion. "You are the most brilliant, fierce, and beautiful woman I've ever met. You see through all my defenses to the man I actually want to be. You make me want to be better, to be worthy of the way you look at me when you think I'm not paying attention. *I see you...*"

Sweat beads on my forehead, and I fight the urge to wipe it away. "I know this is fast. Too fast, probably." I take an unsteady breath at the realization that she may walk away right now.

She's watching me, those green eyes seeing straight through to my soul. I feel naked, exposed, like she can see every stupid mistake I've ever made, every insecurity I've ever hidden behind.

"But I also know that I love you like I've never loved anyone else before." I struggle to find words that don't sound like dialogue from one of my movies. "You mean everything to me. I've loved you since I swung you up from the sandy shoreline and you fell into my chest and stole my heart right then and there, while you were bleeding all over the place, even with the possibility of attracting sharks." I can't help but grin at the memory of her and me at the beach.

Her lips curve into the smallest smile, and hope takes hold inside of me when I see it.

"I'm not asking you to marry me tomorrow, although I would be fine with that. I'm asking if you'll take a chance on us. If you'll say yes to the possibility of forever with me."

I flip open the ring box. A vintage diamond—exquisitely cut—glitters with inner fire, casting prisms of light that dance across her beautiful face.

"This was my mother's," I say quietly. "She wore it for twenty-three years, through good times and bad, through my father's obsession with work and all the pressures of this industry. She told me once that the right woman would make it beautiful again, and she gave it to me on my sixteenth birthday for safekeeping, four weeks before she died. You *are* that woman who will make it beautiful again, Isla. *This* I know at a soul level."

Isla's eyes fill with tears. And I know she finally recognizes the sincerity of this gesture from me.

"I want you to have it. Not because I'm trying to buy your forgiveness or manipulate you into saying yes. But because I cannot imagine it on anyone else's hand. Because you're my person, Isla. The one I want to fight with and make up with and build something real with."

The artificial rain intensifies—a dramatic crescendo to my heartfelt plea. She stares at the ring, then at me. I just wait. I'm not quite sure which way this is going to go.

"Roman," she whispers. "Please, get up."

She reaches down with trembling hands and takes my hands in hers and pulls me to my feet. The crowd is a distant roar that barely registers.

Those green eyes that see right through me are softening, but there's still hesitation there. "I need you to understand something. If I say yes, it's not to the Roman Lysander the world knows. It's not to the heir, the movie star, the brand. It's to the guy who helped me up when I fell, who's seen me angry, and at my worst, at one in the morning, who listens when I talk about my work. That's who I'd be saying yes to." Her voice is gentle, but firm.

"That's all I want to be," I say, my voice rough with emotion. "Just that guy. Your guy."

She takes a deep breath, and time seems to stand still. The crowd around us fades away, the artificial rain a distant backdrop to the thundering of my heart. I can feel each beat in my fingertips, in my temples, at my throat.

"If we do this," she says slowly, "it has to be real. Not a PR strategy, not a Hollywood romance. *Real.* With all the messy, complicated parts. I won't be a chapter in your memoir or a steppingstone in your career. I need to know you are in this for the long haul, Roman. That when it gets hard—and *it will get hard*—you won't run."

"I won't run," I promise, meaning it more than any line I have ever delivered. "I'm done running, Isla. I want the real thing. With you. All of it."

I take the ring from the box and, with infinite tenderness, slip it onto the third finger of her left hand. It fits perfectly—as if it were forged for this very moment.

This impossible, beautiful collision of us—these two broken souls—that found each other on a beach.

"Perfect fit," I say.

"It's so beautiful." She gazes up at me, still uncertain. "But it was your mom's..."

"Yes, and she would want you to have it."

I stay focused on Isla. "So… will you marry me, Isla Jane Ryder? Just say yes. To me."

She studies me for what feels like an eternity, those green eyes searching mine for any hint of deception.

"Okay then," Isla says, her voice steady despite the tears shimmering in her eyes. "Yes." The word is a quiet vow, a promise whispered against the backdrop of a cheering city. "Yes, Roman Alexander Lysander, I'll marry you."

The rooftop erupts—a symphony of cheers, applause, and popping champagne corks. Tom the DJ, cued by some unseen signal, transitions to Ed Sheeran's "Perfect".

I pull Isla into my arms and kiss her like she's the last breath of air I'll ever need.

"I love you," I murmur. "I love you, and I'm going to spend every day proving it to you, Isla Ryder."

"I love you, too." It's an admission of joyous surrender. She smiles up at me.

The relief and uncontainable joy I feel is immense. It's like my life just started with this woman saying yes to me.

And the world rights itself. The chaos recedes. There is only the two of us.

"You beautiful, impossible man." A watery laugh escapes her. "Do you have any *idea* what you've just done?"

"Hopefully, the *right thing. For once.*" My smile is shaky but hopeful.

She glances around at the sea of faces, the recording phones, and the sheer spectacle of it all. "You've just proposed to me in front of half of Hollywood. There's no taking this back."

"I don't want to take it back. I want everyone to know. I want the whole world to know that you're mine and I'm yours."

She studies my face carefully, tilting her head ever so slightly. The tell of hers I love so much and instantly recognize now. "You really mean it," she says in newfound wonder. "You're actually in love with me."

"Desperately. Completely. Irrevocably, even if it's absolutely insane, given the circumstances."

A genuine laugh bubbles up, free and joyous. "The circumstances are pretty fucked up, yeah?"

"The worst. We're a walking conflict of interest with trust issues and abandonment complexes. We should probably run screaming in opposite directions. But I'm not running." I give her a challenging look.

"I'm not running either," she says back to me and sweetly smiles.

And just like that, the weight of the world lifts from my shoulders. All I can see is Isla, all I can feel is the perfect rightness of this moment as I pull her into my arms.

Our lips meet, and our kiss is everything—tender and passionate, a promise and a beginning. My hand cups the back of her neck, feeling the warmth of her skin, the silky texture of her hair. The scent of her perfume—something floral and sophisticated—fills my senses.

Someone in the crowd murmurs, likening my performance to Matthew Macfadyen's Darcy in *Pride and Prejudice*, and I can't help but grin against Isla's lips. The irony isn't lost on me—even in my most authentic moment, people see a performance.

But for once, I don't give a damn what they see or think.

The night spins on, a whirlwind of music and laughter. As we dance beneath muted fairy lights to the sound of artificial rain, I hold Isla close, feeling the steady beat of her heart against mine. The weight of what we've just committed to—not just to each other, but in front of

Hollywood's elite—should feel terrifying. Instead, it feels like coming home.

The joy and celebration reaches raucous levels—Hollywood loves their newfound queen and always loves to celebrate.

Some producer I worked with years ago is already in a corner, no doubt pitching our story as the next big rom-com to a studio executive.

Tomorrow will bring challenges—the media frenzy, professional complications, and my father's inevitable reaction. The headlines write themselves: "LYSANDER HEIR PROPOSES TO PR GURU: GENUINE ROMANCE OR PUBLICITY STUNT?" The stakes for *Vendetta* and both our careers have just been raised exponentially.

But tonight, with Isla in my arms, her head resting against my chest as we sway to the music, I can't bring myself to worry about any of it. My shirt collar is damp where her tears have soaked through, and I can feel the steady rhythm of her breathing against me.

She pulls back slightly to look at me, her eyes serious despite her smile. "And just so we're clear—I'm still running *Vendetta* my way. Your twenty million bought you a seat at the table, not creative control."

I laugh, feeling lighter than I have in years. "I wouldn't have it any other way." My hand traces the curve of her face. "Besides, you're the genius behind this whole operation. I'm just the guy holding your hand."

She rises on her tiptoes to kiss me again, and I know with absolute certainty that whatever comes next—whatever headlines, whatever challenges, whatever storms—we'll be together and that's all that matters.

<hr>

Later, when the joyful celebration has subsided and fragile peace has settled over the terrace, she looks up at me with mischief dancing in her eyes. "You know this doesn't fix everything, right?" she asks, twisting the ring on her finger. "We still have a lot to work through. Trust to rebuild. You still owe me a proper apology for some of the things you said. *In private, of course.*" A playful smile touches her lips.

I laugh. "Well then, we should get going so I can start apologizing in all the ways you'd like me to. In *private*, of course." I kiss her. "And yes, I'll spend the rest of my life making it up to you, if you'll let me. Plus, there's that lifetime promise of cake corners—for you and you alone."

"I'll hold you to that." Her smile widens, genuine and radiant. "But

Roman? What you did tonight… the honesty, the vulnerability, the complete disregard for what anyone else thought… that's the guy I fell in love with… *yesterday*, at the beach."

I'm stunned by her admission. It's a gift all its own.

This beautiful secret we will always share.

I kiss her again—a slow, lingering kiss that speaks of home, of forever, of love found in the most unexpected way. On a beach.

Love.

It's real.

And that's all that matters.

———

The End

acknowledgments

I would like to thank all of my fans who still leave me notes on Facebook or send emails telling me how much one of my stories affected them.

And for all of you who keep in touch and reread my novels, since it has been a long while since I've put a new book out: *thank you.*

This book is also for those of you who leave reviews for my books on your blogs and other fine on-line book retailers, especially you, because reviews make an author's world go 'round. We need to hear the feedback, feel the love, field the hate (*sometimes*) because there is something to be learned even from the harshest critic, as well as the most avid fan. *Thank you for that.*

It was the continual encouragement like yours that brought forth the idea of writing another novel because I know you are still in my corner. Cheering me on. Thank you.

So. Here it is, a new novel, *The Image Maker, Book 1* in the Hollywood Hearts series, *finally*, a bit late and then some, for all of you... Thank you so much for believing in my work and in me as a writer. I appreciate the support you all provide, but mostly; I treasure all of you for being a part of my *writerly* world.

Katherine Owen

playlist – the image maker

FINAL CUT

Playlist for *The Image Maker*

I listen to a lot of music while I write, so I put together a list of songs that I listened to while writing *The Image Maker*. As you will see, I used some of the song titles for quite a few of the chapter titles.

Here's that song list—***The Image Maker* - Final Cut**. Enjoy!

- **Chapter 1 - Catch and Opportunity** "Same Mistakes" - Laurel
"Same Old Love" – Selena Gomez

- **Chapter 2 -** No **Roots** - "No Roots" – Alice Merton

- **Chapter 3 - Resurrection** - "Young And Beautiful" - Lana Del Rey
"Beautiful People Beautiful Problems" - Lana Del Rey, Stevie Nicks
The Chain" – Fleetwood Mac

– **Chapter 4 - Your Eyes Open** - "Your Eyes Open" - Keane

- **Chapter 5 - Malibu Landing** - "Born Without A Heart" - Faouzia
"West Coast" - Lana Del Rey

-**Chapter 6 - Soul Meets Body -** "Soul Meets Body" - Death Cab for Cutie

- **Chapter 7 - Blood In The Cut** - "Blood In The Cut" K. Flay
"Blue Jeans" - Lana Del Rey
"Same Old Love" - Selena Gomez
"Dreams" – Fleetwood Mac

- **Chapter 8 - Too Good To Be True** - "Too Good To Be True" - Kacey Musgraves
"Snow On The Beach" - Taylor Swift, Lana Del Rey

"West Coast" - Lana Del Rey

"Just What I Needed" - The Cars

- **Chapter 9 - I'm Not Over -** "I'm Not Over" - Carolina Liar

"Wouldn't It Be Good" – Nik Kershaw

"Cake By The Ocean" - DNCE

- **Chapter 10 - Lucky -** "Lucky" – Britney Spears

"Ocean Eyes" - Billie Eilish

- **Chapter 11 - Come As You Are** "Come As You Are"– Nirvana

Roman Lysander's Dedicated Songs to Isla Ryder at his birthday party:

"Come As You Are" – Nirvana

"Blood In The Cut" - K. Flay

"It's All I Can Do" - The Cars

"Perfect Day" – Hoku

"Fade Into You" – Mazzy Star

"Meant To Be" – Bebe Rexha

- **Chapter 12 - Please Please Please -** "Please Please Please" Sabrina Carpenter

"A Drug From God" – Grimes, Chris Lake

- **Chapter 13 - Meant To Be -** "Meant To Be – Bebe Rexha

"Come As You Are" – Nirvana

"Blood In The Cut" - K. Flay

"It's All I Can Do" - The Cars

"Fade Into You" – Mazzy Star

"Perfect Day" – Hoku

- **Chapter 14 The Malibu Experience** - "Come As You Are" - Nirvana

"California Nights" - Best Coast

"It's All I Can Do" - The Cars

"Fade Into You" – Mazzy Star

"Perfect Day" – Hoku

- **Chapter 15 - Snow On The Beach -** "Snow On The Beach" – Taylor Swift, Lana Del Rey

"Birds of a Feather" - Billie Eilish

"Fade Into You" - Mazzy Star

"Perfect" - Ed Sherman

"Deep In Your Love" - Bebe Rexha, Alok

"Soul Meets Body" - Death Cab by Cutie

"Landslide" – Fleetwood Mac

- **Chapter 16 - Catalyst -** "Catalyst" - Anna Malick

"Sin x Secret" - Charlotte Lawrence

"Love Is A Wild Thing" - Kacey Musgraves

"Fresh Laundry" - Allie X

"Landslide" - Fleetwood Mac

"Wild Side" - Laurel

- **Chapter 17 - Love, Save The Empty -** "Love, Save The Empty" - Erin McCarley

"Borrowed Time" - A Fine Frenzy

"Hurricane" – MS MR

"Fresh Laundry" – Allie X

- **Chapter 18 - la di die -** "la di die" Nessa Barrett, jxdn (feat. Jaden Hossler)

"Cornflake Girl" - Tori Amos

"Blood In The Cut "- K. Flay

"Paper Love" - Allie X

"Pretty When You Cry" - Lana Del Rey

- **Chapter 19 - Sit Still, Look Pretty** - "Sit Still, Look Pretty" – Daya

- **Chapter 20 - Wreck of the Day** - "Wreck of the Day" - Anna Malick

"Complicated" – Avril Lavigne

"Delicate Weapon" - Grimes, Lizzy Wizzy

- **Chapter 21 - White Horse** - "White Horse" -Taylor Swift

"Flowers" – Miley Cyrus

"Cornflake Girl" - Tori Amos

"Stupid Girl" - Garbage

Part 3 Love, Where Is Your Fire? "Love, Where Is Your Fire?" - Brooke Fraser

- **Chapter 22 - Gold Dust Woman** - "Gold Dust Woman" - Fleetwood Mac 2004 Remastered

"Ghosts of You" – 5 Seconds of Summer

"Everybody's Changing" – Keane

"Bitter Sweet Symphony" - The Verve

- **Chapter 23 - I Remember Everything** - "I Remember Everything - Zach Bryan, Kacey Musgrave

"Somewhere Only We Know" - Keane

"Creep" - Radiohead

- **Chapter 24 - Hold Back The River -** "Hold Back The River" - James Bay

"When Doves Cry" - Prince

"Cold Heart" – Elton John, Dua Lipa, PNAU

"Save Your Tears" - The Weeknd, Ariana Grande

"Alrighty Aphrodite"– Peach Pit

"Do It Again" – Steely Dan

- **Chapter 26 - Nothing In My Way** - "Nothing In My Way"—Keane

"Do It Again"—Steely Dan

"I Remember Everything"—Zach Bryan, Kacey Musgraves

- **Chapter 27 - Looking for Water** - "Looking for Water" - Alex Parks

"Slide Away" - Miley Cyrus

"Born Without A Heart" - Faouzia

"Vampire" – Olivia Rodrigo

"Leave The Pieces" – The Wreckers

"Uninvited" – Alanis Morissette

"Flowers"- Miley Cyrus

"High By The Beach" - Lana Del Rey

- **Chapter 28 - Uninvited** - "Uninvited"– Alanis Morissette

"Cold Heart" – Elton John, Dua Lipa, PNAU

"Please Please Please" - Sabrina Carpenter

"Love Like Mine" - Stela Cole

"West Coast" - Lana Del Rey

"Vampire" – Olivia Rodrigo

"Wake Me Up When September Ends" – Green Day

- **Chapter 29 - Save Your Tears** "Save Your Tears" - The Weeknd, Ariana Grande

"Wake Me Up When September Ends" – Green Day

"A Sorta Fairytale" - Tori Amos

- **Chapter 30 - Perfect** - "Perfect" - Ed Sheeran

"Bitter Sweet Symphony" – The Verve

"I'm Good" - Bebe Rexha and David Guetta

"Save Your Tears" The Weeknd, Ariana Grande

"Watch Me Shine" - Joanna Pacitti

"Perfect Day" - Hoku

"Birds of a Feather" - Billie Eilish

- **Chapter 31 - Slide Away** "Slide Away" - Miley Cyrus

"A Sorta Fairy Tale" - Tori Amos

"i hope ur miserable until ur dead" – Nessa Barrett

"Vampire" – Olivia Rodrigo

"You Learn" – Alanis Morissette

"Mariners Apartment Complex" - Lana Del Rey

"Watch Me Shine" – Joanna Pacitti

"The Reason" - Hoobastank

- **Chapter 32 - The Reason** - "The Reason" Hoobastank

"Chasing Cars" - Snow Patrol
"Every Breath You Take" - The Police
"Just What I Needed" - The Cars
"I Want To Know What Love Is" - Foreigner
"Perfect" - Ed Sheeran
"Ordinary World" - Duran Duran
"Perfect Day" – Hoku
"Birds of a Feather" – Billie Eilish
"Waiting For A Girl Like You" - Foreigner

Please note there is more information and links and the playlists for both the Work-in-progress Play List for *The Image Maker* and ***The Image Maker – Final Cut** at* Spotify as well as my website and this blog post. ***Thanks for reading!***

Visit my website for links to the original work-in-progress play list. www.katherineowen.net

about the author

"I believe all I can do is inspire (or, is that "grind"?) both my readers and myself in what I construe as reality. Someone has to capture the sad, emotional, angsty love stuff that often collides with fate. It might as well be me. Apparently, I am THAT writer."
~ Katherine Owen

Katherine Owen is the author of *The Image Maker,* her latest release in the Hollywood Hearts series. Owen also wrote the bestselling Truth In Lies Series which includes: *"This Much Is True", "The Truth About Air & Water",* and *"Tell Me Something True"* as well as standalone novels: *"Seeing Julia", "When I See You"* and *"Not To Us".*

For more information about her novels, her writing, and everyday happenings, visit her website www.katherineowen.net, where she sometimes uses edgy language and mild sarcasm in observing life as a writer.

Get in touch with her via her contact page at the website or her Facebook fan page. She'd love to hear from you.

Want to know first about her next novel release? Join her mailing list. https://www.katherineowen.net/newsletter

instagram.com/katherine__owen
facebook.com/KatherineOwenauthor
pinterest.com/katherine_owen

other books by the author

OTHER BOOKS BY KATHERINE OWEN

The Hollywood Hearts Series

The Image Maker – Book 1

The Image Breaker – Book 2 (Fall 2025)

The Image Keepers – Book 3 (Fall 2025)

The Image Masters — Book 4 (Winter 2025)

The Truth In Lies Series

This Much Is True (Truth In Lies, Book 1)

The Truth About Air & Water (Truth In Lies, Book 2)

Tell Me Something True (Truth In Lies Book 3)

Standalone Novels

When I See You

Seeing Julia

Not To Us

Works-In-Progress

Saving Valentines (Fall 2025)

The Image Breaker – Book 2 (Summer 2025)

The Image Keeper – Book 3 (Fall 2025)

Another WIP (still untitled)

More information about the books including play lists, excerpts, and extras at:
http://www.katherineowen.net.

thank you & a request

Thank You & A Request

Life is unbelievably short, and your book list is probably pretty long, so *thank you* for spending some of your precious time reading *The Image Maker, Book 1*, in the *Hollywood Hearts series*.

If you share your thoughts about the book by leaving a review, please know how much I appreciate your time and effort for doing so. *Thank you!*

—*Katherine Owen*

www.ingramcontent.com/pod-product-compliance
Lightning Source LLC
Chambersburg PA
CBHW031732180726
48283CB00005B/1480